Blood Relative

Blood Relative

Blood Relative

Carolyn Hougan

FELONY & MAYHEM PRESS • NEW YORK

All the characters and events portrayed in this work are fictitious.

BLOOD RELATIVE

A Felony & Mayhem mystery

PRINTING HISTORY
First edition (Fawcett): 1992

Felony & Mayhem edition: 2022

ISBN: 978-1-63194-278-5

Manufactured in the United States of America

Cataloging-in-Publication information for this book
is available from the Library of Congress.

To Elisabeth Case and Samuel Johnson

ACKNOWLEDGMENTS

Several people made useful suggestions and contributed helpful comments during the writing of *Blood Relative*. My thanks to Jim Hougan, Daisy Hougan, Joanne Bario, Devorah Zeitlin, Scott Miller, Deidre Sampson, Joy Davis, Linda Sullivan, Eric Yoder, and Daniel Zitin.

The icon above says you're holding a copy of a book in the Felony & Mayhem "Hard Boiled" category. These books feature mean streets and meaner bad guys, with a cop or a PI usually carrying the story and landing a few punches besides. If you enjoy this book, you may well like other "Hard Boiled" titles from Felony & Mayhem Press.

For more about these books, and other Felony & Mayhem titles, or to place an order, please visit our website at:

www.FelonyAndMayhem.com

Blood Relative

Part One

BUENOS AIRES
August

Chapter One

ROLANDO
The Cattle Tick

WHEN I FIRST hear the news, I don't feel the slightest exhilaration. The truth is, I gave up on finding her a long time ago. Oh, I've indulged in my fantasies of "reunion," but I was sure they were just that—fantastic, improbable.

But here it is. My mother promised a "surprise" at lunch. Suddenly, she's announcing it.

"Remember that woman I told you about? The head of the adoption agency that we traced to Spain? Well, the trip to Madrid seems to have paid off," she says in a determinedly casual voice. "We have…a really solid lead."

I can see it in her too, the stiff grip of restraint. Neither one of us can believe it, that this could be the real thing at last. It must be like winning the lottery: the initial stance is incredulity.

The effort to keep her hopes down subdues my mother's normally buoyant manner. Her smile is no more than a nervous gesture. It's as if she's trying the news out on me; if I believe it, maybe she will too.

She lights another cigarette. Her eyes bounce around the room until her focus finally settles on her own fingernails. She gives them a hard stare, as if assessing the skill of her manicurist, then leans toward me and exhales so forcefully her face is momentarily obscured by smoke.

Her voice comes to me through the haze: "We even have her name."

I am a man more driven by passions than most. The obedience and compartmentalized thinking required by my military career were not easy for me to acquire. But because part of its discipline is the routine concealment of emotion, a military education proves invaluable when you have a secret to keep. Even as a young cadet, one is taught to maintain an emotionless posture—taught, even under scrutiny, even when deliberately provoked, never to show anger or fear, embarrassment or even amusement.

In my case, it is this ingrained habit of deception that has made it easy all these years for me to keep from my mother the true ambition of my heart. It makes it easy now for me to control the surge of excitement that finally comes, that almost swamps me in a rush of adrenaline. It makes it easy for me to keep my face from betraying my feelings, to keep from my mouth and eyes the glazed rapture of the hunter who has sighted his prey.

Of course, my mother would misread my expression anyway. She'd take it as one of simple happiness that at long last we had hope of finding the lost remnant of our family.

I copy her manner and keep my voice matter-of-fact. "But that's fantastic. After all these years, I have to say I'd almost given up. I didn't think we'd ever find her." Even as I'm saying this, I don't believe it's true, that we've really picked up her trail. It's still sinking in.

"It was a stroke of luck that this woman took her records with her to Spain," my mother goes on. "If she'd left them here, I'm sure they would have been destroyed. Amazing when you think about it—that she should lug them overseas. I guess she was afraid...afraid to keep them, afraid to throw them away..."

The waiter materializes lifting the bottle of wine from the bucket in a smooth motion. My mother puts her fingertips over her glass and gives a tiny, almost imperceptible, shake of her head. The waiter comes around to fill my glass, giving the bottle a sharp little twirl as he finishes pouring. For some reason the waiter's flourishes irritate me so much that I find myself enraged. I have an impulse to grab his wrist and push him to the floor. I take a deep breath. I am not under control after all. Correction. I am under control, but only just.

"...still amazes me that so many people who do illegal things want to keep *records* of their transactions," my mother is saying. "The soul of the bureaucrat prevails, I suppose." She stubs out her Marlboro.

I say nothing. My mouth feels as if it's full of sand. I guzzle the glass of wine.

"I gather she was quite frightened, this poor woman, but they reassured her. Some of the things she did were illegal, but they're hardly going to extradite her for them. Not when there are murderers still walking around free." A blood vessel ticks in her temple. "Why don't you come back to the office with me after lunch? I'll make you a copy of the papers."

She's not talking about her office at the newspaper, but her other office. Although she is nominally the publisher of *Acción*, she rarely goes there anymore, preferring to spend her time looking for the missing.

The waiter slides the plates in front of us. The smell of the meat brings saliva into my mouth and I realize I'm quite hungry. "I'm very curious," I say at last. "What is it? Her name, I mean."

"Mariah," my mother says, struggling a little with the unfamiliar pronunciation. She spells the first name for me. "Mariah Alicia Ebinger."

"Evinger," I repeat, but she corrects me.

"Ebinger. With a B."

She is talking about María. She is talking about her granddaughter—my niece—who disappeared more than ten years ago during the so-called "dirty war" here in Argentina. Sad to think this is what Argentina is famous for now. Our country used to be known for beef, polo, the gauchos, the tango, the glamour of Buenos Aires. Now we are famous for our two recent wars. First came the dirty war and "the disappeared," a word to which Argentina gave a new meaning. Second was the humiliating war with the British which we lost so badly that it is known not as the war of the Malvinas, but by the name the victors call their defended islands: the Falklands War.

Even these events are old news now, although the grandmothers and mothers (including my own) still march every Thursday in the Plaza de Mayo, the dates of the disappearances inked to their white kerchiefs, the deteriorating photographs of the missing pinned to their breasts. And the disgrace of our total defeat by the British—this too has begun to blur and dim with time.

Our most recent fame is less dramatic. Today, our celebrity depends on our notoriously unstable currency. That, and the entertaining spectacle of a nation so amazingly mismanaged that in a matter of decades a country once among the ten most prosperous in the world has sunk until it is now on a level with Yemen.

"Mariah Alicia Ebinger," I say, the syllables sliding out between my teeth. Speaking the name seems to exhaust my breath, and I gasp quietly as my mother nods to show I have pronounced it correctly. "And where do they think she is?" I manage. "Any information on that?" I pat the napkin on my lap, then cut a small piece of meat and begin chewing it. Although I am now forty years old, I'm self-conscious of my table manners when dining with my mother.

She shrugs, takes out a cigarette, taps it, first one end, then the other, against the pink linen cloth. "This is preliminary information," she says. "The parents were North American, so we are *assuming*..." She stops and smiles ruefully. Even this sort of half smile transforms her. She was a famous beauty in her youth. At sixty, too thin and quite gray, she is still a woman people look at twice. "We are checking with emigration. We have a source in the U.S. Embassy, and we are hoping to find some kind of paper trail there. In the meantime, the logical place for her to be is in the States."

"Big country," I remark.

"But so much is computerized there, it is not like trying to find someone in...oh, Paraguay. Every child must have a social security number. The investigators don't think it should prove very difficult. We have the parents' names too, and their social security numbers. They lived here for almost two years, so we actually have quite a bit of information about them, including at least one U.S. address—where their belongings were shipped when they left Buenos Aires. Of course, that information is quite old, but still..." She pauses and sighs, shutting her eyes for about thirty seconds. It's a prayer, I think, a ritual appeal to the heavens. I don't believe she's even aware of doing it. She opens her eyes and goes on. "It's hardly possible to remain hidden in the United States—unless you live on cash, unless you live like a fugitive. The credit bureaus there have huge databases that the investigators make use of." She pushes the food around on the plate with her fork. "I am told also that Ebinger—that this is not such a common name. If she is there, they expect to find her within a month."

"You're also assuming she's alive."

A mistake. I shouldn't have said it. I shouldn't have raised that possibility, the literal dead end. Her expression twists briefly in pain and then flares into anger. "You know, Rolando, I understand that it is part of human nature to wish that others suffer our own misfortunes, but it is not a part of ourselves that we should encourage."

I feel my face flush with blood. She has read me right, of course. Why should my own Elena and Liliana be dead and this one be alive? If only my mother knew how badly I "wish others to suffer my own misfortune," she wouldn't be sitting here with me. Black rage boils up in me at the thought of Mariah Alicia Ebinger; dark venom pumps through my veins. I try hard to maintain control, breathing through my nose to calm myself down. A trick of yoga, taught to me by Liliana.

"I didn't mean it that way," I manage in a wounded voice. "I want to find her as much as you do, you know that. I guess I don't want to get my hopes up. I'm guarding against...against...false elation."

My precarious voice leads her to mistake my emotion for filial hurt. She reaches for my hand to soothe me. "Please forgive me, Rolando. I'm very hard on you." A sigh. Her skin feels like paper against mine. "I feel the same way. I'm not permitting any dreams of reunion. I'm not expecting *anything*. I'm prepared for the worst, believe me. But even so, I don't *feel* she's dead. The documents suggest that she was taken away from here, and if she was taken away from here, it would be—" She picks the word carefully. "—*surprising*... I think it would be surprising if she did not survive."

A brown-haired boy of about ten, who has been lurking a few feet away with a basket of long-stemmed red roses, approaches the table. He must be new at this to wait so politely for a break in the conversation rather than sliding the flowers under our faces or standing right at the table's edge with a pathetically needy expression. Then again, maybe it's my mother. Something about her elicits good manners; even cab drivers treat her with careful courtesy.

"A flower for the lady?" the boy asks shyly.

I raise my hand in a dismissive gesture and he begins to drift away when my mother detains him with a finger on his sleeve.

"What's your name?"

"Martin." He looks at his feet.

"Well, Martin, how much for all your flowers?"

I don't know what she's up to. Her house is always full of flowers; she has some steady arrangement with a florist.

The boy looks up with a shocked expression. "*All of them?* Let's see, each one is two hundred fifty australes, I have—" He starts to figure it out. He squints. "For all of them, I can give you a bargain. Six thousand."

My mother smiles. "A deal."

I watch the boy's face develop a troubled expression as he starts to gather the roses together. He has no paper, no way of wrapping the huge bouquet. I'm with him; I can't see how my mother is going to manage. He frowns and looks at his basket, worried that somehow my mother had thought it was included in the transaction.

She touches his hand and shakes her head. "They're not for me." She counts out six thousand-austral notes and holds a seventh up in the air. "This is for your delivery charge. I've had some good luck today and I want to celebrate with flowers—I want you to give one or two to each woman in the restaurant. You can explain that they are from me."

We watch him, going around, placing the roses in front of the women. He meets some resistance at first; everyone thinks it's a hustle of some sort. But he keeps gesturing back to my mother, who smiles steadily as she receives the barrage of nodded thank-yous and smiles and little salutes of acknowledgment that come her way. We leave the restaurant on a groundswell of goodwill.

After lunch I decide I will go to her office, as she suggested. It's an unusually warm day, and a few people are taking advantage of the balmy weather to sit at La Biela's outdoor tables. Mother has to stop and kiss a friend. Then of course she must introduce me and we have to talk for a minute or two. Finally we're released to resume our stroll. There are no taxis in sight, and we walk a little way down Junin, a mother and son, her arm hooked through mine. People smile at us; we make a handsome picture. I am in uniform, and, despite everything and the debacle of the war, the uniform still inspires admiration. The people have not lost the habit of esteem.

Across the street the wall that contains the cemetery is almost, but not quite, high enough to hide it completely. Above the wall protrude the very tops of the roofs of the mausoleums, the architectural embellishments, the knobs, the angels, the crosses, the spires. I wonder if this is the only place in the world where the fashionable living feast so very close to the fashionable dead.

Finally a taxi swims around the corner and my mother halts it with a tiny peremptory gesture. The car has some problem with the exhaust system. We don't try to talk above the racket.

Unlike my mother's plush office at the newspaper (where she so rarely goes), this one has a humble look, furnished as it is with odds and ends from attics and basements. Except for its state-of-the-art computers, and the age of the women, it might belong to a student group. It also has some of the untidy exuberance of a campaign headquarters. Really, these women are amazing—tireless, relentless, undaunted by the most depressing odds. The search for the missing has uncovered in them huge reservoirs of energy.

Everyone greets me with affection. They are brimming with happiness for us. "Great news," says the usually taciturn Elenora Castelli, beaming. "It's wonderful, isn't it, Rolando? Isn't it wonderful?" Mrs. Higuera actually kisses me on the lips. For a moment, among these women, I am caught up in the general surge of happiness. I actually feel a bogus moment of bliss.

"Unbelievable, isn't it?" I say to the room at large. "We may actually find her after all this time."

"You never lost faith," Señora Higuera says, touching the cross resting on her bony chest. "You and your mother never lost faith."

"We don't *know*," my mother admonishes, not wanting to risk offending providence with premature happiness. This subdues them, and we retire to her cubicle. The walls around us are amateurishly covered in lavender burlap—which is itself nearly obscured by pinned-up photographs of the faces of the missing. As my mother hands me the papers, the tacked-up photographs give me the uneasy sensation of being watched.

I handle them: the birth certificate, the papers from the Agencia Palomar, some documents from the United States Embassy. My mother makes copies for me. When I get up to leave, she clasps my hand between her two and then we embrace. When we separate, she holds on to my sleeve for a moment, as if to detain me. With her other hand she touches her knuckle to a tear that glitters in the corner of her eye. Then she produces a smile so brittle it almost breaks my heart.

As soon as I leave my mother, my composure deserts me and I stumble down the street without thinking. I end up at the Plaza de los dos Congresos. Some kids are kicking a small red ball on a tattered patch of grass. The fountains are not operating, which gives the square a sad, closed-for-the-season look. A group of men in suits rushes past me, hurrying toward the Parliament building. I spot a free bench and collapse on it, disturbing a clutch of pigeons. They lift up halfheartedly from the pavement, then settle back and resume picking at the remains of a discarded sandwich. I stare at the birds. Each one of them seems for a moment to have the face of my dead child.

I sit on the bench, breathing heavily, knowing that I have crossed some invisible boundary into the territory of the deranged. It's as if only the hope of revenge has held me together all these years. Now that it seems more than a dim hope, now that it seems a real possibility, my husk of control is split, I'm emerging from it a madman. My heart is beating so hard I have the sensation that the bench is shaking underneath me.

Not long ago I read an article by a naturalist, one of those reverent ruminations on the oddities of nature. The writer mentioned a small animal—not an insect, as he took pains to point out—called the cattle tick. It can remain on a stalk of grass, on a twig, on a tree trunk, inert, for as long as eight years. In eight years it never feeds, it never moves, its bodily processes proceed so slowly it is almost in a state of suspended animation. It might as well be dead, but it isn't dead. Then one day along comes a warm-blooded mammal. Triggered by the smell, the cattle tick launches itself from its twig and leaps onto its prey, fastening its beak into the host's skin and gorging itself on blood.

Sitting on the bench in the Plaza de los dos Congresos, I am like that cattle tick. I have a whiff of Mariah Alicia Ebinger, and the bloodlust is on me.

Chapter Two

ROLANDO
The Red Couch

I DON'T CONSIDER RETURNING to work. I look for a telephone and spot one across the street—near the El Molino Tea Room on Callao.

Looking up, above the tea room, at the soot-blackened oars of the windmill embedded in what is now an office building, I remember my mother showing me this oddity when I was a child. She'd pointed out that a hundred years before, it really was a windmill, a source of power, and not just a sign, a kind of decoration for a tea room.

Once, on an outing with Elena, I told her the same story my mother had told me—how the first balloon flight in the country was launched not far from here in the 1800s. But the French balloonist had the bad luck to crash into the windmill. I embellished on my mother's story, sketching for

13

Elena an image of the balloon impaled on the arms of the windmill, its rapid deflation (I made rude noises for Elena, which made her shriek with laughter). Then I told her how the balloonist was stranded, like a cartoon figure, hanging on to an arm of the windmill and whirling around and around until the windmill keeper managed to turn the oars out of the wind.

"Oh, no!" Elena had squealed, pushing her hand against her mouth to keep from giggling in the face of such disaster. "Was he all right?"

"By some miracle, he was," I told her, "he was perfectly all right. But—" I whirled her around in my arms. "—he was very, very dizzy." She giggled and giggled, her laugh spilling out, her head thrown back, hair flying, her little cheeks flushed with excitement. Then we went into the tea room for chocolate cake. The thought of her sitting across from me, studying the menu, which she could not yet read, revives the old ache inside. All over the city she waits for me like this, in ambush. I remember exactly her four-year-old's solemnity as she gave her order to the waiter, a man with a mustache who made a huge fuss over her. I remember a little later, chocolate frosting smeared around her adorable lips...

The light changes and I'm slow to react. I'm jostled, I stumble, I'm tugged along with the crowd as it surges across the street.

I hunch under the protective plastic dome of the telephone, which is not really adequate to screen out the traffic noise, and call my assistant, Tomas Lozano. My fingers are clumsy as I fit the token in the slot. Excitement has destroyed my small motor skills.

"Capitán," Lozano says.

It's difficult to imagine a creature such as Tomas Lozano without the hierarchical structure of the navy to configure his life. Observance of rank is so embedded in the man's psyche that even his voice, over the telephone, sounds as if it's at attention.

"I'm not feeling well, Lozano. Please cancel my appointment with Cruz and give my apologies to General Arbela—I'm afraid I'll have to miss the meeting." I'm almost shouting to make myself heard.

"I am concerned, Capitán," Lozano replies, alarm pitching his voice even higher than usual. "You are seriously ill?"

Lozano knows that the afternoon's gathering is not one I would miss due to some minor affliction. Some months before, a committee had been ordained by the new government. The press was attentive; appointments were carefully considered, then made. Today is the group's inaugural gathering.

Composed of military officers, members of the new government, and delegates both from the press and various human rights groups, the committee is to make recommendations about ways to heal one of our country's festering wounds. The matter at hand is how to maintain strength and morale in the military services and at the same time placate the segment of the civilian population still clamoring for punishment of what are now being called the military's "excesses" during the "Process of National Reorganization." It is an emblem of the committee's stance, and perhaps the public mood as well, that the word "excess" has replaced the word "atrocity." It's not surprising, either, that the phrase "dirty war," a name the junta itself chose, has given way to the less evocative "process."

When the committee was being formed, my name was one of the first to come up. First of all, I am a captain in the navy, the branch of the armed forces widely perceived as responsible not only for the most brutal "excesses" of the dirty war, but also for the national humiliation over our military defeat in the Malvinas. But I am also a celebrated victim of the "Process." My position in the navy did not protect my family during the dirty war. I lost my wife and child, not to mention my sister, to those very military "excesses." (It is often put this way, that we relatives of the missing have "lost" our loved ones, as if we have misplaced them, like so many sets of keys.)

To round out my suitability for the task force, I have potent connections to the press. Ours is an old and powerful family; its most visible activity is the ownership of *Acción*, the liberal daily of which my mother is the publisher.

The committee's job will not be simple. More than twelve thousand citizens were killed in the dirty war. Although demand for punishment has diminished over the years, there still remains a well-organized and vocal segment of the citizenry vehement in its desire for vengeance against the military.

But a substantial portion of the military in Argentina does not consider itself the servant of any elected government, but the true and natural ruler of the country. And it has enough power that if Menem were to act against it—for instance, revoke the general amnesty—there would certainly be another coup. Then too, if every military man connected to the murky abuses of the dirty war were to be prosecuted, not only would the court system be overwhelmed, the three branches of the service would be virtually stripped clean of officers.

Inside the telephone's plastic hood, someone has scrawled dozens of examples of the anarchist symbol, the circled A. Also NO A INDULTO, NO AL TERRORISMO ECONOMICO—complaints about the wage and price freezes that the Menem government has introduced to try to control inflation.

"You are unable to attend the meeting? You are seriously ill?" Lozano repeats in his squeaky, alarmed voice.

I invent something embarrassing because I know Lozano will believe it. Like many rigid souls, Lozano could not conceive of inventing an excuse that would compromise his dignity.

"A violent but let us hope short-lived stomach virus," I tell him. "I...I don't think I can safely sit in a meeting room without bringing disgrace to the navy. I'm gushing shit, Lozano, I'm a fountain of diarrhea."

"Ahhhh."

"Please see that the memorandum I prepared is delivered to General Arbela immediately, and...ah...explain the problem as you see fit."

"Yes, sir."

"I'll call you later today to see if anything urgent has come up."

"Can you be reached..." Lozano starts. I hear the stiff clatter of the typewriter in the background. "...at your flat?"

I pause. In the telephone booth facing mine an impatient woman is making a call. All I can see are her elegantly shod feet—in navy and red alligator-skin shoes—one of them tapping rapidly. "Yes, but I don't have a telephone in the bathroom."

"Ah. Exactly," Lozano says in his fastidious voice. "Will you call in the morning?"

"Absolutely."

I return to my apartment on Quintana. We lived here—Liliana and I—in the years before Elena was born. When we bought the house in San Ysidro, we kept the flat in town as a pied-à-terre, for those times when we didn't want to make the trip out to the suburbs.

The doorman, Alejandro, hurriedly turns down his radio as I come in and offers me one of his hesitant smiles. "Good afternoon, Alejandro. How's it going?"

He shrugs and smiles again. Although we've known each other for five years, he's still too shy to talk to me.

I take the elevator up.

Now I live here again. I used to force myself to go out to the house periodically, but I haven't been able to face it in months. Maybe it's been almost a year now. The servants always greeted me with their hurt and reproachful faces—not understanding the vortex of rage and grief that going there stirred in me. I would like to tell them to just move into the main part of the house, to live in it as if it were theirs—because I never will, I'll never be able to inhabit those rooms again—but it would just make them worry and feel uncomfortable, they wouldn't be able to do it. It's too bad, because I don't plan to sell the house. I don't plan to do anything with it. It will just stay there, a museum to my loss. The servants have become my curators.

I pour myself a whiskey and drink it in a swallow. Then I recline on the couch, my head propped up on the armrest. The couch of soft, fragrant red leather was Liliana's favorite place to sit and read. It's so easy to picture her slim figure seated here. She liked to slip her shoes off and draw her feet up, her legs bent at the knee, parallel, her toes digging into the space between the side of the couch and the cushion.

I am commonly perceived to have suffered, grieved, and recovered—the natural progression. The stages have been studied by now; there is an entire literature describing them: disbelief, denial, anger, grief, acceptance.

I am commonly thought to have stood up well.

No one knows. No one knows about me. I have not passed through grief to acceptance. I have not passed through anger to grief. I am stranded in anger, I wallow in it; it is the only thing that sustains me. Only in my dreams of revenge do I find any comfort for my debased and wounded heart.

The comforting smell of the leather rises around me and my eyes drift closed. I always do it here, on Liliana's favorite couch. There is the familiar sense of blurring, and then I let them flicker through my mind, the things that happened to Liliana, to Elena. The rage builds slowly, like a drug, seeping into my veins, sifting into my capillaries. Visions of retaliation percolate through me. A red flush spreads over my face and chest; my hands are hot.

Always before, I have imagined the girl, I have imagined Mariah Alicia Ebinger, in a plain room, a seedy room, an interrogation room, perhaps, lit by a fluorescent light. Maybe because I have a name for her now, maybe because for the first time she seems actually within my reach, a new vision comes to me with the force of revelation.

It's night and it's raining, a steady drizzle. There's a smeary reflection of lights on the wet pavement. I pull up to an aging, slightly seedy motel. I am in the United States; I'm driving an anonymous late-model Detroit car. It looks like every other car you see. It has the plastic smell of a new car and also the odor of air freshener masking tobacco smoke. Moro is in the back with the girl.

I register at the office where a sixtyish man takes my money and fishes a key from under his desk. His eyes are permanently bored. He looks like a man who's seen everything—and more than once.

I repark the car in front of our room. It's not a room, actually. It's a unit, self-contained, one of a dozen identical tiny houses. There's no clerk to see the girl; there's no one at all to see me untie the straps binding her legs together. Moro opens the door of the unit; I help the girl from the car. A trench coat is draped over her shoulders. My arm is around her, pulling her head toward mine. We look like a family—a husband and wife, a brother. The collar on her trench coat is turned up. Even if someone were looking, I don't think it would be possible to tell that she's gagged.

The unit is basically one room, with a bath and a kitchenette. Moro brings the luggage in from the car and turns on all the lights. The main room has wall-to-wall carpeting in a serviceable tweed brown. There are two double beds with floral spreads. I put the girl on one of the beds and tie her legs together again. She is submissive; the struggle is out of her. There is a television that pivots on a wood-toned stand, some nondescript lamps, a small table and two chairs.

Most motels are close to highways, and this one is no different; there is a constant ebb and flow of traffic noise. I find the sound soothing, like surf. Moro turns the television's volume up, but not so loud that anyone will complain. There's canned laughter, inane theme music, a run of advertisements. He flicks through the channels and settles on a quiz show.

I leave the girl gagged, although this will deprive me of her screams. I sit next to her on the bed and explain to her at length why it is that she has to suffer and why she has to die. I see from her terrified but vacant eyes that she believes me and is without hope.

Moro helps me hold her down, but I myself must inflict the damage on her, even though it is very distasteful for me. I plan to hurt her as much as possible before actually killing her because I believe that only her agony can relieve my own pain. At times I am weeping. At times, I have to close my eyes.

Perfect revenge requires that I rape her. Although I have read that rape is an act of anger and not of sexual desire, always I am unable to imagine myself violating her. So my dream of revenge ends simply, in an execution. At the end, I am calm. My hand does not shake. My eyes do not squeeze shut. I administer the coup de grace; a single bullet to her temple and it is over.

Chapter Three

ROLANDO
Fraternity of the Deranged

❦ ❦ ❦

SLOWLY, THE SMELL of the leather couch and the corrosive odor of my own sweat revive me from my trance. This fantasy of revenge, which began years before as little more than simply wishing the girl dead, has turned into a detailed reverie. It's almost a ritual, a kind of religious observance—and it has the same effect. I feel momentarily cleansed, elevated.

I get up renewed and revitalized. I take a shower and change my clothes.

It's always best to use a public telephone for these purposes, and this time I don't even mind. I raise my hand to salute Alejandro as I pass, and when I get out to the street, I walk the four blocks to the closest telephone so jauntily that I'm practically whistling.

21

I haven't seen Hugo Moro in a long time, but his telephone number remains in my memory. I feel a little foolish, but you never know about telephones, so I identify myself by my old code name. "It's Adrian."

Hugo Moro has been the instrument of my vengeance before, and he is not surprised to hear from me. He skips over the small talk that would begin most conversations between once-close associates who have not seen each other in over a year. Small talk is not part of his repertoire, and anyway, he knows what this is about.

"Ah," he says. "Either you've found another one or you just miss my company." His laughter stutters over the line.

I arrange to meet him later that evening. He asks that I come to his place, and although I know it's an act of obeisance, I agree.

Since he's quite insane himself, I'm curious to know if he'll detect the change in me. Will he see that I've stepped off the precipice, that I've joined him in the fraternity of the deranged?

Hugo Moro first came to my attention years ago during my stint in Naval Intelligence—we were both in our twenties—although at that time I never made his acquaintance.

His debriefings were occasionally contained in the dossiers I studied. His interrogations were always the most thorough and the most productive, and after a while I began to look for his signature first, to see if I should pay particularly close attention. Initially I thought him simply an exceptional interrogator. It's easy to imagine how some of the men must have laughed at my naïveté, how they must have rolled their eyes at my earnest enthusiasm for Moro's skill. "You know," I remember saying more than once, "this Moro is really good, isn't he?"

Much later I learned that Moro obtained his excellent results through coercion, or let's be accurate, torture. "He

gives a new meaning to the phrase 'hostile interrogation,'"
was the way I heard it first. In retrospect, it did seem to
explain his results.

Years later I had reason to reassess my thinking about
the reason for Hugo Moro's success. Torture, it would seem,
is a tool like any other; results depend upon the skill of its
use. Hugo Moro was an exceptional torturer, and when I
finally met the man, I understood the reason why: he lacks
some essential human component in his personality.

I recently read in the science section of my mother's
newspaper that the genetic defect responsible for cystic
fibrosis has been identified. The flaw that causes the disease
seems such a tiny genetic mistake, that out of more than
a hundred proteins metabolized by the body, there is one
that cystic fibrosis sufferers cannot metabolize. The whole
of the rest of the body and all its complex processes can be
quite perfect, but the lack of the ability to process that one
protein undermines the entire organism. That minuscule
genetic defect is invariably fatal.

Hugo Moro is also missing something crucial, some
key component. In his case the lack of it doesn't kill him;
it just keeps him from being entirely human. I don't know
the exact psychological designation for his condition.
Psychopath? Sociopath? I'm sure there's a term for what's
wrong with Hugo Moro and just as sure that someday
medical science will identify its cause. Neurotransmitters
not firing in sequence, damaged dopamine receptors,
elevated serotonin levels, something like that.

As I got to know Hugo Moro, I realized that he was
an exceptional torturer not because he was willing to inflict
excruciating pain on his fellow human beings, or because
he was willing to kill rather than be denied information—
he had plenty of company there—but because he did these
things with all the detachment of a carpenter striking a nail.

Most of the poor boys who happened to be fulfilling
their national service during the years of the Repression had

expected to do so filing papers, marching in drills, participating in staged maneuvers. They had not pictured themselves, for instance, inserting an electric cattle prod into the anus of a middle-aged dentist and asking him repeated questions about the whereabouts of his daughter. By and large, they did not make a smooth adjustment to their new role.

I wasn't involved in any of this, but later I heard the stories. Some of the boys crumpled under the pressure, simply unable to comply with what was required of them. Others, those who showed an aptitude for it, exploring whatever latent sadism was in their characters, eventually became just as ineffective. Only those who followed orders reluctantly got good results, but the process eventually brutalized them as well and they too became either sadistic or incapable.

Moro was different. His subjects rarely died unexpectedly. Detached from the emotions that battered the other interrogators, he was sensitive to the physical condition of his subjects. He never went too far, but he went, apparently, just far enough.

Moro's apartment is in San Telmo, across from the huge park. It's convenient to the polo fields—he's a fan—and also he keeps in shape jogging over there. He's something of a fanatic about his body.

The building has an intercom system. I push his number and very promptly he answers. I speak into a brass grid: "It's Adrian." He buzzes me up.

His place is surprisingly cozy—at least it surprised me the first time I saw it. I'm not sure what I expected—black leather furniture, I suppose, expanses of chrome and glass. Instead the apartment has an English country look. Polished wood, overstuffed furniture, porcelain dogs flanking the fireplace. He greets me at the door, in a T-shirt and purple sweatpants, barefoot. He's very handsome, a fact that always startles me when I see him because I tend to forget it between times. To me, there's something wrong with his face, some telltale blankness—the sort of thing you see in a woman who's had an unfortunate face-lift, all the expressiveness of her features removed with her wrinkles.

"Hey," Moro says, "*Capitán*. Come in."

"Please," I remind him. "Call me Rolando."

We've been over this ground before. For some reason, he finds it amusing to call me Captain, as if our relationship is based on rank. It's his idea of a joke.

He rolls his eyes up to the ceiling. "I forgot." He dips his head and presses his lips together to contain his smile. "Come in, Rolando."

He's set out some hors d'oeuvres on the coffee table in front of the fireplace: smoked trout, prosciutto draped on wedges of melon and stuck through with toothpicks, a little bowl of olives. He gestures toward them but I go past, toward the window. Already I want to get out of there.

"Glass of wine?"

"Sure."

"Red? White?"

"Ohhh...white, I guess."

"Great. I have a Chilean chardonnay that's..." He bunches his fingers together like a bouquet and kisses the tips of them. These gestures of his are all new. It's as if he's been watching old Italian movies.

There's a row of shelves near the windows and on top of them are plants, his collection of small oriental statuary, and an aquarium. He hands me a glass of wine and watches me carefully as I sip. Actually, it's delicious.

"It's good. Very good."

He smiles at the confirmation. "I own part of the vineyard."

I am sure Moro was not the only person of his position to come out of the war a wealthy man. One can imagine the riches offered to a torturer, if only to distract him for a moment, if only to postpone for ten seconds the next bout of agony. I pay Moro quite well, but he often reminds me he doesn't really need the money. His reasons are different. He's actually said it—"I love my work." He claims it's the only thing he likes better than polo.

I attended a match with him once. He's hardly the typical polo fan since he lacks allegiance to any team or even to a player. What he admires is the complexity of the action, the rapid positional shifts, the flow of events on the field.

As for his work, what he means by "loving it" is only that it fully engages him. This time, of course, his role will be different. I am not hiring him to interrogate or to punish, only to help me, to arrange things. I suddenly realize, in a rush of anxiety, that he might say no.

He's waiting for me to tell him what I want, and he smiles at me his cold, unearthly smile. Without intending to, I take a step away from him and look out the window. It's unsettling to be enclosed in a room with Moro. Not that he's untrustworthy or unpredictable; in an odd sense he's totally trustworthy and predictable.

In a way, it's like being with an alien. He knows what desire is, or fear; he knows what should make him pleased and what should make him angry. He recognizes these emotions in others, and assesses their strength with an exact calibration. It's just that he's never experienced them. He's learned to mimic emotional responses by watching other people, and mostly he's successful. He seems sad when he should seem sad. He chuckles on cue and smiles and appears amused when he knows something is supposed to be funny. There is one particular laugh of his, a childish cackle, that I think genuine. He only laughs in that way when his sense of irony is struck—it's not amusement, exactly, it's when he's impressed by the collision of intentions, the crossed wires of fate.

He sprinkles some fish food on top of the water. The fish have large, extravagant tails and rise immediately toward the flakes on the surface. "If you give them too much," he tells me, "they'll die. They don't know when to stop eating."

"Like goats."

"On the other hand, if you don't give them enough, they tend to eat each other. They begin with the tails. Most things are the same, I've found. There's surprisingly little slack in the world."

"Yes." I'm thinking of his own speciality, the application of pain. Too much, Moro says, and the subject will say anything and the information given is unreliable. Not enough, and there's also not enough—as he puts it—"incentive" for honesty.

"I theorize that in their natural habitat, food sources are not so concentrated, they have to work harder for their nourishment."

"You're probably right."

He can tell I'm uneasy. He's particularly acute at detecting discomfort. "You didn't come here to talk about fish appetite," he says. The automatic smile on his face lends him not a trace of warmth.

"No."

He dips his head to the side and raises one eyebrow.

I have trouble meeting his eyes. "I've had some news," I begin, staring at my hands.

Of course, nothing concrete can be done until I get the girl's address. What I want Moro to do is to make general preparations. I explain to him in some detail what I require, and after a moment's consideration he agrees. We briefly discuss the price for his services. Then I give him the manila envelope, which contains the documents my mother gave me, several small photographs of myself, and some cash.

He looks at the cash, our own currency, with some distaste. "My fee will be paid in dollars," he says.

"Of course. This is for immediate expenses."

A large ginger cat hops up on the sill and looms over the aquarium. The cat taps his paw against the surface of the water and then shakes it, annoyed that it's wet. "Another glass of wine?" Moro asks, stroking the animal, which arches its back and sets its tail straight up.

"Why not?" I agree.

The big cat hops down and follows Moro into the kitchen. When he returns, and gives me my glass of wine, Moro holds his own up toward mine. "To success, then."

The fish dance in captivity. The cat rubs Moro's leg. The air in the room seems to be shrinking away from me. I feel it as a physical sensation, a strange pressure against my skin, as if I'm in a vacuum. I wish I had refused the glass of wine.

"Success." I take a big gulp of wine and wonder if Moro will be insulted if I leave before I finish it. It's a ludicrous notion; I don't believe Moro is capable of having his feelings hurt. The cat is playing with the surface of the water again. The fish swim serenely, unaware of the threat. I take a deliberate look at my watch. "I really have to go."

Moro pads to the door in his bare feet and pulls it open. A smile hovers around his lips. "Ciao," he says. In the elevator, I feel as if I'm escaping.

Chapter Four

ROLANDO
Fresh Blood

I'M LATE; I hurry across the Plaza Saw Martin. It's a warm day and the huge rubber tree is full of small children whose nannies and mothers sit on the benches around the perimeter, enjoying the sun. The children themselves are not visible; they can only be heard, chattering and laughing inside the branches and leaves of the tree, as if they are a flock of birds.

Another meeting with my mother. We've had plenty of these over the last six weeks, commiserating with each other on the lack of progress of the investigation. Despite my mother's prediction that it would be easy to locate any resident of the United States not living as a fugitive, finding Mariah Alicia Ebinger has not proved so simple. We take turns counseling each other in the art of waiting. One of us is always saying it: we must be patient.

I catch sight of her, across the square, gliding toward me. Even if she were encased entirely in garbage bags, I think I would recognize my mother by her elegant walk. She raises her hand and quickens her pace.

Patience has proven difficult for me. Every day that goes by with no news of Mariah Ebinger, something inside me twists tighter. There are possibilities my mother and I don't discuss: that the information from the woman in Spain was incorrect, that the name itself, which we were so thrilled to learn, might be a red herring. We never mention, either, that our girl might be dead after all, that she might have perished in some tragedy, although the thought hovers over us, a brooding shadow of doubt. My mother, particularly, is deft at skirting this treacherous ground whenever we veer toward it.

In the meantime, waiting has stranded me in a permanent state of distraction. I'm losing cohesion; portions of my mind seem to be drifting away. Someone will be talking to me and pause for my reply, and suddenly I'll realize I haven't been paying attention at all. I'll be walking somewhere and I'll stop in confusion, forgetting where I'm going. In the last couple of weeks people have begun asking me if I'm ill. You'd think after waiting so long, I'd be used to it, I wouldn't mind, but in fact I find myself totally unnerved. Learning the girl's name has created some terrible urgency within me.

My mother crumples her eyebrows anxiously as she approaches. She's dressed in a pale green linen suit, the color of young leaves. "Rolando," she says in a worried tone and kisses my cheek. She tilts her head and takes a motherly look at me. "Are you all right?"

I can hardly tell her that it's only during my sessions on the red couch that I feel as if I'm inside my body. I can hardly explain to her that my real life has become insubstantial; only my dreams have the punch of reality.

I fall back on the cliché. I do a lot of that these days; I'm too exhausted for original thought. "Just tired," I tell my mother. "I'm quite tired. The committee," I say vaguely.

I hail a taxi and give the address of the laboratory. She places her thin hand over mine and we ride in a companionable silence. Today we are to donate fresh blood so DNA slides can be prepared. Samples were drawn years before in case we should happen to die before the girl was found, but new blood is drawn when possible. It's time-consuming, the preparation of these slides, and expensive, so expensive that blood samples are kept, but the slides themselves are not made up until it seems likely the evidence will be needed for comparison. With the girl herself beginning to seem a chimera, the very fact the procedure is being done seems auspicious. It makes us feel confident our lead is substantial after all.

Indeed, there is a comforting solidity to the whole laboratory process: going to the white clinical room, baring our arms for the withdrawal of blood. As we watch the technician write our names on the test tubes in his meticulous hand, our blood seems already evidentiary, destined to be critical in a judicial outcome, drawn only for the purpose of review by experts.

My mother and I are a rapt audience as the technician explains to us the process of extracting the DNA from the blood, the tedious business of stripping away the fluid's other components, the staining of the slides. When he tells us that DNA can also be obtained from semen, from hair, from scrapings of skin under the fingernails of victims, I become slightly uneasy about the samples of my blood I am contributing for posterity. But I can hardly ask for them back, and the way it is planned, there will never be a reason to connect me to the girl.

Then he shows us prepared slides from another case, the grandparents' DNA and that of their grandchild. As he explains how their genetic relationship was confirmed, my mother is enthralled. Her face is illuminated by a smile of such delight and excitement, for a second I can see what she looked like as a child.

Even I am intrigued to see the fuzzy bands of different thicknesses, the telltale imprint of heredity, although I never intend there to be any joyful confirmation of identity in the case of Mariah Alicia Ebinger.

Back in a taxi, the hint of a smile, a serene, almost beatific smile, plays at the corners of my mother's mouth. I know she is dreaming of a rosy reunion with her only grandchild. Having a sample of her blood drawn has lifted her, has pumped her heart full of hope. When she looks at me, her expression collapses into worry. "Really, Rolando. Are you sure you're all right? You don't look well. Have you been drinking too much?"

I manage a shrug. "Perhaps."

"Please," she says, squeezing both of my hands. "Don't lose heart. I know we are going to find her."

I nod and construct a smile. "Yes."

❖ ❖ ❖

I am just sitting down, just in fact lowering myself into the chair at my desk, when Lozano buzzes. My mother, on line one. I'm puzzled. I left her not half an hour ago. What can she want?

Her voice is urgent, emotional: *"They've found her."*

"What?" A film of sweat forms instantly on my hand, and the receiver nearly slips from my grasp. "Where?"

"In Wisconsin."

Wisconsin. Beer. The name "Milwaukee" comes crashing into my head. And that's it, that's all the information stored in my brain that connects to the word Wisconsin.

"I don't even know where Wisconsin is," I confess to my mother in an amazed tone.

"It's near Chicago, in the Midwest, near the Great Lakes."

"Wisconsin," I say. Suddenly we both laugh. It seems preposterous that "Mariah Ebinger" should be found living

in a place neither one of us could locate, in all probability, within a five-hundred-mile radius.

"Oh, Rolando, I don't know. If it's her, I don't know if I'll be able to wait. Do you think she'll remember us?"

"I really don't know. Do they usually?"

"No," she says in a tiny voice. "But I thought maybe..." Her voice evaporates and I hear several short, shallow breaths as she struggles for composure. "Listen to me," she says in a disgusted tone. "Of course she won't remember me, not at first. And I want to rush it, just like everyone I've ever counseled."

"Can I have it? The address?"

"Of course we have to confirm," she warns. "We can't even begin, we can't even send the initial letter until we confirm. Still...oh, Rolando. Can I see you? Could you manage dinner tonight?"

"Of course. I want to be with you. But—"

"What is it?"

"The address. I just want to see it, written down, in black and white. Just to look at it."

"Of course you do. I understand." She speaks the words and numbers. My hand does not seem to be attached to me. I watch it in the act of writing, as if it belongs to someone else.

2302 Elm Street
Janesville, Wisconsin 53404

At six I'm outside Retiro, waiting for Moro. Commuters are rushing to the trains. There's plenty of graffiti on the walls outside the train station, long-winded graffiti protesting the plan of the government to privatize the railway.

I buy a paper to have something to do while I wait. The major story, as usual, is about inflation. Runaway inflation, galloping inflation. Inflation in this country is always pictured as a horse that the government can't quite get its reins on, a polo pony, perhaps, gone berserk.

What I really want to do is jump on a plane and launch myself at 2302 Elm Street, Janesville, Wisconsin. But no, I can't simply disappear for a few days. I will follow the plan Moro and I have made. Earlier, as soon as I finished talking with my mother, I put in for leave, to be taken in two weeks' time. Everyone senses the strain I'm under. They all thought it was a great idea for me to take a short vacation, and I know my mother will agree.

Moro looks better and better as I look worse. He's gaining some kind of presence, a celebrity aura. He saunters toward me wearing an unconstructed silk suit and a gray turtleneck.

We take a walk along the river. I give him the slip of paper with the address written on it.

"I can't leave immediately," Moro says.

"What? Our arrangement was that you'd be ready to go at a 'moment's notice.' "

Moro rubs his jaw. "I had a tooth that abscessed. I'm in the middle of a fucking root canal."

A disappointed "No!" lurches from my mouth. Now that I look at him, I see that his face is swollen on the right side.

"I don't want to be on some fucking plane if this tooth acts up. I'm on antibiotics now. The dentist tells me the infection should be cleared up by the weekend."

I am literally speechless. I can't believe Moro is muttering something about a "permanent cap."

"I want you to leave now, tonight."

"Fuck you, *Capitán*."

I lunge toward him and grasp him by the shoulders, pushing him against the railing. He doesn't even tense his muscles. He finds my urgency amusing; a little laugh rolls out of him. *"Cap-i-tán,"* he says in an admonishing tone.

"Re-lax. We have plenty of time." His flesh seems oddly dense under my fingers. I release him and lean against the railing.

"Plenty of time," I repeat vacantly.

He's right of course. Weeks ago I asked my mother to outline the procedure for me—what happens when a child is located—so that Moro and I could make our plans. In fact, the process is very slow and deliberate. Every effort is made to reassure the "custodial parents," to involve them in a "non-adversarial" way. Every effort is made to cushion the child from the trauma. Lavish counseling is provided for each step of the way. My mother has made a life of this in the past ten years, explaining the procedures, counseling restraint, caution, patience.

Our legal position, she has pointed out, will be muddy at first. Child custody law in the United States is flexible; disposition depends less on legal concerns than on the court's perception of "what's best for the child." The girl is a U.S. citizen after all. Without cooperation from her guardians, even obtaining a blood sample for DNA comparison will require a court order.

I want Moro to make this solo trip for the purpose of reconnaissance, to minimize the time I myself will have to be away from Buenos Aires. Moro will do a dry run: rent a car, find his way from the airport, scout suitable motels, locate the house. He'll conduct surveillance on the family for a few days to ascertain the girl's habits. The ideal thing, of course, will be to determine a way we can take her alone. That way, after we kill her and dispose of the body, she can join the ranks of teenagers who simply disappear from their lives.

Moro has already acquired the necessary false passports, the visas, the tickets. When it is time for my trip, I am to fly to Bariloche to do some serious hiking and fishing, to truly get away from it all. It will be a real wilderness trip; I'll be out of touch for a week. Moro has briefed me both on the cover trip and on the actual way I'll get out of the country without detection. I'll take the normal boat trips and cross the border into Chile at Lago Frias, on my real passport, which will then be held in Chile until my return. I'll leave Santiago on false papers, fly to the United States and back, and then cross back into Argentina on my real passport. Moro has been thorough. Anecdotes of the false trip are steadily accreting in my mind. I already know the types of fish I have caught and where, which animals I will likely have seen. I already know the name of my mythical guide.

"*Capitán.*"

I can't quite focus on Moro. I see him through a quivery haze that makes it appear his face is melting. I realize belatedly that there are tears in my eyes.

"If all goes well with the tooth, I'll leave on Monday."

"Fine."

"I should be back by the weekend, Monday at the very latest." He raises his hand in a little salute. I watch him saunter away.

"Bon voyage," I manage. By the time the words come out of my mouth, he's almost a block away.

JANESVILLE, WISCONSIN
October

Chapter Five

MARIAH
Moving Target

I CAN'T REMEMBER WHEN I started having these dark moods. At first I thought it was just some quirky hormone kicking in, an adolescent thing. I put it down to that. I thought it was a more advanced form of sadness, stronger because I was older, but that I'd get over it. Sometimes now, when those bleak moods come on me suddenly like the pulses of a dark heart, I even shake my head or tap myself on the temple, as if my mind is a vending machine and it's just a question of jostling a loose wire back into contact and I'll be my old self again.

This time at least I have a reason for the mood. I feel it gathering force as soon as my father gets the words out. "Well, Mariah," he says. "It's that time again."

I don't know what he's talking about. "What?"

He flicks a glance to my mother. "We're moving."

They give me a moment of silence to let it sink in, and it does. The way I feel is: paralyzed. My mother must see it in my face because she goes for diversion. Ordinarily stingy with praise, she starts complimenting me. "Oh, Mariah will be all right," she says to my father with a quick, dismissive chop of her hand. "She'll be sad for a while but she'll bounce back. She's very *resilient*."

Nice that she's got it all figured out.

She looks at me nervously and then goes on, upbeat. "You haven't even told her where, Arthur. Tell her where."

"Washington," my father says, "Dee Cee. Well—to the Washington, D.C., area. The nation's capital. A capital idea, huh?" He follows this lame pun with his usual throaty chuckle.

He calls himself a "punaholic." Puns jump into his head and he can't keep from saying them, even though I've never heard anyone laugh at one of my father's feeble puns. He claims it's a compulsion, like biting your fingernails. My mother and I have developed a stagy groan as our response, and we perform it now in perfect unison. My mother flashes me a smile.

Every couple of years, just as we're settling into some town, just as my mother is getting the knack of the best places to shop and lining up a full schedule of piano students, just as I'm making solid friends and bringing my wardrobe and slang vocabulary up to local standards, my father's company transfers him.

His company does time management studies, so once some factory or corporate headquarters has been studied, and reports and recommendations made, it's time for Dad to move on. He says it's the nature of his job that we have to move a lot—like military people—but the truth is he *likes* it. No matter how happy he is where we are, he greets each move with unwavering enthusiasm. As he puts it, he sees each change as an "opportunity."

"I like it here too," he's saying now. "I like Janesville very much." His hands are jammed into the pockets of his khaki pants. He keeps a little penknife in his pocket; he's twirling it around in there. He looks straight into my eyes. "Don't think I *want* to leave, Mariah. That's not the point."

Even though he's saying the same things he always says, the standard moving speech, there's something funny about it, something wrong. He's got this pasted-on smile; his enthusiasm sounds forced.

We're standing in the kitchen. There's an unmistakably weary look in his eyes as they scan the walls where he's hung (with my help) the white lacquered pegboards that hold my mother's large collection of cooking equipment. I can see that mentally he's already beginning to dismantle the kitchen. The pots and pans and utensils will be placed in large boxes labeled KITCHEN GEAR in green Magic Marker. The screws and spacers and pegboard hooks will be held in Ziploc bags taped to the backs of the pegboards with strong transparent tape.

"I just thought—" I start, but something about their faces makes me stop. Suddenly, they look so old and fragile, so worn-out. I get the feeling that if my mother, in particular, has one more thing to deal with, she's going to start to cry. So I dredge up a smile. "I just have to get used to the idea," I say. "You know."

My parents are old. I was born when my mother was forty-four, the late but successful result of what she calls "fertility therapy." I'm sixteen, so that means she's sixty.

"Well this move is different. This time it really is a special opportunity," my father says. The deal is that he's leaving his company and going to work for a new one. "You probably didn't think some new outfit would woo your old dad, did you? You probably thought I was marching straight toward the Boorstein and Smathers retirement watch. I kind of thought so myself." He pauses and rocks back on his heels. "But it seems to me an opportunity is not to be resisted. It is to be recognized and then exploited."

"Do you want some hot chocolate?" my mother asks. She dips her head toward me in her nervous, birdlike way as if I'm still very small and she wants to minimize the distance between us. "It'll only take a minute."

I know that if I accept her hot chocolate, my father will launch into a talk. There's nothing he likes better than having "talks," during which he hands on to me some of his hard-earned wisdom. He has that gleam of anticipation on his face now; he rolls back on his heels in an expectant way.

"No thanks," I tell my mother in an apologetic voice. "I think I want to go for a walk."

Her eyes meet my father's; it's a significant glance that seems to reassure both of them.

I pick up my jacket off the back of one of the bentwood kitchen chairs.

"I know it's hard," my mother says suddenly, turning from the stove where she's sautéing onions.

My hand is on the door. I really want to get out of there.

"Nonsense," my father says. "She's going to love Washington. It's chock full of museums and such. It's a fabulous city, just fabulous. Have a nice walk, sweetheart."

I walk to the end of our street, Elm. Funny, because the elms all died years before, someone told me, of Dutch elm disease. Sturdy maples, each one staked and mulched, with protective brown tape spiraling up their trunks, line the street now. They're still small trees, their trunks about as thick as my wrists. The big old frame houses look exposed, the way houses do in new developments, too big for the surrounding landscape. It's as if some model railroad scenery's been thrown together from different types—the trees from HO gauge, the houses from a big Lionel set.

The maples have turned yellow tinged with red, and each one has a perfect, symmetrical shape. They look like flames. A blue car passes me, cruising slowly down the street, as if the driver is in unfamiliar territory, checking house numbers. As soon as I turn the corner onto Rutledge, I begin to run toward my friend Helena's house. The maples flash by me on either side. I run the four blocks fast, even though my Dock-siders aren't broken in yet and my feet hurt. I stumble up the wide front steps past the pots of lavender mums her mom put out there. Once inside, Helena and I don't speak until we've clattered up the stairs and are in her room. I throw myself onto her bed and dramatically bury my head in my hands. "We're moving."

"Ohmigod," Helena says in the way we all say that phrase, the voice trailing away on the "god" part, as if dozens of times a day we are robbed of speech. "When?"

I roll over on my back on her white eyelet bedspread. Directly above me, taped to the ceiling, is a poster of Andre Agassi, the tennis player. "I forgot to ask them. Six weeks. It's usually about six weeks."

"But I don't *want* you to move," Helena says. This is one of the main things she says all the time: "But I don't *want* a C on my report." "But I don't *want* to have a pimple." "But I don't *want* a D Hall."

Suddenly, it makes me want to hit her. Tears begin to come into my eyes and I close them so Helena won't see. She'll miss me, and I'll miss her, but I'm crying not because I hate to leave Janesville and my friends, but because we're moving *again*, and this time I'm not sure I have the heart for the effort. Tears begin to slide out of the corners of my eyes, and I know that soon I won't be able to keep myself from sobbing.

"Does Bobby know?" Helena asks in an excited voice. It occurs to me not for the first time that Helena views her life as a soap opera. This is an episode: Mariah Moves Away. But it's my *life*, I think, and with that corny thought, a little moan comes out of me. Andre Agassi seems to be swimming down toward me through my teary haze.

I jump up. Helena is thrilled by my wet eyes. "I've got to go," I lie. "I promised my mom…"

"Ohmigod," she says. "I can't believe you're moving. I can't believe it." I run down the stairs.

I sprint the six blocks to the woods down off Claremont Avenue, and by the time I get there, my cheeks are wet and stinging cold. I push through the brush until I get to the clearing where Bobby and I sometimes go. The afternoon light is harsh and throws sinister shadows. The shadows look evil, as if menacing things are hiding in them, just waiting for the dark to come and enlarge their territory.

The pile of rubble that is the debris of our romantic encounters—stubs of Barclay menthols, which Bobby smokes, squished Coke cans, a few wine cooler bottles— looks pathetic and sordid to me in the sharp light.

I spend a few minutes picking up cigarette butts and bottles and tossing them into the underbrush. I even start scuffing up the ground. I stop when I think what it reminds me of: a cat covering its shit. Then I sit down in the white mesh patio chair Bobby dragged there from someone's curb. The white plastic coating is coming off, revealing the rusty metal grid underneath. I pick and pull at the plastic while I sit there thinking.

I'm sixteen years old and I've lived in six different places.

Albuquerque, New Mexico.

St. Paul, Minnesota.

Raleigh, North Carolina.

Memphis, Tennessee.

Portland, Maine.

And Janesville, Wisconsin.

Our life wasn't really much different from place to place. We always lived in the same kind of middle-class neighborhood, and as far as I could tell, we always had about the same amount of money. I always made friends; I went to school. Sometimes I fit in right away and sometimes it took a while, but I'm adaptable, as my mother said.

I don't remember New Mexico because I was too little, but I remember the rest all right, and I go through them in my mind, thinking of each house and yard and the special places and friends in each place. Memories rise to the surface of my mind, like bubbles on a pond: the way Miss Mallory, my teacher in Raleigh, wrote on the board, the exact curve of her fancy capital letters; my friend Anita in Memphis, who gave me a gold cross with a rhinestone chip when I left. And when we drove away, she stood in the middle of the road and waved and waved until I couldn't see her anymore.

I sit in the mesh chair like that for a long time. Already I'm beginning to remember Janesville as if I'm not there anymore.

It's fall. It's October 7, 1989, to be exact. The leaves are turning color but they haven't yet started coming off the trees in quantity. The clearing still has a hidden, sheltered feeling, which it will soon lose.

We've had a warm fall and then a cold snap. The abrupt change in the weather seems to have clarified everything, as if the cold made the world contract into focus. Every blade of the dry, browning crabgrass, every leaf and twig and berry, seems miraculously, spectacularly clear. I close my eyes and turn my face up into the sun. Even with my eyes closed I can see patterns of light and darkness on my eyelids as the wind tosses the branches of the trees around.

I open my eyes. The sky is an intense blue. The expanding diagonal line of a jet trail cuts it in two. There's something about that blue sky and the angle of that jet trail that makes tears surge into my eyes. A huge convulsive sob pulls right out of me, so unexpected and so powerful that it topples me right over on the ground. Even while I'm lying there, weeping, I don't get it. I can't understand why the look of that jet trail in that blue, blue sky just about breaks my heart.

I don't know how long I'm there like that, right on the ground, sobbing like a little baby, but I'm carrying on hard enough that I don't hear Bobby. When he touches my back, it scares me so much, I think my body may explode from the shock. "Helena told me," he says.

I hurl myself into his arms and let him hold me. I know he thinks I'm weeping because I'll be losing him, and it isn't true, but easier to pretend that's it. I could never explain why a patch of blue sky and a jet trail made me feel like the world was coming to an end.

I feel so much better in Bobby's arms anyway; just the warm feeling of him and the familiar, tangy smell of his sweat takes the fear away from me, and in a little while I'm back in some kind of reasonable shape and telling myself I'm all right.

Bobby Bailey is a sweet guy with a good sense of humor and I like him a lot but I don't think I *love* him. I'm sure I'll recognize love by the crushing intensity of its effect on me. As proof that I'm not "in love" with Bobby, I haven't given in yet either to my own body or to Bobby's constant begging. I mean, we haven't as the books say, consummated our relationship. This is not because I'm afraid of getting pregnant or we're afraid of getting AIDS or herpes. We've learned all about safe sex and birth control in Family Life education at school. Bobby has condoms with him all the time in case passion overcomes me. It's only my feeling that I ought to be in the grip of a major obsession, unable to resist, that's kept me from following my natural inclinations.

"Baby," Bobby says. "Is this for sure?"

I nod my head.

Bobby sucks in his breath and heaves his shoulders. "We could run away," he offers.

We both know this isn't going to happen, but it's still the perfect thing to say. Bobby is the president of his class. He plays the major sports: football and basketball. His mother is some big deal in the PTA. His father is a pediatrician. They're rich and live in a big house on Welander Drive. Bobby is going to attend his father's alma mater, Duke, and become a successful doctor. He'll drop Bobby (this is already happening) and become known as Rob or Bob. He isn't going to run off with anyone and scratch out a living in the Sun Belt.

I shake my head and the breath goes out of him. Our hands are twined together and he raises them to his mouth and kisses my knuckles. He lets his head drop back and then he sighs. When he brings his head up again, he looks at me with a concerned expression. For a second, I can imagine him twenty years older, a doctor; he'll look at a patient like this.

When I shut my eyes, I can still see that patch of blue sky and the jet trail and I can still feel the desolate lurch of my heart.

"I'm going to miss you so much," I tell him.

Bobby nods in a solemn way and ducks into the bushes. Our stuff—a blanket, the package of cigarettes, matches, a bottle opener, some wine coolers—is in two green plastic garbage bags. Bobby brings out the blanket, actually an old cotton sleeping bag. It has a pattern of rocket ships against a navy blue background. I watch him spread it carefully on the ground, squaring up the corners in an obsessive way that reminds me of my father. We lay down on the blanket fully clothed. I can feel the hard knot of his erection through his blue jeans, like a fist under his zipper. We fool around for a while, and, just thinking of moving and everything and leaving Bobby, I almost go over the edge of my resistance. But I don't, and then the feeling goes away.

Bobby moans and moans; strange sounds come out of him. "Please," he says, "oh please." I have to admit that after a while I just don't feel anything anymore. It's like I either have to keep going all the way or else I have to shut down totally. Bobby has better concentration. He unzips himself. He lets his penis out into the air, something he's never done before. I'm amazed at the way it looks but I'm not turned on. I stare at his penis as if it's a medical illustration. Still, I know what he wants and it doesn't seem fair not to do it. I put my hand around it and move it around. He comes almost instantly. An almost painful sound squeezes out of him. He says, "Oh, baby, oh, baby."

I rub my hand around in the grass to get the stuff off of it. Afterward, we sit there on the raggedy sleeping bag, rocket ships all around us, and share a wine cooler. It tastes like Kool-Aid or those waxy boxes of fruit punch my mother used to pack in my lunch.

The sun is setting. A pinkish glow hangs over the horizon. Bobby walks me home through the fading light. He's unbelievably grateful. He keeps stopping to kiss me. We hold hands. I can feel his pulse in his fingers, the heat of his blood. It seems to me that the fact of my moving away is pressing us together, and I start thinking how maybe I really do love him after all. Now that it's too late, his kisses make me feel helpless and almost sick to my stomach. I'm weak with desire.

At my gate, he presses his forehead to mine, as if our thoughts might mesh and merge across the barrier of our skin. He draws back from me and stares at his feet. "Mariah," he begins, but then the door swings open and my father come out.

" 'Hello young lovers wherever you are,' " he sings in a lunatic baritone as he walks toward us.

"Hi, Mr. Ebinger," Bobby says.

"I guess Mariah has told you that we're moving on," he says to Bobby in a matter-of-fact voice.

"I wouldn't say 'moving *on*,' Dad," I mutter in a sullen way. "Just moving. I'd say *moving*."

He dips his head toward me. "Nice semantic distinction," he says, hitching his head to the side and making a little noise by pulling his tongue away from his front teeth. I hate that noise. "I guess we can thank the Janesville school system for that. Well, Bob, it's not quite time for goodbyes yet, but I want you to know it's been a pleasure knowing you. Dolores and I think you're a fine young man."

He sticks out his hand toward Bobby. I just can't stand being there with them for another second. I yank my hand away from Bobby's and run up the front walk.

"She's upset," I hear my father say.

"Yeah, well," Bobby says in a wary voice.

In the house, my mother is coming from the kitchen toward the living room, probably to answer the telephone, which is ringing. Her startled face confronts me near the front stairs. She's holding a wire whisk, and her white cooking apron is smeared with brown. For an instant I have the insane feeling it's blood on her apron, she's killed someone and now she's going to attack me. I go up the stairs as fast is I can and throw myself into my room. I actually lock the door.

I'm in there thinking I'm crazy, crazy, crazy. I'm saying to myself, stop it stop it stop it stop STOP IT and all the time my heart is jumping in my chest and I can hardly breathe.

It's quite a while until I calm down.

Maybe I'm really sadder about moving than I feel, I mean really, really sad, and this is how it's coming out. It's created some central instability or something.

Chapter Six

MARIAH
Seen From the Air

IT ISN'T SIX weeks until we leave Janesville; it's not even a month. Three weeks, that's about it. The new place in Washington—actually it's in Virginia—where my dad's going to work is in a hurry to get him out there.

The time goes by in a pleasant blur. Everyone's nice to me, and why not? I have no power in the scheme of things. It's nice, in a way, to be free from the side-choosing and social-balancing-act part of high school. Even if it is a little bit like being dead.

Between school, and fooling around with Bobby, and helping pack, I don't have much time to brood about moving. Besides, although I wouldn't admit it, I'm beginning to give in to the idea of a new place. My mind makes dreamy forays into what my dad would call a shipshape future: I'll always hand my homework in on time, I'll shave my legs every morning, etc. Also, of course, I'll immediately find girlfriends I like and trust...

We're good at moving; we've got it down. Our folded boxes stay with us from move to move, and we long ago learned it's smart to put the same things in the same boxes, so you don't end up with scratched-out, scribbled-over labels. We have checklists of boxes; early on, we lost important family stuff (all my baby pictures, for instance), and since then we even *number* the boxes. There are other lists, too, that cover everything from transferring my school transcripts to providing an envelope for the realtor to forward our security deposit.

This time everything happens so fast. The day after my dad announced we were moving, a guy from the real estate agency came to measure the rooms, check the condition of the paint, that kind of thing. Our house was immediately listed for rental. Outside there's a blue and red sign swinging from a wooden arm.

The agent, Jack Walls, reminds me of a little dog, a terrier or something. He has this eager look and he scratches his head a lot. He brings people through to look at the place, which really makes you feel strange. If we're around, they avoid looking at us and talk to each other as if we're not there. "We could put the sleep sofa there." "I like the dining room, don't you?" They open all the closets; they even look in the medicine cabinets. Jack smiles a lot and makes professional comments: "The traffic flow is fabulous for entertaining"; "...plenty of storage, and then you have the pull-down stairs to the attic too."

My dad calls the people who might rent the house "tourists." He comes home and asks my mother: "Any tourists today?"

This morning, when I left for school, a man was outside taking photographs of the house. He snapped me just as I came out the door. It was one of those things like on vacation, when you step in front of some people posing in front of some sight. I was sure I'd messed up his picture.

"Oh God," I said. "I'm sorry."

His mouth formed a precise smile; it reminded me a little bit of Jack Walls's smile. He put his camera back in his camera bag. "I'm from the property management company," he told me. "You know, the rental people. They need a picture of the house." He had a slight Hispanic accent.

"I thought it was already rented." I'd heard my dad talking to Jack on the telephone last night, something about a credit check and then "no more tourists traipsing through."

The photographer shrugged. "I don't know. They don't tell me that kind of thing. This was on my list."

"Maybe you should get another shot. I mean, I think I'm in that first one."

He wagged his head. "No, no problem. I took some before you came out." He hitched the bag up on his shoulder. "Well," he gave a little wave. "See you 'round." He turned and then stopped. "Guess not." He laughed. "Since you're moving. Where you going to?"

"Virginia," I said. "Near Washington, D.C."

"Oh yeah? I got a friend out there. Ar-ling-ton." He said the syllables like that, very evenly, with a little pause between each one.

"Where the cemetery is." My dad bought some guidebooks to the D.C. area and I'd been looking at them. Arlington Cemetery—it was one of the major sights.

The man looked puzzled for a second and then laughed again, a kind of weird laugh. "That's right. That's where President Ken-ne-dy is buried. So where you going? Near there?"

I shrugged. Helena was waiting for me. I wanted to get going. "Alexandria."

He shook his head. "I don't really know the area." He leaned up against the porch like he wanted to keep talking. It was awkward; to leave I had to squeeze by him.

He followed me down the walk. "Moving soon?"

"Next week."

He opened the gate for me and closed it behind us. "Well, good luck," he said with a little dip of his chin.

"Thanks."

When I got halfway to the corner, for some reason I turned around. He was leaning on his car, looking straight at me. I was a little embarrassed to be caught turning around. I gave him a half wave and turned back away. For some reason, he creeped me out.

My last night in Janesville. Tomorrow is it: moving day. Even though it's a Sunday, Bobby talked his parents into letting him have a farewell party for me. He promised it would be over early.

It was supposed to be a small party, but it ends up jammed, wall-to-wall kids. Bobby made a guest list for his parents but he just lets everyone in anyway. At first I keep overhearing these urgent conversations between Bobby and his mother. His mother nods her head discreetly toward some weird-looking dude and says, "Was he *invited?*" Bobby pretends he can't quite remember: "I think so."

For the first time in my life I get drunk, so my impressions of the party are kind of fuzzy. Kids keep talking about the future, but it isn't my future they're talking about. They talk about assignments, projects, the winter dance, Christmas parties, all stuff that's going to happen after I'm gone. I feel set apart, almost as if I'm not really there. It's as if I'm seeing it all from the air.

Bobby and I do some heavy making out in the laundry room until his little sister walks in on us, at which point he says, "Mariah spilled some Coke on her skirt," although I don't know how this is supposed to explain what we're doing. Helena barfs out on the patio. In the end a boy named Andy Rabin tries to drive his Mazda up the flagstone steps in Bobby's front yard and Bobby's mother totally loses it. Soon after that, Dr. Bailey kicks everyone out.

Bobby walks me home, squeezing my hand so hard it makes my knuckles hurt. "I'll write you every day," he swears. We walk slower and slower the closer we get to my house. Eventually we stand on the porch, immobilized for what seems like an hour, glued to each other, one long kiss. We say, you know, how much we'll miss each other, and then finally I just touch my finger to his lips and say "Bye" and stumble inside. My face is all raw and burning from where his beard rubbed my skin. I run upstairs to my window and watch him walk away. He walks very slowly and dejectedly at first, but when he gets halfway down the block, he breaks into a kind of determined lope and then he disappears around the corner.

The phone starts ringing. Before I get halfway down the stairs my father answers it. "No," I hear him say, "you've got the wrong number."

I wake up with a hangover. I'm surprised that being hung over is almost as disorienting as being drunk. The main problem, apart from the sickening pain in my head, is that something's wrong with whatever usually keeps my body in balance. I keep leaning over just an inch farther than I should and almost falling. My parents are too busy to notice how messed up I am.

The hangover does blunt the force of my sadness, which is a big help. I can see why the Irish get plastered at wakes. By the time the funeral rolled around, you'd be too hung over and wiped out to give in to bursts of emotion.

I'm sad Bobby didn't cut school and come over, even though I made him promise not to. I have to admit I'm disappointed that he's not more unhappy about losing me. I want him to do something crazy. His sweetness isn't enough, his hopes that we might "go to college together," his claims that he'll "never forget me." I want him to be freaked out, really wrecked, but instead he's only sad.

The thought of Bobby sweeps through me with such a jolt that I suddenly squeeze my eyes shut. I only just keep myself from sobbing. I sit in the dining room, rigid, drinking Coke after Coke, watching the movers stagger down the stairs with our furniture.

Professional movers are never the hefty types you expect. This bunch is no different. There's a skinny old black man who looks very tired and keeps clearing his throat all the time. There's a young, wiry white boy with an acne-scarred face, his hair caught back in a ponytail. He sneaks looks at me, thinking I don't notice. The boss of these two is a thirtyish, athletic-looking guy who wears an electric-blue Adidas warm-up suit and huge Nike high-top shoes. He's the strongest-looking one, but he does the least work. His shoes seem unbelievably big and clean. Blindingly clean. I can hardly stand to look at them.

My mother keeps giving them food and coffee and sodas. She flutters around her furniture. "That's my crystal in there. Be extra careful, please." When she isn't worrying about the furniture, she worries about the moving men. "Oh, that looks *heavy*. Maybe you should get one of the others to help you, maybe you should rest." She pitches in, over my father's protests, picking up lamps and lamp shades, footstools, light stuff, dragging it all out to the curb.

My father gives constant advice. "If you'll turn that chair counterclockwise a quarter rotation, I think you'll find it much easier to fit it through the door." "Can I make a suggestion? Take the door off the hinges. It'll take a few minutes but it will be well worth it."

It's freezing in the house with the doors wide open, and I wander through the emptying rooms in my ski parka. The rooms look grubby without their furniture and curtains, all the stains and nicks revealed. Bright squares and rectangles show where pictures and mirrors hung, even though they didn't hang there for very long. We only lived here in Janesville for about two years.

I collapse on the blotchy beige rug in my room, but lying down turns out to be a mistake. It seems as if the floor is moving, and my head starts throbbing and I feel like I might throw up. I decide I'll go for a walk. I stop to tell my father.

"That's it," he's saying to the man in the running suit and the boy in the ponytail, who are about two-thirds of the way up our basement stairs, one behind, one in front of our washer. This house didn't have a washer/dryer, so we had to buy a set. I guess the new house doesn't have one either or else my dad would have sold these. "Like that," my father says. "*That's* the ticket." The man in the running suit is on the downstairs end of our Maytag, which I see is going to barely fit through the basement door.

"Get out t'way," he says in a loud, desperate voice. My father hops nimbly to the side and the machine wobbles through the opening. It teeters there, on the edge of the stairs, and the boy with the ponytail struggles to balance it while the other man gets into a new position. The boy stretches over the machine with his arms hooked over its back. The pure white flesh of his lower back is revealed in the gap between his jeans and his jacket. You can see just the beginning of the crack of his buttocks. He keeps hitching his neck back, as if he can somehow close the gap and cover his exposed flesh, but of course he can't do anything about it without letting go of the washer. I look away.

Then the man in the running suit gives a big push from the stairs and the boy with the ponytail staggers back, crashing into my father, who didn't move back far enough. The movers stand there, breathing heavily.

I roll my eyes at the boy so he'll know that the whole family isn't stupid enough to stand directly in the way of two men trying to get a major appliance up the stairs. But when I turn to my father, his eager, engaged expression makes me feel disloyal.

"A walk," my father says, smacking his lips together. "Hmmmm." He looks at his watch. "Don't be too long. Our ETD is about three-thirty."

I give a little nod and go out. It's Monday, a school day. We never move on weekends—it's more expensive then. I consider going by the school, but then I think *what for,* to look at the bricks? So instead I head for the woods off Claremont Avenue. When I get there, I sit in the white mesh chair and drink a wine cooler, which is slushy with crystallized ice. I stay there for a long time, but after a while I get cold and I head home. *Home.* The thought of our empty house as home makes a crazy little laugh push out of me.

When I get back, the movers are in the kitchen drinking beer. "It's *Miller* time," I say. The little laugh comes out again.

"You bet," says the older black man warily.

My father barges through the kitchen door. "Where have you been?" he demands.

I put on an expression of puzzled innocence that's one of my specialties and push the fingers of my right hand against my breastbone. "I was *walking.*"

"You don't just go gallivanting off for an hour and a half. Your mother was worried sick."

"I wasn't *gallivanting.*" A smile forms on my mouth. I know the smile will cost me but I can't stop it. The wine buzzes in my head. The boy with the ponytail belches softly into his hand. "I was walking," I say. "I was *thinking.*"

"You didn't *think* about your mother, did you?" my dad sputters. "You know how she is. She convinced herself you'd run away. She even went driving around looking for you. She's got enough on her mind, don't you have any consideration?"

We finally roll off around three-thirty.

"Any last requests?" my father asks. "Want to cruise by the school?"

I shake my head. School will be just getting out. I hate the idea of having somebody see me now, when in their minds I'm already gone. "Let's just go."

We speed through the wintry dusk in our Toyota Camry, a purchase heavily researched by my father. He's a cautious consumer; he reads *Consumer Reports* cover to cover. He has firm opinions about water heaters, hair dryers, outboard motors.

I watch out the back window as Janesville recedes. It looks faded, in the dusky light, already a dimming memory.

"So long, Janesville," I say.

My mother leans over the backseat. "You're really sad about leaving, aren't you, honey?"

I shrug, but she's right. I'm having trouble not crying. "Umm-hmm."

"But you're looking forward to Alexandria," my father says in an upbeat voice, "right?"

"I guess I don't even get to be sad," I say, in a voice that's too loud for the car.

"Not much point in giving in to it," he says in a reasonable voice.

"*Arthur*," my mother says.

"Does everything have to have a *point*?"

My mother can't tolerate friction, especially in a confined space like the car, so she jumps in before we really get going. "Stop it, you two, *please* don't bicker. *Please*." She looks over the seat toward me and gives me the sweetest little smile.

Her hair is thinning as she grows older, and with the sun behind her, her scalp is clearly visible through her skimpy hair. Suddenly I can also see the form of her skeleton under the thin skin of her face, and the sight of her that way, so fragile and somehow unprotected, makes me feel even worse, even sadder. She reaches over the seat and strokes my hair with her thin hand and gives me that sad little smile again. "I'm sorry that we have to move, Mariah. I wish…"

She doesn't finish the thought and I curl up in the backseat, pretending to sleep. I'm trying to remember Bobby's face, to fix it in my memory, but instead I keep seeing my mother's skeletal grin. It's only a short time until the light fails completely. We hurtle on through the bleak Midwestern night.

BUENOS AIRES
November

Chapter Seven

ROLANDO
Domestic Help

I'M IN BED with Carla when the phone rings. She grabs for it and answers as if she's my maid.

"Carrera residence." Pitching her voice high. She thinks this kind of thing is cute. "Whom shall I say is calling?" Her accent is all wrong for domestic help.

"Give me the phone, Carla." She moves the receiver to the other ear, away from me.

"Who? I see." She holds her hand over the receiver. "There's a man named 'Blondie' who wants to speak to you." She lowers her lashes and looks at me out of the corners of her eyes. A flirty grin. "Is there something you haven't told me about yourself?"

Teasing banter is about as deep as it gets between me and Carla. Although her perceptions and comments often reveal her intelligence, she long ago decided to position herself in life as a dumb blonde. Usually I encourage her because the artificial quality this posturing gives our relationship suits me fine. I get to keep my distance.

I can't encourage her now. My heart flutters in my chest like a moth batting against a light fixture. "Blondie" was Hugo Moro's nickname in the old days, his idea of a joke, since his hair is quite black.

Moro is back from the States, right on schedule. He's been gone exactly a week. I give Carla my no-nonsense look and hold my hand out for the telephone receiver. She slips it into my palm with a pout.

"Did you?" I sputter. "What did you—?"

"She's pretty, your little teenager," Moro says. "Looks something like you, although she's not so light-haired; her hair is as dark as mine. Still, the family resemblance is strong. I did manage to get a snapshot."

The thready beat of my heart is almost alarming. A snapshot. After so much time. *A photograph.* Moro told me he planned to take one for practical purposes—so that I would recognize the girl, so that he and I would have the option of operating independently. Somehow I failed to imagine what it would mean to me. To be able to see her face. I'm light-headed; blood sizzles in my ears. I discover that I'm standing up.

"I'll be right over."

"*What?*" Carla says. She flounces off to the bathroom, tossing me an irritated look.

"Not now," Moro says in a fuck-you voice. "Let's make it tomorrow."

"*Tomorrow.*"

He's toying with me and I know it, but I can't stop myself from pleading. "I want to know what you found out. I need to—"

"Hey, I've been out of town, you know. I've been in fucking airplanes for about eighteen hours. I've got things to do. Get my cat from the vet's, for one thing."

"Your cat."

He relents. "I guess I could make it later tonight. Ten-thirty," he says in a take-it-or-leave-it voice. "My place."

I say okay, but he's already hung up.

Carla comes out of the bathroom naked. She's outrageously attractive, in a brassy sort of way, and here, so far from her own country, she's had free rein to pursue her notion of herself as a bimbo.

She poses, hand on hip. "*Where* are you going to come right over?" she complains. "What about me?" She stretches out next to me and begins nibbling my earlobe. Now she'll want to seduce me, to prove to herself how irresistible she is.

More and more, lately, I've been impotent. But this time, maybe because I'm so distracted by the thought of seeing Moro later, by the thought of a *photograph*, I relinquish myself to Carla's seduction and find myself capable.

When we're finished, I take a shower. Carla doesn't like to shower after making love. She likes the smell to stay on her; she likes walking around afterward with the crotch of her underpants damp, with semen stiffening in her pubic hair. She often confides sensual details like this to me, announcing them with a sort of ingenuous pride. It makes me think she's read a book about it—*How to Lead a Sensual Life*, something like that.

I must say I find Carla distinctly odd. At first I thought it was a cultural thing, but now I'm not so sure. She's from the States, a Californian. She has that California look, blonde and blue-eyed. Sometimes, even as I touch her, she doesn't seem quite real to me. Her skin seems too perfect, an analog developed through genetic engineering. From a distance she resembles a Barbie doll.

She's a trade representative for a computer firm; I met her several months ago at an embassy party. We had lunch the next day and immediately afterward became lovers.

She's still in bed when I come out of the bathroom. My clothes are draped over my rather ornate valet stand. It was a present from my father for one of my birthdays, eighteen, twenty, something like that. No doubt it was selected by his secretary, her taste ran to the baroque. Carla doesn't move, even when I'm almost finished dressing.

"Come on, put some clothes on. I'll take you out to lunch. Your choice." My pants are baggy and I cinch my belt in tighter. For the last couple of months I've been steadily losing weight.

She stretches and moans, sensuously of course. "All right." She sits up. "Do you have to wear that? I feel like I'm going to lunch with a Boy Scout."

She's talking about my uniform, which she dislikes. Apparently, the military has never figured in her erotic fantasies.

"I still can't believe I'm seriously involved with a man in the *navy*," she says, rolling over on her back, stretching her arms up over her head. It's only recently that she's begun to risk this exposure. She's had breast augmentation surgery; only in this elongated position are the scars visible. Actually, although I dislike the lumpy way the implants feel, I find the little silvery threads of the scars quite touching. I like to run my tongue along them, although it makes Carla nervous. "The navy," she says again, shaking her head.

"Perhaps if you think of it in Spanish," I say, "as the *armada*—"

She lets out a peal of raucous laughter. Her laugh is singularly shrill and unattractive. "The *armada*." She sits up, giggles on, out of control. "Oh, God, no. The *armada*. Oh, God, I'm going to wet my pants." Another shriek. "If I *had* pants." More laughter.

Despite myself, I'm offended.

After a few more rollicking chuckles, her laughter subsides. "You have to understand, Rolando. How can I explain this? To a person educated in the United States, there's only one 'armada,' and that's the *Spanish* Armada, the guys that were defeated by the clever little English boats

led by Sir Francis Drake. So when you say 'armada'—"
Giggles interrupt again. "I mean, I'd be thinking of you
sailing around in those old Christopher Columbus type
boats with the square sails."

"Surely this is your cultural deficiency, isn't it? If you
want to have lunch, get dressed."

She steps up behind me and puts her hands around
my waist, pressing her body against me. She's on tiptoe,
her chin on my shoulder. "I'm sorry, baby," she says in
her little-girl voice. She picks her panty hose off the back
of the chair, sits down on the side of the bed and begins
bunching up the fabric into her thumbs. "I don't mean to
make fun of your uniform or your navy. It's just that in
the States, men of your class do not generally pursue a
career in the military." She stands up, thinking about it for
a second, pulling the panty hose on, smoothing each leg in
turn. She turns her back to the mirror and twists her head
around to study herself from the rear. "Maybe that's just
post-Vietnam."

"I suppose two hundred years of civilian rule is bound
to diminish the reputation of the military," I remark. "Here,
we try to seize power every now and then, just to keep our
stock up, just to maintain the level of respect."

She looks up at me and raises her eyebrows. "I don't
know that that's such a good idea. To joke about it, I mean.
After all that's happened."

"You don't understand us, Carla." She looks up at me
with an inquisitive little frown. When she forgets to pose,
she really is adorable. "When our populace *elects* a government, when it actually *picks* its leader, it wants everything.
An end to inflation but without austerity measures; more
jobs, more pay, more benefits and less taxes. No one can
possibly do it, and so gradually, with no consensus about
priorities, everything goes to hell. Then we"—I thump
myself on the chest—"have to step in and straighten things
out. We get to screw things up for a few years, and the hue

and cry for elections begins all over again. This is simply
the way it works, our form of checks and balances."

"I wouldn't call what happened the last time you were
in power here 'straightening things out.' "

"Nevertheless, I give the present government a few
years—four, five at the most—before there's another coup."

"After all that happened. *No way.* I just can't believe
that."

I shrug. "You wait. What you don't understand is that
we're crazy down here."

I sit down next to her and put my hand on her breast.
I kiss her neck. "We're crazy about skin like this." I make a
line of kisses all the way down the tendon on her shoulder.
"We're crazy about girls named Carla."

"Oh sugar, you just got *dressed*."

"A fully dressed naval officer can still make a California
girl scream for mercy." My hand dips down inside her panty
hose; my finger slips inside her.

She yelps. "You need to cut your nails."

"I'll make an appointment with my manicurist." I push
her shoulder gently and her upper body falls back against
the bed. I suck her nipples, apparently too hard, because she
makes little displeased sounds.

"Be gentle," she urges. "I'm about to get my period;
they're very tender."

She tries to sit up, but I push her back down. "But we
just made love," she complains. "You said you were in a
hurry."

I'm surprised myself, especially given my recent lack of
potency. I haven't pushed myself on a woman since I was a
teenager, but I can't seem to help myself.

I'm afraid it goes on for a long time too, me slamming
into her. A couple of times she works hard, moving under
me, moaning like she loves it, biting my neck, tonguing my
ear, but eventually she just lies there and endures me. When
it's finally over, I'm embarrassed and full of remorse. "Oh,

God, Carla, I'm sorry. I don't know what's the matter with me. I'm sorry." She remains limp, so I wash her off gently with a lukewarm washcloth. She's not interested in smells now. She whimpers, actually, while I'm doing that, she's that chafed.

By the time we get to the Plaza, she's perked up a little. The real experience was unpleasant and painful, but she's already transforming it into something else—a paean to her desirability. Also, she likes to think of me as a sexual predator. The word "insatiable" comes up a couple of times. She shifts around coquettishly, making comments about her soreness.

She perks up, but I have to say I don't. Even my basic human appetites seem unreliable. Carla excuses herself to visit the ladies' room. "Order me a mineral water, please, when the waiter comes."

The room is full of Anglos; there's scarcely any Spanish in the air around me. When the waiter does arrive, I order a double whiskey for myself, a mineral water for Carla. He asks does she want still or bubbly water, but I can't remember her preference. I take a guess: "Still."

Carla enjoys the admiration she inspires as she completes her rather elaborate walk back to me. I see that she has completely redone her makeup.

"You look awful, Rolando."

I raise my whiskey. "Thanks."

"I'm worried about you. Why don't we take a *real* vacation? You and me. We could just lie on some beach, soak up the sun. I give you Carla's guarantee you'd come back rested and restored. I can't believe you'd rather track around in the woods shooting animals."

The waiter arrives with our drinks and stands attentively, ready to take our food order. I forget, between the time Carla orders and when the waiter turns to me, what it was that I'd decided to eat. I'm forced to open the menu again and order the first thing my eyes fall upon. "And bring me another whiskey. No, maybe a half bottle of wine. What are you having, Carla? Do you want red or white?"

"I really don't want any wine."

"Well, I don't care. Just some wine. I don't know. Red, I suppose."

"Anything in particular, sir?"

There's a strange feeling in my head, a bubbling pressure that makes it difficult to think. I can't think of a single kind of wine. Not a varietal, not a brand, nothing. "What...whatever. The house wine would be fine," I manage.

"Really, Rolando," Carla asks earnestly. "Are you okay?"

Chapter Eight

ROLANDO
Permutations of If

AFTER LUNCH WE walk down Florida Street, which is crowded with shoppers. Although every other story in the newspaper seems to be about the country's dire economic situation, the populace still seems to have plenty of time and money for shopping, We walk between two segments of the long line snaking out from Robertino's, where everyone from tourists to shopkeepers goes to change their dollars at the unofficial rate. The length of this line—today it stretches all the way out of the arcade and halfway to the newspaper kiosk—is a fairly accurate daily indicator of the currency's inflationary trend.

There are the usual street entrepreneurs. We fend off the kids trying to press into our hands slips advertising the leather factories. We edge by the circle of onlookers watching a man painting with his foot. I catch a glimpse of his work, a clichéd rendering of two tango dancers. It's not good, of course, but that's hardly the point; the point is not art, but triumph over adversity. Despite myself, I feel a little burst of sad admiration.

Farther down the street a larger crowd surrounds the bird fortune-teller. I've seen this one before, but we stop to take a look just the same. It's a one man/one bird show. The man has an accordion strapped to his chest, and on his shoulder perches a bird. I don't know what sort of bird it is, nothing fancy, something like a small pigeon. In front of the man is a table covered with a frayed lavender cloth. Several crumpled-up wads of paper are arrayed upon it in a circle. The man extends his finger to the bird on his shoulder, and transports the bird delicately to the center of the board. He then accompanies the bird's jerky steps with little flurries of accordion music. When the bird at last lowers his beak toward one of the crumpled papers and pecks at it, the fortune-teller plays a kind of accordion crescendo, picks up the paper and unfolds it. The bird gets to keep the seed the fortune was wrapped around.

"You must be careful today," the fortune-teller reads. "I think you should blindfold the bird," a tall man in an Adidas shirt says quite seriously. This makes the crowd hoot with laughter, and the man looks around with surprise. His friend elbows him in the ribs.

"Who's next?" the fortune-teller asks. A woman holding a child's hand raises her index finger.

I hail a taxi on Lavalle and give Carla's office address to the driver. Instead of jumping in, Carla insists on kissing me goodbye in her usual passionate way. Shoppers flood past us, and traffic builds up in a honking clog behind the taxi. I'm embarrassed—I'm in uniform—but I submit, out of remorse for my earlier behavior.

I have a conference at three at the Naval Club and an hour to kill before then. I buy a newspaper at the kiosk on the corner and go into the Café Florida for a cup of café con leche. The lead story is about Daniel Scioli's hand.

In his spare time, when our president is not coping with his unruly people and the even more unruly currency, he ceases being President Menem and becomes Carlos Menem, sportsman. He plays amateur soccer at a fairly high level and races motorboats for some team sponsored by a motor oil. We like this boyish, muscular quality in our president; his energy is reminiscent of John F. Kennedy's youthful vigor. He seems like a man who knows how to have fun and we like that too.

On Sunday the newspapers carried a big story about one of Menem's sporting endeavors. It was accompanied by a photograph displaying him—the famous muttonchop sideburns, the amiable smile—standing triumphant next to his racing partner, Daniel Scioli. The two had just won a race, and between them they held aloft a trophy.

Just one day after celebrating that victory (the story I'm reading now emphasizes), Scioli's racing career is probably at an end. Sunday afternoon Scioli was in another race, partnered by a different member of the team (Menem being back at the helm of the country). Scioli's boat flipped over and his hand was severed by the propeller. Divers searched the bottom in an effort to recover the hand, but found nothing.

It is a scene I imagine with some difficulty, the team of divers scouring the ocean floor for a human hand. I wonder what else they found down there: did they find the bones of the corpses dropped into the river during the troubles?

There are bones down there, I know that. Everyone knows that, although no one knows how many.

When a regime engages in the slaughter of human beings and expects to keep that a secret, disposal always represents a major problem in logistics. Think of the Nazis. Murdering millions of people was simple in comparison to the difficulties of disposing of their bodies. Here in

Argentina, death never became an industrial process, as happened in Germany. For one thing, the number of dead was not so great that the problem *had* to be addressed as a matter of policy. Here the efforts were haphazard: hasty burial in paupers' graves, cremation in oil drums, and eventually, the most popular solution, burial at sea.

Toward the end of the worst of the "abuses," there was a hurried attempt to get rid of the evidence before the human rights organizations came to call, and the number of so-called "doorless flights" picked up. The dead and apparently sometimes the living were loaded into the cargo bays of military transports and simply dumped over the middle of the Río de la Plata. The graffito on the bridge near Retiro is fading but still discernible.

DO YOU KNOW THE IDENTITY
OF THIS CORPSE FLOATING DOWNSTREAM?
IT MAY BE YOUR SON OR YOUR DAUGHTER.
IT IS SOMEBODY'S SON OR DAUGHTER.

After a few hours doctors advised the divers to cease searching for Daniel Scioli's severed hand. At that point, experts pointed out, it would be festering with microorganisms and could no longer be reattached.

I wonder how Daniel Scioli will approach life now that he has no hand. Will he go over and over the event in his mind, revising it to a different outcome? If he'd taken the wave a little differently, if he'd been in another boat, if he'd had a cold that day, if his partner had been driving and not himself, if he'd been thrown just another foot from the vessel... As I well know, there are a million permutations of "if" with which a victim can torture himself.

When I think about the past, I often contemplate my life as a construct, a maze leading me to the present unenviable moment. Looking at it that way, I find it so easy to see the thousands of instances where a different decision, a turn this way or that, a conciliatory gesture, a slight softening of my stance, could have changed everything.

For instance, I remember that pivotal dinner. It was a family affair, my mother's birthday, in fact. I was there with my wife, Liliana, and my daughter, Elena; my sister, Gabriela, was there with her husband, Victor, and their daughter, María. Liliana and Gabriela had been friends as schoolgirls; in one of those pleasant parallels, the little girls were also great pals.

So while we had drinks, the girls were having a wonderful time playing dress-up. My mother had set aside a section of her study for the grandchildren. There was a mound of stuffed animals, an old filing cabinet full of coloring books, games. She'd filled a steamer trunk with dress-up clothes: old costume jewelry, old dresses of hers and clothes of my father's. She'd also purchased some new items: ballerina gear, plastic knight's armor, a doctor's scrub suit and stethoscope, a workman's hard hat. The little girls started out dressing in recognizable outfits—a doctor, a businessman, a rich lady— but then they got the idea of mixing up the costumes and came giggling out in outfit after outlandish outfit, pressing their chubby little fingers to their faces and squealing with delight as we fussed over them and praised their wit. My mother got out her camera. I still have one photo of Elena in my wallet. She's dressed in a particularly bizarre but adorable combination: the knight's breastplate; the ballerina's tutu. She's grinning from beneath the brim of a fedora.

I'd made a pact with Liliana before we even left our house that afternoon. I wouldn't talk politics, I'd be on my best behavior for my mother's birthday. Friction had been increasing between my sister and me for months. It was probably unavoidable since ideologically we were on opposite sides of the fence. Victor was Gabriela's childhood sweetheart; they had married when Gabi was only eighteen. He was an assistant professor of history—Argentine history was his specialty—at the University of Buenos Aires. Gabriela herself was a student there, having returned to pursue her law studies when María was about two years old. Victor was a leftist, a supporter of the Montoñeros—something he had in common with many academics. It was a little surprising— and probably due to the fact that both he and Gabriela came from "good" families—that he hadn't been fired already.

The university was a natural focus of any regime's propaganda effort, and therefore especially subject to the wild political swerves that beset the country. Under the current regime, entrance requirements had been tightened, student activists and left-wing faculty dismissed, the curriculum revised. Many seemingly bland texts were banned, including the *Encyclopaedia Britannica*, for instance, which committed the sin of identifying the islands known here as "The Malvinas," by their imperialist alias, "The Falklands." Barely qualified but politically reliable men were appointed heads of departments to guide the student population back to "Christian thought."

It was a little amazing, given these circumstances, that Victor, a known leftist, had been able to hang on to his job. More than a year after the junta had seized power, Victor was still being permitted to lecture on Latin American history at an institution which had recently condemned Darwin's *On the Origin of Species* as "un-Christian."

Since it was my mother's birthday, I can remember the date of that fateful dinner exactly. April 23, 1977. I wasn't the only one trying to keep the peace for my mother's sake; Victor was on his best behavior too. More than once, during dinner, I saw him start to say something and then clamp his jaw shut with a forced smile. It's ironic, of course, that it was Mother, naïvely striding into the political territory that Victor and Gabriela and I were so cautiously trying to avoid, who started everything.

She mentioned that one of *Acción*'s reporters, Violetta Rausch, was missing. Several neighbors had seen her taken from her house and thrown into a car. "I thought this was going to stop when the military took over, these awful kidnappings. It only seems worse now."

"Stop?" Gabriela said, with a nasty little laugh. "That's a joke, right, Mom?"

My mother's eyebrows, delicately tweezed into elegant arches, curled into an expression of genuine puzzlement. "What do you mean, Gabi?"

Gabriela stared at her plate and tossed a nervous look at Victor before replying. "Tell me, Mama, do you think your colleague Jacobo Timerman was kidnapped by left-wing terrorists?"

Timerman, publisher of *La Opinion*, had gone missing several days before. "In his case," my mother said, "I thought the right wing probably took him. We can't seem to quite get rid of anti-Semitism in this country."

Liliana reached under the table for my hand and squeezed it. I kept calm.

Gabi looked again at Victor. Her voice was tight and nervous. "Mother, frankly I'm shocked that someone as intelligent as you are isn't aware of this, but hundreds of people have disappeared since the coup. Victor and I know so many students and staff at the university who have simply vanished. There's even a word for it now, these people who are disappearing—the students say they are *chupada*, sucked up. You can't get any information about them from anyone; they've been sucked into the void. But it isn't terrorists from the left *or* the right who are taking them. It's the government."

"That's the most ridiculous thing I ever heard," I said. "And I ought to know."

Gabriela snapped right back at me. "I hope you *don't* know, but frankly, it's hard to believe. It's happening right under your nose, Rolando. How could you *not* know?"

I tried to make light of it and turned to my mother, spinning a finger around near my head as if to indicate Gabi's foolishness. "She's lost her mind."

Victor also tried to defuse the situation. "That's not fair, Gabi. You're really not being fair. Most people honestly don't know. Most people, like Ana, believe the propaganda, that the Montoñeros are doing the kidnapping, that the old right-wing death squads are still operating. The propaganda has been very effective."

"Wait a minute, here," I interjected. "You're actually accusing the government of kidnapping citizens. And what is it supposed to be doing with them?"

"Holding them in secret detention centers," Gabi said without hesitation. "Torturing them. And sometimes killing them."

I laughed. "As for questioning people, this is part of the effort against terrorism," I insisted. "I suppose you are saying we should not interrogate terrorists. As for torture and murder, this is fanciful even for you, Gabi. You always have swallowed leftist propaganda whole."

"It's not terrorists," Victor said quietly. "It's just students, Perónists, anybody."

"You are seriously proposing that the government is kidnapping ordinary citizens. For what reason? We don't have time for that, I assure you."

"Violetta Rausch was not a terrorist," my mother said. "I don't believe she was even a leftist."

I turned to my mother. She'd pushed her plate aside, most of the food uneaten, and was smoking a cigarette. She looked at her fingers.

Things deteriorated rapidly after that. I accused Gabriela and Victor of working against the people's best interests, of supporting terrorism, of undermining the government. I accused them of having blood on their hands and trying to shift the blame to someone else. Liliana tried to buffer the growing hostility between us. "I'm sure

Rolando doesn't mean you and Victor *personally*..." Both
Gabi and I told her to shut up, and she left the room in
tears. Gabriela accused me of stupid loyalty to the military,
of underestimating the power and greed and stupidity of
the junta, of playboyism, of blindness, of supporting state
terrorism. "Just like a Wehrmacht officer," she spat out.
"You know what's going on but you prefer not to pay attention. As long as it doesn't personally touch you. As long as
your hands are clean."

"I don't know," my mother was saying.

"Just in my own classes," Victor put in, "five students
have disappeared, not to mention one of my T.A.s."

"You're calling me a Nazi?" I demanded of Gabi.

"I'm not calling you a Nazi exactly."

"Oh, not exactly, I see. Thanks so much, Gabi. Not
exactly. A fascist, would that be more accurate?"

"That's hardly the point. The point is you should open
your eyes, Rolando. You could be a force for the good. This
is a serious situation."

"You're saying I can join the efforts to destabilize the
country"—I looked from my mother to my sister to my
brother-in-law—"or I can continue to be a fascist collabo-
rator, is that it?"

Gabriela actually shrugged. By this time I was standing.
I'm not sure exactly why I became so upset. We had political
disagreements all the time, Gabi and I, and no matter what
names we called each other, or how heated the discussion
became, it had always remained simply a disagreement of
an ideological nature. Something had stiffened within Gabi,
that was one thing. There was no goading, no humor in her
remarks that evening. And her accusations had less to do
with my political opinions than they did with my personal
integrity. Secretly, I had always felt that my mother found
me slightly ridiculous, slightly ineffective, that her love for
me had a patronizing edge to it, that she found me less
worthy of admiration than Gabi, Gabi who seemed to be

without human weaknesses. Now I was being accused of being part of some vast governmental conspiracy to kidnap innocent people, and my mother was looking at her finger-tips and saying, "I don't know." It wasn't a neutral "I don't know," either. It was clear that my mother agreed with Gabi. And some repressed but still potent flame of sibling rivalry was fanned back into life.

For lack of anything else, the clichés are faintly descriptive of the way I felt: my blood boiled, I went stiff with rage. I left the room, without a word, and went to find Liliana and Elena.

"Rolando," my mother called after me.

"Can't we even have a simple political discussion," Gabi asked, "without Rolando becoming offended?"

There were two more attempts at family dinners after that, both disasters, both ending with Gabi and I screaming at each other, Victor stiffly trying to stay out of it, and Liliana, the little girls, and my mother in tears. So this is how we became estranged, my sister and I.

Then, after all the invectives Gabi had hurled at me, I simply couldn't stand the thought of Liliana being with her, the two of them trying to figure out how to bring me around. Shy little comments Liliana tried out on me from time to time led me to believe that Gabi had been working on her, twisting Liliana around to her way of thinking. Eventually I forbade my wife to see my sister.

It was hard—it was impossible—explaining to little Elena, who was scarcely four years old, why she could no longer see her best friend María, but after a month or so of Elena's complaining and whining, she seemed to forget about her cousin and her aunt, and she stopped begging to see them. A couple of times, I caught Liliana hastily hanging up the phone, or speaking in such a stilted way—she was a terrible liar, Liliana—that I guessed she was concluding a forbidden conversation with my sister. Once, Liliana tried to pry out of me, in bed, when I was in a cozy, post-coital mood, what it would take to accomplish the restoration of normal relations between Gabi and myself. I told her that since as far as I was concerned I was entirely the injured party, it would take a full-scale, abject apology by Gabriela before I could even consider forgiving her.

I trusted Liliana, I trusted her to do as I asked. I had no idea she had disobeyed me; I had no idea she was visiting my sister behind my back.

When I think of it now, it's clear that Gabriela won, as she always won. And in winning, she took from me not only my illusions, but in a single stroke, everything I loved. From the grave she both vindicated her argument and confirmed its truth in the cruelest possible way.

Chapter Nine

ROLANDO
Invisible Scabs

OF ALL THE things a man does in his life, his highest priority is still the same as the caveman's: to mate, to produce offspring, to protect them until they reach maturity. It is in this, my deepest human duty, that I failed completely. And I was unprepared, not only for the loss of my wife and child, but for my own failure. When I learned of Liliana and Elena's death, I descended into a bleak spiral of guilt and rage.

For months I operated within a fog of grief. I don't know when the notion of exacting revenge implanted itself in my mind. It's a natural response, of course, although most people let it go eventually. A few, like my mother, even manage to transform their vengefulness into political or social action. I was different. I couldn't forget, I couldn't forgive. I clung to the idea of personal vengeance, I nurtured it, I relied on it.

It began to seem that I was alive only to get even. I grew to believe that retribution might lift me from my despair, and if not, once my revenge was exacted, I could commit suicide a happy man. Instead of fading with the passage of time, my vindictiveness grew imperceptibly. I cannot place it, exactly when it happened, but one day I found myself truly obsessed.

The peripheral figures responsible for what happened to Elena and Liliana were easy targets. Easy to identify because of my access to the files, and easy to find, due to Moro's connections. Moro debriefed them, and in this way we learned a good deal. In this way we discerned María's role. As for the others, after their interrogations, Moro had no trouble disposing of them. Eventually María was the only one left.

But for so long that central figure of my dream of revenge was inaccessible to me; the honest truth is that I thought she was dead. Now that I know she's alive, Mariah Ebinger is all I think about. Within my mind, her domain is expanding all the time, as if she's a cancer in my consciousness. Sometimes, lately, I am unable to think because her name repeats in my head in a dull robotic whine: Mariah, Mariah, Mariah, Mariah.

Occasionally, even now, I remember that she was just a child when it happened. Just for a minute or two, I know that I'm insane. Nothing makes me more uncomfortable than these lucid intervals. When I'm in the middle of one of them, I can hardly stand being inside my own skin. I scratch at it like a junkie, I pick at invisible scabs, I pull at my hair like one of the poor homeless creatures I've seen hunched against the walls down by Retiro. I feel the way they do, needing to touch myself continually—even hurt myself—for reassurance that I still exist.

The rest of the day passes slowly and deliberately, the dull minutes dragging themselves past their indifferent spectator, me. I am so impatient for my meeting with Moro, I am so impatient to see the photograph, it brings back to me the way I felt as a child, before I was conditioned to endure the relentless pressure of boredom. I remember long tedious stretches in church, and certain classes in school when we boys sprawled insensate at our desks, stupefied by monotony.

Every time I look at my watch, it seems that no time at all has passed. The sullen, stubborn crawl of the seconds makes me feel physically ill. The afternoon proceeds at this crushingly dull pace. I beg off my appointment. I can hardly concentrate on persuading a nervous general to be less inflammatory in his public statements. The truth is, I can hardly speak.

I arrive at Moro's half an hour early and pace up and down the block until time for the appointment. It's such a relief when Moro pulls open his door. Just the sight of him soothes me, dispels half of my anxious tension.

He stands aside, without returning my effusive greeting. His face is pinched with fatigue. He doesn't bother with wine this time, or hors d'oeuvres.

"So?" We sit down across from each other. "I want to know *everything*."

"You won't be pleased. Except with this." He slides a manila envelope across the table toward me.

I barely hear him. I pull open the metal clasp of the envelope and tumble out the photograph: a pretty girl looks at me with a slightly startled expression. A weird and embarrassing sound emerges from me, something like the sound a cat makes when it sees a bird through the window. Moro is saying something again.

"What? I didn't hear you." I can't stop looking at the photograph.

"I said she's moving. We'll have to start from scratch."

"What do you mean she's moving?"

"What do you think I mean? I mean that she's fucking moving to a fucking different house in a fucking different city. I mean that she's moving a thousand miles away from where she is now, that's what I mean."

The pressure of my fingers has dented the edge of the photograph. I try to smooth it out but I have done too much damage. "Do you know...do you know *where*?"

"I know the name of the city. I got that out of her."

"You *spoke* to her?" My eyes keep flicking down to the photograph, as if I'm afraid it will disappear.

"It would have been so easy there," Moro says in a wistful voice. "She was always going into the woods to meet her boyfriend."

"If you know where she went, it shouldn't be so hard to find her again." This is a hopeful comment, trotted out by some optimistic part of my mind that remembers my mother saying something of the sort.

"I'll tell you this: it would have been a hell of a lot easier if she'd stayed put," Moro says. "I did a little checking at the local library there. She's not moving to some little town. It's a big place, over a hundred thousand people."

I find that I am standing up now, clutching the photograph to my chest as if it might act as a shield. The severity of the setback is dawning on me. This means the whole setup is down the drain. Even assuming we find her immediately, Moro will have to travel to the States again, reconnoiter all over again. I'll have to rearrange my leave. The tickets to Chile, the trip to Bariloche, the whole deal is blown.

A black cloud, a hopeless disappointed gloom, descends over me, a devastation so acute that a puny wail escapes from me, a cry so defeated and strange that even Moro gives me a sharp look. I am struck down by the news, my legs wobble, it is only luck and the habit of upright posture that allow me to keep my feet.

Part Two

ALEXANDRIA, VIRGINIA
March

Chapter Ten

MARIAH
Gee Dubbaya

MY SCHOOL IN Alexandria is called George Washington High School, G.W. for short. This is pronounced with a semi-Southern accent I quickly master: Gee Dubbaya. George Washington's name is all over Northern Virginia. You see his silhouette everywhere too—the patrician nose, the little ponytail. Mount Vernon is less than ten miles south of our house. My father, of course, has already planned an outing.

G.W. has more than 2500 students. I've never gone to such a big school. The first day, when my father takes me there to get me registered, even his jaunty, toed-out walk slows as we push through the front door. A huge surge of noise washes over us as we step inside.

Dad stands there for a moment, stunned by the decibel level. The noise doesn't bother me, I'm used to it. It's the

same in every school. The hard surfaces in the hallways—
tile and metal lockers and linoleum—make the sound of
hundreds of kids milling around even louder.

A bell rings. Everyone starts rushing to get to home-
room on time. Locker doors slam all around us, an
explosive sequence of metallic clangs. Everyone has to shout
to be heard; everyone's doing it now.

"Hey. Jamar. Jamar! Borrow your English book?"

"You won't believe this—"

"—geometry quiz."

"Catch you at lunch."

"That motherfucker lays one finger on me—"

"New skirt, Katie?"

"—don't be failin' no health."

My dad is kind of nondescript-looking. I mean, you
wouldn't notice him. His predominant color is khaki. Beige
skin, light brown hair. He wears khaki pants and a muted
plaid shirt. Only his blue eyes stand out. He bounces me an
alarmed look.

Kids are rushing by; he looks helpless. Finally, I tap
a sleeve belonging to a huge girl with rosy cheeks, who
directs us to the office.

Besides the sheer size of G.W., another thing that's
different from my old school in Janesville is that at least
half the kids in these halls are Black. I stare at their fabulous haircuts: zigzags razored into the short hair behind
their ears, hair that extends straight up from the sides of
their heads kind of like dark chefs' hats, hair shaved up
the sides and back and tufting out at the top in a kind of
pineapple look. They strut past us as if we don't exist. In
all the other schools I'd transferred to in the middle of an
academic year, I'd been immediately pegged as the new kid.
This place is too big for that; I'm invisible.

We pass a bulletin board displaying antidrug messages.
There are slogans and substance abuse hotline numbers and
brutal cartoonish illustrations: O.D. victims with pinwheel

eyes; gigantic syringes dripping huge droplets marked AIDS; a drawing of a person, zigzagged down the center, split in two. Both halves are falling off a cliff. The caption says: "Don't CRACK up." My dad scrunches up his face and tosses me another look.

It takes about half an hour to conclude the formalities of enrollment. The guidance counselor has sleek gray hair brushed back from his head. His hair is separated into little triangular points like an animal's pelt when it's just come out of the water. His name is Emmet Page and he looks a little bit like Kenny Rogers. Emmet Page does the talking; my dad and I smile and nod a lot. When it's time for him to go my dad looks deeply relieved. He gives me a make-the-best-of-it smile.

It takes me about a month at G.W. to figure things out—who to be friends with, the crucial alterations to my wardrobe and slang. I have to get, for instance, some black cloth Chinese shoes with straps. These were unknown in Janesville. I have to get rid of the thin, woven cloth bracelets ("I haven't seen one of those in an age"). They don't say "OHmigod" here; they say "ohmyGODDDDD."

This is such a big school, no one notices me in the halls, but in each class, everyone knows me as the new girl. Before my newness wears off, I try to make friends with as many people as I can.

I'm mostly in Honors Classes, which in this school system are called "Phase Four." Lots of things have different names here. For instance, Home Ec is "Teen Life." Typing is "Keyboarding." Shop is "Exploring Technology." My father says the curriculum is a masterpiece of euphemism.

"Minorities" actually constitute a majority at G.W. Besides the large number of Black students, the school has a lot of kids who don't exactly speak English. Most of them are from El Salvador or Nicaragua, and some of them don't really know how to read and write even in Spanish. There are a lot of Asians too, from Cambodia and Vietnam. As

I've learned from P.E., some of the Hispanic kids, the ones that don't speak English, wear hidden religious ornaments, which they touch secretly. When I try to imagine being in this big school and not speaking the language, and not even knowing how to read in my own language, I just can't picture it at all.

My new best friend is Darlene Cullen. I'm lucky she likes me because she's really popular. She happens to live two blocks away and we have three classes together, so it's easy for us to be friends. We try out for the soccer team and we both make varsity.

She has strawberry-blonde hair and even strawberry-blonde eyebrows and eyelashes. Her parents both work for the government. Kids hang out in front of her house, which is about a half mile from G.W. No one is supposed to go inside but sometimes Darlene sneaks me in.

She's a little bit fat, which bothers her a lot. She's always throwing down half-eaten things, a Moon Pie or a Twinkie: "Can you believe I'm eating that? *Godddddd.*"

I tell her my father's theory about why people eat too much: that in ancient times, people who could eat a lot had an advantage. They could survive shortages in the food supply. "Great," Darlene says. "So I'll be able to tough it out better than most if famine strikes Northern Virginia." I have to agree the threat seems remote.

Darlene is very funny about her name. "I mean what kind of a name is that for two *lawyers* to give their only kid? I mean when you met me, could you believe my name was *Darlene?* This is a name—I mean the only kind of job you can imagine with a name like Darlene is one where you have to *wear a name tag.*" I'm laughing; there's something about the way Darlene talks that always starts me laughing.

"You have an aunt or something named Darlene, right?"

She shakes her head. "No. They came up with it on their own. They just looked down into the bassinet and the perfect name jumped out at them." She stands up, pretending to be her mother, putting a prissy look on her face. *"Darlene,"* she gushes. *"Let's call her...Darlene."* She sticks out her lower lip and sends a jet of air up toward her bangs, which lift and then fall. "Sometimes I'm surprised my mother ever had a baby. I mean you'd think it would have been too *messy* for her."

"I think your mother is nice." This isn't true. Her mother wears expensive clothes and a permanent frown. She hasn't managed to learn my name yet. I'm "one of Darlene's little friends."

"Give her time." She picks up the Moon Pie and hands it to me. "Don't let me eat this, okay? Don't let me see where you throw it away." She groans at her weakness.

There aren't as many couples here as there were in Janesville. Kids socialize in big, mixed groups, they don't pair up so much. Our group goes everywhere together—to the movies, to Baskin-Robbins, to basketball games, on field trips—like a tribe.

At first I keep my distance from the guys anyway, in loyalty to Bobby. I show everybody his picture, I tape it in my locker, I talk about him, I say maybe he'll come for spring break.

For a while Bobby and I write letters back and forth two or three times a week and tell each other "I love you" during our telephone calls. Darlene keeps me informed of local interest: "Taylor has a crush on you but he's still seeing Holly." "Andrew Arnold likes you, Mariah. Now he's *hot*, you've got to admit." Then Bobby and I stop writing so much. Maybe we talk to each other once every couple of weeks.

In March, I receive a cream-colored envelope addressed to me in Helena's careful round handwriting. Inside, I read that Bobby is "seeing" Angela Wellington.

He calls a couple of days later. We talk for a while before he gets around to Angela Wellington. I talk about G.W., Darlene, Washington. He talks about our old friends, a local tragedy—a kid we knew slightly who got badly injured in a car crash. When he springs the news, he gets through it in a tight voice, as if he's holding his breath. "Mariah, there's…someone else." His voice brings him back to me. I can just picture him sitting there, talking himself into calling me. It's so Bobby to call me like this, to do the right thing. Thinking of him sitting there, I really am sad; tears start dribbling out of my eyes.

"Helena told me."

We both stop speaking. The silence fills with faint crackles and squeaks, as if our connection might fade before we actually say goodbye. Bobby says quickly: "I'll never forget you."

When we hang up, my throat is aching; I'm starting to cry for real. My father looks up as I pass him on my way to my room. His eyebrows bunch up. "What's wrong, honey?"

"Bobby and I broke up." I rub my eyes.

"Of course you broke up," he says in his entirely reasonable voice. "He's in Janesville." He flips his hands to one side. "You're here." He flips them to the other side. "You're sixteen years old, for crying out loud."

I want to go to my room, but I have to stay there and listen to him. He rolls back on his heels and starts talking about Reality. He talks about distance, time, age, expectations. He's trying to comfort me, as if these *facts* can somehow make me feel better. The buzzer goes off in the kitchen. My mother opens the oven door. She's humming the Hallelujah Chorus. My father keeps on talking. All of a sudden I just can't stand it anymore, the sound of his voice drilling into my brain. "Shut *up*, Dad," I say. "Could you just shut the fuck up?"

I launch myself toward the front door. My father is yelling something after me. I make out the words: "young lady."

At Darlene's house her father answers the door. He's a redhead, like her, with an open, genial face. He senses something is wrong, and I step in through the door he holds open. "I don't believe Darlene is here, Mariah, but—"

Darlene's mother steams into the room, fixing the clasp of a gold bracelet. She doesn't even look up at me. "She's out with some boy named—let's see—Nixon? No, I would have remembered that. Dixon? I think that's it. Charlie, we've got to get a move on."

I wander from Darlene's house down toward the Metro stop. I find a few crumpled dollars in my jeans pocket and buy a fare card. On the train I sit opposite the map of the Metro system. Ribbons of color represent the different lines; I stare at the confused knot of downtown. I close my eyes. The motion itself is soothing. As we move smoothly along the miles, Bobby recedes from my mind.

The train is almost empty. Two Black women sit in the middle of the car, their heads inclined toward one another, talking. Every once in a while, one of them laughs good-naturedly, but I can't hear what they're saying.

A disembodied voice mumbles at the stations: Braddock Road, National Airport, Crystal City, Pentagon. Past the airport, the train plunges into a tunnel. I try to pinpoint the exact moment we pass under the river, and I think I do, sensing a distinct change in the air pressure, but of course there's no way to be sure.

Chapter Eleven

MARIAH
Gypsy Moths

I GET OUT AT the Archives stop and head for the
Washington Monument. It doesn't look far, but it takes me
longer to get to it than I expect. I stand near its base for a
few minutes. A group of German tourists collects around
me, meeting up after a trip to the top. They talk loudly,
using a lot of sweeping hand gestures, and take turns
posing for photographs with the obelisk as a backdrop.
Together we watch the circle of flags around it snap and
toss in the wind. One of them says, *"Wunderbar."*

I cross Seventeenth Street and walk along the Reflecting
Pool toward the Lincoln Memorial. When I get there, some
little kids are taking turns sliding down a smooth slab of
marble next to the flight of steps, whooping and giggling
in the fading light. I mount the cream-colored steps. The

seated figure of Lincoln appears as I pass between two
huge Doric columns at the top. He looms above me, sitting
serenely in his enormous chair.

Lincoln is dressed in his normal outfit (except for no
top hat): frock coat, bow tie, stovepipe trousers, all of it
in creamy-white marble. He looks impossibly white and
solid, an embodied ghost. His huge hands rest on the end
of the arms of the chair. They seem to have some muscular
tension, as if he's about to grip the chair and push himself
to his feet.

A man's voice behind me says reverently, in a Midwestern
accent: "He was a great man."

"You bet," chirps his wife.

I have a momentary image of Lincoln rising to his feet
and staggering through the Mall, like the marshmallow
giant in *Ghostbusters*.

I walk across the Memorial Bridge toward Arlington
Cemetery. My feet are starting to hurt. Traffic rushes by;
joggers lope past, breathing heavily. In front of me, up on
the hill, the eternal flame at John F. Kennedy's grave winks
and twitches in the wind. Below me, the brown, muscular
water of the Potomac, swollen with spring rain, moves
silently toward the sea.

I get on the Metro again, then wander back home. As
soon as I catch sight of my house, I know that my parents
will be not just pissed off, but worried, so I'm prepared for
the vigil that greets me as I come through the door. My
mother is sitting, tilted forward in the Boston rocker, literally wringing her hands. Her red-rimmed eyes stare at me.
"Oh, thank God," she says in a relieved quaver. I'm afraid
she might actually fall to her knees.

"I'm sorry," I say reflexively.

My mother is a born worrier; she lives with fear. Any
deviation in routine makes her imagine the worst. If my
father is an hour late, she's ready to call the hospitals.
Forget traffic jams, losing track of the time, getting lost.

The intensity of her dread never changes, so it's hard to take her worrying seriously all the time. She can get as worked up about a splinter—"I've heard they can work their way to your heart, I'd better call the doctor"—as a nuclear threat. But looking at how wrecked she is, I get a surge of guilt.

My father stands with his hands on his hips and taps his foot. "I guess you've got some explaining to do."

"I said I was sorry."

"Don't you *ever* tell me to shut up."

"I'm sorry I'm sorry I'm sorry," I say loudly, through my teeth. They exchange looks. My voice tries for the earnest, regretful tone I know they want. "I'm *sorry*. I mean I really am totally sorry. You know," I say vaguely. "I was upset."

"Where were you?" my father snaps.

"I went to the Lincoln Memorial."

He gives me a sharp look, trying to tell if I'm bullshitting him or not. I stare at my feet. I'm wearing an ancient pair of Tretorns with holes near my little toes, tiny explosions of frayed canvas.

"You know you're going to have to be grounded," my father says. "And I mean *grounded*. No soccer, no dates, no dances, nothing. Do I make myself clear?"

"I'll get kicked off the soccer team."

"You should have thought of that," my father says flatly.

"Can I go to my room?"

The telephone rings, as I head for the stairs. I'm closest so I pick it up.

"If that's one of your friends," my father says, "you can't talk now."

"I'm sorry," I say into the receiver. "Could you repeat that?" A high-pitched voice asks if he is speaking to Mariah Ebinger.

"This is Mariah." I don't recognize the voice.

"Ah," says the voice, and then the connection is broken.

"Who was that?" my father demands.

"I don't know. He hung up."

"Dinner is really overcooked," my mother says. "Maybe we'll just have some sandwiches."

I guess I want to show my dad the downside of grounding me, so when I'm not at school or doing homework, I just stay on the couch, watching television. I pick programs my father hates: *Wheel of Fortune, Jeopardy, Double Dare*. The air in our family room is filled with breathless lists of prizes. "She's also won a set of Pierre Cardin luggage, a Jules Jurgensen watch, a La-Z-Boy recliner..." Audience enthusiasm strikes me as forced. I develop strange attachments to contestants.

"Alan is an aerospace engineer. What exactly do you *do*, Alan?"

"Joan is a computer consultant who enjoys reading and rock climbing. She's single and she *enjoys* it. Now what does *that* mean, Joan?"

I notice that I seem to root for the men and dislike the perky women, which probably reveals something bad about me.

The women seem well-prepared, coached, looking to rack up winnings. The men act as if they're not quite sure how they ended up sitting someplace decorated in primary colors.

I'm not unhappy when the men lose. I like watching them shrug their disappointment away, as if they're better off anyway. What would they *do* with a Broyhill dining room set? The women don't handle loss as well; they smile in a tight-lipped, bitter way, as if they knew all along nothing good was going to happen to them.

When there's no game show on, I watch MTV or sitcom reruns: *Cheers, Family Ties*. We're surrounded by bursts of canned laughter.

One thing: I'm getting over Bobby. I tell Darlene to let Ryan Ferguson know I "like" him. He's going with Miranda Bates, but everyone knows they're breaking up, especially me, because Ryan Ferguson has been heavy-duty flirting with me for about a month. He's always stealing my shoes on the bus. I'll be dangling my shoes from my toes, letting the heels scuff against the floor, and then suddenly I'll feel one sliding away from me and a little while later Ryan Ferguson will hold it up, acting amazed. "God! Look what I found. A *shoe*. Did anyone lose a shoe?" He goes through a little Cinderella routine before he gives it back to me.

I've never lived anyplace where spring is so beautiful. The houses in our neighborhood are old, from the thirties. There are tons of big oak trees, and under them, dogwoods and redbuds and lilacs and endless drifts of magenta and pink azaleas. But the trees are in trouble, my father has told me, because of gypsy moths. He came home from a community meeting on Wednesday and told me I could look forward to "plenty of work" on Saturday.

I make a plan. I'll work my butt off on Saturday and then I'll get Darlene to just "drop by." She can pretend she's returning my geometry book. If she gets there at the right time, after a long afternoon of me working hard, I think I can get my dad to lift my restrictions. Darlene promises to try to get Ryan Ferguson to come with her.

So I spend about six hours on Saturday doing yard work with my dad, pulling ivy down from the big oak trees in the yard, scraping off the little tan masses of gypsy moth eggs. I hold the ladder for him while he climbs up and scrapes the high ones into a coffee can.

"It's kind of like what happened with the killer bees down in South America," he says from the top of the ladder. "Hold the ladder, will you honey?" I brace it. "It's not level down there," he adds, as if I need to be persuaded he's in danger. "Anyway, Mariah, it was a French scientist who first imported the gypsy moth from Europe. This fellow worked in Boston. Just like the misguided soul who imported the African queen bees to improve the common Italian honeybee, this gentleman was attempting to breed a new and improved type of silkworm. Hand me that trowel, would you?"

I hear the slap of the screen door. "For heaven's sake be careful," my mother says.

He begins climbing down slowly; the ladder *is* unstable. When he gets close enough to reach me, he hands me the coffee can and I dump what's in it into another can full of Clorox.

"God, this is gross." The eggs foam in the bleach.

"Same old story," he goes on, moving the ladder to the next tree. "Some of the caterpillars got loose, and ever since, they've been chewing their way south, defoliating their way across the country. Bill Windler next door says it was like Borneo here last year, thousands and thousands of moths in these backyards. And when they're in the caterpillar stage, you can hear 'em, munching away up there in the trees. You can actually hear their *excrement* falling. Bill says it sounds like it's sleeting."

I work hard all afternoon, stuffing ivy and raked-up leaves into green plastic bags, bracing the ladder for my father, sometimes climbing up myself to scrape eggs off. This is heaven for my dad: telling me interesting things while we work hard together.

When we're through, I drag the garbage bags to the driveway and line them up neatly. "We've probably removed a million eggs, don't you think, Mariah? Each one of those egg masses is supposed to contain five hundred to a thousand eggs."

The phrase "egg mass" alone makes me want to puke.

"That's a *million* caterpillars," my father says, shaking his head. "Can you *imagine* that? A *million* caterpillars just from our little backyard. And we probably didn't get half of them. They're going to spray, of course. The city is going to do aerial spraying."

I'm just getting out of the shower when Darlene shows up. Perfect timing. I'm rubbing my hair with a towel as my father opens the door. Ryan Ferguson stands behind Darlene, slouching against one of the little porch columns. He's wearing a green-and-gray-striped rugby shirt, baggy shorts and docksiders, no socks. He's holding a couple of baseball gloves. He's looking at me. He has a way of turning his head to the side and looking at you out of the corners of his eyes. It's much more personal than a direct look, as if he was just in the process of turning away when his eyes caught on you and he couldn't help himself.

"Hello, Darlene," my father says. "I'm afraid Mariah's still grounded."

Darlene sends her customary little jet of air up from her lower lip. Her bangs lift and fall. "Oh I know, Mr. Ebinger. She loaned me her geometry book and I wanted to return it."

Ryan steps forward from the column and holds out the book.

"I'm Ryan Ferguson," he says in an assured voice. "Nice to meet you, Mr. Ebinger."

"Sorry," I say. "This is my dad; Dad, this is Ryan."

They shake hands. Ryan says: "We were hoping 'Riah could come and play softball. We're having a little pickup game down at G.W." The use of a nickname, which no one has ever called me, seems very strange, but it does have a certain effect, implying that Ryan and I are some kind of old buddies.

And softball—this is the kind of wholesome, outdoorsy stuff my dad wants for me. He rolls his eyes up to the sky for a moment, as if consulting heaven for advice. Then he jams his hands in his pockets and rocks back on his heels. "Oh, what the heck," he says. "Go on ahead, Mariah. Your glove's in the shed." He smiles, pleased with his generosity.

A block from the house I toss my glove up into the air and catch it. Just walking next to Ryan Ferguson makes me giddy. "Softball," I say. "That was the perfect touch."

Ryan gives me his sideways look. "I know what dads like," he says.

"Good clean fun," I say.

"There you go," Ryan says, and points his finger at me.

"So what should we do?" Darlene says. "Go to Old Town?"

Ryan looks at me.

"I've been in my *house* for two weeks. I don't care."

"There's only one thing," Darlene says.

"What's that?"

She starts to laugh; she can hardly talk. "What are we going to do with these stupid gloves?"

We walk under the railroad tracks near the Metro. A man in a suit gives us a wary look, as if he suspects us of abusing "controlled substances."

Ryan moves along in a kind of pigeon-toed stalk, very deliberate, almost a swagger. Ever since I got Helena's letter, I've been warming up to the idea of Ryan Ferguson. Now it's like all my nerves are on tiptoes; I can hardly stand the effect he's having on me. I can imagine those things—pheromones or whatever you call them—surrounding him in a cloud. I can imagine this chemical reaction taking place in the air between us.

"I know one thing we could do," Ryan says. "We could go down by the river and actually play softball. I mean we could play catch anyway." He takes my hand and begins stroking my palm with his thumb; I get these little rushes of sensation in my chest.

"No we *can't*," Darlene says.

"Why not?"

"No *ball*. Remember?" She holds up her glove. "These were part of our plot to free Mariah."

"Well, that is…ah…a consideration," Ryan says in the flawless Ronald Reagan imitation he perfected in World Civ. "But…ah…young ladies, don't ever think that something like a lack of a ball is…ah…a prohibitive factor." He mimes that he's flipping me a ball. I pretend to catch it and toss it back toward him. He mimes a leaping save, then rolls one to Darlene. We pretend to toss it around a few more times, making increasingly difficult catches, laughing like crazy. In the process of making a diving save, Ryan hurls himself on the sidewalk, scraping his arm.

Darlene and I make a big deal about his blood. He winces, pretending to be in excruciating pain. A lady in purple is walking toward us. "Please don't hurt me anymore," Ryan pleads. *"Please,"* he sobs. The lady frowns and picks up her pace as she goes by.

I'm laughing so hard I'm practically crying.

Chapter Twelve

MARIAH
Aberrant Data

WITHIN TWO WEEKS, Ryan Ferguson and I are an "item," as my father puts it. This is different from the way I felt with Bobby. Ryan and I are in the exact center of the world. This is it: I'm in love.

The clichés compare it to being sick and being disoriented. They all seem to be true. I'm breathless, head over heels, I'm lovesick, I feel like I'm running a fever, my feet don't touch the ground. My head is in the clouds, I'm starry-eyed, I'm moony, I'm in a daze.

Since I'm never without the thought of Ryan somewhere in my mind, my concentration span shrinks to almost nothing. I keep losing the thread of conversations. Complicated tasks—geometry proofs and chemistry labs—are almost impossible. School nights, when I have to stay in after dinner, are the worst. I grab the phone before it completes the first ring. When it's not him, I experience it as a physical sensation: a sinking feeling, a plummeting pain in my chest. When it *is* him, we talk for hours, but when I hang up from these conversations, I can't remember a thing we said. Our voices make a connection on a different level, like the murmur of blood in our veins.

I collect relics of Ryan like he's my religion. There's a little shrine in my room: three pictures of him, the notes he's written me, a lock of his hair, his crew jacket.

We still hang around with our group, we still go places with them, but we're not really with them, we're with each other. We're always touching. We drape ourselves over each other like pieces of clothing. If we could find some way for every inch of our bodies to touch, we'd do it. My body is in a constant state of turbulence. This isn't like Bobby, who I was always able to resist. I have no resistance against Ryan Ferguson. It's just a matter of time. I'm fizzy with desire.

But it's not easy for us to be alone. My mom is always at home, and by the time Ryan gets done with Crew, his dad is home. This is a city. There are parks and a few patches of woods, but just when you think you're alone, a jogger will loom up out of nowhere and whip past, breathing evenly.

It will be much easier once Ryan can drive, which will be in July. He already has a car, which he and his dad fixed up together, an old silver Toyota, waiting in his garage. Whoever owned it before had an obsession with the word "touch." It's plastered with bumper stickers: Touchamatic, Keep in Touch, Rock with the Touch-tones, Touch and Go Banking, WKFW: The Lite Touch.

We go to movies. We try for movies that are on their way out of town and not crowded. We sit in the worst seats, in the corners. In the front corners we tilt back in our chairs; the images loom over us, huge, foreshortened. In the back corners we can really see only half of the screen. We see movies like *Naked Gun*, *Tequila Sunrise*, and

Beaches, months after their original releases. We end up half undressed, our faces flushed. We come out of movies looking like we've run a few miles on a hot day. Somehow, I lose my bra in *Naked Gun*.

A basic human urge is to fit aberrant data into a coherent worldview. Anything that cannot be understood must be squashed in somewhere. Where it fits just depends on your frame of reference.

My World Civ teacher, Mr. Vail, introduced this idea last week. He was talking about myth and religion, but then we got into science too. For instance, until the knowledge base grew, the rising and setting of the sun made people believe that the sun circled the earth daily, and even that was only after they figured out that the earth was round. Before that, they thought gods dragged it through the sky or that the sun itself was a god and could appear or not on its own "lordly whim," as Mr. Vail put it.

Mr. Vail says everything is like that. We human beings always try to fit information into what we already know. Columbus didn't know about the continents of the Americas, so when he hit land in the Caribbean, he thought it was part of India. Mr. Vail's point was that we like to have everything explained and we try hard to make everything fit in, even if it really doesn't. He says it's only the rare, revolutionary thinker who is able to get free of conventional thought so the facts themselves can create a new frame of reference.

So what happened this morning, when I went crazy—it's easy to think it was because I'm overstimulated (as my father puts it) from spending so much time with Ryan Ferguson. It's true that I'm obsessed with him, that I'm not getting enough sleep. It's reasonable to think I got to some kind of emotional critical mass, and one unexpected thing caused my mind to go over the edge.

We all hope this is it, especially me.

Here's what I remember. The sound from the sky was not just loud enough to wake me. It was amazingly, spectacularly loud. A look at my alarm clock. Six A.M. I got up and ran to the window, and looked out into the frail light. The sound kept getting closer and louder, even when that didn't seem possible. There were big helicopters, two of them, flying low and slow, beating directly over our house, hovering above our trees. They would fly over just a little way and then swoop back.

I can't explain what happened. The sound became so loud, it drove everything else from my mind. It was like the sound was the only thing in the world.

I screamed but I couldn't even hear my own voice. Then the beat of the helicopters' rotors seemed to go right into the center of my heart, and somehow the beating of my heart got mixed in with it, so when the helicopters started going away, it was like my heart was going away too. I guess I fainted or something.

Anyway, the next thing I knew I was flat on my stomach under my bed, even though I don't remember getting under there, and my heart was going like crazy and I was shaking all over and I couldn't seem to get my breath.

I had to be at school at 7:45 for Early Bird P.E., and when I didn't come down, my mom yelled up a few times for me to hurry. I heard her but it was like her voice was in a dream or something. It didn't occur to me to answer her; I knew without trying that I couldn't speak. Eventually she came up and found me there, under the bed.

She freaked, of course. Anybody probably would have freaked, faced with the sight of someone they loved twitching away under a bed for no good reason. She wanted so much for there not to be anything really wrong that her first reaction was to be mad at me, as if this was some kind of joke I was playing. "What do you think you're doing, Mariah? You're going to be late for school! Come on!"

She went on like that for a while; then all of a sudden she stopped and ran off yelling my father's name. I was aware of all this, but it was like it was happening to someone else.

"See," my mother said, coming back into the room with my father. "Oh God, Arthur. What should we do? What's the matter with her?"

My father knelt on the floor next to me and began stroking my hair. "It's all right, honey, it's all right. What's the matter? Come on, it's all right. What's the matter?"

After a while the terror loosened its grip on me and I stopped shaking and started simply to weep. My father held me and stroked my hair some more. I pushed my face against his chest and took what comfort I could from his stiff embrace.

By the time I recovered enough to go into the bathroom to wash my face, my parents were already groping for explanations. Phrases drifted through the hiss of water. "...seeing too much of that boy," my father said. My mother suggested "panic attack." I heard the word "overtired." I wanted them to be right.

When I come out of the bathroom, my mother says maybe I should skip school. Even my father, normally opposed to the idea of missing school for anything less serious than pneumonia, is willing to go along with this. They exchange an odd, furtive glance.

But the truth is, I'm fine now. Already I have trouble remembering the way I felt, that terrified girl under the bed. I agree with my parents. I haven't been getting enough sleep; I *am* overstimulated. One thing I'm sure of: I don't want to skip school and stay home.

"I was probably having a nightmare," I say. Then I have an inspiration, an explanation. "You know, I did see *Platoon* last week, over at Darlene's. Maybe I was dreaming about that. I mean, you know, the helicopters..." This didn't make sense really. In *Platoon* the helicopters were always a good sign, coming to get someone out. "What were those helicopters *doing* anyway?"

"You remember, honey," my mother says. "They were spraying. For the gypsy moths."

"Why did they have to come at six A.M.?" I ask. "You'd think they'd wait till people were *awake*."

"The earlier it is, the less wind," my father says. "Also, fewer people are out of doors at six in the morning. While the spray isn't *toxic*..."

I look at my watch. "I can make it in time for second period if we hurry."

My mother: "You have to eat first."

My father isn't quite willing to let my "panic attack" go. He has quite a bit to say, at breakfast, about adolescent psychic energy, how it's associated with poltergeists and other so-called possessions.

"*The Exorcist*," my mother mentions.

"Most of your demonic possessions," my father concurs. He wiggles his eyebrows. "The devil did it; the devil made me do it. Projections. That's what the psychiatrists contend."

I'm eating Rice Krispies. I'm paying attention to the noise the pieces of cereal make as their surfaces contact the milk. It sounds like a very soft rainfall.

My dad starts in on the Salem witch trials. "All those overexcited young ladies," he says. He spreads orange marmalade on his English muffin. "Repressed sexual energy—that's one theory."

"I thought it was Cotton Mather," I say, "stirring the people up. You know, it was kind of a rallying point, uniting everybody against the devil."

"That's interesting," my father says, frowning. "I'm not familiar with that theory."

I know about the Salem witches. I did a paper on them in the ninth grade. "Anyway," I say, "I thought it started with some West Indian woman who was a slave. She told the girls voodoo stories. It was like the most exciting stuff they'd ever heard. They got so into it, their parents figured they must be bewitched."

My father rubs a finger on his cheek. "But their *energy*," he says, "their hysterical energy. It undoubtedly came from repressed sexuality."

"Oh, Arthur," my mother says. "That's just pop psychology."

"Maybe, maybe not." He starts talking about other mass delusions: flying saucers, the persistence of certain myths like Atlantis.

My attention floats free of the conversation and settles on its usual object, Ryan Ferguson.

Friday night a bunch of us are going ice-skating. Saturday, Ryan has a crew meet in the morning, but then a bunch of us are going to bike down to Mount Vernon. Saturday night...

"Did you hear what I said, Mariah?"

"What?"

He looks not at me, but at his hands. "I *said* that for the foreseeable future, you may only go out with Ryan Ferguson once a week. That's it. Saturday night, I know you've got some party on, but that's it, that's all. You're obsessed with that boy. It's not healthy. He's a nice young man—don't get me wrong—I like him. But you've gone overboard. I don't think—"

"But Dad, that's not fair." Blood whizzes in my head. "I mean that's just not fair. I need to see him. I mean—"

"You don't *need* to see him. You're confusing need with want, Mariah. It's a different thing, as you will someday learn."

I try to keep from crying. Tears don't get you anywhere with my father; they work against you. "It's just not *fair*."

"Fair," my father says. He shakes his head. "Fair has nothing to do with it. You're forgetting that an hour ago you were lying under your bed totally out of control."

"But I was *dreaming*. I *told* you..."

His chair scrapes. He stands up. My mother is bustling around in the kitchen, slapping pans into cupboards. She doesn't want to get into it, take sides. The garbage disposal grinds away. There's no point in talking to my father. It's very hard for me but I keep my mouth shut.

Since I'm going to be late, I ask him to write a note to the attendance office. I unfold the white sheet in the car as we drive silently toward school.

Mariah had a dentist's appointment this morning.
Arthur Ebinger

This is what my father calls a "white lie."

Chapter Thirteen

MARIAH
White Lies

I KNOW ABOUT WHITE lies. They protect you without hurting anyone else.

So I don't give a moment's thought to obeying my father's rule about not seeing Ryan Ferguson. I don't even think about it long enough to make a decision. It's what Mr. Vail calls a priori; it's already made.

I see that deception will have to become part of my life. My mind is already going ahead, figuring out ways to see Ryan without my father knowing. Tonight, for instance, I'll say I'm going ice-skating with Darlene. I'll just get Ryan to meet me there.

I know my father thinks restricting my time with Ryan is "for my own good." He just doesn't know how it is with me and Ryan. I could never explain it to him in a way he'd be able to understand.

Anyway, words aren't designed to tell what falling in love with Ryan Ferguson has done to me. It's like trying to describe how cantaloupe tastes, or what sweat smells like. You really can't do it. When I'm with him, everything is spinning around in a luscious whirl, like even my actual molecules are alive in a way they never were before. Even just doing nothing is thrilling, if you know what I mean.

I can just hear me saying that to my dad. Sure. He'd go: "You can't be in love when you're sixteen, Mariah. You don't even know what it means." No. I know *exactly* what he'd say: "What you mean, Mariah, is that you're boy crazy."

I hand my note to the woman in the attendance office, who makes out an Admit & Tardy slip for me.

"Get your teeth cleaned?" she asks.

I smile. "No cavities."

It's during classes. The halls are so quiet I almost tiptoe. I carry one of those five-by-four bright yellow student passes; if you don't have one, the hall monitors are on you in a second. I stop off at my locker. I have a picture of Ryan taped to the inside. I touch the picture's lips with the tip of my pinky.

Ryan's about five-nine, but his wide bony shoulders and huge feet make me think he's going to get a lot taller. He's skinny, even skinnier than me. His hair is ashy-blond, a little curly. He has hazel eyes and dark, strong eyebrows. I love his mouth. He has a freckle on his lower lip, and large white innocent teeth with tiny spaces between them.

Everyone looks up when I come into the Geometry room. Ryan gives me a "Where were you?" look. I roll my hands through the air; I'll tell him later. Mr. Clagg is talking about polyhedrons.

Ryan walks me to French. We drift to a stop across from the French room, where there's a bank of lockers. I lean up against one. Ryan fences me in with one arm. He makes a kind of little room for us with his body, a little private space. I give him the one-minute version of why I was late.

"My father thinks I'm seeing too much of you, so don't come by tonight, just meet me at the rink."

"And I thought the man *liked* me."

"He does. He just thinks I had the nightmare because of…" I force the air to buzz out between my lips and giggle and hide my face in my hand. "Because of…repressed sexuality."

Ryan laughs.

"I'm *serious*. He went on all about the Salem witch trials, adolescent girls…all that stuff."

Ryan tilts his head down and to the side, his sideways look. He makes a slow little kiss with his mouth. I put my hand over my face again. I'm blushing, my skin is hot. Our free hands never stop moving, our fingers lace in and out, twining, rubbing. The bell rings.

"Shit, I'm going to be late," Ryan says. "See you at lunch."

I'm a good skater; there were plenty of outdoor ponds in Janesville where we all used to go, and plenty of cold weather. But Ryan isn't so good, and we lurch around the rink together, falling a lot. More than we have to, really— this becomes an excuse for letting our bodies collide. A bunch of the group is there and we collide with them too. We gather in little knots around the rink, laughing and knocking each other down. I try to teach Ryan how to skate backward; I push him along and support him, but he doesn't trust me, and every time he turns his head to look behind him, he loses his footing and we both fall.

It's crowded. Little girls in skating skirts practice their spins and turns in the middle of the rink. A few middle-aged men skate swift, effortless circles at high speed, one hand tucked behind them. I admire the compact way they cut through the air. A gray-haired man with a big belly also skates in the middle ice, doing difficult, elegant double jumps, smiling continuously, like a performer.

At the break, Darlene and Stolly and everybody else go inside to play the video machines and get some food. Ryan and I sit in the bleachers watching the Zamboni machine smooth the ice. I know I'm not the first person to notice this, but it reminds me so much of a snail, the way it leaves its trail of slime behind. It's chilly. I like watching the fog come from Ryan's mouth, his visible breath.

"So did the helicopters wake you up this morning too?"

"What helicopters?"

"They came to spray for the gypsy moths. You know."

"They did? I slept right through it, then."

"How could you sleep right through it? It was—it was like totally loud."

He shrugs. "My mom always said I could sleep through anything short of a nuclear attack."

After a while people begin to filter back in. They stand peering over the glass, watching the Zamboni machine close in on the center.

"I really like you, Mariah," Ryan whispers in my ear. "I'm crazy about you."

His words float around my head in a swirl; a dizzy whoosh zips through me. We kiss, barely touching our lips at first. I run the tip of my tongue along the underside of his top teeth, letting it ride slowly along the ridges. His tongue comes into my mouth, just exploring at first, then thrusting in.

A lady behind us coughs a loud, fake cough and we remember where we are and pull apart. I feel like I'm out of breath. Darlene and Stolly come back from the snack bar.

"He threw the locker key into the trash can with our trash," Darlene says. "He just dumped everything on the tray right in there."

"Yeah, it was real smooth," Stolly says. "We're in there rooting around in other people's *garbage*."

"Ketchup was the worst," Darlene says. "I'm serious."

For the rest of the hour, Ryan and I do spectacular, exaggerated falls. Darlene awards us points based on the degree of difficulty. Finally the skate guard kicks us all out.

We go to Pizza Hut. Stolly makes an outrageous salad out of jalapeño peppers, chick peas, and watermelon chunks, which he actually eats. Taylor Blair talks some older guy into buying him a pitcher of beer and pours it into everybody's Coke glasses. We laugh a lot. We talk about what we're going to do in the summer. Stolly drops Ryan and me off near George Mason, the elementary school three blocks from my house.

Ryan and I sit on the swings for a while, stepping ourselves around in circles, twisting the chains up tight, then letting them spin us back down. Then Ryan starts pushing me. I get going so high the heavy steel framework the swings are suspended from thumps at the top of my arc, its legs lifting out of their sockets. I stop pumping, lean way back so my body is horizontal. My hair hangs straight down and sweeps along the ground.

Then I sit up, scuff my feet to slow down, and jump off. Ryan kind of catches me; he has his hands on my waist. I can hardly stand the way I feel when he touches me, like I'm going to twitch right out of my skin. I twist and run away.

It's dark but the moon lights up some things: the metal bars of the swing set, parts of the jungle gym, the edges of the slide. "Mariah," Ryan calls. "What are you doing? Come on."

There are three or four big concrete cylinders scattered around the playground. They're over on their sides, tunnels for the kids to play in. I crawl into one of them and sit hunched up, my back curled against the side.

"Where are you? Come on, Mariah."

My breathing is all around me in the tunnel, as if I'm holding my hands to my ears. I'm a little worried. I want

to make love with him, but everything's so great right now.
What if it doesn't work out? What if I don't like it? I'm
prepared for disappointment. (Mr. Krieg, our Family Life
education teacher in Janesville: "Doing what comes naturally isn't always so easy. That's one reason farmers and
breeders increasingly use artificial insemination. Don't get
the idea, which books and movies can give you, that this
will be like a personal earthquake. Initial intercourse may
be less than pleasurable, even painful." Helena: "I thought
big deal, is that *it*?")

My heart is going crazy. Should I tell him I never slept
with anyone before? Should I ask him if he did?

I hear him coming; my heart feels like it's going to
jump right out of me. He takes my hand and pulls me out
of the tunnel. "I don't know about you and that dude from
Plainsville—"

"Janesville."

"Yeah, well..." A plane rumbles by overhead; the
lights blink. "I slept with Miranda."

I run away from him, grab the rings on the swing set
and flip myself upside down. I balance there, with my feet
straight up, my hair hanging down around my head. I'm
happy he told me, but at the same time I'm not happy to
know. He comes up behind me and I flip back down, but
do it wrong, so we end up falling down together. The rings
come swinging crookedly back, over our heads.

"Hey," Ryan says. "I never felt this way about her."
Everywhere we're touching, I can't stand the way it feels.
"I'm crazy about you. I'm really crazy about you."

"Bobby," I start. "We never..." The moonlight touches
parts of his face: his forehead, his cheekbone, the ridge
of his nose, his chin. I want to tell him it's okay about
Miranda. I want to tell him I'm crazy about him too, but
it turns out I can't talk; it's like my throat is full of water.

I hear a dog barking. I hear the thin whine of a TV or a
radio, far away. I hear the wind rushing through the leaves.

When I look up, the branches of the trees are thrashing around, like the trees are shaking their heads, shaking their long hair.

He kisses me on the mouth. "Mariah," he says.

There's somebody way over at the end of the school-yard, walking their dog. The dog's collar makes a chinking sound as they go along. Then the sound stops. Ryan pulls me over to a piece of playground equipment that looks like a turtle. The shell was built for climbing on, but we get underneath it. You can't tell in the moonlight, but the hexagonal metal sections are painted bright yellow and orange. A woman's voice says: "Good *dog*." The chinking sound starts up again and keeps getting closer.

Ryan's next to me; we're touching all along our sides. The wood chips under us poke into my back. We don't move. The woman and the dog go right past us. The dog stops and gives a low woof. She fusses and coos at it in baby talk: "Come on, Chelsea, you're a good *dog*, izzn't you a good dog. Yesssss. Come oh now, come on home now, good *dog*."

When she's a ways away, up near the building, Ryan props himself up on one elbow. First he holds my head in his two hands for a second, then he takes his finger and licks it and runs it over my lips, very slowly, all the way around, as if he's putting lipstick on me. It feels like my lips don't have any muscles in them, they're so loose; it's as if everything about me is spreading apart, opening up. His finger draws my lower lip all the way over to the side, and then slowly his finger goes down the middle of my chin and then down between my breasts, and everywhere his finger goes it's like the flesh beneath it is melting, humming and burning with pleasure way down to the middle of me.

He puts his mouth over my right nipple, right through my T-shirt, and he bites it very lightly. Then he starts pulling off my pants and my underpants. I've been resisting boys taking my pants off ever since I was twelve, but now

I can hardly stand the way the cloth feels against my skin. I wish they would just disintegrate, just dissolve away. But then when they're off and I have just the air against me, I can hardly stand that either.

Then Ryan's pulling down his own pants, and then he's fumbling with something, which I hope is a condom, because I can't stand this, I really can't stand this. And when the tip of him touches me, I'm so excited I'm out of my mind, I'm lost in a kind of blur of sensation, I'm totally gone.

After it's over, I just lie there, with the wind rushing through the trees and another jet rumbling by overhead. I can't talk; I can't even move. My arms and legs feel dead, anesthetized, as if their ability to feel anything is used up. It was an amazing feeling at the end, kind of like an electric shock that feels really good instead of terrible. I think of the Robert Palmer song, "Addicted to Love," and I can see that Ryan and I will be doing quite a bit of this from now on.

Chapter Fourteen

MARIAH
The Diamond Pivot

DECEPTION IS PUTTING a strain on me. First I have to avoid talking about Ryan, then I have to make up some story to fill up the time I'm actually with him. In a funny way, it's making *me* suspicious. I can't help thinking my mom and dad are trying to catch me. One of them will ask an innocent question, like: "Did you enjoy the movie?" And I'll be about to answer and I'll stop and my mind will go flat with panic while I try to remember: What did I say? Did I say I'd gone to a movie? Which one?

I haven't blown it yet but it's hard on me. I have this bruised look under my eyes and I've lost a few pounds. My mom even took me to the doctor last week because she thought I might have mono or anemia, but of course it turned out I was fine.

121

There was something soothing about going to the doctor with my mother. Especially since the week before, I'd gone to a clinic downtown in D.C. to get a prescription for birth control pills. That was like such an adult thing for me to do, going to the birth control clinic. I was proud of myself but it was so hard. I had to keep giving myself little pep talks to keep myself going. When I got through the door, I was so tired I almost fell asleep in the orange leatherette chair. I was afraid when they called my name I wouldn't be able to get up, I wouldn't be able to move.

When the counselor interviewed me, I couldn't seem to talk. She asked things like: "Do your parents know about this relationship?" I had to shake my head no like a little girl. "Are you using some protection now?" I nodded my head yes. My eyes kept filling up with tears. When she touched my arm, the pressure traveled. It felt like a fist pressed to my throat. "Are you sure you're ready for this, honey?" I knew I had to say some words. It was like I had to pass a test. The words bunched up behind my lips and came out in an angry mutter: "I'm sure." I sounded exactly like my father.

I'm beginning to spend a lot of time at Ryan's house. He lives with his dad. His parents are divorced and his dad has custody. His mom lives in Bethesda and he sees her about once every two weeks. He used to spend every other weekend with her but now he doesn't want to, so they just have dinner together or go somewhere every other Wednesday. I've met her twice. Both times she took us to Roy Rogers and she seemed nervous. She smiled a lot in a twitchy kind of way. I mean her smile came and went so fast, it didn't stay on her face more than a split second at a time. She had three little brackets on either side of her mouth, marks from all that smiling. She wore a lot of makeup and asked me to call her Betty. Of course, Ryan's parents are young. His mom is only thirty-five; she had Ryan when she was eighteen years old.

I know that Ryan's dad has guessed what's going on between us, because he always makes a lot of noise whenever he comes toward a room we're in. I mean, he's always coughing or whistling or talking to himself: "Now where *is* that Phillips screwdriver, damn it?"

I can tell he doesn't mind. If anything, he's *proud* of Ryan. I mean, when Ryan first introduced us, he shook his head admiringly and said: "Way to go, Ry. She's *real* pretty." Once he chuckled, "Oh, Ryan's oversexed, like his father."

He acts like a kid himself. Ryan hates the way both of his parents try to act so young. But his dad really gets off on it when someone thinks they're brothers. And his mom— both times I was with her she told the same story about how someone couldn't *believe* she was old enough to have a boy Ryan's age. She used exactly the same words: "So he said, 'You must have been a *child bride*.' " Ryan rolled his eyes at me.

Ryan thinks because they got married so young, his parents feel like they missed out on their youth and they have to make up for it now.

Once Ryan's dad got started about the perils of getting married young. "Of course we 'had' to get married," he sad. "Betty and I."

"Jeez, Dad," Ryan said. "Give me a break."

Mr. Ferguson looked at me. "Ryan knows that the one thing Betty and I have never regretted for one second is him. He's the one good thing about it, the good result of a bad situation. Betty and I, we were just in the grip of perfectly natural impulses..."

Ryan stood up. "Dad, come *on*."

"This is *important*, Ryan. Just bear with me." The skin crinkled up between his earnest eyebrows. "With Betty and myself there we were, pregnant, and of course we were stuck with that thing that is imprinted on the hearts of Catholics—

that sex is a sin, it's really only for having babies." Ryan pushed his hand through his hair and looked at the ceiling. "Look, I know you're embarrassed," his dad said. "But the thing is that we have to get *over* that. What I'm trying to get at is that I think the new way of doing things is a real improvement."

Ryan's dad is a lawyer; he's in "transportation law," whatever that means. He comes home in these great-looking suits, but the first thing he does is change his clothes. He wears jeans, or sweatpants, or Adidas shorts. He likes to do things with us, like shooting hoops, or going to Baskin-Robbins, or even just sitting with us and watching MTV.

He likes me because he thinks I'm smart. He likes it that I can talk about glasnost or the civil rights implications of AIDS testing. "I was getting worried about Ry," he said once. "He seemed to be attracted only to airheads. I mean Miranda, sweet girl, God love her, but a mind like a dandelion."

He finds my intelligence reassuring. He thinks that by having everything out in the open, by practically giving us permission to fuck, he can protect Ryan from getting what both he and my own parents would call "too serious." He's wrong of course. Ryan and me, we're in deep.

Sometimes we lie on our backs on the floor of Ryan's family room and fantasize how we could get really away, really alone. We could make up a story that we're going hiking with some school group on the Appalachian trail. We could stay in one of the shelters, live on trail mix and freeze-dried dinners. Or we could run away to Ryan's uncle's place in West Virginia and live in a trailer. If Ryan's dad ever heard us talking like that, he would just shit. And my dad, forget it.

Exam week.

My dad is really bossy. If he catches me listening to the radio while I'm studying, he makes me turn it off. If I come downstairs to take a break, he looks at his watch and sends me back up: not time yet. My mom nurtures me the way I imagine Japanese mothers do: she darts in with trays of nourishing snacks, she irons my favorite clothes, she runs my bath, she buys me huge twenty-stick packs of gum.

To tell you the truth, I'm a little worried about these finals. I'm having trouble concentrating, and I know the marks will go on what I'm always hearing about: my permanent record. My father relentlessly brings up college admissions boards. I always imagine groups of stern men and women poring over my grades, deciding my fate.

Still, it's hard for me to study. It's as if I exist in a different world from the one where the exams are important. The things I'm trying to cram into my brain, like Avogadro's number and mole theory and the law of tangents, buzz around in my mind like bees trapped in a house, bouncing off the windows, crazy to escape.

I try. I force myself; I grip the book in my hands and stare at the pages. Sometimes I can't do it at all, I can't even focus, the words just float away from me, dissolve into the air. My mind stays suspended in the space they left behind until images of Ryan, and me, drift into it. I think of his face, then of the freckle on his lower lip. Then I picture us somewhere, like in a tent, in a campground. These imagined scenes are very detailed. They seem much realer than the concepts and words I'm trying to fix to my mind. If we're camping, I see the stitching in the canvas, the tent pegs driven into the brown earth, the exact way the bushes look, our sleeping bags rumpled up on the floor of the tent. Ryan's in his underwear, just waking up, rubbing sleep from his eyes. He sees me; he smiles a lazy smile.

Then I catch myself, with the kind of jerk of consciousness you get sometimes when you're just falling asleep. Sometimes I've read halfway down a page, and not a word of it has sunk in. Sometimes I've been reading the same sentence over and over again but it's just stayed words, it never got to mean anything to me.

I only have one exam the first day and it's P.E., which I'm not worried about. It's just P.E., for one thing, and anyway, it should be easy. We had one quarter of health and the rest is just the rules of sports, which I know cold. Still, I'm tired, really wrecked. I stayed up very late last night studying for my chemistry and geometry finals, which are both tomorrow. That was my dad's idea, studying ahead; then tonight, before my two toughest exams, I can get that "good night's sleep" the study guides always talk about.

Dad drops me off at the corner of Braddock and Mount Vernon. I cut across the vacant lot on the corner. It used to be a gas station, then somebody told me it was a dry cleaner's for a while. The building is all boarded up. The asphalt of its parking lot is crumpled and breaking up in spots, turning back into gravel. Big weeds grow up through the cracks.

I usually kind of admire weeds that sprout up through concrete or blacktop, I admire their strength. I think it's amazing they can find the one weak spot to break through, that little green things can crumble something hard like concrete, something hard enough to break your bones. But today the sight of the weeds poking through the cracks, the whole derelict look of the place, makes me sad. There was something there, and now there's nothing, now it's desolate, running to ruin. It makes it seem like all human endeavor is pointless.

I hurry and at the crosswalk catch up with two Hispanic girls, Elisa and Yolanda, who are in my P.E. class. We say hi back and forth and talk about how we're not ready for the P.E. exam.

And then something so weird happens.

Elisa speaks English really well, but Yolanda doesn't yet. All of a sudden Yolanda gets this worried look on her face. And she asks Elisa something in Spanish: *"Cambiamos ropa hoy o no? Me olvidé mís calcetines blancos. Tienes otros? Uno más F para no tener ropa y no voy a pasar."*

She's worried that we might have to dress out for P.E. and
she doesn't have her white socks, which you have to have,
along with your gym suit, or it counts as an F for the day.

Elisa replies in a not-so-sure voice: *"Creo que no."*

Then this comes out of my mouth. I tell Yolanda not
to worry: *"No cambiamos hoy. No cambiamos nada más
este año."*

It sounds like me but it doesn't sound like me.

Elisa stares: *"No supe que tu hablas español, Mariah!
Por qué no nos dijiste?"*

I get a very weird feeling, like my flesh is freezing up
under my skin. I don't answer her. The silence seems dirty.
My feet start going before I even think of moving; I'm
running across the street, away from them. I hear myself
yell, "Gotta go to my locker."

I don't go to my locker, I don't stop until I get into the
ladies' room, into a stall. I hang my backpack up on the
hook and then I sit down. Maybe it didn't happen. That's
what I'm thinking: maybe that didn't happen. My legs are
shaking. I put my hands on my knees to try to press them
still. I'm thinking: maybe that didn't happen, maybe that
didn't happen at all.

But I can still hear Elisa's voice. What she said, in
Spanish, was, "I didn't know you spoke Spanish, Mariah.
Why didn't you tell us?"

And here's the thing, here's the thing about my
speaking Spanish: I don't.

I *don't*. I'm sitting there in the bathroom stall.
Thoughts are flying through my head.

I'm possessed by the devil.

I'm speaking in tongues.

Someone else has invaded my brain.

One thing is for sure: this is wrong; this is all, all
wrong. I'm sitting in this bathroom and I know that I'm a
person whose life was going along all right, and now it's
taken a sudden U-turn, a one-eighty, what my dance teacher

in Janesville called a diamond pivot. I can't get Elisa's voice out of my mind: *"No supe que tu hablas español, Mariah!"*

On the back of the stall door, written diagonally, in black Magic Marker, is this:

Party hardy, rock 'n' roll
Drink a pack, smoke a bowl
Our love is great, our sex is fun.
We're the class of '91!

I want to see if I can do it, translate it. I don't get every single word, but I can. *I can.* And when I can, I get a feeling like a huge fish is flopping over in my stomach. My mouth fills up with vomit and I try to keep it inside while I jump off the seat and turn. I throw up. It gets all up my nose. I'm kneeling there over the bowl, grabbing toilet paper, coughing, trying to get the vomit out of my nose, and my brain is finishing up that stupid rhyme: *Somos la clase de noventa y uno.*

Chapter Fifteen

MARIAH
Retrieval

I USE ONE OF those folded brown paper towels they have in the bathroom to wash my face. When I wet it, it gets limp and slimy and gives off a sharp smell. I hate the way it feels against my skin, like a big piece of pond weed. I put on some lipstick. I fix my hair. It seems important to look normal.

I head for the gym. I thought about going up to the nurse's office but I knew what would happen. First they'd take my temperature. This is like a ritual. They always do it, even if you go in for a scraped knee. Next they'd call my parents. My mother would come and get me and I'd have to start explaining. I can't imagine explaining this to my mother. I can't imagine explaining this to anyone.

I'm better off sticking it out at school, going on with the day that's planned in my head: the P.E. exam, lunch,

129

then Journalism. That's it: we have early release all week. In Journalism the final edition of the G.W. newspaper counted as our final exam, so we're just going to have a party. I have a tin of my mother's Toll House cookies in my backpack.

But walking toward the gym, the Spanish words for things keep popping into my mind. I look at my shoes: *zapatos*; at the floor: *suelo*. *Esquina, ventana, libro.*

I try to keep it from happening. I think of other things so there won't be any room for those words. I put a picture of Ryan in my mind and concentrate hard on that, but it's no use. The words for the parts of the face line up on my mental picture of Ryan, just like on vocab sheets from French class: *ojos, naríz, labios.*

The main building of the school is air-conditioned, but the annex and the gym aren't. I go out the side door from the main building, where my locker is, and cross the parking lot. It's only eight in the morning but already the sky has the flat white glare that makes these hot days different from the ones in Janesville. In Janesville, hot days came with a full, ripe look, the sky a brilliant blue, everything practically growing in front of your eyes. Here the heat seems to take the color out of everything. The sky goes pale, the trees and the grass look drab and exhausted, as if they're using all their energy just to survive. It seems to me everything must grow secretly, at night.

When I go through the door and into the gym, it's even hotter inside. The humid air presses against me, so dense it seems to stick to my skin. Suddenly I can taste the vomit in my mouth again, as if the heat has reconstituted it.

The bleachers are pulled out; the kids are scattered around, talking. Mr. Carruthers and the other P.E. teachers stand in a little group in the middle of the gym floor. They wear sleek red warm-ups with stripes down the legs and arms and stand with their feet well apart, knees slightly flexed, the jock stance. Their arms are full of mimeographed exam sheets. They look so capable, as if they could handle anything at all, I have a sudden urge to ask them to help me. It comes to me in Spanish: *ayúdame, por favor...*

Elisa and Yolanda are sitting in the front row, down at the end. Elisa spots me. I see them bend together; their heads almost touch. I pretend I don't see them. I lean forward, let my hair fall in front of my eyes. I keep my eyes down as I climb the bleachers, all the way up to the top row. I want the wall at my back, something to lean on.

Ryan and I both have B lunch. When our eyes meet, mine go skidding away from his. When our hands touch, my palm is greasy with sweat. I wasn't going to tell him, but he knows right away something's wrong. I think how I'd feel if Ryan told me: hey, a weird thing happened, I speak Spanish now.

Sure.

He gives my hand a squeeze, asks, "What's the matter?" and I see I'm going to tell him after all. The noise in the cafeteria churns around my ears. I'm trying to think of how I can put it. Somebody's voice sticks out clear from the cafeteria roar: "That fucking Mr. Roper, he gave me a fucking D."

"What's wrong?" Ryan asks again.

I start: "This morning, when my father dropped me off..." But then the rest of it evaporates; the words back up in my throat. It comes into my head how Yolanda said *"Cambiamos hoy?"* and my voice, saying Spanish words, and I feel the same way all over again. My heart squirms in my chest. There's a heavy swerve in my stomach. I squeak my chair closer to Ryan and press my face into his shoulder and start to cry. At first it's like a little pulse in my eyes, the tears just sliding out, but even though I'm trying not to, soon my shoulders are shuddering and I'm sobbing, I mean pretty soon stuff is even dripping out my nose.

"Shit, Mariah, what's the matter? What's happening? Are you pregnant? Is that it? I swear to God it'll be all right. Whatever you want, I swear to God, we'll make it be all right."

I'm shaking my head. Cafeteria noise has died down in our immediate vicinity. Ryan pulls me to my feet.

He speaks to one of the cafeteria monitors. "I'm taking her to G-two." Guidance-2 is where you go for hotline counseling, if you're having drug or alcohol problems, if you're being abused, if you're suicidal. But he doesn't take me there. We go outside and we sit in the shade at the side of the building. I start pulling up grass with my hands, which for some reason seems to calm me down.

"I'm not pregnant," I say. "That's not it."

I can sense his relief, but I'm not relieved. I could understand being pregnant; anybody could understand that.

"Well, so—you're not *moving*, are you?" he asks with sudden anxiety. I shake my head.

I keep on ripping out grass. He puts his hand on top of mine to stop me. I raise my hand up, with his on top of it, until the back of his hand is pressed to my lips. I suck a little ridge of his flesh into my mouth and push my tongue against it until I realize that what I'm doing is like sucking on a nipple.

"Maybe G-two is what I need. Maybe I'm going crazy." Tears collect in my eyes again. I'm thinking we have to get back inside soon. I don't want Ryan to get into trouble. He gives me a little upward nod with his chin, like *tell me*, and so I explain what happened with Yolanda and Elisa.

"*What?*" he says. "Jesus Christ."

I don't say anything.

"Say something in Spanish."

I say the first thing that comes into my head, which turns out to be the Lord's Prayer. It comes out expressionless and fast, a ritual mumble. "Oh, God," I say in English, and suck in my breath to keep from crying again.

Ryan doesn't say anything; he just frowns.

I look at my feet. "We'd better go back," I say. "I don't want you to get into trouble."

"There must be some logical explanation," Ryan says finally. "Maybe you had a Spanish babysitter or something. I've heard of that, kids growing up bilingual."

I shake my head. "I don't think I had a babysitter. My mom always worked at home, you know, teaching piano."

"Maybe when you were little, she had a job. Where did you live before this?"

"You mean before Janesville?"

"Yeah."

"A lot of places."

"California? New Mexico? Someplace they spoke Spanish?"

"I *did*. You're right. I *did*." I warm up to Ryan's idea in a hurry. "I lived in New Mexico. I don't remember it at all, that was when I was a baby."

"Maybe that's when you learned to talk. I mean that's when you *do* learn to talk, right, when you're a baby?"

His idea is a ray of hope, a reasonable explanation. It turns out the cliché is correct. I feel better right away, and the way I feel better is like a weight lifting off me.

"You should ask your mom and dad. I don't know why you'd remember it all of a sudden like that. But they say that your brain never forgets anything; it's getting to it, it's *retrieval* that's the trick. Remember that guy in the assembly?"

I do. He's talking about the memory man, a guy who came a couple of weeks ago to give an assembly. He got a bunch of kids up on the stage, and got them to remember things by pretending to walk through a house, thinking of crazy visual cues.

"Didn't he talk about memory triggers? Maybe something Elisa or Yolanda said, or the way they said it, sort of unlocked your mind. I mean it's gotta be something like that, right? What else could it be?"

"I don't know." I look at my hands. "It freaked me out." The more I think about it, the more I like Ryan's idea. It holds me up the rest of the day, like a life jacket.

My mother is making one of my favorite dinners, enchiladas. *Enchiladas.* Right. I convince myself she probably learned to make them when we lived in New Mexico. I'm setting the table in the dining alcove. My father is in the living room finishing up the newspaper.

"So, how'd the P.E. exam go?"

"Great. It was easy."

"Won't be long now," my mother yells from the kitchen. "Put the salsa on, okay sweetie?"

"Do you feel like you're all set for chemistry and geometry?" my father asks.

I finish laying out the silver, get a spoon for the salsa. "I don't know about all set," I say. "I'm pretty well prepared."

" 'Pretty well prepared,' *hmmm.* That doesn't exactly exude confidence." He folds the newspaper. "I don't want to see your grades slipping. If they do, that boyfriend of yours will become an ex-boyfriend pretty quick."

"Quickly," I say. "You need an adverb to modify an adjective."

A warning glare comes to me over his glasses. "Maybe you've been watching too much TV," he says. "I don't think that's cute." I go into the kitchen to help my mother.

So we're all sitting there, passing around the rice, the refried beans, the enchiladas, when I bring it up. I'm so convinced Ryan is right, that really, I'm just looking for confirmation. "I was just wondering. Did I ever have a Spanish-speaking babysitter?"

What happens is not what I expect.

I expect my mother's face to get a puzzled expression. Then I expect her to say, "*Why, yes dear*, why do you ask?" and so on, spooning rice. Instead she gets a shocked, alarmed look and says no in a breathless voice. She throws my father a stricken glance. It seems like a long time before he finally speaks. "What prompts you to ask that, Mariah?"

I don't know why, but immediately my instinct is to lie. I don't exactly lie, but I offer them my story with a shrug, as if what happened to me that morning when I understood Yolanda and Elisa was only a little surprising, not a total wipeout shock that literally made me puke.

I tell them Ryan's theory that maybe I had a Spanish-speaking babysitter. "But I guess not," I say, "which makes it *really* weird."

I don't miss the panicked, horrified look on my mother's face. When she puts her knife and fork down, her hands are shaking so badly, the silverware rattles loudly against the plate.

We all pretend not to notice.

"Hold on," my father says. "We did live down there in an area where half the population is of Hispanic descent. You didn't have a babysitter per se, but maybe you had a little Hispanic friend in one of your preschools. Odds are you did." He turns to my mother. "Your mother would know more about it."

My mother speaks hesitantly, as if she's translating for someone else. "Come to think of it—you know one of your nursery school *teachers* was Hispanic. Miss…*Alvarez*, I think it was. Of course, she always spoke English to *me*, but who knows what she spoke to you kids? Half the class was Spanish-speaking. At *least* half. You might very easily have picked it up from there. And there was a little girl named...*Luisa!*...who was one of your little buddies." My mother's gaze keeps straying over to my father, as if she needs to touch him with her eyes every minute or so for reassurance.

For the next couple of minutes, I sit there listening to my mother re-creating this toddler named Luisa and this teacher named Miss Alvarez. If I hadn't caught that wild look on her face a minute before, I'm sure I'd be believing her.

I'm lying too, or at least keeping back information. I don't tell them I *spoke* in Spanish; I don't tell them about the Lord's Prayer mumbling out of my mouth. I sit there, pushing the food around on my plate, waiting until it seems like time's up and I can leave the table.

"May I be excused?" I get up quickly, without waiting for an answer, take my plate to the kitchen, scrape it off. I say something about getting up there and cracking my books.

I feel a little better in my room, but not for long. The gypsy moths are hatching from their cocoons now. In the day, the yard is so full of them that sometimes you have to push them aside in the air to get through to empty the garbage or something. When I lie down on my bed, I turn and see that there are about twenty brown moths crouched on the wall above my headboard. They look creepy hunched up on my wall like some kind of disgusting fungus.

There must be a hole in my screen. I spend a good twenty minutes capturing moths in a tennis ball can and letting them out through the bathroom window. I know I should kill them, but I can't get myself to do it. When I'm done, my hands are covered with brown powder from their wings. I find the hole in the screen and patch it over with Scotch tape. I keep thinking I got them all, but every time I go to lie down on my bed, I hear another one, underneath the box springs, caught under the dresser. I can't stand the way they sound, the soft trapped beating of their wings.

I have a bad feeling, a terrible feeling in my mind. If my mind was like a body, it would be like it was running out of air, like it couldn't catch its breath.

What I need is Ryan. I tell my parents I'm going to Darlene's to borrow a book. My father, who ordinarily would give me the third degree about leaving my room on exam night, surprises me by not raising any objection.

I feel so much better when I get outside. Just the space seems to make me feel better. I call Ryan from the 7-Eleven and go to the schoolyard to wait for him. I sit on the jungle gym with my eyes closed. Some kids are shooting hoops on the blacktop behind the school, and I listen to them, their shoes squeaking, the ball thumping steadily against the asphalt, the occasional slap when the ball gets passed, the ball on the backboard, the clang of the ball on the rim. "Hey Freddy, Freddy, Freddy, Freddy!" someone yells. Ryan comes up behind me and puts his hands over my eyes.

We walk off toward the woods behind the tennis courts with our arms clamped around each other's waists. It's still so hot out; when my hair moves, I can feel the sweat on the back of my neck. The trees rustle in the soft heavy air.

"So are you all right? What happened? Did you ask your parents? You know, about the babysitter?"

But I don't want to talk. I just want to touch him, the comfort of his flesh.

"So come on, what happened?" Ryan insists. "You didn't ask them, did you?"

"My mother lied to me. She looked scared to death. She just looked scared to death." I stop walking. I'm almost going to cry again, but it's like I'm too dried out to produce tears. "All I can think is I must be adopted or something. Or else, I don't *know* what. I mean, I speak *Spanish* now. I mean, what is *that*?"

He pulls me against him and hugs me. *"Adopted?"* He squeezes my hand. "You really think? I mean..."

"I don't know."

"Jesus." He shakes his head. "Man."

"But it's so *stupid*. Why wouldn't they tell me something like that a long time ago? It's not like them. They're not idiots. They must have known you can't keep a secret like that forever. Especially since I couldn't exactly have been a *baby* when they got me if I already knew how to talk. I mean, they're the kind of parents who would tell you all along how special you were to be adopted, how you were *chosen*. I just don't get it."

"So...you going to ask them?"

"God, I don't know." I try it out. "Mom, Dad, there's something I have to ask you. Oh *God*. Are you my mom and dad?" That feeling in my head again, like my brain cells are running out of air. *"Oh God*, Ryan, oh God."

"Let's go right now. I'll come with you."

Instead I kiss him hard on the mouth, and then the next thing you know his tongue is in my ear, then he's sucking my neck. We go on for a while, leaning up against the tree. Through his pants I can feel his erection.

"Where can we go?" I say so he'll know what I want. It's not even dark out yet.

"Are you sure? What about—"

I kiss him on the mouth to shut him up. It's too late anyway. There's like a point of no return and once we're there, it's easier to find someplace than to be all messed up for hours.

"But what about..."

"Ryan." We talk about going up to the park behind the Baptist church, but it's a long walk, it'll take too long. Ryan thinks of the vacant house, over on Allison. There's

a shed in the backyard. The house is sold but the new
people haven't moved in yet.

When we get there, there are no neighbors around;
thank God, because we're in bad shape. It's one of those
metal storage sheds built in the shape of a barn, that's where
we make love. It smells like pesticides and fertilizer. After
Ryan comes, I hold on the root of his penis to keep it in me
for a while. I want to just stay like that, with him inside me,
and he can tell it, he lets me. When we finally get up, I feel
so much better. The door of the shed opens with such a loud
squeak it makes us laugh. We walk back to the schoolyard.

"So, what are you going to do? You want me to come
with you? You going to ask them about it, about being
adopted?"

I take a breath, chew on my lip. "I don't know."

"I think I better come with you."

"I think you better go home and study. I'll be all
right." Now, this second, it's beginning to seem fantastic
to me. Adopted? It can't be that. There must be some other
explanation.

"You sure?" Ryan says.

"I'm okay." Right this second, I can't even think of
a single Spanish word. I can't even think of the word for
goodbye even though I always knew it, everybody knows
it, it's something totally common.

"If you need me, promise you'll call. I mean if you—I
mean for any reason—you call me and I'll be right over,
okay?"

"I will."

"You promise?"

"I promise."

Ryan kisses my mouth and then he kisses my fingers
and then I actually start to hurry home to study. I think
of the word, then, after he's gone: *adiós*.

I'm walking slower and slower as I get closer to home,
scuffing my heel against each segment of concrete until

pretty soon I'm hardly moving. The sun's going down; there are bright pink tufts of clouds through the trees. I walk over a segment of sidewalk stained blue-black with mulberries. When I stop to think about it, it's just about hilarious. I mean there I am—my whole life is turning inside out on me. I'm not the person I always thought I was. For lack of any other explanation, I'm thinking I must be adopted, which means my parents have been lying to me for years. So what do I do? I go out to make love to my boyfriend. And then? I'm actually on my way back home to study chemistry.

So I'm walking home and I get around to it— thinking about how my mom and dad might not be my mom and dad; I get around to that word and what it means: *adopted.*

I'm thinking of my mom's terrified face. I'm thinking of Spanish words coming out of my mouth.

I reach the sidewalk in front of my house and I just stop cold. I look up the flagstone walk at the pretty little house with its trim white shutters and neat plantings of flowers. Light shines steadily out from the windows. A buttery glow spills onto the lawn. The house is closed up, cooled by the humming air conditioner. I hear the other air conditioners humming too, the one from across the street, the one from the house next door, all of them churning away. Everyone's inside, in their sealed houses. Every forty seconds or so the distant rumble of a jet from National vibrates the air. A few moths bat against the light over our front door.

I imagine my mother sitting in the wing chair, working on her needlepoint, my father sitting in his leather recliner, reading *The New Yorker.* I shift my weight from foot to foot. I can see the ceiling fan in my room upstairs, slowly turning. I imagine my chem book open on my desk, my notes scattered around it. What I can't imagine is myself going in there.

The night's falling, softly and slowly. It never really gets dark here; there's too much light for that. The days just fade into a twilight that has a strange pinkish-orange tinge from the mercury vapor lamps. I turn my back to the house, and first I'm walking but then, before I know it, I'm running, I'm going faster and faster.

Chapter Sixteen

ROLANDO
A True Democracy

THE MOTEL IS ideal—almost exactly as I pictured it. It's
such a perfect rendition of my vision that when we pull up
in front, I have a strong sense of déjà vu. I take it as a good
omen. It's as if my reveries on the red couch were prophetic,
not fantasy. I can almost feel everything coming true.

The motel is called the By George! The man at the
desk, who checks us in, has no larynx. He speaks in an
electronically amplified voice, accomplished by inhaling air
and then exhaling through a microphone held against his
throat. Despite myself, I keep peering at his neck to see if
he has a hole, a visible aperture.

"You're probably wondering about the name," he says.

Moro nods noncommittally. The clerk explains to us
that "By George" is a play on words, a reference to the first

142

president of the United States, George Washington, who lived not far from here. I don't really understand.

The explanation takes a while since the man has to stop speaking and inhale air between each sentence. If he were reciting the multiplication tables, I'm sure we'd stand there and nod and smile. It would seem impolite to do anything but listen attentively to someone taking so much trouble to speak. When he's finished, Moro asks if we can have one of the rooms at the back. The man squints at his list, takes in some air. "Quieter back there, all right." More air. "I can give you number twelve." We nod and pay for two nights in advance. He holds out the key but doesn't immediately relinquish it. He's back to the name again. "It seemed like a natural, you know," he says a bit wistfully. "We'll stay here, by George!"

Moro and I smile and nod appreciatively. He drops the key into Moro's hand. He inhales and broadcasts another, parting, sentence: "Don't let the heat get you down, now."

I find myself wondering. If I was afflicted with the loss of my larynx, would I bother with small talk?

I'm heartened by the perfection of the motel because things did not start off well. We're twenty-four hours behind schedule. I almost lost my mind when Pan Am canceled the flight. I knew it didn't really matter—there are three extra days built into the schedule as a cushion—but I was crushed with disappointment anyway, having to stay in Santiago another night when I was mentally set to be jetting toward my rendezvous with Mariah Alicia Ebinger. It didn't help that we chose a hotel where I was extremely unlikely to encounter anyone I knew. Economy class.

The By George! is located on a very busy multilane road known as Richmond Highway. It is also called Route 1. This is common here, for roads and streets to have both names and numbers. Route 1, I learn from Moro, is a highway that runs all the way up and down the east coast of the United States. We could get in our rented Ford Mustang, exit the motel parking lot, and drive all the way to Florida without making a turn.

We cleared customs in Miami. Miami amazed me. I felt as if I hadn't left South America; everyone around me in the airport was speaking Spanish. The flight from Miami to Washington arrived at ten, on time. We rented two cars and drove to Alexandria in less than twenty minutes. One of the cars is a spare. Before coming here we parked it at a crowded shopping center half a mile down Route 1.

Moro drives around to the back of the motel and parks in front of number 12. We get our small suitcases from the trunk. The suitcases are inexpensive canvas ones and everything inside them is anonymous. There are no identifying laundry marks, no unusual items, no personal gear, nothing that can be traced to Moro or me, nothing to connect us to Argentina. Moro fits the key in the lock, pushes the door open with his foot, precedes me inside. We're met by a wash of stale, chilled air.

"Perfect, isn't it, Captain?" Moro says, offering me one of his strange smiles. You wouldn't really call it a smile, what he does with his mouth. He pulls his lips apart, displaying his teeth. He rubs his hand over the stubble on his face. "I'm going to take a shower."

I pace around the room, touching things—the windowsill, the bed, the television, the water glasses.

Moro made all the preparations during his last visit. He purchased the guns and other equipment and stored them in a rented facility. (We might not need weapons, but clearly it's best to be prepared.) He scouted motels, ascertained the location of the Ebinger house, mapped out a route, drove there. He found a good place to leave the extra car.

Acquiring the guns was no problem, he told me. Permits were necessary, but Moro had obtained identification solely for the purchase of weapons, after which it was discarded. Moro told me it was easier to buy the weapons than it was to rent the cars. He could have bought an arsenal. Even semiautomatic weapons are readily available here.

"A true democracy," he said.

Moro finds it ironic that the world's largest democracy has trained so many members of the Latin American military in the most barbaric and repressive techniques. Like so many other Latin officers, he himself acquired his special skills in "interrogation methods" at U.S. expense, attending training sessions at the U.S. Army school in the Canal Zone. This education is provided by the Alliance for Progress. I guess you could chalk it up to fear of Fidel.

The equipment is stored in a place called Springfield U-Store-It. It's in a bleak industrial area and consists of two cinder-block buildings. Moro goes inside and emerges with a black duffel bag. We eat lunch at a place called The Three Little Pigs, and then we return to the By George! Moro insists we take a nap.

He sleeps for a couple of hours, but I can't; I just lie there, staring at the ceiling. I bought a *Washington Post* this morning from a vending machine and I try to read it, but I can't concentrate. The front page has a photograph of a group of Romanians standing on top of an enormous felled statue of Lenin. Ropes crisscross the statue, making the figure look not so much felled as captured. The photograph might easily serve as a book jacket for *Gulliver's Travels*.

When Moro wakes up, we head over to the motel's restaurant/lounge, the Buried Hatchet. It bears out the colonial motif. The tables are rough-hewn; the bartender wears a tricorn hat. Special menu items are marked with little red hatchets.

Of course, I wonder about the symbolism of the hatchet. Moro elicits the explanation from a cocktail waitress: some story about George Washington, as a boy, chopping down a cherry tree. When questioned about this act, he admits it. The waitress tells this story in such a way that I can tell it's a cherished tale, meant to reflect well on the founding father; I just can't understand why. That's the way it is here; everything has to be explained to me, and even then I don't get it. This sense of foreignness never leaves me, not for a second. I could live here a hundred years and never get used to it. Even the colors of the neon lights seem slightly off, a different, alien palette.

There's an army base two miles from here that seems to supply most of the clientele for the By George! It's a popular spot for assignations. I think it's a brilliant choice by Moro for this reason. Dreamy couples, preoccupied with sex, stroll in and out of the units, drift over to the lounge. They don't pay attention to anyone else.

We're both bursting with nervous energy. The thought of returning to our unit for a few more hours is so claustrophobic, we stay a long time in the lounge, eating, nursing beers, eating some more, waiting.

The noise is intense. A video machine provides a counterpoint to the jukebox's heavy rock and roll. The music is so loud, the tables vibrate. The perky, inane melodies of the video game float above the din, annoyingly clear. It doesn't seem romantic to me, but the dreamy couples sit holding hands under the table, staring into each other's eyes. Asian girls with bodies like children. Black girls with fabulous bodies, asses sticking out behind balanced by breasts jutting out in front. White girls with plucked, querulous eyebrows look pallid and dim in comparison, as if they've been kept indoors too long. They seem aware of their pallor and wear too much makeup to compensate.

I keep thinking: How can this work? How did they ever think this country could work? All these different people pushed together. Compared to this, everyone in Argentina looks exactly the same. It's bracing, somehow, to be sitting here, in this exotic company. Even if a place like it existed in Buenos Aires, I would never go there. Except for Carla, I'm accustomed to the company of the well-bred and the overpaid. Our topics of discussion center on politics, polo, and methods of preserving our power or our money. Sitting in the Buried Hatchet lounge, I overhear conversations bordering on the surreal.

"Mary Lou's gonna get her butt sucked."

"What you say?"

"Lip-o-suc-tion. Get her butt sucked, you know. She saving money for that."

"Now can you imagine saving your money to get your *butt sucked*?" This girl is sipping a drink that has a tiny paper umbrella propped on the edge. She twirls it between her fingers thoughtfully. "There's plenty of men like a good-sized butt."

"Can you imagine having the fat sucked outta you?" her companion replies. "Can you *imagine*?" Her whole body ripples with displeasure, an incredible display of muscular fluidity. "Ewwwww. I think it's disgusting."

From there the two embark on a discussion of Michael Jackson's plastic surgeries.

In the booth behind me a man is talking to his date about what seems to be some kind of vicious system of massage.

"So Kathy gets me to go to this person that helped someone in her office with his back."

"A chiropractor?"

"No, this was some kind of German thing. I forget. I'll tell you, it was a trip. First of all, I have to take everything off except my underpants."

"What? Wait a sec. This is a *masseuse*, right?"

"I'm telling you—no. This is some kind of...body manipulation system. This is a big woman could kill you with her bare hands is what this is. I'm laying on this table and I'm like whoa! I'm half afraid she's going to karate-chop my neck, you know."

"So what happens?"

"She starts in on me with her hands. It feels like an army marching over my back."

You can't seem to avoid small talk with Americans. You ask them for a room, a pack of cigarettes, a light, some gasoline, and the transaction is not complete without some other exchange of information. Their interest is almost generic, part of an aimless and shallow curiosity. This is what they ask: Where are you from? Uruguay, we might answer, or Venezuela, or Chile. The specific country makes no difference to them, the continent is sufficiently precise. Ah, they generally reply, with a little categorizing smile. South America. Did you have a good trip? What airline did you fly? What are you doing here in the D.C. area? We tell them we're here in the United States to look into computer systems for our business at home. Our cover story, bolstered by our briefcases full of computer brochures, doesn't interest them at all.

The way it's worked out, Moro does most of the talking. They find my accent, which is British (for a time, I went to school in England), surprising. To be Hispanic in this country is to live within a certain set of expectations. I don't fit the bill. I throw them off. My voice seems to convey some kind of disdain. I can see it in their eyes. Their eyes narrow: *Who do you think you are?* I'm a man with a story, but it isn't a story they want to hear.

So I let Moro handle as much as possible. He sounds like a Cuban, I guess, or a Mexican. He doesn't worry them; they peg him as one more hustler.

Another characteristic of the population here: they're poorly dressed. People will wear absolutely anything, the most unflattering clothing.

The best-looking people are Black. The most stylish of all, surprisingly, are the soldiers dressed in camouflage gear. Dressed to blend in with the jungle, their attire seems perfect for the stupefying heat, for the concrete and neon sprawl of Route 1. They look as if they could plunge into any kind of trouble and set things right.

After the Buried Hatchet closes, we have no choice but to go back to our room. We sprawl on our separate beds, watching the television. Moro flicks from channel to channel with a remote control device. It's attached to the television by a cable. Various ordinarily movable objects turn out to be securely connected to the room. The lamps are screwed into the tables. The coat hangers are of a construction that does not allow for removal. The telephone is bolted to the chest of drawers.

On one channel is a talk show. The host is interviewing a collection of individuals whose common characteristic is "gender identity variation." Little signs flash under the participants as they speak: intersex, eunuch, transgender, transvestite. Information scrolls along the bottom of the screen providing the phone numbers of support groups for each specific subgroup. The age of specialization.

"I've got everything you've got—and some more," one perky-looking man announces to the host. The audience laughs nervously. Moro changes the station.

The sporting channel shows a "Monster Tractor Pull," vehicles with enormous wheels dragging stupendous loads. Dueling for the New Age, testing the strength of machines.

Gorbachev is on the all-news channel, accompanied by a translator. The Russian is speaking about the Baltic republics, appealing to the crowds in Lithuania. He asks for restraint. The halting pace of the translator lends an odd drama to the proceedings. It's as if he's continually searching for the right word and may at any moment give up and lapse into silence. The faces surrounding him keep an anxious attention on him, like parents at a child's stumbling recital.

Gorbachev is succeeded on the screen by George Bush. Bush is striding toward a helicopter. He stops to answer questions shouted at him by reporters. First the president

goes through a kind of set piece for the photographers:
swivels his head, crumples his mouth into a smile, waves.
The air is turbulent; strings of his hair fly about. The first
question put to him concerns strategic arms reduction, and
he sounds piqued, as if he's responding to a neighbor who
has complained about his dog. His lips appear to be too
large for his mouth. "Well, we're *trying* to do something
about this. We just have to have some patience." He invokes
"the American people" and then ducks under the turbulence and boards the aircraft.

A woman in a bright yellow jacket opens her mouth to
speak, but before she can say a word, Moro turns the television off. It makes a sparkling sound, as if someone has
flicked a few drops of water on a hot fire, and the screen
goes dark.

Moro smooths his hair back from his temples. "Let's
go, *Capitán.*"

Chapter Seventeen

ARTHUR
The Cozy Lie

ALL ALONG I maintained to Dolores that we should tell her, but it never seemed the right time, somehow. It's a familiar story, I guess—time marches on, and what was once merely difficult becomes impossible.

When exactly is the appropriate time to tell a child that she's not really "your" child? Do you tell her when she's six? While you're teaching her to tie her shoes? At six, when she's in first grade, when she's learning to write in cursive, carefully curving her letters, putting touching little curlicues on the capitals? Do you tell her while you're helping her learn to ride a bike? While you're running along beside her, awkwardly holding the seat and the handlebars until she gets some sense of how to balance on two wheels? Do you tell her then? When exactly do you shred the bonds of

151

trust that have been knitted together over the years? Do you wait until she's older, as Dolores always insisted, claiming that Mariah needed to reach a certain level of maturity before she could learn the truth? But then, when she was twelve, stumbling through adolescence toward womanhood, she seemed even more vulnerable, in a way. I can see her right now, the first time she got shoes with little heels, how excited she was, her touching, wobbly walk.

We couldn't do the obvious and tell her right from the beginning, which is what all the books and the experts recommend. We didn't have her right at the beginning, for one thing—I mean she wasn't a baby when we got her. We wanted a baby, of course, but there wasn't a baby to be had, and when we were offered Mariah, well, despite her pathetic state, and her age, we said yes immediately. We had been waiting so long, see. It was easy to deduce by then that we should have started trying to adopt earlier, really in our early thirties—we would have had a good chance then. But we kept hoping Dolores would get pregnant. Hope. You know how it is. Sometimes hope is not the balm of future happiness that soothes an inadequate present. Sometimes hope is no more than a pernicious form of procrastination.

Her "real" name was María, incidentally. We were told that. That was about all we were told. *"La niña se llama María."* The one paper we got, a birth certificate, gave her name as María Aguilar de Carrera. We were told that her parents were dead.

We thought it would be less confusing for the child if we kept the names close, yet we still wanted an "American" (by that I mean North American) sound to her name, so we just decided on Mariah. It seems like a funny notion, thinking about it now. I wonder how long she remembered the real sound of her name. I wonder how long she just thought we couldn't pronounce it correctly.

For a couple of years, by then, it had been pretty clear that there was little chance of our getting a baby from a legitimate adoption agency. Too old, that was the thing. And what can you do about that? It's a condition that keeps getting worse. The competition for children put up for adoption was ferocious, and we got on the list late, and the longer we waited, of course, the older and less "suitable" we got. It wasn't just our age. Our frequent moves counted against us as well, seeming to disclose some basic instability of our potential family. I could always see the disapproval in their faces as they perused our residential history, the lifting eyebrows, the tightening mouths, the mulling "hmmmmms." One woman actually asked (with a straight face) if we'd considered getting a dog. ("They're a lot of company.") It was very discouraging. That's why we agreed to go down to Argentina in the first place.

I'm a time-management expert. Until recently I worked for Boorstein and Smathers, and in the early years we did a good deal of consulting for the State Department. We'd be brought in by A.I.D., usually. Sometimes we were able to boost production by as much as fifty percent; it was amazing. They'd never heard of time management in some of those places. Myself, I'd never been assigned abroad, but when a team was being selected to be sent down to Buenos Aires, I put in for it. Even though the political situation down there was, well, *unsettled*, I put in for it. Everybody was surprised—it was mostly junior personnel who took jobs abroad. It was a step down for me, really, careerwise.

It was the baby thing, of course. We had the idea that maybe in Argentina things would be easier. But even down there, we got nowhere with legitimate adoption agencies. By the time we'd been there a year, I'd have to say we were hooked up with some fairly shady operations. We were frankly waiting for a baby to buy. Even so, we were running out of time. I was only a few months from the end of my stint there, in fact, when in the most roundabout way, we were offered Mariah—for a certain sum. It wasn't much. She wasn't a baby, after all, but a totally withdrawn four-year-old. She was almost five, in fact; she was just shy of being five years old.

It was unbelievably difficult arranging to get her out of the country; it was a full-time job for a month. You never saw so much red tape, but we finally got the papers. I did notice that the Agencia Palomar seemed to have cut quite a few legal corners, but, hey, we weren't complaining. As far as getting her an American passport was concerned, connections in the State Department were invaluable. Without them, we might have been stuck down there for *years*. Her name was legally changed, right then and there. It was on her hard-won American passport: Mariah Alicia Ebinger.

Getting back to telling her about how she was adopted—believe me, we couldn't have started at the beginning with her. She wouldn't have been able to make any sense of the notion of adoption. It took months of coaxing and all of Dolly's seemingly endless patience and boundless love to even get the poor thing to stop going rigid whenever we touched her. She didn't say a single word for over a year, if you can imagine that, not a word! We were very concerned that she would never recover from whatever it was that had happened to her, that she had suffered some permanent damage. Looking at her now—she's outgoing, she's popular, she's a regular all-American girl—it's hard to remember the way she was. Incidentally, we never learned just what had happened to her, although it was clear she had suffered some terrible trauma. You can appreciate that we weren't in a position to press for details.

So at dinner Mariah just floored us with that little story about understanding Spanish. We'd long ago concluded that she would never remember her early life; we thought that door was shut for good. When she came to us, Mariah didn't remember anything about herself, let alone remembering what had happened to her. And I mean literally—she had amnesia. Up in St. Paul we took her to a bunch of doctors: a psychiatrist, a couple of psychologists.

We were so worried about her. They gave her batteries and batteries of tests. The tests reassured us on one front; nothing *physiological* was wrong with her. She wasn't brain-damaged in any way.

This first guy we went to, Borchardt, I think his name was, he told us that what Mariah had was a sort of stress-related amnesia. And the way she withdrew into a shell sometimes—those he called pseudocatatonic episodes. Stress amnesia was quite common, he said, in adults as well as children. It happened when something traumatic had befallen someone: a car crash, a violent accident, a fire, a murder. You know, these crackpots that go and shoot up a McDonald's or something—sometimes the witnesses blank out, they don't remember anything, the whole event falls into a kind of black hole in their memory. It happens to soldiers too, Borchardt said. The way he explained it to us, he presented it almost as a healthy, healing thing, the mind repressing what it couldn't tolerate knowing. Most people regained their memory eventually, although sometimes they didn't. Sometimes their minds kept certain experiences walled up forever.

"Give it time." That's what Borchardt recommended, just to give it time and probably the whole thing would resurface, and at that point we'd be able to deal with the grief or the fear, or whatever it was that was afflicting Mariah. Borchardt suggested therapy for her, and we pursued that for a while but the therapists never elicited any kind of breakthrough, and Mariah never did regain her memory. In retrospect, I kind of wonder if we shouldn't have taken her to a Spanish-speaking therapist, assuming one could have been found in St. Paul. But I didn't even think about that at the time; it never occurred to me. Hindsight, that wonderful beast.

There is no question in my mind that Mariah is recalling something now; that's what the understanding of Spanish has to mean. Her mind is beginning to unlock itself.

We rarely spoke Spanish around her, by the way, even when we first got her, although both Dolores and I speak it quite well. Early on, we learned that she was calmer, less fretful, when we spoke to her in English. She actually seemed to find the sound of English soothing. It was very perplexing, because we assumed she couldn't understand a word we were saying.

Anyway, once she emerged from her withdrawal, it seemed risky to dredge up emotional stuff that might send her right back into her shell. So we left it there, in the dark, her past. Dolly was especially adamant that we shouldn't upset the applecart and in matters dealing with Mariah, I tended to follow her lead. After all, the truth was we had very little information to share with her. Eventually, of course, Mariah did ask questions about her earlier life, about when she was a baby. Not to put too fine a point on it, we started inventing a past for her to cover the one she didn't remember.

After a while these stories began to seem real, you know what I mean? Think about it. How much do *you* know, I mean really know, about your early childhood? Isn't it just stories, really, that your parents have told and retold? It got so that sometimes I could picture, I could almost *remember*, a baby Mariah saying her first words— "Dadda" and "doos" (for juice). Some part of me almost recalled the day she rode down some steps on her Big Wheel (the explanation for a large scar on her knee), the time the swing hit her on the head (small scar, right temple). Sometimes it seemed to me that I really was there when she was eleven months old and took her first tottering steps. In a way, we gave ourselves her babyhood this way, telling those stories. When the time came that Mariah started wondering why we didn't have any baby pictures of her, we told her that when we moved from New Mexico to Minnesota, the movers had lost some of our boxes and one of them had contained all our photo albums.

As soon as the door closes behind Mariah, who's off to her friend Darlene's to get a book, Dolores rushes into the living room.

"What are we going to do, Artie? Oh, God, why now? Why all of a sudden now?"

I stand up. I put my arms around her. We stand there in the middle of the room, me patting her in a stiff way. I've never been adept at comforting people. "Look, it's not the end of the world," I say, although it is the end of the world as we know it; the world defined by the cozy lie. "In some ways, it'll be a relief."

"How?" Dolly sniffs. She lowers herself carefully onto the couch, her head in her hands. "A complete disaster," she says. A sob rips through her. She doubles over like someone who's been smacked in the stomach. "How are we even going to *start* to tell her? 'Honey, there's something we've got to tell you, there's something we've got to—' " Her voice keeps drifting up into the upper registers until finally, like the voice of a soprano with laryngitis, it cracks into inaudibility.

"We won't have to keep worrying about it," I say. "That's one relief. And we won't have to stay one step ahead of the people looking for her."

"They'll take her away. They will," she says in a breathless monotone. "They will. They'll take her away from us."

"Honey, she's not a baby, you know. She's not going to want to *go* away. She's sixteen years old. She's in *love*. By the time the legal dust settles, she'll be ready to go to college."

Dolly shakes her head. "She'll hate us for this. She'll just hate us. She'll never forgive us. God. We should have told her; we should have *told* her, Artie. Oh God."

I sit down next to her and take her hand in mine. Her hands look twenty years older than the rest of her. All that chopping and cooking and washing up. She's a reckless, enthusiastic cook. Inspired, but careless. At least a dozen times a day she takes a sharp breath or mutters a quick little "damn." Cutting herself, burning herself. Her hands have paid the price. Papery skin stretched over the bones. Brown irregular spots. The fingertips of certain fingers are criss-crossed with tiny cuts, much like the battered surface of her favorite cutting board. I raise her hand up to my mouth and kiss her knuckles. She squeezes back until the bones in my hand hurt. "She might hate me," I tell her, "but never you. She couldn't hate you. All you've ever done is love her." She catches her breath up into her throat. Her teeth clench to hold back the tears. "We'll tell her when she gets back," I say firmly.

"Oh God," Dolly says. "Oh God, Artie, oh God."

We settle into waiting, anxious for Mariah to get home so we can get it over with, but dreading it all the same. We sit there on the couch as if waiting somewhere public, for a train, say, or at a doctor's office.

I'm restless. I keep getting up and adjusting the thermostat, walking from room to room, tidying the newspapers. A couple of gypsy moths crouch on the wall above the fireplace. I capture them and flush them down the toilet. I watch them struggle against the surface tension of the water until the suction of the vortex catches them and pulls them down. Kind of gruesome, but what are you supposed to do? The damn things are destroying the trees.

When Mariah went out, she said she'd be back in half an hour, but her half hours tend to stretch on for quite some time, so although we sit there, waiting for her to come through the door, I'm not surprised when an hour comes and goes and she still hasn't shown up. Even after an hour and a half we aren't particularly worried. Just anxious, dreading the confrontation when she does come home.

By nine-fifteen two full hours have gone by and I am concerned. Where *is* she? Dolly gets up and paces. A few times she putters around in the kitchen for a while and then comes back and resumes her post. Once she even goes outside and looks up and down the street. Dolly is a gifted worrier anyway. She worries about everything; random events seem inherently threatening to her. By nine-thirty she's muttering, "Something's happened to her, I just know it, I just know it."

At ten, Dolly is a basket case, and at her urging I call Mariah's friend Darlene. There's a little hesitation in the girl's voice when I ask her if Mariah is there.

"Well, did she come over to borrow a book?" I persist. "She left here around seven-fifteen. She said she was going over to your house to borrow a book."

Hesitation again. I can almost hear her thinking: Should I cover for Mariah? "Well…"

"Please," I say. "We're a little worried, actually."

"I really haven't seen her since this afternoon. I'm sorry, Mr. Ebinger."

I call the boyfriend, Ryan. The father answers, and when I ask for his son, he says the boy is "studying for exams right now, Mr. Ebinger."

"Art."

"Art. I'm sorry we haven't met. Of course, I know Mariah quite well. A wonderful girl—you must be very proud of her."

"Thank you. Yes. I am. Ah, *is* your son there?"

"Is it something urgent or could I have him call you back? I hate to interrupt him when he's actually working." He gives a little suburban laugh.

"I'm afraid it really is urgent."

"Is something wrong?"

"My daughter is missing," I say stiffly. "Would you mind? I mean, I thought your son—"

"Of course not." Hastily. "I'll get him."

The boy admits he saw Mariah around eight, but says they'd parted company before nine o'clock at the elementary school. She was headed back home. "Jeez. She should have been home a long time ago." Alarm replaces the curiosity in his voice. It's the alarmed tone that persuades me of his veracity.

"If you hear from her," I say, "her mother is very worried. *Please* tell her to call."

"You know," he starts in a nervous voice, "she was...upset, you know... Jeez, I gotta go look for her."

His father must have been standing right next to him because I hear him so clearly: "You will *not*, Ryan Ferguson."

"Dad, Mariah's *missing*. I gotta go look for her." Then he speaks into the receiver: "Goodbye, Mr. Ebinger."

I hear the father yell his son's name and then the connection is severed.

Chapter Eighteen

ARTHUR
Swimming Upstream

IT'S FUNNY HOW an idea can get a hold on someone and then come to dominate that person's life. I mean one day it's not there, even as an idea, and the next thing you know, it's *everything*, it's the very focus of your existence. I mean when Dolly and I were in our twenties, out in Seattle, for the first few years after we were married, we never gave a thought to having children. We took precautions against it, in fact. What a word. *Precautions*. It's amazing how fast a word can get old-fashioned.

I guess it shouldn't be surprising that the idea of having a child should come to obsess someone. It's probably the second most basic drive—to reproduce, that is. After survival. Many animals—plants too, come to think of it—only survive up to the point of reproduction.

161

Take salmon. They swim thousands of miles just so they can spawn in the little stream where they were born. They practically kill themselves—well, some of them *do* kill themselves—fighting their way upstream, fighting all that water. I've seen them, out in the Northwest; it's something, I'll tell you, the force that drives them. They give a ferocious fight if you hook one. You have to get them at the mouth of the river, of course. Once they hit the fresh water, the taste goes out of them.

We human beings are not so different in behavior from our colleagues in the animal kingdom. Just compare us to birds, for instance. Around the neighborhood, I can get myself into a bird frame of mind. Women sit in their beauty shops with awful-smelling stuff in their hair, to make it curly, to make it a different color. What is that but preening? And you have the men—like me—out there mowing their lawns, caulking, painting their trim, cleaning the gutters. Nesting.

I'm thinking about birds, I guess, because Dolores reminds me of a bird. I mean, if I had to pick a member of the animal kingdom that is most like Dolores, it would definitely be a member of the avian class. She has those same quick, alert eyes. There's a lot of nervy speed in the way she moves. When she's sitting, only the smallest part of her seems to be touching whatever it is she's on—perching, you see. Everything she does is quick and deft and precise. She has that high energy, as if she could just shoot off into the sky if she wanted to.

Anyway, when we were in our twenties, Dolly and I, we were both working hard and loving it. We were just about as happy as two people could be. I was one of the very earliest time-management people; the field was in its infancy then. I was out at Boeing. We were so gung ho about what we were doing, you just wouldn't believe it. We thought we were inventing the wheel. We streamlined everything; we pulled worthless chunks of time out of thin air and turned them into productive hours. It was like magic. And Dolores—she had her own career in music. She played with the symphony. She's a multitalented woman, you know. Now she kind of dissipates her natural gifts, in what I think are (not to make a pun), trivial pursuits like cooking and knitting and teaching piano to children of no discernible talent. But back then she played the viola *and* the piano on a professional level. And we were very social in those days. Dolores loved to throw a party, and was she good at it! She would toss together these amazing feasts, and on a shoestring budget too. I never called her Dolores in those days. The name seemed too dark and heavy for someone like Dolly, someone so bright and cheerful. I mean in Latin *dolor* means sorrow, grief. In Spanish it means pain.

No, the name Dolores didn't begin to suit her until later, after the baby bug hit. You can imagine the scenario easily enough. Couples we were friendly with began to have babies. I was thirty-three; Dolores was thirty (we'd married at the somewhat advanced, at the time, ages of twenty-eight and twenty-five). Suddenly it seemed imperative to "begin our family." That's the way it was thought of in those days, as a gradual building process, adding one child at a time until the family was complete. We expected to have three or four kids; we hadn't quite decided.

So we stopped "taking precautions." In those days, when the pill was just a research mention on *Time*'s science page, and the word "legal" never preceded the word "abortion," the fear of unwanted pregnancy was so strong that we just assumed that as soon as we stopped taking precautions, Dolly would get pregnant like the next day. Well, of course, that didn't happen. Every month she greeted the evidence of her menstrual period with disappointment edging toward despair. After a couple of years her inability to get pregnant began to dominate our emotional life.

Knowledge about human fertility has advanced a great deal since, but even then there was plenty to do. Dolly kept strict charts of vaginal temperature; her secretions were monitored for texture; detailed records of menstrual patterns were maintained. We "had intercourse," as the doctors always described it, at optimal times.

There wasn't really anything "wrong" with either one of us. If some physiological insufficiency *had* been identified, the hope factor would have been eliminated and we probably would have adopted a child then, when we were still young, when it would have been relatively easy. Instead we suffered through another ten years of struggling to conceive, living in an oscillating monthly cycle of hope and failure.

Dolly went to a couple of dozen different doctors and every damn clinic she could find. She took all the different types of fertility drugs. Once I had a dream that she had twelve babies. It was a dream come true and a nightmare all at the same time. A radiant Dolly graced the cover of the *National Enquirer,* her head on a pillow, surrounded by this huge litter of babies. The babies resembled little pink pencil erasers. I was shown on the following page in an inset guiding a hand truck stacked high with diapers through our front door. I was wearing a cardigan and a wry smile. I resembled a brain-damaged Bing Crosby.

As I said, once Dolly got it into her head that she had to have a baby, her pursuit was fabulously thorough. Although we're not Catholic, Dolly and I traveled to Rome, where her womb was blessed by the pope. She consulted an astrologist. We had sex during particularly auspicious stellar configurations. There was more, embarrassingly more—an herbalist, a psychic, you get the picture.

So when the chance came to get Mariah, I'll tell you, it was like a dream coming true. Damaged as Mariah was, the day she came to us was still one of the happiest days of my life, because it signaled an end to the accelerating lunacy I've just described. We finally had a child upon whom Dolly could lavish the thwarted but apparently boundless supply of mother-love stored within her.

A knock at the door pulls me from my reverie. Before I even move to get up, Dolly is there opening it. It's as if she's been catapulted from the couch, she gets there so fast. I glance at my watch. Ten-thirty. For the first time I'm really worried, I'm actually afraid. Mariah bent the rules often; she rarely broke them. Where *is* she? Even from where I sit I can feel the gush of hot moist air pour into the room as Dolly pulls the door open.

It's that boy, Ryan.

I stand up. I can see the fear drain away from Dolly's shoulders. She was prepared for the worst, the police, the whole television sequence: "Mrs. Ebinger? I'm afraid I have some bad news for you..." Anything else is a reprieve.

The boy's smooth, innocent face is distorted with concern. His skin is flushed, as if he's been running; sweat is beaded up at his hairline. "Is she here? Did she come back?"

Dolly's hand flies to her mouth and she catches her breath. "No," she says in a tiny voice.

"I thought she was all right," he says, not exactly to us. "She was upset but I thought she was all right." He starts out the door but I stop him with a hand on his arm.

"Hold on," I say. "Wait a minute. Whoa."

He doesn't want to stop but his good manners win out over his inclination to bolt. "I've got to find her, Mr. Ebinger." He's almost as distraught as Dolly.

"Hold on a second. You said she was 'upset' when you saw her. What's that all about?"

He looks back and forth from my wife to me. "You must know," he says finally. "She figures she must be adopted." Dolly sags into me.

"Oh God," she says. "Oh, God, I knew it. She's run away." Her voice is high and unstable. "I just knew it."

"I'll find her," Ryan says.

"Let me drive you," I offer. "Please."

He pulls away. I'm actually holding his arm in quite a strong grip, but he yanks himself free. "No," he says, in a surprised voice.

"Please," I say urgently, but he's already halfway down the steps. When he reaches the sidewalk, he breaks into a run.

"Oh God," Dolly says. Her face is hidden in her hands and she's whispering, babbling really, into them. "We should have told her a long time ago. Oh, Godddddd. It's my fault, it's all my fault. I just wasn't brave enough. She'll never understand, she'll never *understand*, she'll never...she'll never...she'll—"

"I'm going to drive around and look for her." I take Dolly's elbow and lead her over to the couch.

"Let me come," she pleads.

I know she doesn't want to be left behind with just her fears, but I persuade her that it's a bad idea to leave the house empty. What if Mariah calls? Or the boy, Ryan? What if Mariah comes back and no one is there?

"I'll find her," I say, with a great deal more conviction than I feel.

Outside, the streets look not so much empty as deserted. As I turn on the car, I realize I have little idea of where to search. I decide to start at the school, G.W. It's the only place that occurs to me, besides Ryan's or Darlene's. I drive down Braddock and turn into the school's large deserted parking lot. The neat empty rows, striped white for angle parking, make me think of huge fish skeletons. I park up against the chain-link fence that separates the parking lot from the football field.

It's an ominous night. Thick, low clouds churn across the sky. The full moon blinks on and off behind them, a stuttery illumination that is distracting and hallucinatory, like a strobe light. Occasionally, the moon, as if with a huge muscular effort, shakes itself entirely free of the heavy clouds and for a moment casts a steady, rather sinister light.

I wander around, calling Mariah's name. My voice sounds thin and tentative, as if it lacks the force to carry through the hot, heavy air. At times the trees shake and rustle in the rushes of muggy wind and my voice disappears entirely. There's rain in the air, maybe a thunderstorm.

I spend about fifteen minutes there at the school, feeling increasingly foolish shouting my daughter's name. Several groups of young men, most of them Black, approach me to see if they can help. I describe Mariah and ask if they've seen her, but of course they haven't. Although no one is rude to me, I can tell they think my behavior idiotic from the sniggering conversations I can't help but hear. ("He looking for his daughter." "How old is she?" "Teenager." "Shit, man, it's not even eleven o'clock." "She supposed to be home studying." "Yeah, she probably studying something, heh heh heh.")

Finally I give up and just drive around town, hoping I'll see her on the streets. It's aimless driving, a token effort; I feel compelled to look but I am devoid of hope. Occasionally I call her name out the window. After about half an hour of this, I turn for home. I don't want to leave Dolores alone any longer. I contemplate the next step. First I'll check with the boy, Ryan. After that, I suppose, will come the police.

Chapter Nineteen

ARTHUR
Remembered Posture

FROM OUTSIDE I hear Dolores pounding away at one of those mournful Chopin preludes. The piano is just about sobbing. The music stops instantly when my hand touches the latch, and by the time I pull open the door, my wife's anxious face is there to greet me. Her pathetically hopeful expression slumps instantly to one of despair when she sees that I'm alone. She turns from me without a word.

"I guess she hasn't come back here either," I say, pointlessly.

Her hand goes up to her hair and forages there, as if for a thought. "No." She crumples onto the couch. "I was so sure you would find her," she says. "You've got to find her for me, Artie. You've just *got* to."

Dolores has a touching faith in me. Actually, she has a touching faith in all men. She was raised to depend on them. I jingle the keys in my pocket, a sound I always find reassuring. "Don't worry, she'll show up. Remember when she broke off with Bobby? She went off for hours and I had to ground her. She'll be back soon."

Outside, the trees thrash in the wind, and far away I hear the persistent low rumble of thunder. I put in a call to Darlene, hoping she's heard from Mariah. A female voice fairly bristling with self-confidence and self-involvement displays a perfunctory interest in my plight and then rapidly lets it be known that there's no possibility that her obedient, safe, sleeping child—who in case I've forgotten, has an exam in the morning—will be awakened in order to answer questions about my missing one. This is the mother about whom Darlene complains regularly and apparently with cause.

Just as I set the receiver down, preparatory to calling Ryan's number, the phone jangles and I feel that nasty jolted sensation—not unlike an electric shock—that occurs when one's expectation is confounded by an out-of-sequence event. It's as if the future is snapping at my heels. It's the boy's father, Ferguson.

"Is my son there?" he demands.

"He *was* here," I reply. "About an hour and a half ago."

"I suppose he's out somewhere with your daughter," he mutters. "God*dammit*. Or..." He hesitates and his voice backs off from its belligerent tone. "...is she there?"

"No, I'm afraid she's not." I'm actually immensely cheered that the boy hasn't returned home. It probably means he's with Mariah, and despite my efforts to keep her from seeing too much of him, I like Ryan Ferguson and I'm hopeful he'll have a calming effect on my daughter.

"Jesus Christ," Ferguson moans. "Right before his geometry exam. He's got to pull a B in the thing. What happened? Did they have a fight or something? God, their *timing*."

I definitely don't want to go into this. "I really don't know, Mr. Ferguson."

"Larry," he corrects in a distracted voice. There's a low menacing roar of thunder outside. A crackle of static jitters on the line. Ferguson wheezes out a sigh. "Look, if he shows up there, tell him to get his buns back here, would you?" Another distant but rugged drumroll of thunder. "Maybe the rain will bring them in," he adds in a hopeful tone and then hangs up.

I tap my fingers on the telephone table and turn to Dolores. "I think she's with her boyfriend. That's good news, don't you think?"

"Oh, yes," she says eagerly. "Oh I'm so glad she's not alone. He'll keep her from doing anything too crazy."

I'm not so sure.

Mariah, unlike her mother, has not been raised to so readily put herself in the hands of others. Dolores comes from an almost aristocratic background, albeit one that lost its money a generation ago. The money may be gone, but the manners and expectations endure. Indeed, one of the characteristic expressions of her family is: "You're in good hands with..." Not Allstate, of course. You're in good hands with Brown, the orthopedist; with Blasingame, the stockbroker; with Popkins, the real estate agent. People like Dolly don't so much consult professionals as put themselves in someone's care. This implies a responsibility on the part of the stockbroker or orthopedist or whatever that stems from a nearly extinct sense of shared community.

While the rest of us expect decent treatment only by the implied threat of lawsuits or press exposure, members of Dolly's class generally expect to be taken care of, not only by professionals and merchants, but by the institutions of society. And there does seem to be some invisible network that prevents the shabby-genteel from totally falling through the cracks.

My own background is totally unlike Dolly's. I'm one of those oddballs, a self-made man. At least I can say that, beyond their genetic contribution, my parents failed to have any great influence on my life, unless you count negative examples.

I grew up in Shamokin, Pennsylvania. My father spent his whole working life as a coal miner. For the last two decades, at the apex of his career, if you can apply that word to a life in the mines—and why not?—he operated a power shovel. Each day in my parents' life was like a windup toy. They started out in the morning, and then the obligations of the day took them over, and by evening they had ground to a halt, hopefully somewhere near their bed. My father was routinely cruel to my mother and his children, not, I think, due to any inherent brutality in his nature, but because in his world, kindness was usually perceived as weakness.

There were two ways my father had "fun." One was to get totally blotto (on payday) at a local tavern called Millie's. The other was the week in the fall spent hunting with his buddies, a leap back to the good old hunter-gatherer days. They would come back, stubble-faced, bleary-eyed, smelling of beer, a field-dressed buck lashed to the hood of the Chevy.

I can't say some sudden revelation or some inborn flash of genius or even a revulsion against the life I've described propelled me free of Shamokin. I'm slight in stature, and as a boy I had a big mouth, a combination that had predictable results. I discovered the public library one day while being pursued by a huge, irate tough named Mike Lastowski. The librarian stared him down, and I remained there until it closed.

The librarian (her name was Miss Manino) and I forged an unlikely bond. I appealed to her powerful didactic instincts. She provided me with reading lists, taught me how to use the card catalog, and gave me the run of the library. While she took a great deal of pride in my academic achievements, my family found the new scholarly me threatening and boring at the same time. It was Miss Manino who helped me with the endless paperwork involved in applying for college entrance and financial aid.

So, Dolores and I floated toward each other from opposite cultural corners. Dolores was as taken with my self-reliance as I was with her manners and cultural grace. She admired my knack with a slide rule and my know-how about automobiles; I admired her French accent and her ability to hum Mozart.

I sent round-trip airplane tickets (their first flight) to my parents, the only representatives of my family to attend our wedding. They appeared pinched and nervous in the pew of Grace Episcopal Church, shifting restlessly throughout the ceremony. I knew they could hardly wait to get outside and have a cigarette.

Later, at the country club reception, my father's hands— the creases and crevices of his fingers as permanently blackened by coal as if they had been tattooed—stayed resolutely in his pockets except for those obligatory occasions where they shot out quickly for a shake. He looked around warily, with a strange grin on his face, and shifted edgily from foot to foot. My mother, dressed in a frilly pink outfit topped off by some kind of fur stole, which she refused to relinquish despite periodic attempts to relieve her of "her wrap," drank too much, and told baby stories about me ("I was changing Artie's diaper and he got me—pow!— right in the eye").

Dolly sits on the couch, peering out the window. I must confess I still find the effortlessly good posture of her thin, bony shoulders quite touching. Outside, the rain falls steadily. Every now and then a car hisses by on the wet pavement and Dolly's shoulders perk up for an instant as if she expects the car might stop and disgorge Mariah. I go over, sit next to her, take her hand in mine.

It's eleven-thirty. "At midnight," I promise, "I'll call the police. In the meantime, how about a brandy?"

She nods, and when I bring the drink, she hunches over it, cupping it in her hands as if it's hot and she is severely chilled.

At quarter to twelve I call Ferguson. "I'm going to call the police and report Mariah missing."

"Damn."

"Do you want me to leave Ryan out of it?"

"How can you leave him out of it? You can't leave him out of it. The first thing they're going to ask is does she have a boyfriend."

"Well," I say.

"Wait another hour or two, maybe even until morning."

I tend to agree, but I don't think Dolores can withstand another hour of inaction. Putting the matter in the hands of the police, while unlikely to do any real good, will at least provide the illusion that something is being done.

I promise to call Ferguson in a while. Back on the couch next to Dolores, I feel compressed, inert. I want to call the police and yet I don't want to call the police. Ferguson may be right about it being too soon. Those scoffing voices on the playground come to mind. How late would it have to be before someone Mariah's age would seriously be considered missing? I'm a bit embarrassed to call, a little afraid they'll think my fears ridiculous. At the same time I'm annoyed with myself. My daughter is missing! We're in a terrible crisis and my predominant emotion is to be *embarrassed*. I sit next to Dolores, who is fairly pulsating with anxiety, and my mind is in this stew of indecision. A dozen times I imagine I hear a hand on the latch. Once, this impression is so strong that my emotions go through a rapid transition, from worry to relief to anger. I even stand up, ready to make an annoyed interrogation of what I assume will be a chagrined Mariah. But of course she isn't there—it's just the wind, lifting up the brass mail slot, rattling the door.

At one A.M. I can't stand it any longer. I put in the call to the Alexandria Police Department. Half an hour later a patrol car slides up to the curb. A policeman emerges and walks slowly and deliberately up our flagstone path. Halfway up the walk he smooths his hair back with his palms.

"I'm Officer Hultin," he says, and I introduce myself and Dolores. Hultin is thirty-five, maybe forty, with heavy five-o'clock shadow. His, short dark hair is slicked back with some kind of grooming aid. He examines me with cynical blue eyes. I can smell tobacco on his breath. His uniform has knife creases in the trouser legs that look sharp enough to cause injury. On the whole, there is something reassuring about him. His eyes don't miss much. He looks to be a man who'd be hard to surprise. The tidiness of his uniform is heartening too, and the precision of his gestures, even the fact that he's armed. He seems to be ready for just about anything.

Dolly doesn't appear to feel the same way; she's past the point where anything as insubstantial as reassurance will make her feel better. She quivers on the couch, holding a hand to her face. By this time, she's really fallen apart. It's just habit—a certain remembered posture, a framework of manners—that keeps her from babbling. I do the talking.

Officer Hultin writes everything down in a tan stenographer's notebook. His handwriting—the first thing he does is to write down a case number, his name and telephone number, and hand it to me—is excellent but requires him to write rather slowly. I assume he's attended Catholic school; it's been decades since the public schools have bothered with penmanship.

He asks a few questions about Mariah.

Height and weight? Five-five, a hundred and five.

Color of eyes and hair? Brown and brown.

Has she ever run away before? Dolores objects. "We don't know she's run away, do we?"

Has she ever been *missing* before? "No," Dolores huffs indignantly. "Never." I think of the day she broke up with Bobby but decide not to mention it.

Officer Hultin wants to know if Mariah was upset. We go over that ground without explaining exactly *why* she was upset.

Can we pinpoint the time we last saw her? Seven-thirty, more or less.

Can we describe the clothes she was wearing? Cutoff Gap blue jeans and a pink T-shirt. Anything on it? Two sharks with buck teeth and glasses and the words "Shark Nerds." I watch his hand write, in his careful cursive: Shark Nerds. "It's from that cartoon," Dolores says in a distant, spacy voice: "Far Side."

He takes down the names and telephone numbers of her friends. We go over my contacts, earlier that evening, with Darlene and Ryan. He jots down the information about where Mariah attends school. He asks for a recent photograph. I hate giving him the photograph, a school picture, Mariah beaming steadily for the camera. I can imagine a swirl of future horror in which Mariah's features are fuzzily reproduced on milk cartons, on grocery store bags, on mass-mailed flyers with offers for inexpensive luggage on the reverse sides. The details I've just given Hultin will be reproduced below her face, and the plaintive, shot-in-the-dark plea: *Have you seen me?*

Hultin closes his steno book. He explains that surrounding jurisdictions will be alerted immediately and that her name and photograph will be recorded with the area clearinghouse in Springfield.

"But what, actually, will be done?" I want to know. I divulge that her boyfriend might be with her. He looks in his notebook.

"This Ryan Ferguson, you mean."

"Yes."

"That puts a little bit different light on things, know what I mean?"

"Well, I'm not *sure* she's with him." I hasten to explain the sequence of events, and how the boy had gone out looking for Mariah too. "The last time I talked to his father, Ryan had not come back home, so I was thinking…"

"I see." He taps his pen on the notebook. "She have money with her? You checked to see if any of your funds are missing?"

"She wouldn't take our money," Dolores huffs. "She's not like that."

"When people get upset, ma'am," he explains patiently in his hard, matter-of-fact voice, "they don't always do things their usual way. She have a bank account?"

"Yes."

"Give me that number. We'll check and see if there's been any recent withdrawals."

"I don't even think she took her purse," I say. "She said she was going out to borrow a book from her friend."

He sighs. "She didn't do that, did she, sir? She called her boyfriend instead, right? I'm not saying she planned to run away. It's just we don't know until we check."

I look in my wallet; Dolores explores her purse. We're not missing any money. We find Mariah's purse, a scruffy brown thing, in her room.

I escort Officer Hultin to the door. The fact that Mariah never ran away before seems consequential to him. "Chances are, she'll be back sometime this morning. If that happens, or if you hear from her, call the station immediately and tell them. Always give the case number when you call in." He starts to turn and leave but he suddenly has a thought: "You just moved here recently, that correct?"

I nod.

"How recent?"

"November."

"If she's not with this boyfriend...any chance of her going back where you lived before?"

"Janesville, Wisconsin." I shake my head. "I don't think so."

"Well. That's another thing we'll check on if she don't turn up this morning. We'll alert Janesville. We'll worry about that tomorrow if we have to."

I thank him. He shrugs. I find his practicality comforting. The fact that he has a routine to adhere to makes our position seem less terrifying.

"I don't really think she took off on you, Mr. Ebinger. My guess is she'll be back soon. I hope you and your wife won't even have to talk to me again, except to tell me she's home safe."

All of a sudden, his optimism depresses me. I don't want policemen having hunches about my daughter.

"I hope you're right."

He gives a little salute and a nicotine-stained smile. I watch him walk in an efficient but unhurried way to his car.

Chapter Twenty

ARTHUR
A Sickening Vibration

WE SIT THERE on the couch, keeping our vigil. Every once in a while I nod off. When jolted awake by some slight noise, a tick of the thermostat as the air conditioner kicks on or off, a moth batting the window, or by the unconscious reflex of my body realizing that if it tilts over any farther, it will fall, for a moment I can't remember why Dolly and I are sitting there transfixed in the yellow light of our living room.

The very stillness of the night immediately conveys the lateness of the hour. Even the omnipresent, dull roar of traffic from 395 is muted to a low hum. Then in a sudden surge—*Mariah!*—I remember, and instantly I'm awake. Each time, I check my watch. It's two-ten, two-thirty, five of three. Each time, I remain alert for a while until fatigue, with the monotonous persistence of an ocean pounding at a cliff, renews the slow erosion of my consciousness. I'm once again fully submerged in a dreary, dread-laced slumber when the sharp rap on the door wallops me awake again.

I rub my eyes and try to shake my mind free from fatigue as I walk stiffly toward the front door. Before I reach it, the sharp rap sounds again.

I'm expecting the person at the door to be bringing news of Mariah. I know it's not Mariah herself because she'd never knock on a door in that peremptory manner. Maybe she's being escorted by someone—Officer Hultin, Mr. Ferguson, even Ryan. So it's with some eagerness that I pull the door open on the two men who plunge through it as soon as I give them the opening. One of them pushes me roughly against the wall inside the foyer and the other strides past me toward Dolly.

Even before he speaks, I'm not sure how, I know the man is an Argentine. It's his shoes, perhaps, or the set of his mouth (his tongue molded to a different language), I don't know. He's about thirty-five I guess, quite handsome in a dark, Latin way, except for his thin-lipped mouth, which is too small for his face and gives it a pinched expression. He looks at me dispassionately as he holds the knobs of my shoulders in his big hands. I'm momentarily speechless. Literally. My tongue lolls in my mouth, useless. My head had hit lightly, but shockingly, against the wall as he pushed me out of the way to get through the door.

What I am is frightened. The fear hits me quickly and then creates a sickening vibration in my chest, as if I've been struck by an invisible arrow, its shaft still quivering. Finally I manage to say, "Hey."

"Where is the girl Mariah Ebinger?" he demands in his high-pitched, accented voice.

"Who the hell are you?"

He thrusts me back against the wall again and my head grazes the plaster. "Where is she?"

"She's not here. We thought *you* were her. I mean we're waiting for her," I sputter. "She's missing."

"What do you mean, she is not here? It is three-thirty in the fucking morning. *Rolando!*" He propels me in front of him, holding my arm behind me, his fingers fastened around it just above my elbow. He steers me toward the living room with this firm, aggressive grip. I see the man he referred to as Rolando standing over Dolly, just looking at her. This one is lighter-haired, a little older, maybe forty.

"Watch him," the one holding me orders his friend before rushing upstairs. The man called Rolando shifts nervously from foot to foot. He seems slightly embarrassed. From upstairs we hear doors opening and slamming shut. The other man comes back down the stairs, fast, shaking his head. "*No está,*" he says.

He approaches Dolly, and with a sudden, almost casual motion, lifts his hand and cracks the back of it across her face.

"Where is she?" he demands.

Dolly screams. A howl of rage comes out of me and I lunge toward the man, but he turns and viciously throws his elbow straight into my stomach. A belt of pain tightens horribly in my abdomen, and the howl from my mouth repeats itself, an involuntary yelp like that of a cat or dog when you step on its tail.

"Hugo?" says the older man, Rolando, in a querulous voice.

Hugo says something in Spanish, so rapidly that I don't catch the meaning.

Dolly's red-rimmed eyes glare out over the hand that she holds in front of her injured face. She manipulates her cheek with her fingertips, probing for damage. "Mariah is not *here*. You can hit me if you want but she is *not here*. What do you *want* anyway?" Her tone is admirably defiant; I feel an absurd surge of pride.

"Let me explain," I say, in an insanely placating tone, as if once everything is straightened out, we'll have no more problems with these men.

"Yes, that would be an excellent idea," says the man called Hugo, who has come behind me. He grabs my arm by the wrist and gives it a little tug upward, producing just enough pain to remind me that I am in his power.

"Normally, we're asleep at this hour," I start, stupidly. "The reason we're up is that Mariah has run away. Earlier this evening, she ran away."

"Don't fuck with me," the man behind me says. "Where is she?" He jerks on my arm again, this time quite hard. The pain in my stomach has subsided to a dull throb, but this yank upward on my arm opens a new seam of pain in my shoulder. A moan falls from my mouth; tears jump involuntarily into my eyes.

"Stop that!" Dolly says, and immediately Hugo releases me and steps toward her. He smacks her in the face again.

I take a step forward. "Now, wait a minute!" I am rewarded with another blow to my stomach. The blast of pain makes me double over.

Hugo, who has been responsible so far for all the violence, issues some rapid instructions in Spanish to his curiously reticent partner. This time I get the gist of it. Rolando is to "watch" Dolly (*"la mujer"*). Moving stiffly, the man called Rolando approaches Dolly and puts a tentative hand on her arm.

Dolly is bent over, snuffling, and when she straightens up I see that she's bitten part of the way through her lower lip. It seems swollen already. Blood wells up on it, and wiping it, she rubs it onto the soft skin alongside her mouth. It gives her a tawdry look, as if she's smeared her lipstick. "Why are you doing this?" she whimpers.

Even though they don't seem to have the slightest trouble understanding English, I repeat what I said before, very slowly and deliberately this time. "Mariah has run away."

"To where? Where did she run away?"

"Well, we don't *know*."

Hugo releases my arm and steps toward Dolly, arms wide, as if to embrace her. He opens his hands flat and claps them hard on either side of her head, against her ears. I lunge toward her, but Hugo turns calmly to restrain me. When I still try to get toward Dolly, he yanks my arm up behind me. A plume of white blossoms in my head. I make a strange, horrible sound like a very sick man trying to clear his throat. Something in my shoulder has given way. Shoulder separation, is what I guess.

"Look," I say desperately, stretching my hand out in a gesture even though this small motion causes a sickening flush of pain. "This is not a story I'm telling you, this is the truth. Look, even the police were here. *Look*." I make a move toward the piece of paper that Officer Hultin left for us, which is on the end table next to the couch. This time my arm feels the pressure soon enough, and my body instantly freezes, before the pressure graduates to pain.

"*Policía?*" Hugo says, interested. "Why?"

"Because Mariah has run away, that's what I'm trying to tell you. We filed a missing person's report on her."

Hugo releases my arm and steps back against the doorway to the dining room. His mouth opens to reveal a gap-toothed smile which then expands into a laugh. He sounds genuinely amused. "Mis-sing pear-son," he says, chortling, shaking his head from side to side. "Mis-sing pear-son. *Oye, Rolando!* Poof! *Desaparecido*." He finishes with a nasty, rat-a-tat-tat laugh.

"Shut up!" Rolando picks up the piece of paper from the end table. My mind is busily trying to assess these men. Their hands are manicured. Their clothes appear to be brand-new. Rolando speaks English flawlessly, and with a British accent, which puts him firmly in the ranks of the Argentinian upper classes.

"So," Rolando says in a resigned voice, his eyes flicking up from the white piece of paper, "when did this happen?"

"Tonight."

He shakes his head slowly from side to side. His voice is barely audible. "I cannot believe it."

"Fucking Pan Am," Hugo says. "Pan fucking Am."

Rolando looks at me. His large brown eyes suddenly seem terribly fatigued. "We were scheduled to be here last night, you see." He laughs soundlessly, then shifts his gaze to Hugo. "Now what?"

Hugo shrugs. "We tie them up." From a black duffel bag I had not noticed before, he extracts a length of thin rope and a thick roll of silvery duct tape. His hands are strong and dexterous. On the ring finger of his right hand, he wears a heavy gold ring with a diamond-centered star engraved in it. I watch it flash into sight and disappear as he works. He's efficient and completes the task in about a minute. Dolly and I offer no resistance. You might say the fight's gone out of us.

It isn't until Dolly and I are both bound, a process that almost caused me to faint when Hugo jerked my arms behind my back, that I begin to reconsider my initial impression, which is that these men are emissaries of the famous Mothers and Grandmothers of the Plaza de Mayo. You see, when Hugo cackled his nasty laugh and said the word *desaparecido*, I did get the joke.

Chapter Twenty-One

ARTHUR
Unexplained Intentions

MOST PEOPLE FROM the States are probably like I was: they have no idea what Argentina is like. Before Dolly and I got down there, I guess I expected a bigger Mexico—Mexico being the only Latin American country I'd ever visited. But except for the common language, Argentina is nothing like Mexico. It's more like France or Italy. And physically, its inhabitants are mostly European stock: Germans, Spaniards, Italians. There's nothing to mark out a visiting *norteamericano* from the crowd, nothing to visually identify him, except that we are not usually as stylish as the natives.

The political situation in Argentina was what the State Department termed "unsettled" when Dolly and I arrived in 1975. Argentina's president at the time—granted, she was mostly a figurehead—was "Isabelita" Perón, the third wife of Juan Perón. In 1973, Perón had returned to Argentina from almost twenty years of exile in Spain, just in time to die on his native soil about a year later. Before succeeding her husband, Isabelita had been her husband's vice president. Before that, she had been a nightclub dancer in the Happy Land Bar.

Nightclub dancing was not ideal preparation for the duties of running a large country, and the serious problems already facing Argentina when she assumed the presidency did not improve under her leadership. During Isabelita's short presidential stint, inflation accelerated at an appalling rate. By 1976, when Dolly and I had been there for about a year, it had reached an annual rate of 800 percent. Think about it. January 1, a fella buys a TV set for five hundred bucks. A year later, it's going to cost him four thousand. Who wants to save money under conditions like that? Who wants to bid a contract?

That wasn't all of it. Although Perón attracted support from both the right and left wings, it was the left wing that was more responsible for Perón's return to power. The two factions among the Perónists had already split apart even before Perón's plane landed at the airport in Buenos Aires. The huge crowd—several hundred thousand strong—gathered at the airport to welcome *el líder* back from exile soon turned on itself. Right-wing Perónistas fired into the larger contingent of left-wing Perónistas. Over two hundred people, most of them students, were killed. Word was, Perón did not even reprimand the right-wingers.

Disenfranchised by Perón, the left began engaging in guerrilla warfare. There were brutal incidents almost daily, and they were followed by predictable counterattacks and retaliations from the extreme right. The news in Buenos Aires read like today's news out of Lebanon—explosions, assassinations, kidnappings. In the final week of the civilian government, there were forty-three political murders and almost fifty bombings in the capital city.

If you've never lived in a city or a country where the situation is "unsettled," I can tell you that although everyone was worried, there was little direct effect on most of the people in Buenos Aires. It was less threatening, in most ways, than daily life in a big U.S. city.

But everyone *was* waiting for the military to step in and restore order, and do something about the economy too.

So to say that the 1976 coup was bloodless is to understate it. It was almost sweatless. Not a single shot was fired. Business went on almost as usual. If there were tanks and soldiers on the streets, people simply stepped around them. Some even shook hands with the soldiers in congratulation. On the evening of the coup, Dolly and I went to a dinner party, just as scheduled. There was such a pervasive sense of relief that Jorge Luis Borges, in a quote that would later become infamous, said, "Now we are governed by gentlemen." Within our own U.S. Embassy, the military takeover was considered an overdue step in the right (not to make a pun) direction.

The junta that took power was a triumvirate, one man from each branch of the armed services. Naturally enough, the new government felt it had carte blanche to deal with terrorism. Repressing the threat from the left was practically its mandate. The now-famous "dirty war" was declared against subversives. What the dirty part turned out to mean was that the military did not feel constrained to follow any of the accepted rules of conduct for a government.

They did succeed in putting an end to left-wing terrorism. But kidnappings, murders, and torture, this time conducted by the government itself, increased rather than decreased under the junta. It was one of those things where the cure proves immeasurably worse than the disease. They called it the "Process of National Reorganization." The ominous sound of that is about right; the rooting out of terrorists quickly became nothing more than state terrorism. Eventually twelve thousand people disappeared, most of them entirely innocent of any political activity.

Words with new meanings emerged, to describe what happened to these vanished people—the now-famous *desaparecido*—and also the word *chupada*, which means "sucked up." People were sucked up into the Process of National Reorganization and were often never seen again. When mothers, fathers, brothers, coworkers, and friends made inquiries about these missing people, they were simply told there was no information, or that the missing persons had been kidnapped by leftists.

It wasn't true. The people being abducted, without any kind of due process, were really being held by the government in secret prisons and detention centers, where they were systematically tortured. Many were killed and then either buried in nameless graves or dropped from cargo planes into the Río de la Plata.

It's amazing, but Dolly and I knew nothing of this when we were in Buenos Aires. The horrible facts did not surface until later. We left in the middle of the worst of it too, in 1977. At that time most people still trusted the junta, still believed the government was putting Argentina's house in order. They would have scoffed at rumors of atrocities, even if rumors had been circulating, which they were not, at least not in our circles. Press censorship was successful; people bought the government propaganda, which blamed everything on left-wing terrorism.

But twelve thousand people can't disappear without eventually raising an outcry and some attempt to find out what happened to them. People really didn't know what to do at first. I mean, they'd make inquiries about missing loved ones, and the government would just slam the door shut, saying it knew nothing. After a while that many doors slamming shut makes quite a racket, I guess; eventually the truth had to come out. In the end there was no evidence that the disappearances were due to "left-wing terrorists," and evidence began to accumulate that in fact the government itself was responsible.

The first to make a visible protest were a few mothers and grandmothers of missing persons; feeling they had nothing left to lose they began gathering and just walking, in big, slow circles, in the Plaza de Mayo, the square in front of the presidential palace in Buenos Aires. Later they began to pin photographs of their missing sons and daughters, their disappeared grandchildren, their abducted nieces and nephews, to their clothes. These protests were not mentioned in the censored newspapers; there weren't any articles about the *desaparecidos* themselves either. Dolly and I never heard of the Grandmothers of the Plaza de Mayo when we lived in Buenos Aires.

But last year, in Janesville, I saw a PBS documentary about them. My heart nearly catapulted from my chest during a segment about the children. The narrator interviewed a series of women who were seeking their children—well over a hundred of them—who had disappeared during the three worst years (1976 to 1979) of the junta's rule. A massive, exhaustive inquiry into the whole "dirty war" was being made by the new Argentinian government. No effort was being spared in tracking down the disappeared, and a special push was being made in the case of the young children and infants listed among the missing. The separate endeavor of the Mothers and Grandmothers was a supplement to this huge national inquiry. The search for the missing children was being carried out with the assistance of computer banks and DNA matching.

Mass graves were being exhumed, and many missing persons were accounted for this way, including some of the children. Other children were tracked down and found to be living with people—sometimes neighbors, sometimes childless military couples—who had adopted them.

Sometimes, during the "Process," the government thugs arrived at a house and seized only the parents, leaving the terrified children behind to fend for themselves. Neighbors usually took those children in, and then passed them on to relatives of the missing parents.

The disappeared children had generally been kidnapped along with their parents. Witnesses testified in the hearings how the children were often forced to watch their mothers and fathers being tortured—and vice versa. Sometimes the children were then given away, or sold, after their parents' deaths. There were horrible cases where pregnant women had been kept alive only long enough to bear their babies. A few days after giving birth the women were killed; the infants "disappeared."

In most cases, the parents of the children were dead; it was their *grandparents* who were looking for them. With DNA typing—the sort that is sometimes used in courts here to identify rapists—positive identification could be made with just a sampling of the grandmother's or grandfather's blood and the blood of the child.

Riveted to the television, I felt an extraordinary pain in my chest, as if my heart were giving birth to another heart, a dark companion to my loving heart. And that dark heart instantly knew the truth that my other heart denied: Mariah didn't rightfully belong to us. Watching that documentary, part of me knew it with a sickening certainty, that Mariah was one of them, one of the disappeared.

I never did tell Dolly about that documentary; I never even mentioned it. But there was no hiding the story of Argentina's nightmare (and its implications) from her. Articles and documentaries about those years of terror began to appear—even a critically acclaimed movie, *The Official Story*. Then one day, we were at the supermarket checkout counter. Dolly picked up a *Life* magazine and began leafing through. She stumbled upon an article that told the life stories of several Argentinian children tracked down by the efforts of the Grandmothers of the Plaza de Mayo—children brought up in total ignorance of their actual identities.

One look at Dolly's stricken face and I knew her mind had accomplished the same sickening leap as mine had when I saw the documentary.

So when the letter from a woman claiming to be Mariah's grandmother arrived, I was unprepared, but I was not truly surprised. The tone of the letter was polite and official. The dry sentences explained the reason for the inquiry and gave a brief history of the short life of María Teresa Aguilar up to the time she disappeared. She had been traced, through the confessions of a repentant "adoption counselor," to the Agencia Palomar. Records at the American Embassy in Buenos Aires and exhaustive inquiries led to our current address. Requests were made for certain information about "your adopted daughter" Mariah Alicia Ebinger. Assurances were given that intricate psychological counseling efforts and the full consent of the child, along with the advice and assistance of local health and human services authorities, would precede any attempt to reunite the child with her blood relatives in Argentina, if the requested DNA typing (they were prepared to get a court order) proved her to be María Aguilar de Carrera, who had disappeared from Calle Valentin, San Ysidro, Buenos Aires Province, on December 12, 1977. The letter closed with a moving exhortation that we should not add to the dimensions of the tragedy suffered by Mariah's family by becoming what amounted to accessories after the fact.

To tell you the truth, I could not, at first, even show this letter to Dolores. And when I finally did, she broke down badly. I called a physician; she had to be sedated. Tranquilizers were prescribed, and frankly, she's been using them ever since.

I knew that I was behaving very badly, even unforgivably. I did know that, I knew that. But I still decided not to respond to the letter. I would keep it, and once we had a chance, in our own time, to set things straight with Mariah, I would contact the Grandmothers' search committee.

I planned the move immediately, and I did everything I could to make it difficult for anyone to locate us after we left Janesville. Within two days of the arrival of the letter, after a blitz of telephone calls, I was in Washington, D.C., trying to secure employment. A week after that I was weighing job offers. I gave notice to my stunned superior at Boorstein and Smathers and later misinformed them that I had taken a job in Boston, rather than the real one I had taken in Virginia. I made complicated arrangements for the forwarding of mail, which involved two outfits; one in St. Louis, Missouri, and another in Arkansas—places where mail is sent, repackaged, and forwarded. There were loopholes in my scheme, of course. I could hardly forbid Mariah from writing to her friends in Janesville, and I didn't. I wonder if it was through Bobby or Helena that the men found us.

For a while Dolly and I just sit on the couch, adjusting to the indignity of being bound. The way we're tied tends to make us sit up rather primly, knees together, posture impeccable. We're bursting with questions, of course, but we've been warned not to talk, even to each other. Hugo brandished the wide roll of duct tape and made a gesture across his own pursed lips that was entirely convincing.

Rolando and Hugo smoke a cigarette each. Hugo prowls around in the refrigerator, and makes some sandwiches, which the two men eat. As Rolando takes small, neat bites of his sandwich, interspersed with sips of Miller Lite, I can't contain myself any longer.

Although I'm surprised that emissaries from the Grandmothers of the Plaza would behave so roughly, that letter I received back in Janesville from the "Grandmothers" is the only connection I've been able to make with the fact that these men are here looking for Mariah. If I were searching for a lost child, and finally found those I considered to be her captors, who had not responded to a gentle, reasonable letter, but instead absconded with the child, I honestly don't know how I would behave. To these men, we are no better than kidnappers.

I begin, in a resigned tone, to state my case: "I just couldn't answer your letter," I say. "Please try to understand that we needed a little more time to prepare Mariah."

Both men appear puzzled. They stare at me.

"But you are from the Grandmothers of the Plaza," I say stupidly. "Aren't you?"

In his explosion of laughter Hugo practically spits out the liquid in his mouth. He chokes for a little while, trying to keep from spraying beer all over. *"Abuelitas,"* he manages finally, using a Spanish word that means "little grandmothers." He can hardly contain his amusement. He rolls his eyes at Rolando, who allows a small, pained smile to form on his mouth but says nothing. Hugo jumps up and crumples the beer can in his hand. He totters toward the kitchen, walking as if he is very old. *"Abuelitas,* yes, I like that. *Abuelitas."* We can hear him in the kitchen, opening the refrigerator, popping the top of another can of beer.

"But I thought—" I start.

"Shut up," Rolando says matter-of-factly. "No talking."

I don't know how long it is that Dolly and I have been sitting here. An hour? Two? It seems a very, very long time, but it's still dark, so it can't have been so long, really. Every once in a while our eyes meet. Sometimes Dolly is agitated, rolling her eyes toward the men, crumpling her eyebrows in concern, mouthing Mariah's name. Sometimes she's calm, with a tough set to her mouth. Her pretty, fragile face is beginning to show more signs of the abuse she's taken from Hugo. There is some puffiness around the eyes and a purple bruise rising to the surface of her left cheekbone in addition to the swollen lip. The agony in my shoulder has retreated into a kind of steady but tolerable ache, although whenever I shift my body on the couch—a tricky maneuver, given that my hands and feet are bound—I create new bursts of pain. The couch is an uncomfortable one anyway, wicker with a thin cushion.

Suddenly I sense that Dolly is sitting more tensely, more alertly. The darkness outside has been for some time imperceptibly shading to what has been forecast as a gray, polluted dawn. I hear a car outside on the street, stopping and then starting, stopping and then starting. Dolly rolls her eyes toward me with immense agitation and then she bellows: *"Helppppp!"* An amazingly loud sound. A second later I hear the familiar slap of the *Washington Post* landing on the sidewalk out front.

"Coño!" Hugo shouts and jumps to his feet. Within a minute, first Dolly is gagged, then I am. Dolly offers no resistance, and mine does no good because no matter how I try to squirm, Hugo, with Rolando's steadying hand in assistance, has no trouble securing the wide strip of adhesive across my mouth. Then, as punishment, Hugo claps his hands together again—very hard this time—with Dolly's head between them. She seems to lose consciousness for a moment; when she revives, her eyes pour tears. For the next several minutes I watch helplessly as she sniffs and snuffles, in a valiant effort to avoid the indignity of having snot running down her face. A thin trickle of red blood comes from her ear.

My head fills with successive, abortive, horrible ideas. Before I can fully explore the terrifying corners of one, a new one occurs to me. The men have made no effort at disguise, and I worry about what that portends for Dolly and me. That worry evaporates in the sudden full-blown image of Mariah coming through the front door. Expecting her hysterical mother and angry father, she will instead confront not only the truth about her past and the evidence of her "parents' " possessive and deceptive love, but these two disastrous men and their unexplained intentions.

A while passes in this dreadful reverie. The sky is no longer brightening but a steady overcast gray. Then Dolly begins shifting about on the couch next to me and making urgent noises through her gag. She finally succeeds in attracting the attention of Rolando and, with a rather brilliant effort—involving, as it does, only her eyes and certain small, restricted motions of her body—manages to convey that she needs to urinate. Rolando and Hugo have a discussion about it. It seems to me that Hugo prevails, because at the end of it he turns toward us and lifts his eyebrows; his face splits in a nasty simile. Dolly squirms and pleads with her eyes for what seems like a very long time, but the men say nothing. I notice that Rolando keeps his eyes averted. I try to show Dolly my love and concern with my eyes. She has a weak bladder; I know she's in discomfort from that as well as from the contusions and whatever else happened to her when Hugo clapped his hands on her ears. My own muscles are stiff and aching from the stress of remaining in the same position for hours.

The two men speak to each other softly in Spanish from time to time; I can't hear them well enough to understand.

Rolando reads a copy of the *Washingtonian*. On the cover is Suzanne Kent Cooke, overweight and vindictive, and her adorable daughter. For a moment Rolando stops reading. He lifts a hand to his brow, the thinker's pose, and something about the form of that gesture copies a habitual motion of Mariah's so exactly that I suddenly realize what should have been obvious the moment I clapped eyes on the man. He looks like her, he looks a great deal like Mariah, he's obviously some relative of hers.

Before I can think about the implications of this realization, I'm distracted by a new bout of ferocious—but of course constrained—motion from Dolly. I'm afraid she's going to succeed only in hurling her body off the couch. But then her frenzied motions subside and from the sudden quiescence of her body and the collapsed droop of her head, I know that she's lost the battle with her body and wet herself. It's an event to which our captors remain oblivious.

A few minutes later, poor Dolly's urine having made its slow process through the cushion beneath us, its sad, humiliating drip seems to foretell our doom. These men have not shown us a single shred of kindness. They aren't capable even of ordinary human decency. Their reaction to my question about the Grandmothers continues to puzzle me. If they haven't come to restore Mariah to her loving family, why are they here? I can't figure out what it means that the man has such a powerful resemblance to Mariah. Is he her father? Her real father? Is this treatment by way of punishment for the travail he and his wife suffered, deprived of their daughter?

I know that they're going to keep us like this until Mariah comes back. And who knows what kind of shape Mariah will be in? Perhaps her whole early life will have returned to her in a sudden rush of memory. In any case, she'll be filled with confusion. She may even be filled with hate for us—that would be natural, I suppose. But I know that Mariah, no matter how angry and betrayed she feels, will never be able to look at us in this pathetic state without compassion. She would never enjoy seeing us degraded like this. I have a brief flurry of hope. Mariah's sweet face jumps into my mind and I know that seeing us in this pitiful condition may blunt her anger at us, may hasten her forgiveness. She'll save us; she'll make the men untie us.

I've been pinning my hopes on the man Rolando. He hasn't really laid a hand on either Dolly or me, and in fact he seems to be in some discomfort when Hugo abuses us. But despite the fact that he is not indifferent to our suffering, he has certainly proved himself unwilling to intervene and prevent it—or even to alleviate it. In some strange way, too, it seems to me that Hugo is acting in his behalf. I've been thinking Rolando is Mariah's father, but suddenly I know beyond a doubt that he is not.

He stands up and stretches lithely, extending his arms over his head. My ears must have gradually acclimated to the Spanish the men are speaking, because although he doesn't speak in a voice any louder than the one he used before, this time I hear him quite clearly.

"Why don't you try to sleep for awhile," he tells Hugo. "I'll wake you if the little bitch shows up."

Part Three

Part Three

Chapter Twenty-Two

MARIAH
Wrong Number

I'M NOT SURE where I went at first when I stumbled away from my house. I was so distracted by thinking about everything that I just ran for a long time, not paying attention. Bushes whizzed by me, cars, houses. I ran for such a long time that I got a pain in my chest, but whenever I stopped running, I started thinking, and that was even worse than the pain, so I started running again.

When the thunderstorm came, I was down by the Braddock Road Metro station. I tried to go inside but it was closed for the night, so I sat in one of the bus shelters and watched the storm flash over the river.

When the lightning stopped, I walked over to Ryan's house and stood across the street for a while. The lights were still on. He was studying, probably. I didn't have a good idea of what time it was, but I knew the Metro closed at midnight, so it had to be later than that. Just being that close to Ryan seemed to console me and I kind of wanted to stay there, sitting on the curb opposite his house, until he went to bed. I wanted to watch the lights go out one by one as the invisible Ryan moved through the house. But I was wet and I got so cold I had to start walking again.

I went over to the vacant house on Allison and sat in the equipment shed for a while. It had the advantage of being dry, but the insecticides and stuff smelled so disgusting, I couldn't take it for long. So I ended up here at school, sitting on this big mulch pile heaped up at the side of the playground. Back in the spring, the PTA had organized a school beautification project, but they must have overestimated how much mulch they needed because they finished the planting and stuff a long time ago and this huge mound was left over.

The wet mulch gives off a powerful, funky smell. If I close my eyes, it's almost like I'm hidden deep in a forest instead of being smack in the middle of the burbs. All around me the houses are dark except for one over on Clay Street where the bluish glow of a television shimmers from a downstairs window.

Every once in a while a car slides by on Cameron Mills Road, its headlights poking shafts of light through the darkness. I tell myself no one can possibly see me from the road, but my body goes rock still whenever a car goes by. I'm afraid it's my father, I guess, looking for me.

And what if he finds me? What am I going to do? Go home with him? What am I going to do when it's morning? Go to Ryan's? Go home?

Just thinking about it, that pretty soon I'll have to decide something, makes my heartbeat accelerate, makes me feel uncomfortable, as if my skin doesn't fit right. Let alone thinking about the fright in my mother's eyes at dinner, my understanding Spanish, the whole area of my suddenly murky childhood.

So I try not to think, I try to shut my mind up. And I do it, but the effort makes me stupid. So I just sit there, tossing little hunks of mulch toward a thin tree about ten yards from me, paying attention to that. I'm trying to beat my record of twelve consecutive hits. A quick, sidearm motion is the best, kind of like how you throw a Frisbee or skip a stone. Every once in a while I doze off, blank out, but I don't really fall asleep because when I come to, I'm not surprised to find myself right where I am, on this stupid mulch pile, wet and cold.

Footsteps make me sit up. The woodsy smell of the wet mulch rises up around me. I'm alert like an animal, motionless, senses revved up, hardly breathing.

There are outside lights around the school, and as soon as I see him come around the corner I relax; I can tell from the way he walks, it's Ryan. "Over here," I call, and he runs toward me, his feet squishing in the wet grass. He hugs me tight. We have a long kiss. I don't know why, but tears start coming out of my eyes.

"Hey," he says into my hair. "Hey."

"You should be home sleeping," I hear myself say.

"Right," he says with a little laugh. He pulls back away from me and holds my face in his hands.

I squeeze my eyes shut. "I don't feel like being the reason you flunk Bio and Geometry."

He goes on like I haven't said anything. "Your dad called me, you know. What did you think? You were going to disappear and he wasn't even going to call me? He was really freaked out. He's been looking for you, *I've* been looking for you, I mean *everywhere*. I came here three times but I didn't see you. Were you here before?"

Ryan isn't pissed off, not the way my father would be. When my dad's worried about something, his relief when the worry is over doubles back on itself. So instead of feeling happy that you're okay, he gets mad at you for making him worry in the first place.

"I just got here a little while ago." I lean my head on his shoulder. "I don't know. When I got to my house, I just couldn't go in."

"So what now?"

"You really should go home and go to sleep," I say. "I mean it too. What *time* is it, anyway?" I stand up. "I'll go home now."

He sighs. "Look, Mariah, forget my exams. I'll take an incomplete, I'll say I'm sick, don't *worry* about it." The wind shakes a spatter of rain down out of the tree, big fat drops. "It's like five o'clock. Maybe six."

Those times I dozed off must have lasted longer than I thought.

"I came out looking for you around ten, ten-thirty."

"God, Ryan. I'm sorry."

"It's okay. Your dad called the cops—you probably figured that, right? They weren't going to really do anything, though, according to your dad. So what are we going to do now?"

I laugh, a weak exhausted chuckle. "I don't know." Without warning, tears squirt out of my eyes again. This time I feel unbelievably sad. The effort to keep from sobbing makes my whole face hurt.

"Come home with me?" Ryan says. "I'll explain to my dad. He'll be okay about it. I'll get him to call your father or whatever, tell them you're all right."

I'm suddenly cold. A shiver zips up my spine. The air feels disgusting against my skin, like the inside of an eggshell. I don't want Ryan's dad to get involved in this, but I don't want to go home either. I keep thinking there must be some other way, but nothing comes to me. Suddenly I'm so tired. I yawn hugely. Something cracks in my jaw.

"Okay?" Ryan says.

"I guess."

We walk toward Ryan's house with our arms around each other's waists. The blacktop by the school is covered with dirty puddles full of the scum of some kind of pollen. When we get to the street, the gutters are still full of runoff, rushing toward the sewers. An old green Volvo station wagon is going slowly down the street about half a block in front of us. Someone in the passenger seat throws papers out onto the front walks of the houses with amazing accuracy.

The sky, still sullen and damp, is getting lighter by the minute. Along Cameron Mills Road the streetlamps flick off one by one as if some invisible giant is blowing them out. They fade slowly with an annoying electronic whine.

All the lights are still on in Ryan's house. They cast a thin, sinister glow into the brightening air, as if something terrible's happened inside, something that still requires intense illumination so the facts can be established. Ryan knocks on his own door instead of just going in. Within about five seconds his father opens it. We all stand there for a minute, his father with both arms braced against the door-jambs and a little smile on his face. I watch his head nod up and down. He isn't sure how to be, happy or angry. "Where the *hell* have you been?" he says. He doesn't look at me.

"It took me a long time to find her."

"It took him a long time," he says to the air. "Well, I'm glad you did," he says in this weird, hearty voice. "I'm glad you did."

"Can we come in, then?" Ryan says. "Or what?"

His father makes a sweeping, be-my-guest gesture across the threshold and we go inside.

At the suggestion of Mr. Ferguson, I take a hot shower. I put on a pair of Ryan's jeans and one of his T-shirts.

When I go back downstairs, the two of them stop talking as soon as I come through the door of the kitchen. Ryan's face is flushed.

"Feel better?" Mr. Ferguson asks brightly.

"Want some hot chocolate?" Ryan puts in nervously. Neither one of them looks at me or wants my answer. "Or some food?" Ryan goes on. "Here." He pulls out a chair. "Sit down."

While Ryan makes me a cup of hot chocolate in the microwave, his father drums his fingers on the counter. "Well," he says. "Well, well, well, well, well." He hitches his head to the side. "I think we should call your parents, Mariah. I know they're worried sick."

The microwave gives a little ping. I can't think of what to say to Mr. Ferguson so I don't say anything. Ryan gives me the hot chocolate.

"I know how I felt: I was really relieved to see the two of you," Mr. Ferguson continues, flexing his eyebrows earnestly. "What do you say, let's put in that call, okay?" He doesn't quite sound like himself. I recognize his hearty manner; he was like this when I first met him, as if he was trying out for the role of Dad on some TV show. He sounds reasonable yet amused, as if any minute he's going to spring some great one-liner.

"I'll make the call if you like," he says, "if you're not ready to talk to them yet. Just to let them know you're safe, huh?"

I shrug.

He takes it as assent, which I guess it is, and rubs his hands together. "Good." He approaches the phone, clearing his throat. When he realizes he doesn't know the number, he asks Ryan for it, instead of me.

"Never mind, I'll do it," I hear myself say. I'm going to have to talk to them sooner or later. I might as well get it over with. What I don't want is to see them, face to hurt face, eye to edgy eye. Not yet anyway. I hesitate.

Ryan reads my mind. "Can Mariah stay here?" he asks. "For a couple of days?"

Mr. Ferguson's generous hands spread out. "No problem."

The phone rings eight times. Finally my mother's voice comes through the earpiece in a peculiar, compressed tone. I feel guilty and sorry for her and mad all at the same time. "Mom? It's me. Look," I start, "I'm sorry if—"

She cuts me off. "I'm afraid you have the wrong number," she says in a rushed, breathless voice. Her voice rises on the word "number" and gives off an odd little squeak. Then the line goes dead.

I hold the receiver in my hand. "That's weird."

"That was *quick*," Ryan says.

"She hung up on me. I mean, she knew it was me but she said I had the wrong number."

"I don't get it," Mr. Ferguson says. "Why would she do that?"

"I don't know."

"Call back," Ryan says. "Maybe you dialed some other number by mistake."

But the line is busy. Twenty minutes later it's still busy. It's seven-thirty. Ordinarily I'd just be getting ready to go to school. Yesterday I was getting ready to go to school.

Ryan makes us some cinnamon toast. He doesn't do it very well. Every step in the process is deliberate. He looks like a little boy, spreading the butter so carefully. When he's done, he puts the toast out plain, in big squares; he doesn't cut it into neat triangles like my mother.

Mr. Ferguson calls G.W. twice, once to report that Ryan is sick, the next time to report that I'm sick. He lays his hand on Ryan's shoulder as he calls. "So, you rescue a fair maiden, you get a coupla incompletes," he says, strictly to Ryan. Big, broad smile.

At eight I try calling home again. Still busy. A funny look comes over Mr. Ferguson's face. "Ahhh," he says, shifting from foot to foot, "you're not bullshitting me, are you Ryan? You guys aren't...ah...*pregnant*?"

"Jesus Christ, Dad."

"All right, all right, okay, I'm out of line, I just thought..."

"I'm sorry," Ryan says to me.

"I'll tell you what," Mr. Ferguson offers, speaking to a space slightly to my left. "In a little while, I'll go over and talk to them. See what's up. How about that? I'll tell them Ryan found you, you were exhausted, you're asleep. Okay? I mean we can't just hang around here forever. I, for one, have got to get to work." After a meaningful glance at his watch, he looks at Ryan. "I'll bet Mariah would like to lie down in the TV room," he suggests in an ordering tone. "She must be exhausted. In fact, you ought to think about sacking out for a while yourself, and then hitting your books. You're not going to take any *more* incompletes."

There's a funny edge to his voice, and I can see that his tolerance for me—and the trouble I'm causing—is already beginning to fade. The distance in his voice makes it clear how his idea of me has changed. I can't say I blame him for worrying, but the sudden change in my status is depressing. Overnight I've gone from being a desirable partner for his son's adolescent "rites of passage" to being trouble, a fuckup, a mess.

Ryan goes to get a blanket for me. Mr. Ferguson comes back from the bathroom, patting his hair, which is dampened and shows the grooves of his comb.

"Get some rest," he says. He tries for an upbeat smile.

The couch in Ryan's TV room is upholstered in some tweedy, itchy fabric. Ryan forgot to get me a pillow and I think about getting up and asking him for one, but once my body is horizontal, fatigue seems to hold me where I am. It's as if I'm on an airplane during takeoff, as if some force is crushing me into the couch. My thoughts begin to drift and lose connection. For a second I try to grab on to the last shred of consciousness. Ryan is going to bring me a blanket: I should at least stay awake until then. But it's no use; I fall asleep.

Chapter Twenty-Three

MARIAH
Instinctual Reactions

WHEN I WAKE up, the sun is beating on my face; my cheek burns in a slant of light. It takes me a second to figure out where I am and why. I rub my cheek as I sit up, squinting in the gritty light. I wish I had my toothbrush.

Even through the air-conditioned coolness, I can tell it's bad outside, hot and polluted. The light comes through the windows with a poisonous glare. When I spot Ryan, sitting motionless across from me in the wing chair, my body gives a spasmodic jerk. Because he should have moved by then, you know, and said hello, his inertness is scary. Then I realize from his slack mouth and lolling head that he's asleep, it's just that he's fallen asleep in the chair.

The glowing chartreuse numerals on the VCR's digital clock read 10:47. I can't believe it—as tired as I was—that

I only slept that long. Ryan moves his head slightly and mumbles something, talking in his dream. I tiptoe out to the living room, and check the kitchen and the family room, but there's no sign of Mr. Ferguson. Can he still be out talking to my parents? Then I remember him saying he was going to go to work.

I read magazines for a while, comb my hair, drink a Coke. At noon I just can't stand it anymore and I wake Ryan up. He has an indentation from where the welted seam of the upholstery pressed into his cheek. He's so cute, sleepy, I want to kiss him awake, but my mouth feels too gross. I wonder if married people kiss each other before they brush their teeth. Do they just get used to it and not mind?

I make us some toast, pour myself a glass of milk, make Ryan some instant coffee. For a few minutes I'm in a happy fantasy of being Ryan's wife. Finally we talk about what to do. Ryan guesses his dad must have gone to his office, but first we check upstairs to see if he's up there sleeping. "After all," Ryan says, "he was up all night too." We tap on the door, then open it and peer in. But there's no one there. The bed is tucked in, neat and tidy.

Ryan calls his dad's office, but I can tell from what he's saying that his father isn't there. He hangs up.

"His secretary asked me if *I* knew when he'd be getting in. He's already missed one appointment." He pushes his hair back from his forehead. "Could he still be over there talking to your parents?"

"What would they talk about all this time?" I call my house but this time the phone just rings and rings. I imagine it sitting on the telephone table by the stairs, ringing away. No one rushes to answer it. I let it ring at least twenty times. No one is sitting anxiously by it, waiting for news of their missing daughter. "Let's go over there."

I'm going crazy that Mr. Ferguson isn't home, isn't at his office, that my parents don't answer the phone, that I don't have any information about a situation of which I am the central figure. Suddenly I seem stupid to myself too, wandering around all night, pissing and moaning, making Ryan miss his exams, getting his dad thinking I'm a pain in the ass. It seems to me I *am* a pain in the ass.

Thousands, maybe millions of people in the world are adopted. It's a shock but it's not like finding out you have two months to live or something. It's true, my parents should have told me a long time ago. And it's not surprising I went out of control. In fact, I still don't get it. How could they lie to me all these years? My dad, especially, is a cards-on-the-table kind of guy.

But the truth is, I'm already forgiving them. I've always felt like it was up to me to make my parents happy, especially my mother, and I still feel that way and I still want them to be happy. If it's been a shock trying to imagine part of my past without them, I can't imagine my future without them at all.

I can already see my father, his head cocked to the side, his slightly embarrassed look. I can see him rolling back on his heels, preparing his explanation. I can see my mother, dabbing at her defenseless eyes: "Don't be too hard on your father, Mariah." My mother will claim it is really her fault. "I was afraid; I wouldn't let him tell you." Even if this isn't true, it's what she will say. Nothing is ever purely my fault or my father's fault. My mother always intervenes. She likes to shoulder some of the blame, she likes to step in between combatants. Love makes my mother strong.

I get dressed. My underwear is still damp but I put it on anyway. My shorts and my shirt are stiff and wrinkly, but dry.

I'm right about the weather. When we step outside, we walk into a wall of heat. The sun is a nasty ball behind the haze. It's so humid that the evidence of last night's rain has not yet evaporated from the asphalt. By the time we get to my house, which is about a mile from Ryan's, my shirt is sticking to my back. Beads of sweat collect and slip down my spine.

We pass Mr. Windler, walking Beethoven, and he nods hello. "My dad *is* still here," Ryan says in a puzzled voice. He nods toward their white Taurus.

I hesitate at the top of the walk, just where I did last night when I came home from seeing Ryan. I feel a little unsteady although whether it's from the heat or fatigue or my own anxiety, I'm not sure. My skin is the only part of me that's wet. The back of my throat is dry as dust; even my teeth feel dry. We pass a clutch of tiny bugs spinning in a hazy shaft of sunlight. Ryan slips behind me, and gives my hand a squeeze. At the front door, for a second, I'm not sure whether to knock or just go in. I decide to be formal. Ryan holds the screen door open behind me as I reach for the brass pineapple that's the door knocker.

Maybe it's because I'm so nervous that I react the way I do. Maybe it's because I'm practically holding my breath in edgy anticipation of seeing my mother and father. Tears are already backed up behind my eyes. I can feel the pressure inside my head, as if I've been rolled over in a wave and inhaled some seawater. These are the faces I'm expecting at the door, my mother, my father, the heartfelt meeting of our eyes. Ryan's father will be in the house; I don't know how I feel about that. It's only the white Taurus at the curb, the puzzling presence of Ryan's father, the possibility that he might answer my knock, that keeps my tears in check, that stops me from a blind gushing plunge into the arms that open the door, that allows me to keep, as they say, my wits about me.

So the dark-haired man who does come to the door, who smiles through the doorway at me with such an odd look of satisfaction on his face, steps into my life from outside my immediate frame of reference. It's the wrong face; it's not a face I'm expecting. It shakes me out of my imagined sequence. The tears behind my eyes evaporate in a little rush of anger. I'm thinking: shit, I'm ready to throw myself into my mother's arms and now I'm going to have to be polite, now I'm going to have to explain myself to some counselor or policeman, some composed, well-meaning neutral party.

"Ah," the man says in his high-pitched, slightly accented voice, "Mah-rye-ah." His eyes flick quickly away from me toward Ryan, who is still behind me holding the screen door open. There's something so calculating in that rapid, checking motion of his eyes, something so at odds with his smooth smile and the friendly dip of his head as he beckons us in through the door he's pulled open, that my back stiffens and a strange surge of blood rushes through me, leaving my fingers prickling.

We hesitate on the threshold. "Is my dad—" Ryan starts. "Is my dad here?"

"Of course. They are all waiting for you," the man says in his polished voice, inclining his head cordially to the side as he speaks. "Come in." He turns his head away for a fraction of a second and shouts a name. "Rolando!" There's a strange jubilant note in his voice, an inexplicable tone of triumph. Maybe it's this new departure from what I'm expecting (he's calling a *second* counselor or policeman? Why aren't my parents rushing to the door?) that frees my mind and allows the recollection of his face to rise in my memory.

Anyway, when his face swivels back to me, I recognize him. Our positions were reversed at the time: I was coming out of a house; he was outside.

If I was surprised to see Ryan's father's Taurus outside, if I was bewildered when this man answered the door, and startled when he shouted for his companion in such a strange, triumphant voice, it's nothing to the seismic mental jolt I receive as I realize that the real estate photographer who stood outside my house that day in Janesville is here, inside my house, standing here right now, having just opened my front door,

I can recollect him, I can bring to mind that October day in Janesville. I can hear him saying "Ar-ling-ton" in that same hyphenated way he spoke my name when he answered the door: "Mah-rye-ah."

I'm already stepping into the house. It's only the brilliant instinctual reaction of my body that saves us. When I recognize the man's face, it's as if I've seen a snake, caught a whiff of a tiger; something is so wrong there's instant recoil—a blast of adrenaline yanks me back from the man's reaching arms. I collide with Ryan, then grab on to his arm, pulling him back after me. "What the hell?" I hear him say. I practically drag him halfway up the walk until my terror communicates itself to him and he starts running on his own.

The twin mounds of ivy lining the brick walk flash by, flanked by the wet green grass. A feeling from childhood: fear pushing me from behind, a hot breath against my back. I'm at the curb, I'm on the street, I'm jumping up the opposite curb. I hear the slap of the screen door and turn to see the men coming up the walk. Ryan pauses too, and his gaze copies mine. We see the two men. They have guns in their hands.

The guns don't look like toys. I've heard victims quoted on the toylike quality of guns: bank tellers, gas station attendants, bystanders to random violence. "It didn't look *real.*" These guns are not like that; these guns are dense with reality. Their precise shape and color is so authentic, they make everything else around them look hazy and fake.

It's hard turning my back to the guns but I do it. I release Ryan's arm and we rush headlong past a red Subaru in the driveway toward the Shafers' backyard. The idea is to get behind the house.

There's a little gate into the Shafers' backyard; we push through it, and race past the patio furniture, down four steps, past the hammock and toward the back of the yard. The Shafers' little cairn terrier is going nuts, running back and forth on his stiff little legs, shaking his head, baring his teeth in fury. The Shafers' yard is separated from the one behind it by an old and rusty chain-link fence intertwined with honeysuckle vines. It's a little more than waist high. Ryan hurdles it easily but I have to climb it. One of my Dock-siders gets caught on a loose curl of wire at the top. My foot comes free but the shoe falls back over the fence.

There's a thick stand of bamboo in the yard we've just entered and I crash through it, following Ryan. It scrapes painfully against the skin of my arms and legs. Finally we break through into the grassy part of the yard. As we run up the lawn toward the house, I hear thrashing sounds behind me: the men coming over the fence into the bamboo. We reach the front of the house, the driveway. Ryan never stops, and I follow him without hesitation across the street, past that house and into its backyard. There are two little girls, about four or five years old, playing on a yellow-and-green-striped swing set.

"Who are you?" one of them asks.

Ryan never even slows, and I hurl myself after him toward the high stockade-style fence that encloses the rear yard.

"Shit!" Ryan says. He holds his hands down, making a step for me with his laced palms. "C'mon, Mariah! Come on." I step into his hands and he practically dumps me over the fence. I land badly, my left knee hitting a rock.

"Who are you?" I hear the little girl ask again in an indignant voice. "What are you doing in my yard?"

Ryan comes over the fence, lands on the balls of his feet, and pulls me up. When we reach the front yard, Ryan hesitates, looks, and pulls me to the right. A blue Volvo wagon is backing out of a driveway two doors down.

I know where we are: Allison Drive. And I know where Ryan is heading—to the empty house, to the shed where we made love. The woman in the blue Volvo puts the car in forward and starts down the street. One of those yellow diamond-shaped signs hangs in the side window: NOBODY ON BOARD.

It's still half a block to the house with the shed. The woman in the blue Volvo didn't close the garage door. Ryan pulls me into the empty garage. He yanks the handle; the segments slide down.

But when the last panel settles to the floor and we're hidden, I don't feel safer. What I feel is trapped. What if the men saw us duck into the garage? They weren't very far behind us. I imagine bullets punching through the wood of the door, the shreddy, ragged holes they would leave in the plywood. Ryan tries the door into the house, which opens. I pull on his sleeve.

"We'll go out the back door," Ryan whispers.

"What if there are people in here, Ryan?"

"Good. Then they can call the police."

I follow him in, up two steps. We come through a kind of pantry into the kitchen, where a fiftyish man in a bathrobe sits at a round table reading the paper and dipping his spoon into a bowl of Rice Chex. He begins to rise from his chair even before he speaks. His spoon is still in his hand, dripping milk.

"What the hell are you doing in here?"

I feel caught, trapped, frozen.

"Ah," Ryan says, and unfortunately this pause makes what he says next seem both ridiculous and unbelievable. "Men with guns are chasing us and we're hiding from them."

Even to me it sounds as if he's making it up.

"It's true," I shout fervently. "Call the police, call 911. *Please*."

"Get the hell out of here," the man says, wiping his chin on the back of his hand. "You fucking kids, what is this? Is this some kind of graduation prank?"

"Look, sir—" Ryan begins.

"*Please,*" I interrupt. "It's true, I swear to God it's true." The man pulls his bathrobe belt tighter. "My name is Mariah Ebinger," I say in a rush. "I live two blocks over from here on Gallagher." There's a sharp rap at the front door. My voice evaporates.

"Shit," Ryan says.

"Don't move," the man in the bathrobe says. "Stay right there."

"Shit," Ryan says again.

"It's probably not even them," I hear myself say.

There's another insistent rap on the door. "Hold your horses," the man in the bathrobe says. "I'm coming."

We follow him to the kitchen doorway. The house is a split level, the front door a few steps down from where we are and then across a flagstone landing. We stand behind a wrought-iron railing and watch the man unhook the door chain. Almost as son as he touches the doorknob, the dark-haired man seems to explode through the opening, the other man behind him.

The man in the bathrobe grabs the dark-haired man's sleeve. "Hey," he says in a surprised voice. "What the—"

We're already turning, already running when we hear the gunshot.

The sound is loud, so impossibly loud. I have the sickening feeling that it's not a piece of ammunition that's exploded, it's the whole world, starting to go. I stop and stand there, dumb, stunned. Ryan yanks on my arm; we go out the same way we came in. Ryan hurls the kitchen door shut behind us, sprints toward the garage door and jerks that open halfway; we duck under and run.

We crouch behind a brown Oldsmobile parked in the driveway next door. One of the men comes out the front door and goes into the garage. Ryan drags me the few feet until we're behind the edge of the house. Where is the other man? We run for it, house by house, ducking behind houses, cars, front yard to backyard. Then we're at the vacant house, hurling ourselves through the backyard, throwing ourselves into the shed. Ryan pulls the door shut slowly. It squeaks loudly and closes imperfectly, leaving a two-inch seam of light.

Ryan squats on his haunches. I sit, cross-legged, motionless. The seam of light falls in a stripe across my hands, which are folded together as if I'm praying. I'm looking at my hands as if they belong to someone else. I'm surprised to see that they're shaking. That realization leads to another. My whole body is shaking. I seem to be having these thoughts one by one, as if the part of my mind responsible for linking thoughts is not working. Ryan moves. Very carefully he shifts from his crouch and sits down.

Our breathing sounds so loud in the small space. I have an image of the whole shed vibrating with our breathing, expanding and contracting like a cartoon shed, a shed with lungs. I can't stop myself; I begin to shake violently with silent laughter. Ryan grasps my arm in a fierce grip but I'm out of control, water dribbling from my eyes. I snort in huge drafts of air as quietly as possible through my nostrils. I bury my face in Ryan's chest, clench my face, my fists.

Suddenly my father's voice, full of amused contempt, speaks in my head: "Hysterical females." I can see him as he said it one night when Darlene was staying over. I can see him shaking his head. Darlene and I were collapsing in a giggling fit, our hilarity beyond his capacity to fathom.

The thought of my father sobers me instantly. A shot of worry and foreboding pierces me, so powerful it makes me feel physically ill.

Chapter Twenty-Four

MARIAH
Bystanders

WE STAY IN the shed for a long time.

The shed is metal and has no ventilation. In only a little while it's disgustingly hot. As soon as we got inside it, sweat gathered on my upper lip, on my neck, on my forehead. Now I'm damp everywhere, dripping. The smell of pesticides and fertilizers is strong and nauseating. My muscles ache from staying in one position so long. My knee hurts where I scraped it. My toe hurts. The heat and the smell, combined with the fear of discovery and the need to stay silent and motionless, make every minute seem to go on forever.

I keep thinking someone must have heard the gunshot. Will they call the police? It sounds so unbelievable: gunfire on Allison Drive. Personally, whenever I hear loud explosions, I think it's trucks backfiring. Whenever I hear a burglar alarm, I think it's broken. I think everyone's like that. We all hope for the best.

I try to figure out what's happened. The man who stood in front of my house in Janesville—*what's he doing here?* The other man looked vaguely familiar too, but I can't place him. And what do they want? It seems like they're trying to kill me, but that's crazy. I can't think of a single reason why someone should try to kill me. How can I be a threat to anyone? Maybe it's my parents they're after. Maybe I'm just some kind of a loose end.

They shot the man in the bathrobe. Why did they do that? Maybe this is some kind of rampage, one of those things when pressure builds up until the only release is shooting up a McDonald's or assassinating a celebrity or something. But it can't be. For one thing, it's two men. Two men don't go nuts at the same time, I've never heard of that.

Anyway, one of them was in Janesville outside my house. I can't get around that but I can't get it to mean anything either. Critical pieces of information are missing. I try to think it out, but it's like trying to figure out the plot of a movie when you come in half an hour late. I only have the action to go on.

My mother's voice on the phone: "I'm afraid you've got the wrong number." Wrong number. *Wrong Number.* Was that a warning? Or was she just being mean to me? But my mother would have been worried to pieces; she wouldn't do that. My mother, my father, the men with the guns. I'm so tired, I can't get my next thought to stick together.

After a very long time, or what seems like a very long time because it's hard to tell in the shed without even changes in the light to mark the passage of time, I risk a whisper. "How long are we going to stay here?"

Ryan puts his arm around my shoulder, gives me a squeeze, and then immediately takes his arm away. It's too hot for physical contact.

"How long have we been in here?" I persist.

I watch his head move as he lowers it to look at his watch. The strip of light illuminates different parts of his face. "An hour. Two." Now that my vision has adjusted to the darkness in the shed, the light on his face is too bright; instead of revealing details, it blanks them out.

Our whispers are like scratches in the dark air. "I don't think they're going to hang around on the street. Someone would see them. Someone would call the police."

"In their car," Ryan says. "They'll wait in their car until they see us."

"He shot that man. Don't you think he shot that man?"

"He shot at him. I'm not positive he got him."

"His wife will come back. She left the garage door open. She wasn't planning to be gone long. She'll call the police."

"Not yet. No sirens."

I draw a deep breath. "I think my parents are really in trouble," I say. My voice gets away from me. He squeezes my hand.

"I think you're right. My father too. But you don't mean we should go back to your house?"

"We'll go to *your* house. We'll call the police. We'll call 911."

Ryan sucks in a breath. "You mean now?"

"Do you think we should wait?"

"No, let's go," he says without enthusiasm.

He opens the door a crack at first. The friction of metal on metal produces a screech loud enough to make my face tighten into a grimace. My heart is whirling in my chest. It seems to be spiraling up through the flesh higher and higher, toward my throat. I try to think what I'll do if the men are waiting outside. I work to compose my face. I'm trying for a kind of puzzled innocence. I have the crazy idea that if I get my expression absolutely perfect, the men won't shoot.

Ryan pushes the door wide. Another hard shriek of the hinges.

There's no one there. The door swings open on the plain, ordinary backyard. There's only the back of the house, the chimney, the ivy climbing the brick wall. The windows flash in the sun. I stand there squinting.

We consider rapping on someone's front door and asking to use their telephone to call the police, but it seems too much, our story seems too complicated and alarming to explain in the plain afternoon. It's an edgy feeling, though, walking through the empty streets. We keep looking around us, behind us. After about four blocks of seeing no one, not a single car or person, the streets begin to seem not just empty, but strangely deserted.

Ryan squeezes my hand. "Do you think there's been some alert?" he says finally. "I mean are these guys escaped from a prison or a looney bin or something? Where is everybody?"

"I saw one of them before. In Janesville."

"*What?*" We trudge forward. "You what?"

I repeat what I said.

"You're *sure*, you're completely sure?"

"No, I'm making it up."

"I'm sorry. That was an asshole thing to say."

At last we come upon a little burst of human activity. A blue and white bus goes past. Sirens wail from the direction of the highway. A woman in a red dress stands on the front porch of the house across the street calling, "Here kitty kitty kitty kitty kitty. Here kitty kitty."

Ryan puts his arm around me. "I'm sorry."

"That's why I didn't just walk into the house. I mean at first, when it wasn't my mom or dad or your dad, I thought it was—I don't know, I thought it was a social worker or something. But then I recognized him. Right before we moved, he was outside my house in Janesville. I even talked to him. He said he was taking pictures for a real estate agent."

"Mariah."

A police siren suddenly whoops just a couple of blocks away. The sound sends a surge of panic through me. I have the weird idea that if they come this way, maybe I can flag down the patrol car.

"Mariah," Ryan says again.

"What?"

"Do you have any idea... I mean, what is this *about*? Is your dad some kind of a...coke dealer or something? I mean, what is this shit? Do you have any *idea*...?"

All I can do is shrug.

"You just saw the man that one time, that's the only time?"

"That was it."

"And you're *sure*? You saw him in Janesville?"

I don't say anything. Am I sure? Now that I start thinking about it, my mind going back and forth from that morning in Janesville to today at my front door, I start losing how sure I was. Maybe the man today just looked like that other man. I start to cry again. "I don't know."

Ryan rubs his hand up and down my back. "It's okay."

I'm walking strangely and I realize I've lost a shoe somewhere. I'm going along with one shoe off and one shoe on. It gives me a kind of weird, lopsided gait. I take the shoe off and clutch it to my stomach, as if it's important somehow not to lose it. Each time a car goes by, a little blast of fear zips through me.

A gray car goes by so slowly that I'm almost sure it's the men until I see the bumper sticker: INSULIN IS NOT A CURE! I can't imagine the men with the guns in a car with this bumper sticker and I relax.

Inside Ryan's house we immediately go to the phone in the kitchen. I lean up against the refrigerator and listen to Ryan talk.

"I'd like to report a situation of being...the thing is there were some men with guns chasing us. Me and my girlfriend. And—"

"—"

"I don't know if we're in immediate danger. I guess no, but—we think our parents are."

"—"

"No, not right now. You—"

"—"

"All right. All right." He holds his hand over the receiver. "They're transferring me to the police." He shrugs. After about thirty seconds he says: "Yes, that's right." I listen to him spell his last name in an annoyed tone. "We were going to my girlfriend's house."

"—"

"What? Here? You mean where am I right now? Nine-oh-six Bancroft Lane. *What?* 569-7860. *Her house?* One thousand twelve Gallagher Drive."

When the refrigerator kicks on, the unexpected sound makes my heart twist in my chest.

"Anyway we were going to my girlfriend's house where these men with guns...what? Mariah Ebinger. Not Lilah. M-A-R-I—wait a minute. Can we do this later? We think our parents are being held hostage over at Mariah's house."

"—"

"Ebinger," he says through his teeth, "Mariah Ebinger." He spells it. "And there's a guy on Allison Drive that got shot, that we think got shot."

"—"

"Do you want me to go back and ask his name?"

"—"

"That was a joke."

"—"

"It was an hour ago, a couple of hours ago."

"—"

"Since then we've been *hiding*, that's where we've fucking been. Look, he could be bleeding to death for all I know while you're—"

"—"

"This was on Allison Drive, eight hundred block."

"—"

"Yes, I'll hold."

He takes the receiver away from his ear and looks at it, makes a face and then returns it to his ear. To me he says, "I'm glad we're not in critical condition or something. This is not just slow; this is glacial slowness here."

When I shut my eyes, it's almost as if I could fall asleep standing up.

"All right," Ryan says. "Yes, 906 Bancroft Lane. Yes." He hangs up and turns to me, shaking his head. "An officer will be here within an hour."

"Within an *hour*. They're kidding. What about our parents?"

"This sort of doesn't fit their idea of an emergency. It's like our story's too complicated."

I call my house but it's the same as before, the phone just rings and rings. After I stand there for a long time, letting the phone ring, Ryan takes the receiver from my hand and replaces it on the cradle. "I don't get it," I manage to say. Then I'm crying again.

Ryan leads me to the couch in the living room. "God, Mariah, look at your foot." The toes of my right foot are covered in blood.

In the bathroom I stand with my foot in the sink while he pours hydrogen peroxide over my cuts. I'm so tired, it takes a real effort to keep my balance. Pink froth bubbles up on my toes. The sting seems to revive me for a minute, but when it subsides, I'm more tired than ever.

We return to the couch, which we seem to agree is the right place to wait for the police. The couch is covered in a material that shows a pattern of plumy vegetation and birds. The birds are types men hunt: pheasants, quail, ducks. Masculine colors dominate: rust, gold, olive.

The air conditioner cuts off, and in the sudden quiet small sounds stand out: the ticking of the grandfather clock, a squirrel chattering in the oak tree outside. My chin is propped up on the back of the couch, which is in front of a window. The window has mini blinds, which are swiveled to the open, horizontal position. I peer through the slats toward the street.

Every now and then a car swims by in the gauzy light. Dust has collected on the thin convex slats of the blinds, and I push little lines of dust along with my fingertip into tiny mounds. Dust is in the air too, floating in the shafts of light. I feel inert, as if Ryan and I have been sitting here a long time too, dust accumulating on our skin. Ryan squeezes my hand. He tries to give me a reassuring smile but he's so worried it only lasts a second and then his face goes back to being blank, grim and anxious. I squeeze his hand back. I can't let myself think. Every time a thought comes into my mind, I grit my teeth and hum a wild tune in my head to keep it out.

When the mail falls through the door slot with a loud slap, my heart just about jumps out of my body. It's almost funny.

What I'm waiting for is a regular police car, but when the plain blue car rolls up to the curb, I adjust my expectations. Maybe they send ordinary cars when they're just coming to take a statement or whatever. Maybe regular cars are only to patrol the highways, and to go to sites of emergencies, the scenes of crimes. Maybe they don't like to scare the neighbors. But when the men get out, they're not uniformed policemen. They're not plainclothes detectives either. They're not any kind of agents of order.

It's the men with the guns, although the guns are not visible this time. The men look disheveled and angry.

"*Ryan*," I say without taking my eyes off the men. One man is coming up the front walk; the other is angling toward the side of the house.

Ryan yanks me up from the couch and through the kitchen. I watch him grab a Redskins key chain from one of the cup hooks his father recently installed under the kitchen cabinets by the back door.

In the garage is Ryan's Toyota Corolla. "Get in," he says in a stern whisper. He opens his door as well, very quietly, puts the keys in the ignition, then runs back and jerks open the garage door. Back in the car, he tells me to "get down," which I do as he turns the key. Then he reverses so quickly, the side of my head cracks against the inside of the door.

From my window as we turn out of the driveway, I see the men running out of the garage door toward their car. I continue looking out the back window. By the time we reach the stop sign at Russell, which Ryan runs, they're in their car and it's starting to move.

It's not much of a head start but it turns out to be enough, given Ryan's knowledge of the streets. We twist through Fairlington, a huge and confusing condominium complex, with a couple thousand nearly identical brick town houses and a dozen complicated, intertwining streets.

We come out on Quaker Lane, passing a bank sign that flashes the time and temperature. It's 2:47 and 31 degrees Celsius. I try to remember the conversion ratio. Fahrenheit = 9/5 Celsius plus 32? I can't do the math.

We double back to 395 and head south toward Richmond. Ryan takes the off-ramp at King Street and we pull into Chinquapin, a big park full of soccer fields. There's a one-way circle that goes past all the fields and ends up by the tennis courts. We drive around and pull into the parking lot next to the building where the swimming pool is.

I see why Ryan picked this spot. The parking lot's up on a hill. There's only one way into the park and we can see it clearly from here. We can see every car that comes in. Anyone following us will have to drive all the way around the circle to get to where we are. By that time we could be out of here. If they come on foot, we can just go into the building.

We sit in the car for a while. We don't even talk. My knees are shaking and I press my hands against them to make them stop. Finally Ryan sighs. There's a telephone in the building. He's going to call his mother. Then he's going to call the police. I'm supposed to stay out here and watch for the blue car.

The trouble is, the building is closed for maintenance, according to a handwritten sign on the door—which explains why there's only one other car in the parking lot.

We go to Bradlee, the little shopping center half a mile down King Street. There's a bank of pay phones near the Food Giant. His mother isn't home. He leaves a message on her machine that he'll call her back. Then he calls the police. He talks to them for what seems like a long time.

We end up sitting outside the Food Giant on a low brick ledge, waiting for the cops to come. It's just outside the penned-in area where the shopping carts are kept, between the Giant and the state liquor store. A young kid in an Orioles cap, who helps customers put groceries in their cars, is slamming carts together. He pushes a line of about thirty carts through the automatic doors and inside.

Ryan is holding my hand tight. "We'll just tell them everything we know," he says in a reasonable voice.

We're just getting over a major outburst of hysterical laughter. Ryan parked the car way down by Roy Rogers because he was worried about the fact that he'd been driving without his permit. Parking it down there seemed like a smart thing to do, but after walking all the way up here—with the black asphalt burning my bare feet—and sitting down, I got to thinking how funny it was, worrying about driving without a license when we're in the middle of all this. Once I started laughing, and trying to tell Ryan why, we both got going in that goofy way that makes it hard to stop. The words crossed my mind: battle fatigue. It took a while before we could stop cracking up.

The kid in the Orioles cap keeps shooting us looks. He thinks we're high on something.

The automatic doors whoosh open and shut with a sucking sound. People drive up in the pickup zone. The kid in the Orioles cap puts the groceries in their cars. He whistles the tune of "Don't Worry, Be Happy."

"Hot enough for you?" asks one woman, flipping open the back of her Mazda. She's wearing a T-shirt that says: WOMEN BELONG IN THE HOUSE...AND IN THE SENATE. Most of the people who speak to the kid talk about the weather, about the heat.

Now the area in front of the store begins filling up with old people. Suddenly everyone coming out the door is over seventy-five. Most of them are women. They collect in the drop-off area, each with one or two plastic grocery bags in a cart. They come out of the store in ones and twos, taking small tentative steps, moving with deliberate slowness. They lean on their carts for support.

I get it: some kind of shopping expedition for senior citizens. After a few minutes the kid in the Orioles cap has a kind of traffic jam on his hands. He's having trouble maintaining enough space for people to get in and out of the store, and he speaks to a couple of the ladies, gesturing toward the spot where Ryan and I are sitting.

"Emilio is late again," says a woman with a frizz of carrot-red dyed hair. "I like Emilio very much but he's always late."

"So are we in a hurry? I'm not in a hurry."

A woman in pink looks very flustered. "I worry about the perishable items."

After five minutes most of the old people have drifted our way. Half of them are sitting on the ledge. A Black man wearing khaki work clothes comes out of the state liquor store and invites them inside. "I don't want any of you getting overheated out there," he says. "C'mon in here in the air-conditioning."

"Oh, thank you, Bernard," says a woman clutching a handkerchief in her fist. "You're so kind." It's clear that this has happened before. About half of the senior citizens go inside and stand in the storefront window, peering anxiously outside from time to time, looking for the bus.

When the brown police car finally rolls toward us, Ryan stands and holds his hand up, as if he's hailing a cab. The car pulls right up into the end of the package loading zone, in front of the senior citizens who have remained outside.

A woman in a sari comes out the Giant's door pushing a cart on top of which a baby seat is precariously balanced.

The policeman who gets out of the driver's door slams it shut in the way of a man running out of patience. He's about fifty, bald and fat. He walks ponderously around the car. His brown shirt is tucked into his trousers and is just barely large enough to contain his flesh. A bulge of shirt-contained fat, streaked with sweat, laps over his waistband. His pants are too tight also; the stripe up the side buckles and pulls where the fabric is strained around his bulky thigh. He has one of those trooper-style hats on. He wheezes and puffs as he comes close to us, his face red in the heat. A heart attack waiting to happen—that's what my father would say.

The cop who emerges from the passenger door is young and Black and wears aviator shades.

The police car's radio is on; it gives off a long rasp of staticky talk. The fat man turns his head and elevates his eyebrows but nothing else comes from the radio. He looks at Ryan and gives him a sharp upward nod of the head.

"You the boy called in?"

There are huge half-moons of sweat under his arms.

"That's right."

The black man has a faint smile on his face. He circles up toward me. I stand up. My bare feet make me feel embarrassed. The white cop shifts his eyes to me. He looks me up and down.

"What say we all go down to the station?" The faint smile again, this time on the white cop. "You mus' be hotter 'n hell."

I wonder what all this smiling is about.

"I called before," Ryan says. "From my house. But before anyone from the police station arrived, the men—"

"We c'n git all that straightened out," the white cop says, nodding his chin toward the car, "at the station." He nods and smiles, the loose flesh under his chin jiggling. A lot of smiling.

A large white van pulls up toward the spot where the senior citizens are waiting and parks, angled in front of the police car and partially blocking it. The side of the van is marked: POPKIN'S HOUSE SENIOR CITIZEN EXPRESS. It's a fancy-looking van with big smoked-glass windows that are rounded at the corners.

Ryan sticks his hands in his pockets. The supermarket's automatic doors wheeze open and the kid in the Orioles cap comes out pushing a dozen carts.

The white cop puts his hand on the butt of his gun and he looks straight at Ryan. "Get your hands out of your fucking pockets," he says. "*Now.*"

"Hey," Ryan says, his eyes checking over to meet mine. "What the—"

The white van has its side door open and the parade of senior citizens shuffles toward it. A short Hispanic man assists the carrot-haired lady up the steps.

A woman in a black and white print dress, bent over from a dowager's hump, drops her grocery bag.

"Oh, shoot," she says. "I bet I broke my eggs." The Hispanic man bends to pick up the bag.

"Let's take a look, Mrs. Severtson." He produces the half carton of eggs and opens it. "No, look, they're fine. Everything fine."

The black cop slides up next to the Hispanic man. "Hey buddy, we on police business here. How 'bout you move this van?"

"I got all these ladies with their groceries, man."

"I said *move your van*."

"Can't you do your police business somewhere else? This is a parcel pickup zone here. We gotta right to this location."

A rasp of static. The radio squawks: "Car forty-two, your backup is on the way. Over."

"Emilio, one of the eggs *is* broken," the lady with the dowager hump says. "Can you get that young man to replace it?"

"What's going on?" Ryan says to the fat cop. "Why do I get the feeling you're going to arrest us? We're trying to make a citizen's report is all."

"Take it easy, bud. Just take it easy and you won't get hurt."

"I won't get hurt?'

"Move your van *now*," the Black cop is saying. "Or I get it moved for you. I give you that choice. You blocking our vehicle."

"Gimme a break, man. We just going to take a couple a minutes here. C'mon, ladies, let's get it going. This policeman, he want to give me a tic-ket."

The fat cop has his hand on Ryan's arm, levering him back toward the wall. "Take it easy, bud."

"Take it easy? I called *you*, remember that? I called you. What the—"

The white cop's hand is on the hilt of his billy club. "You called to confess, didn't you? I wanna help you with that, son. It's over, son, it's all over now."

I'm not understanding what's happening. Next thing I know, Ryan's pulling me off the curb, behind the senior citizens' van, dragging me through the parking lot toward Roy Rogers.

"Freeze!" the fat cop yells.

"Oh my *God*," someone says.

"Don't shoot, Russell," the black cop yells, "God almighty."

The white cop's voice is high, quavery, out of control. "They're *armed*, Wilson. Armed-and-dangerous."

Running down between the columns of cars, nothing making sense.

"Chris," someone says in a calm, decisive voice. "Get back in the car. *Now*."

Waiting for a bullet in the back, a bullet like a bird, diving into my back with its beak.

"I said *freeze*."

"Russell, don't. I'm telling you don't. You crazy, man? Don't the fuck shoot. We got bystanders."

Chapter Twenty-Five

MARIAH
Queen Anne's Lace

IT'S ONLY SOME kind of amazing luck that we get out of the parking lot without crashing into another car. There are ten more close calls before we're back on the highway, including a weaving jaunt down the one-way service road. Ryan takes the on-ramp to the highway fast, tires squealing. The force of the curve pushes me against the door. As the car picks up speed, it rattles and shimmies. I look at the speedometer: the needle bounce between 75 and 80.

I don't speak. Ryan needs to pay attention to what he's doing. His eyes continually check back and forth from the rearview mirror to the sideview mirror to the road. After a few miles, he completes the difficult merge into criss-crossing traffic where the Beltway meets 395, then keeps merging right toward the Springfield exit. We follow the signs for Old Keene Mill Road.

My heart thumps when we pass a police car, its blue lights whirling. I'm relieved when I see that the trooper is in conversation with some poor guy in a pickup truck.

"I know why they're blue."

"What?" Ryan says.

"Police car lights. They're blue because it was the only color left. Taillights are red. Caution lights are yellow. Green traffic lights are green. They had to take blue."

I happen to think the blue of police car lights is particularly beautiful. The Virgin Mary's color. I think of it in Spanish: *la virgen.*

We drive a few miles. We pass a Kids "R" Us, a High's, a yogurt place, a little strip of stores including one called Hair It Is, and another called Bone-Jour. We don't talk. We pass a golf course, a couple more strip malls, a dozen fast-food places, a group of huge houses under construction.

"Where are we going?" I ask finally.

"Burke Lake."

"Oh."

"We probably should have let those cops take us in."

"They were weird. They scared me."

"I know. I was *stupid*, though. I panicked, I just panicked." He shakes his head. "I'm so fucking stupid."

I don't say anything.

"You hear that one cop say we were armed and dangerous? He pulled his gun too. He fucking pulled his gun. They have rules of engagement. They can only draw their weapons if... I wanted to confess, that's what he said. I wanted to confess."

"You mean they think we...?" I'm too confused; I let the thought drift away.

"They think we did something. Shit." He shakes his head. "We should have just gone with them." The car comes to a stop sign. "I hope we can get my mom on the phone. We really need my mom."

We turn right on Pohick Road and pass a large brown wooden cross in front of a brown building that resembles an ark. Burke Community Church. The sign says, WORSHIP 10 A.M. SUNDAY. Ryan turns left into a little dirt parking lot large enough to hold about ten cars. He turns off the ignition and we just sit there for a minute.

"This is Burke Lake?" I've heard of Burke Lake; it's a huge place, with a golf course, a mini-train, a marina. This parking lot is too small for a place with all that.

"This is the back entrance. My dad and I used to go fishing here all the time. The front way, you have to pay four bucks if you don't live in Fairfax County. Back here, you have to walk to the lake, but it's free."

The car makes a ticking sound. We just sit there for a minute in the stifling heat. For the first time since the man opened the front door of my house, I actually feel safe.

The heat drives us from the car, although it's not much better outside. There's only one other car in the parking lot, an Isuzu trooper. Its bumper sticker says: SOCCER IS A KICK IN THE GRASS. I look at our car, with all its "touch" bumper stickers.

For some reason the bumper stickers give me a pang. I'm feeling so apart from the world where someone has time to think about bumper stickers. Ryan laces his fingers into mine, raises both our hands to his mouth, and kisses my knuckles.

There's a small dirt road leading into the woods. An aluminum gate padlocked to a post in the ground keeps cars from going up the road. A brown sign with yellow letters says:

BURKE LAKE WILDERNESS AREA
CAMPING BY PERMIT ONLY

Ryan and I embrace next to the sign. He rubs his hands down the length of my back, down over my bottom and then back up around my waist, and holds me tight. We stand there hugging until we hear a car crunch over the gravel of the parking lot—which makes us jump apart.

"So now what?"

"We're going to stay here until we get in touch with my mom."

It turns out he has a plan. While my mind, like a laboratory rat, was circling over the same territory in confusion, trying over and over again to figure out what was going on, Ryan's mind was ranging ahead in the likely future, making contingency plans.

"Do you have any money?"

I don't. I left my purse at home, when I went out to meet Ryan that night. It seems weird—it seems so long ago—that I left my chemistry book on my desk and went out to meet Ryan, that we made love in the shed, that I headed home and stood outside and couldn't get myself to go back in. It seems like I've taken a sidestep and ended up in a different world.

Ryan takes his wallet out of his back pocket, flips it open and pushes open the bill compartment with his thumb. He spreads the money out. "Seventeen bucks"—he jingles his pockets—"and some change."

A car pulls into the lot. A man in bright red shorts gets out, leans against it, does a couple of calf stretches, sets his watch, then lopes off up the dirt road.

Ryan opens the trunk of the Toyota. Inside are a tent, some sleeping bags, and other camping stuff.

"We took my car when my dad and I went camping off Skyline Drive a couple of weeks ago, remember?" I do remember. Ryan was away for the whole weekend and I missed him like crazy. "He didn't want to get the Taurus muddy so we took my car."

"You mean we're going to sleep here?"

"If we have to."

He carries the tent; I carry the two rolled-up sleeping bags. We go up the road a few yards, then turn off on a little path. After about ten minutes of walking, we're deep in the woods. We stop and put the sleeping bags and the tent underneath a bush. Ryan camouflages the spot some more, picking up loose branches from the ground to break up the one blatant swatch of blue. He points to some shiny foliage: "Watch out, that's poison ivy."

He stands back from the hiding place and surveys the area, checking in each direction. Then we walk on, through the woods. There's no path; it's not exactly easy going. Suddenly we come out onto a dirt road. Ryan looks around, taking his bearings. He points to a tree with a split trunk that's a few yards up the road. "If we turn in by that split tree, and just walk east, we'll find our stuff. If you go straight up this road that way"—he points—"you get to the lake." My eyes follow his gesture; I spot the bright glint of water.

"Now what?" We're heading back toward the car on the dirt road. It's idyllic. A stand of Queen Anne's lace nods in the soft breeze. Splotchy sunlight sifts down through the leafy ceiling, and small birds constantly chirp and flutter. A jogger comes around the corner. He nods to us, and then moves on, taking smooth, powerful strides. I get a panicky feeling in my chest and squeeze Ryan's hand. I wish we were just walking in the woods.

I keep seeing the man's face at my front door. "Mah-rye-ah." How does he know my name? He never asked my name that time he was taking a picture of the house in Janesville. I'm sure of that, I'm almost positive of that.

"The only trouble," Ryan says, "is the car. Do you think they got close enough to get the license plates?"

"Who? The police? I don't know. I'm not sure."

He shakes his head. "It'd be so much easier if we could keep the car; but I guess...I guess I'd better put it some-where else."

I stand at the entrance to the parking lot, watching for cars signaling to turn in, and I also keep an eye on the path, for joggers, while Ryan removes the license plates from the car. He couldn't find a screwdriver. He's using a dime.

Ryan checked the trunk one more time to see if anything potentially useful was in there. When he saw the fishing pole, he had a brainstorm, and that's how I ended up down here by the lake.

The fishing pole gives me an excuse to be here, sitting down. This way, I'm not loitering, I'm not doing nothing, I'm fishing. I've been sitting here for about an hour, I guess, holding the fishing pole, watching a red and white bobber float on the surface of the water.

I would have gone with him, but Ryan convinced me to stay here, because I don't have any shoes. The plan is that he's going to park the car in one of the strip malls along Old Keene Mill Road, without its license plates, which are now hidden with our camping stuff.

What I wanted to do was set up the tent and stay in there, but Ryan said no. There were specific campsites, and you had to register over at the main entrance to the park. Plus, you had to pay. Seven dollars. If park rangers saw the tent, they'd make us register—if there even were any campsites available. Besides, there was probably some kind of age limit, like you had to be eighteen or something. If we end up staying here, we'll wait for night and set up the tent in a remote part of the woods. But that's only if he can't reach his mother.

I keep looking at the bobber although I'm not going to get a bite. There's no bait on the hook.

I'm thinking how Ryan's mind works so differently from mine, how he developed this entire plan while driving away from the police at the Giant—when I didn't even have what you'd call a thought. He'd remembered the camping gear in the trunk of the car, thought of going to Burke

Lake, planned the removal of the license plates from the car and the relocation of the car, planned to call his mother and what we'd do if he couldn't get her.

The jogging trail is about two hundred feet inland from where I'm sitting. Joggers come by in ones and twos and threes. I can see them through the trees, flashing in and out of sight. Sometimes I can follow their bright clothing halfway around the lake, blinking through the trees. When they're in groups, they talk. Their words reach me in little drifts.

"—assistant quit."

"The older woman?"

"Yeah, the work was too menial."

"Watch that root."

"—just this huge stack of papers, this humongous..."

When we do get ahold of Ryan's mother, she'll come and get us and then we'll go, all three of us, to the police. We need adult help; we don't want to be alone in this any longer. We don't want to be unrepresented by some adult person who can speak in our behalf.

When Ryan comes back, I'm so relieved, I just stand there hugging him for a while. I close my eyes and let my worries dissolve in the sweet blur of comfort—having him back, not being alone anymore. Then he hands me a plastic Rite-Aid bag.

"You got the flip-flops! *Thanks.*" It seemed like some kind of giveaway of guilt, or something, that I didn't have any shoes. A person without shoes can't get along in this society except maybe at the beach; you can't even go into a 7-Eleven. He got Band-Aids for my toe too, and a Coke, which I drink immediately. Even though it's lukewarm, it tastes as good as anything I've ever tasted in my life.

The bad news is he didn't get his mother. She wasn't home, and at work she was "away from her desk." But there's a phone booth over on the other side of the lake, by the marina, and we're going to walk over there later and try her again.

We're both so tired, we end up falling asleep right there, in the woods. Every once in a while I sort of wake up and I'm fine and dreamy until I remember with a panicked startle why we're out here in the woods. Every time, it comes as a shock, the predicament we're in. In my dreams, I guess, everything's still all right.

When we finally wake up, it's getting on toward night, and we start walking on the jogging path toward the marina and the concessions so we can call Ryan's mother. Every minute or two a jogger chugs past. We pass a square stone engraved with the words: NATURE TRAIL. An arrow points into the woods. We go by the area where the campsites are. We can see the tents through the trees, and the harder metallic glint of some camper vehicles. Clothes are strung out on a line. People are talking. The air smells of cooking fires, grilled meat. It makes me hungry. Children run around chasing each other; we can't see them but we hear them giggling and yelling in the fading light. A couple of ten-year-olds zoom by on dirt bikes. A father and two young boys with fishing poles pass us; one of the boys is carrying a string of fish.

We come out of the woods to an open stretch, where the path goes right next to the lake. There are big bunchy clouds in the sky, outlined with sharp ribbons of light. Biblical shafts of light radiate down from them. The sky is rosy and orange, and the color is reflected on the lake. Ducks and geese bob on the polished water. Canoes and rowboats glide in toward the marina as if they're children being called home. We pass a curve of sandy beach where people are packing up their fishing gear. They have big coolers to carry, folding aluminum chairs, tackle boxes, fishing poles. We pass the self-launch area, where two men with mustaches are securing a green canoe to the top of a Cherokee. Fireflies flicker in the woods.

Ryan goes over to the concession stand to call his mom, while I go to the ladies' room. It has no windows and smells of urine. Graffiti is scratched into the metal doors of the stalls.

Carmen and Philip 4ever

Monica from Scotch Plains, N.J. 1989

Don't you worry about sitting on the seat.
The crabs in here jump 20 feet.

Paper towels have overflowed the trash bin and lie on the floor. There's no mirror, only a polished piece of metal. It lacks the clarity of mirrored glass, and when I look into it, my reflection is fuzzy and smeary. I put my foot in the basin and wash it with a couple of squirts of pink liquid soap, which makes my toe sting. I grit my teeth and lift up the torn flap of skin, which has dirt under it. It hurts quite a bit. I dry it with brown paper towels and wrap it up in three Band-Aids.

Ryan's mother still isn't home. We each have a piece of pizza and a container of milk at the concession stand, and then blow fifty cents to ride the merry-go-round. We're too big for it, of course. Ryan's feet dangle down almost to the floor. Still, it's fun riding around slowly in the dark, the colored lights strung out around us. The little kids sit stiffly, waving at their parents, who are waiting outside the fence, tossing big smiles every time their kid comes around. The boy in front of me is tiny. He only lets go of the pole long enough to get his hand momentarily free and then grabs back on again. His mother is the fat woman in the E.T. T-shirt. She smokes a cigarette and every time he comes around, she yells, "Hello, critter. C'mon, *smile*."

We try Ryan's mom again on the telephone. No luck. Now it's really dark. Moths and other bugs make clouds

around the lights of the concession stand. Park workers
are closing up for the night. They wear brown uniforms
with little silhouettes of Virginia stitched in green on their
sleeves. They flirt with each other, bang things shut, snap
off lights, jingle keys.

We drift out, part of the crowd reluctantly heading
home, except we go right past the parking lot and into
the woods near the restrooms. We sit on top of a concrete
picnic table and wait. Doors slam, motors rev, cars drive
off one by one. A few minutes after the last car drives off,
we go back to the telephone and call, but Ryan's mother
still isn't home. We talk about calling Darlene or Stolly but
decide against it. We need an adult.

Ryan decides we'll keep trying but if we don't get his
mom by twelve, twelve-thirty, we'll give up and wait until
the morning. His watch has an alarm. We'll get up super-
early, like six or six-thirty. His mom doesn't leave for work
until eight.

"Does she ever—" I start, but then I shake my head.
"Never mind."

"You mean spend the night out?"

"Yeah."

"Yeah, she does, sometimes, but she doesn't even have
a boyfriend now. Not that I know of anyway. Anyway, they
usually stay at her place. She like needs her makeup and
stuff in the morning."

We go over to the golf course for a while, and lie down
in the springy grass. The moon has a hazy ring around it, a
big misty halo. We make love, very slowly; we both want it
to last and last. Every once in a while we roll away from each
other and lay facedown in the damp cool grass and then we
start up again. I wish it could go on and on; I wish I could go
to sleep with him inside me, but I don't even know if that's
possible. Eventually we can't stop ourselves anymore.

We get dressed. We try the telephone again. The
answering machine. Ryan just about shouts into the

receiver: "This is me again. Where the hell *are* you?" He tells her he's going to call her in the morning. "Don't worry," he says. "I'm all right."

Because we're starting to get cold, we pick our way back around the lake to where our stuff is. The light from the moon helps, but still, it takes us a long time, stumbling along. We pass the campground. Some people are still awake. Light diffuses through the fabric of the tents, so that from a distance the tents look like huge, soft lights themselves, blue and green. We hear the murmur of people talking. A baby starts to cry, abruptly, but then stops. Finally we reach the path that leads to the little back parking lot where we came in.

It's really hard, finding our stuff. We find the split tree all right, but we stumble around in the woods for a long time and we can't find the hiding place. I've given up, and I'm just sitting on a fallen-down tree, when I see a little light flick on. It seems practically a miracle. Ryan calls me: "Mariah."

We're too tired to put the tent up, so we just stretch it out on the ground and put our sleeping bags on top of it. Lying on my back, looking up, I can see the tops of the trees shift in the wind, the leaves making soft rushing sounds. From a distance I can hear the hiss of traffic on Pohick Road. Every once in a while, when the branches shift a certain way, I can see a star, and every time I see it, I squeeze my eyes shut and make the wish that somehow everything will be all right.

Chapter Twenty-Six

ROLANDO
Center of Gravity

IT'S MORO'S SHOW now. It was my obsession, but now it's him calling the shots. I flounder in his wake, increasingly disconnected. Everything is so fucked up.

After Mariah and her boyfriend surprised us, roaring out of the garage in their small gray car, Moro and I drove around for almost an hour in frenzied but hopeless pursuit. It was pointless, of course. They had the traditional guerrilla advantage: superior knowledge of terrain. After we gave up, we drove by the Ebinger house, but the attendants to calamity were already there: official vehicles, clusters of interested neighbors, the morbid agitation of disaster.

Then we left the area in a hurry. It seemed prudent to change cars, and we did, returning the rental car to the airport (to Hertz) and renting a new one (at Budget). Moro had a detailed map of the Northern Virginia area, but we stopped at a store called the 7-Eleven to buy more maps: a Northern Virginia map for me and two detailed maps of Montgomery County, Maryland. Then Moro drove me back to the shopping center where the second car was parked, and I followed him to the motel. Moro spent a good half hour looking at the maps, marking the route he would take (and I would later follow) on both sets. He gave me some instructions, added some ammunition to the gear in the duffel bag, and took off.

After I watch the news, I'm to check out of the By George! We paid in advance; all I have to do is drop the key in the slot. Then I'm supposed to check into a different motel, the Heritage Motor Lodge, which is about half a mile from here. "Pay for two days," Moro instructed. "Keep conversation to a minimum. Nod when you can, try to look confused—as if you don't speak English very well. We let ourselves be known here. That was all right—there was no reason for anonymity, really, so that was tactically acceptable. But everything's changed now."

Everything's changed. Well, he's right about that. I can't believe how fucked-up everything is. I can't believe the girl was out (at three in the morning!) and that when she came back, we let her get away. It was supposed to be so easy. I'd imagined her in bed, dreaming; I would pluck her from her dreams as easily as picking a flower.

In the planning stages, back in Argentina, the possibility of not finding her at home at three A.M. had not entered into our calculations. Everything else had seemed difficult: finding out where she lived, arranging a plausible cover story to deny my own presence here, arranging the transportation, acquiring the weapons, the vehicles, the ID, all of that. But finding her at home, in bed, at three A.M.— that we had taken for granted.

During his earlier visit, Moro had cased the house. It seemed perfect. No alarm system, one telephone, the girl slept upstairs, the parents down. They had ceiling fans, as well as central air-conditioning, which would muffle the sounds as we broke into the back door. It seemed possible that we could abduct the girl without even disturbing the parents' sleep.

When we arrived at the house to find all the lights blazing, and figures walking around, we altered our plans and went in through the front door. It never occurred to us that she might not be there; that simple fact threw all our plans into disarray.

Even now I can't get over it. It seems so unlikely, so unfair, a cruel trick. An adolescent mixture of fury and frustration still bristles inside me, that the one unforeseen contingency, the one thing that could make our plans collapse, should happen. Even so, the situation should have been salvaged. It wasn't so bad that she wasn't home. All we had to do was wait for her; sooner or later, she would return. And she did, but once again she confounded me. Even now I cannot comprehend how she was alerted. How did she know she was in danger? How could just one look at Moro send her fleeing from her door?

And then, after finding her at the boy's house, we let her get away again. Unbelievably, she slipped through our fingers *twice*. I didn't even get to see her, only the flash of her clothes, a glimpse of her hair. I never even saw her face.

After we lost them, Moro put it to me: "Well, *Capitán*, do you want to pursue it or let it go?" His face was impassive.

"How can we pursue it?" I was practically weeping by then, raging at our missed chances. I was almost incoherent with anger. "We'll never find them now."

"You can always pursue it, *Capitán*." Moro said. "Always. Fortunately, I was thorough in my questioning of Ferguson. I got the name and address of the boy's mother. It's the logical place for him to turn."

Thorough. You could call it that. Submerging a man's face in the water thirty, forty, fifty times, never allowing him more than half a breath of air, asking him: "Where would they go? Where would they go? Where would they go?" Until his mind was pulp.

"We could have had hostages. We could have been dealing from a position of strength."

Moro held his hand in the air, as if he might strike me, and shrugged. "Hostages don't give you strength. Hostages are a colossal pain in the ass. No, once the woman died, I really had no choice," he said. "I didn't kill her, remember." He lit a cigarette. "She died."

It sounds like a semantic distinction, but it isn't, I suppose. He's famous for his restraint, his touch, but he couldn't be responsible for someone's medical history. There were cases during the repression too. People died of it: fright.

On the other hand, he did kill the men.

He did kill the men and it was stupid. *Stupid*. And the man in the house, the man who came to his door in his bathrobe. Especially him. His death struck me as particularly pointless. There was no reason to kill him. He had no role in any of this, and nothing was gained by his death. Nothing. I don't know, watching Moro hasn't been what I'd expected. He didn't function like some finely calibrated machine. Something has happened to Moro; I think the machine has a screw loose.

I could make an analogy to watching a race car go around a curve. Everything's fine until the stresses reach a certain point, then the speed is too much for the camber of the road, a wheel comes up, the center of gravity shifts.

Moro was like that. He went out of control.

But when I think about it, a car is a poor analogy. Moro wasn't cold and mechanical at all. His face gleamed with sweat. His eyes were glazed. He stank.

I was unable to look. I could not even force myself to be in the room. When he made them take their clothing off, when I saw he was going to burn them...when he held the cigarette end toward their flesh, I ran from the room, my mind went into free fall, a spinning, sickening descent. They were tied, hand and foot, restrained, but still I heard them thrashing and thumping in the other room. Their mouths were taped shut. They could not scream, but I heard them anyway, inside my brain, shrieking in agony. I had to leave the house. I vomited in the yard. When it was over, when he had killed them, I experienced a strange burst a relief. Moro actually thought to console me. "Don't worry, *Capitán*, most people can't tolerate it, at first. It's a normal reaction."

"No choice, really," Moro had said, about killing them. But that's crazy. There was no reason to kill the men. I don't agree with him about hostages; we could have taken the men in the car, we could have bound them, we could have brought them here to the motel. We could have used them! I think that Moro saw them merely as sources of information, and when he got what information they had, they were of no more use to him.

Of course, he doesn't understand love; he doesn't understand we could have used them as bait.

After I see if the news carries anything pertaining to our case, I'm to join Moro at the stakeout he's conducting. This is the information Moro prised from the boy's father, Ferguson, in his "thorough" questioning: the whereabouts of the boy's mother. It was a divorce situation, apparently. Ferguson tried very hard not to tell Moro, but in the end the information oozed out of him like blood: the woman's name and address, her telephone number. She lives in Bethesda, Maryland, which is a forty-five minute drive from here.

It's a relief, in a way, just to be away from Moro for a while. The first news comes on Channel 5, at ten. I watch the whole thing but there's nothing about us, nothing at all. The newscasters joke with one another. They talk about sports, the weather (it's the hottest June on record), their plans for the weekend. The weekend weather is discussed at great length. The weatherman is teased repeatedly about the current heat wave, for which the others seem to hold him personally responsible. A chart comes on, with little visual icons over each date. Thursday has a sun, Friday a sun half covered with cloud, Saturday a cloud with streaks of rain descending from it. The weatherman and the newscasters kid around with each other, and a sensible Black woman reins everything in and signs off.

I switch channels. I feel so depleted. I let my body flop on the bed and try to summon the reverie: the girl, the things I want to do to her. But I keep seeing the faces of her parents. I keep seeing their eyes, so desperate and pleading. I don't know. I found it difficult even to look at them. I found I didn't want to be there. None of it was what I anticipated.

I never knew what Moro was going to do until he did it. Each time, the violence was so sudden, so unexpected. By the time the knowledge of what was happening came into my mind, the damage had already been done.

The deaths of the parents struck me as unnecessary, even wasteful. What did they have to do with it? Or the man in the house we ran into. He was in his bathrobe. He wasn't expecting disaster. He had a spoon in his hand. He wasn't expecting to die on his front staircase because Hugo Moro used a little bit too much pressure, because Hugo Moro felt just as much like pulling the trigger as he felt like not pulling the trigger. I keep seeing the man. He crumpled right there, spoon in hand, a little smear of milk in the spoon.

The ads finally stop. There's a montage of Washington sights, culminating in a final swoop past the Capitol dome, the White House. After some cheerful, vaguely martial music, another well-spoken Black woman says good evening and introduces herself. She runs through a list of the major stories, promises weather and sports. "After this," she says, and breaks for an advertisement.

It's pretty much the same run of stories I saw on the other channel, but then there it is: a reporter is standing in front of the Ebinger house, speaking into a microphone. The house looks smaller on television. There are figures moving in and out, a yellow ambulance in the driveway. A body is wheeled out onto the tidy brick porch on a rolling metal stretcher. Two men in white uniforms guide it as it bounces down the steps. All of this is happening in the background as a policeman is interviewed. I force myself to pay attention to the policeman but I have trouble understanding what he's saying, A gray blanket is pulled up over the face of the body. Tightly. The body is a tidy package; everything is tucked in. The wind ruffles the reporter's hair, and a flicker of annoyance crosses his face. The policeman is saying: "Two dead, one critically injured."

An enlarged picture of Mariah fills the screen. Her appearance is slightly different than her appearance in my snapshot. This is a more formal shot, a three-quarter shot, a school yearbook photo. A similarly formal photograph of the boy succeeds hers on the screen. The camera returns to the policeman. He dips his head toward the microphone, but tries to look straight out at the camera at the same time. It gives him an odd turtlelike posture. He's saying: "High school sweethearts." He's saying: "Charlie Starkweather."

Who, I wonder, is Charlie Starkweather?

"More details about this tragic multiple slaying on the Morning News at seven. Live from Alexandria, this is Christian Ballenger for Channel Nine News."

The reporter promises a story on Panic in the Panda House "after this." An ad for disposable diapers comes on. A man dressed in a business suit spills a blue liquid on a diaper and holds it aloft by the corner to demonstrate its absorbency.

What the policeman was saying is becoming clear as I think about it. First of all, of the three people in the house, Mr. and Mrs. Ebinger and Ferguson, one of them is not dead. I find this hard to believe. True, I was unable to look at them closely, but I was certainly under the impression that

they were all dead. Moro too. I thought I saw him, fingers
to the carotid artery. I thought I saw him checking pulses.

Second, the police seem to think that Mariah did it.
They think Mariah and the boy killed their parents.

I try to remember everything Moro said, and do exactly
as he instructed. Exactly. It seems important to follow the
rules precisely. I tidy up the room, putting the newspapers
in the wastebasket, pulling the bedspreads flat, puffing up
the pillows. It occurs to me that I'm trying to make it look
as if no one was ever here. Looking it over, this strikes me
as wrong. I don't want the room to look odd. I mess up
one of the beds slightly, retrieve a section of the newspaper
and put it on top of the bed. It looks neat but not too neat.
I leave some computer brochures on the desk. Creating
an impression. A businesslike impression. Every once in
a while, I remember the expression on Arthur Ebinger's
face; the expressive gymnastics his face went through as he
realized his wife was dead come into my mind and I start
breathing fast and I feel my mind whirling toward chaos.
This will sound funny: alternate nostril breathing is the
only thing that saves me.

I drop the key in the slot but the clerk with the laryn-
gectomy spots me and wants to have a parting chat. "You
fellas," he inhales, "really ought to visit in the spring." A
breath. "We're at our best in the spring." He holds up his
hand and rotates his wrist in the kind of wave royalty uses,
an all-inclusive but energy-conserving wave. I wonder about
the circumstances of his adoption of this mannerism until
I step outside and the heat instantly turns my mind blank.
The heat is amazing. My shirt is sticking to my back within
seconds. The air seems dirty and full of menace.

Cars hiss down the highway, an endless dancing parade
of taillights and headlights. It's so hot, I can't even get into
the car at first. It's hard to believe that it's possible for the
inside of the car to be any hotter than the air outside, but it
is. I stand beside the door, letting the heat equalize.

A dull throb drifts out from the Buried Hatchet. A couple walks past me, arms around each other's waists. The woman says: "I rotate your underwear, you know. I always put the new clean underwear underneath the old clean underwear."

"You don't have to bother, honey," the man says in an amazed voice.

It takes me what seems like a long while to figure out where everything is in the car. Finally I fit the key in, turn on the ignition, locate the air conditioner and punch it on. A blast of superheated air drives me out of the car again, and I have to wait for the motor to run for a while before the air conditioner works.

My driving is poor. Everything seems a little different here, the streets a little wider, the markings and signs alien to me. I'm not secure about the traffic laws either, and I drive carefully, hunched tensely in my seat as if I'm an old person, unsure of my vision. The taillights pulsate in front of me from heat distortion.

I make it to the Heritage Motor Lodge without incident, but then I can't get the key out of the ignition. I search the pockets in the doors and look in the glove compartment for a manual that will tell me how to get the key out but all I find are the rental papers. I try putting on the hand brake, shifting into neutral, into reverse, pressing the key into the ignition. I slam the steering column in frustration. I can't leave the key in the car and risk having it stolen, but I can't imagine *asking* for help either. Finally I try pressing a little button near the ignition and the key, sweaty with my frenzied manipulation, magically slides free.

At the Heritage Motor Lodge, I follow Moro's instructions closely. I nod a lot and keep inclining my ear toward the clerk, a blonde woman with eyebrows so severely plucked she has a singed look. She looks past my shoulder, barely noticing me, as if she's hoping for someone more interesting to step into her life.

The room is a room this time, not a unit. I throw my suitcase inside and drop down on the bed to study my map. Then I'm back in the car, driving in my stiff, insecure way, trying to figure out which way to turn onto the Capital Beltway, a road that makes a rough circle around Washington. The signs offer destinations that mean nothing to me. Richmond. Baltimore. I want Bethesda.

More signs for unfamiliar towns: Frederick. Springfield. I wouldn't mind driving to some anonymous Frederick or Springfield, stopping my car and waiting to come to my senses. At the last second, earning the hooting displeasure of the car immediately behind me, I take the ramp toward Baltimore. Instantly I feel it's a mistake, that I've gone in the wrong direction. I get off at the next exit and pull into a service station. The sign is a big white star inside a red circle—Texaco.

This gas station is entirely self-service; there are no attendants to dispense gas or check the oil or clean your windshield. I have to get out of my car and approach a Plexiglas cubicle. When I open the door, warm air washes over me; there's the vague stink of gasoline. Inside the cubicle is a huge man with a pale white face. He has greasy chin-length hair and sits behind the stacks of gum and cigarettes and cough drops arranged in front of him. If I met this man on the street, I'd be afraid of him. It's a relief, in a way, that he's enclosed the way he is. I know the Plexiglas enclosure is there to protect him (and the cashbox) but it seems the other way around, that the customers are being protected. It's as if he's a dangerous exhibit. Next to him is a tiny television, about the size of a toaster. Minuscule black-and-white figures are playing baseball. I speak to the huge man through a circular pattern of holes drilled into the half-inch-thick plastic:

"Could you do me the favor of telling me how to get to Bethesda?"

"Hmmmmm. Bethesda," the huge man says in a surprisingly high voice. He rolls the word around in his mouth again. "Bethesda."

A short man in a three-piece suit, who has come up behind me and is waiting to pay for his gas, breaks in. He taps his shiny loafer against the cement. "I can tell you," he offers. "It's simple. You go along here on Little River Turnpike until you get to the Beltway ramp, and then you follow the sign for Frederick until you see the sign for Wisconsin Avenue, Bethesda. Get off there."

"You sure?" says the huge man inside. "You sure he don't go toward Baltimore?"

"No no no no no. If he goes toward Baltimore, he's going to end up going across the Wilson Bridge, you know, toward the Cap Center."

"Yeah. What I'm saying is he goes across the bridge, he's in Maryland, right? He *keeps* going, he gets to Bethesda, right?"

"Actually…you're right, you're absolutely right." The short man turns toward me, seesawing his palms in the air like a set of scales. "So—you're in luck. You go toward Baltimore, you go toward Frederick. You can't miss; either way gets you to Bethesda."

"But I don't go toward Richmond?" I ask.

"Hell no," says the huge man. "Don't fool around with Richmond. That won't get you nowhere near Bethesda."

A woman in a plaid dress has stepped up next to the short man. "Wait a sec," she says. She holds a credit card between her fingers by its edges, as if she wants to avoid getting fingerprints on it. "Wouldn't it be easier to take the parkway?"

For a second I feel I'll never escape these well-meaning people, that one of them will volunteer to escort me to Bethesda, to the very house on Camelot Drive where I am to meet up with Moro. "Well thanks," I say, drifting back from the window. "Thanks a lot."

I can hear them continuing to discuss the matter as I get back in the car. "Isn't there construction on the parkway, around Spout Run?" the short man is saying. I drive off and leave them to it.

I have trouble judging the relative speed of my car and the other vehicles; there's a tense moment as I merge onto the Beltway.

What if the woman has come out of the house on Camelot Drive already? What if Moro isn't there when I get there? What will I do? Stay? Or go back to the Heritage Motor Lodge? The whole operation is moving beyond my control.

It occurs to me that the police suspicion of Mariah and her boyfriend is bad. Bad. The kids will call the police to set things straight. Or the police will arrest them. Either way, they will be effectively out of reach. It will be the same as if they'd sought protective custody.

Construction on a bridge funnels the traffic from four lanes into two, slowing it to a crawl. The two lanes blocked off for repair are illuminated by incredibly bright lights. The workers, saturated with light, look as if they're on a soundstage, enacting a scene. A large sign welcomes me to Maryland, "The Free State."

I exit the Beltway at Wisconsin Avenue as the short man instructed. Wisconsin: the name takes me back to that luncheon with my mother, that stellar moment when she first told me Mariah had been located in Janesville, Wisconsin. I stop at the street corner to study my map.

The numbers on the houses are hard to see. I drive a couple of blocks on Camelot Drive before I encounter a number that's legible. I'd get out and walk but I'm afraid another helpful American will materialize and offer me assistance. So I keep on driving until I spot Moro's car. I pull up in front of it and turn off the ignition. When I see that he's not sitting inside the car, I'm not sure what to do. He could be inside the town house, along with the woman, waiting for me. Or he could be under arrest. The police could be inside, waiting for me. Possibly Mariah and the boy had driven here already in their gray car. *They* could be inside. The thought produces a rush of sensation in my chest. My eyes scan up and down the street, and it subsides; there's no small gray car in sight. I sit in my Pontiac Sunbird wondering what to do. Should I go knock on the door? Should I wait? I look at my watch. I'll stay in the car, I decide, for half an hour.

The heat seeps in and I have to roll down the window. Something in the motor ticks on; the sound of some type of insect whirs in the background.

My sense of time is unreliable; I have to keep checking my watch. The night edges in around me. I try to close my eyes, drift into the reverie, but the purity of my desire for revenge has been compromised. My attempts to slip into the reverie are impeded—by Ferguson's desperate thrashing in the bathtub, by Ebinger's eyes above the gag, by the urine dripping through the couch, by the bravery of Dolores Ebinger in the face of Moro's brutality. Out of a sense of the woman's need for dignity, I pretended not to notice that control of her bladder had been lost. Moro *really* didn't notice; he drank a beer and belched.

A fissure of sorrow for what has happened is widening inside me. I can no longer ignore my revulsion for Moro and the things he has done. Things I have permitted. Things I have instigated.

Finally I can't stand the confinement of the car any longer and I step out, into the night. It seems portentous, that small step out, as if I'm stepping into a new zone, where different laws are operative.

The door opens before I knock. The sweeping gesture of welcome. *"Cap-i-tán,"* Moro says, in the unctuous voice a maître d' might use for a generous regular. "Come *in*. It's more comfortable inside."

He has his jacket off. The shoulder holster is exposed. It has a brutal look. He holds an open bag of Doritos in one hand, which he extends toward me.

I decline.

"The lady wasn't home yet. I felt conspicuous on the street after a while so I came inside."

"But how did you get in?"

He shrugs. "It was easy."

"On television," I begin, "I saw the news. They think the kids did it."

"Wait a minute." His hand pauses a little distance from his mouth, with a Dorito pinched between his fingers. "You're saying?"

"The police think the kids did it."

"What?"

"And one of them is not dead," I say in a surprised, excited voice, as if there's some pleasure in delivering this news. "One of them is in critical condition."

Moro bites into the Dorito. It seems to make an unbelievably loud noise. "No shit."

"So what if the police come here? Won't they figure the same thing you did? That this is the logical place for them to go?"

"Hmmm."

"I mean if it was your logical deduction, wouldn't it—"

"Hold on," Moro says, and I hear what he's heard outside: a car. Twin oblongs of light slide across the wall and up toward the ceiling, then vanish. "You take the gun, *Capitán*," Moro says, removing it from the holster and pressing it into my hand.

The thunk of a car door. The tapping of high heels.

"Mommy's home," Moro whispers as he glides toward the door.

Chapter Twenty-Seven

ROLANDO
Heat Lightning

THE KEY IN the lock. We can hear her outside, humming. I don't recognize the tune. The smell of tobacco precedes her through the door, which Moro is standing behind. It works just the way I've seen it on television: she steps into the room, he grabs her from behind, hand over her mouth. The humming stops but there is almost no other sound despite her struggle. Then she sees me, or more precisely, the gun, and her strength is compromised by fear. Moro maneuvers her over toward the couch. The motions caused by her resistance and his forceful-ness turn their halting progress into a kind of debased waltz.

"Get me some tape," he says in Spanish, gesturing with his chin toward the green duffel bag on the floor near the couch. "A long piece for her hands and a shorter one for a gag. And a roll of gauze."

She submits quietly to my binding her hands in front of her. Moro reproves me: "Behind is more secure, *Capitán*." But she fights intently, shaking her head wildly so he can't hold it, when she realizes Moro intends to gag her.

"Take it easy, take it easy," he says in his remote voice as he jams the gauze in her mouth. "We're not going to hurt you. We just want to make sure you're a good listen-er." His crazy heh-heh-heh cackle.

As he finishes sticking the wide adhesive tape to her face, smoothing it down with his hand to make sure it adheres, she gives a sharp kick to his shin. Instantly he smacks her across the bridge of her nose with the back of his hand. Water gushes from her eyes.

Moro rubs his shin. "*Cunt.*" He tears off a length of tape from the roll, biting a notch in it to get it started, pushes her back on the couch, and roughly secures her feet.

She snuffles through the gag, her eyes squeezed shut. She brings her tied-together hands up to rub at her tears. My own hands dangle at my sides.

"A little pain is good, actually," Moro says. "It extends the attention span."

The woman has a pretty face framed by dark curly hair. She's slumped on the couch like a sack of rags, still rubbing her eyes with her knuckles. She's trying to fight down the panic and figure out what's happening to her. I see that the piece of tape cut for her gag is too long. On one side of her head it extends past her ear and into her hair. Her hair is stuck to it. I imagine the pain it will cause her when it is removed. The thought produces a skittery discomfort in my chest. I turn away.

Moro is tapping his foot on the floor. It has an ominous sound, even to me. I feel a surge of compassion for the woman and even an odd sense of camaraderie. We're in this together; neither one of us has any idea what Moro is going to do next.

"So, *Capitán*. You wish to explain the situation to Mrs. Ferguson or should I?" I shake my head. I don't even want to look at her.

I noticed the shocked twitch of her body as he said her name. Now she breathes in a rapid, panicked way as she registers the new information, that she is not a random victim.

Moro starts in a businesslike tone. "Now you don't strike me as a woman who's looking for trouble."

She wags her head no decisively, almost eagerly. Her compliance reminds me that during the dirty war, detainees were routinely beaten before interrogation, before they even had a chance to cooperate. The softening-up guaranteed a receptive mood.

"Look what happens when you act without thinking," Moro goes on. "It's a valuable lesson." He pauses to let it sink in. "But let me assure you that nothing *more* will happen to you unless you *cause* it to happen. Do you understand me?"

Enthusiastic nodding. She's in that receptive mood now.

I feel responsible for the pink blotch on her cheek, for the star of blood on her nose where Moro's ring must have nicked her.

"Good," Moro says, as if they've agreed on a deal. "Good." The air conditioner hums.

It's his remoteness. It's Moro's remoteness that really bothers me. He's there, he's focused, he's intelligent, but he's not connected to you except on a very superficial level. He pulls his lips back from his teeth again. His smile. His smile alone seems lethal.

"I've been here for a couple of hours, and you've received three telephone calls. Altogether there are five messages on your machine. Kind of unusual, don't you think? I mean it's late for telephone calls, I'd say, wouldn't you?" He takes the cigarette package out of his shirt pocket and taps one free. "Actually, I know who's calling you." He lifts his eyebrows and looks directly at her. "Your son."

It's as if an immense jolt of energy courses through her. Her eyes expand with alarm and her body seems to surge with power. I would not be surprised to see her somehow rip free of the tape on her hands and feet, despite its strength. Moro plays the messages; we sit there listening. Each one is preceded by a beep.

"Hello, Mom? It's Ryan. God. I wish you were there." We hear him breathing for a while. *"I'll call back, okay?"*

"Why do you have to be out?" A sigh. *"Damn. If you get there, stay there, okay? I'm in trouble."*

"It's me again. I'll call back."

"It's me, Ryan again. Where are you? Don't call Dad, okay? That's one thing. Uhhhhh. I didn't have a fight with him, it's nothing like that, just— I'll...explain it when I talk to you. Just don't call him, don't go there, okay? I'll call back."

"This is me again. Where the hell are you? Look, it's midnight. I can't call anymore tonight, I'll have to call you in the morning. At the crack of dawn, six or six-thirty, so be ready for that, okay? I love you, Mom. Don't worry, I'm all right."

Moro presses a button. The tape rewinds with a high whine. The messages erase. The liquid crystal display of the machine's message counter reads zero.

Moro lights a cigarette and exhales slowly. "I expect he'll call again." He takes another deep drag. Smoke floats out with his words. "You didn't catch the late news, did you?" She shakes her head almost despairingly. The gag is crumpled into the opening of her mouth, giving it a caved-in, toothless look. "I didn't either," Moro goes on. "But my colleague did"—he gestures to me—"and apparently

your son—Ryan, isn't it?—well it seems he's wanted by
the police."

The woman looks back and forth from Moro to me,
confused. Then confusion gives way to further agitation.
Her agitation starts to build in me as well, as if my nervous
system has formed some sympathetic bond with hers. My
heartbeat accelerates. My hands clench my knees in such a
bleak and anxious grip it makes my bones hurt.

Moro sighs. "The police think your son murdered his
girlfriend's parents."

The woman tries to make eye contact with me, but I
can't bring myself to look at her.

"Mariah Ebinger's parents," Moro goes on. "Do you
know her?"

Mrs. Ferguson nods.

There's an alarming lightness in my chest, as if my
heart is dissolving.

"Well, he didn't murder them, of course," Moro says,
dragging on his cigarette. "I know that for a fact."

Moro is completely relaxed. He has one knee crossed
over the other. He might be sitting on a bench in San Telmo
discussing the different species of aquarium fish he hopes
to acquire, or a polo match, or the best chardonnays. The
woman, on the other hand, forced to sit and listen to him
without being able to express any but the most primitive
response, is so compressed by tension that she looks as if
she might explode. It seems cruel to me, Moro's indolent
recital of the facts. Every hour, I learn something new about
him that I don't like.

"So we're going to sit here until Ryan calls again."
He makes a circular, inclusive gesture with his cigarette-
holding hand. "The three of us. And when he calls, you're
going to tell us where he is. So that's pretty simple, right?"
He drops his cigarette into the plush beige carpet and lets
it smolder there for a moment until he grinds it out with
his swiveling foot. I am as shocked as the woman must be

at this casual barbarity. "Oh, oh, oh," he says. "I almost forgot. I want to put your mind at ease about yourself and your son. We're not interested in you, we don't care about you, we have no interest in harming you. I don't want you to be *frightened*. It's the girl we want, you see. His girlfriend, Mariah. Not you. Not your son."

The woman looks more confused than relieved. The pungent smell of burned wool from the rug hangs in the air. I hasten to reassure her.

"It's true," I say earnestly. "We won't hurt you. We won't hurt your son." I speak with decisiveness and authority, hoping I'm communicating my wishes to Moro. I don't want anything to happen to the woman or her son.

The window shimmers through the gauzy drapes. The sky outside is shaking with light. It takes me a moment to figure out what this is: heat lightning.

"It's an old score to be settled with the young lady," I hear myself say. "It doesn't involve you at all." I smile at her, trying for reassurance, but my words strike me as insane. "A score to be settled." "Young lady." I try to revive in my mind the sweetness of Liliana's smile, the adorable face of Elena. I pull out my wallet. I would like to show my photographs of Elena to the woman. To show her what has been lost.

But of course the identification inside is not in my name. And smiling out at me from the plastic window is not my sweet Elena but a photograph of a little boy I've never seen before. Moro has provided all this. There is a photo of a woman too, and another little boy. "Pocket litter," they call it.

"The thing is, Mrs. Ferguson," Moro says in a polite voice, "—or may I call you Betty?" He lights another cigarette. "The thing is, Bet-ty, that I must warn you about giving anything away to your son over the telephone."

Her face is wrenched up. Tears are dripping from her eyes. It's as if her face is a sponge, being squeezed.

"This is what Mrs. Ebinger did, attempt a warning, and—of course, in her case, there was some justification for the risk because it *is* her daughter we're after—but anyway, I was forced to..." He sighs and looks up toward the ceiling. "Well, never mind."

I had returned the gun to him earlier. He picks it up now and looks at it thoughtfully. Then he holds it to her ear, twisting the barrel so that it is lodged within her ear. She grimaces and holds her head very still.

"Let me tell you how it's going to work, Betty. When the telephone rings, we'll let it ring exactly three times. Three. At the end of the third ring—*exactly*—you are to pick it up. The captain will be picking up the extension in your bedroom." He leans down and blows along the gun barrel; I see the curly hair near her ear puff and twirl from his breath. "I don't think you'll make any mistakes, will you, Betty?" He wiggles the gun slightly and she shifts her head minutely, half an inch to the left and another half an inch to the right. "You'll find out where he is, you'll take us to him. And then—" He withdraws the gun and smiles. "—we'll leave you and your son tied up and locked in your car, in a location where you will surely be discovered within a short time."

She nods almost imperceptibly. There's a red circular impression of the gun barrel visible in the delicate flesh and cartilage of her ear. Moro replaces the gun in his shoulder holster.

The night drags on. Moro sits on a blue leather chair. I sit on the beige couch next to the woman. We watch television. *The Night of the Iguana* is on. Richard Burton, Ava Gardner, Deborah Kerr. It occurs to me that Richard Burton and Ava Gardner are dead. Even Mrs. Ferguson appears to be watching intently, involved in the fate of the old poet, the teenagers, the defrocked priest, the played-out woman making do with tropical diversion. The movie is interrupted amazingly often by ads for obscure devices and services.

We sit in suspended animation, waiting for the telephone to ring. Every once in a while Moro yawns, I stretch, one of us clears our throat. Moro saunters into the kitchen, makes some coffee, eats an orange.

I want the phone call to come and I don't want the phone call to come.

Once, we release the woman's feet and allow her to use the toilet. I volunteer to help her, hoping to protect her from Moro, but the procedure is still humiliating for both of us. I have to pull down her underpants, lift up her dress. I turn my head while she urinates. She could kick me easily but I know she won't. I pull the panties up again. She tries to catch my eye, but I refuse to look at her.

Moro insists on retaping her feet. "Why take the chance?" he says when I say I don't think it's necessary. It occurs to me that Moro could turn on me just as casually as he pulled the trigger on that man who came to his door in his bathrobe.

The movie finally comes to an end. I almost cry when the old poet finally dies. We start watching something called *Little Darlings*. It's about girls at camp having a contest to see which one can lose her virginity first. The night fades into a milky dawn.

When it rings, it sounds as if the telephone is inside my brain.

Chapter Twenty-Eight

JACK HULTIN
Rigmarole

YOU COULD HAVE knocked me over with a feather, honest to Christ. When McVay called me in because the responding officers found that note at the Ebinger house with my name on it and the case number, I couldn't hardly believe what he was telling me. A double homicide? Plus assault with intent? I almost shit. I would have bet real money that by the time I did the follow-up on the Ebinger case, the girl would be back home.

The key to it being she didn't take her purse. When the parents told me that, I just about closed my notebook up right there. Teenaged girls don't hardly go to the bathroom without their purse, I can tell you that. Let alone run away from home.

The way I saw it, this was one of those impulse deals. The girl got mad; she took off. You get a feel for these things after a while. The family for one thing. The parents weren't mad—they were worried. That's unusual, believe it or not. Most of the time, in a runaway situation, the parents being worried is not what makes them call the authorities. Calling the police is a way to step up the stakes, play hardball, put the matter on a serious footing. Normally, there's been trouble with the kid before, the parents are already in some kind of intervention program, there's drugs, there's a juvenile history, there's something.

But not with this Ebinger girl, see. This was the first time; the girl had never run away before. I did my best to reassure the parents, in fact, because when a girl's been missing for a few hours, you're not thinking foul play or anything like that, not when she's sixteen years old and there's reason to believe she's off with her boyfriend.

So when McVay calls me in and starts asking me to fill in between the lines, so to speak, of the missing person's report I filed on Mariah Ebinger, naturally I'm curious. He puts me off; he won't tell me anything until he finishes questioning me. Doesn't want to "compromise my perceptions" is the way he puts it. That's McVay for you. He always talks like that, we call him "the professor."

So McVay's sitting there telling me two people were found dead in the Ebinger house and a third is hanging on by a thread, and it just floors me, I'm like *what*, you gotta be kidding. The mother is dead, McVay says, the *boyfriend's father* is dead. Arthur Ebinger is in intensive care. Clinging to life. And there's *another* guy on Allison Drive, two blocks away from the Ebinger address, got shot the same day. I hear he's gonna make it, but he's still unconscious. It might be days before we can question him. Officially, the incidents are not related, but no one buys that. That's a crock anyway because the boy himself, Ryan Ferguson, reported the Allison shooting on one of his 911 calls.

I don't know who leaked the initial story to the press but they are naturally having a field day. Maybe you can't keep a thing like this quiet for very long—too many people involved. The press is saying killing spree, night of terror, Dog Days murders; they are bringing up that teenager and his girlfriend who went on a killing binge twenty years ago or whatever, they are really going to town on this. Headquarters is a goddamned zoo with these reporters and cameramen and cables and lights and all. And the press don't know the half of it yet.

The M.E.'s report came in last night. It isn't just these kids killed their parents. What we're talking about is *torture*. You won't be hearing about that on your evening news because the lid is clamped down on this thing tight as a tick. And it better stay that way. You start letting out details and you get nutball confessions like you wouldn't believe. You start releasing specifics and you got no easy way to say "this guy is full of shit" because he's confessed, say, to using a rifle when the murder weapon is a revolver or whatever. Chaff from the wheat, like the professor says.

Of course in this case the natural suspects are the kids. But they are just suspects, no matter how the press is playing up the crazed teenaged lovers angle. There's some conflicting data which the press is cognizant of, but they are not bothering with it. Why muddy the waters, I guess they figure. But you can't ignore that two times the kids called 911. I heard the tapes with my own ears. It was the boy did the talking. Now why go and do that—call the authorities—if you just committed murder? You tell me.

Another thing: he didn't sound guilty, if you know what I mean. He sounded *worried* is what he sounded. The whole deal doesn't really make sense. He makes one call from his house, and in that call he reports that he suspects foul play at the girl's house on Gallagher, he suspects a man's been shot on Allison Drive, he claims he and the girl are being pursued by gunmen. Of course, by the time the police got to his house, responding to that call, the two kids are gone—which don't sit right.

Naturally, the responding officers go to the girl's house, and the door's right open, and just inside the door Arthur Ebinger's lying there on the brink of death, and then there's the two bodies. Next thing you know, there's an ambulance, the crime scene boys, all that. Naturally, the neighbors come out. Some of them are questioned briefly right then and there. Turns out one guy saw the kids at the house that morning when he was out walking the dog. Saw the kids, but never saw any two men the boy was talking about. That's why they put the APB out on the kids. When the kids called again, from the Giant, the responding officers, knowing what happened in that house, were nervous as hell, you can appreciate that. Still, it's hard to credit them letting the kids get away. The way I hear it, their vehicle being blocked was a contributing factor.

And the kids taking off like that—that really sealed it. Add to that the girl running away in the first place, which indicates some trouble in the family. And the fact is, you got no alternate suspects, your problem, in a word, being *motive*. So even though it's funny—the kids calling in, and especially calling in *twice*—you gotta think it's them that did it.

What we're thinking here is drug-induced. I mean most likely PCP involvement. Followed by remorse, which explains the telephone calls to 911. Maybe the kids were hoping the parents were still alive, that it was some kind of nightmare or whatever, that they *dreamed* it, that they didn't really do it. And then they had second thoughts about turning themselves in—or those fuckup troopers scared them off or whatever.

Press ever gets hold of the M.E. report, it will really be a circus, I'll tell you. Dolores Ebinger. Cause of death: heart failure. Victim found bound and gagged. Bruising around the face. Blows to the head. Concussion. Heart failure. We're talking about a lady who got scared to death here. This is bad enough.

But then Ferguson. Cause of death: suffocation. Cigarette burns in the armpits, genitalia, anus. Water aspirated in lungs. In other words, Ferguson was tortured, as was Ebinger.

I asked to be assigned to the case because of my early involvement, and McVay says, hell, yes, you specialize in Juvenile anyway, don't you Jack?

Arthur Ebinger is under armed guard at Alexandria Hospital. I checked on his condition this morning first thing. He's still critical but he's "stabilized," according to his doctors. We are to be notified immediately if there's any change in his condition.

Something's been nagging at me since last night, but I just couldn't put my finger on it until this morning. What it is I'm thinking is we got two kids here, we got four parents, right? What's wrong with this picture?

I'm thinking what about the boy's mother? Arthur Ebinger is under armed guard, the girl's mother and the boy's father are dead, but what about the fourth parent, the mother? If he has a mother, which no one has mentioned, the deal being the boy lived with his old man. It stands to reason someone besides me has thought of this angle, but I can't remember anyone mentioning the other mother to save my life. At the risk of him thinking I'm an idiot, I'm going to bring this to McVay's attention.

The neighbors have been questioned. That's how we found out the Fergusons were divorced. Mariah and Ryan both had address books, and we're working on compiling a list of their friends. Plus Schwartz is going down to the high school later this morning to explain the situation to the principal. We're hoping for full cooperation from the school. They'll want to organize some counseling effort too. The kids will be freaked out over this.

McVay has salt-and-pepper hair, never a hair out of place, and he always wears a suit. I swear to God the paper on his desk is six inches thick, though. I mean, his personal grooming is to a high standard, but his office is a pigsty. He was so friendly to me yesterday, but now when I knock on the doorjamb, he doesn't even look up from what he's reading: and when he does, I swear he can't even place me.

He says: "Yes?"

"I was thinking—"

He still doesn't look up, keeps writing. "Good. Increasingly rare activity."

I laugh, but he doesn't. "I was thinking about his mother," I say tentatively.

Now he does look up. "Whose mother?" He makes a rolling, hurry-it-up gesture with his hands.

"Ryan Ferguson's mother."

"Yeah," he says, meaning get on with it.

"Probably someone has already thought of this, but just in case, I was thinking...we posted a guard on Arthur Ebinger, but what about her? I mean probably someone has followed up on this, but..."

McVay sits straight up, pushes a button and yells into his intercom: "Schwartz! Get in here." Fifteen seconds later Mike Schwartz pokes his head through the doorway.

"Yo."

"The boy's mother. Ryan Ferguson's mother. Who is she? Where is she?"

"How the hell do I know?"

"Take—" He points to me.

"Jack Hultin."

"Take Hultin here and fucking find out. Find out who she is, where she lives, come back to me, don't take any action."

Of course it doesn't take us long, just a quick look in the Ferguson study at the address book sitting right there on the desk and we find her: Betty Ferguson. An address on Camelot Drive in Bethesda.

"She would have to live in Maryland, damn it," McVay complains with a sigh.

Jurisdictional problems are a way of life here, with D.C. and Maryland and Virginia in each other's pockets all the time. Cooperation is good except for once in a while. A few months back some jokers from D.C. Vice rounded up all the prostitutes on Fourteenth Street and drove them across the bridge to Virginia. I mean drove them like a cattle drive. Herded them. That must have been something, I'll tell you. Can you picture all those hookers in high heels—don't a single one of them wear flat shoes, I guarantee—marching across the bridge, carrying their shoes? I'll tell you the shit hit the fan over that one.

But that's unusual. We don't try to shove our problems off on each other, and we assist and help as much as possible. Still, it would have been simpler if Mrs. Ferguson lived in Virginia.

Bethesda. McVay details me and Schwartz to be the liaison officers. We brief the Montgomery County guys about the case, what we're dealing with here. There's a lot of rigmarole with this stuff of course: judges, search warrants, go-aheads from above. You can't just go busting into somebody's house, even for their own good.

We do a drive-by first, which points up nothing. There's no cars in the driveway. There's one car out front, could belong to anybody on the street, but we get DMV to ID it anyway. Turns out it's a rental. We take that down just in case it figures somehow. The kids, now, they're not old enough to rent a car.

Got to be drugs. Got to be. Everything is now, just about everything. You go to the courthouse, see how many cases don't have a drug component, you're gonna come up with zip, just about zero. I don't put the Montgomery County guys in the picture about the torture, but even without that they're thinking PCP. Any one of the more bizarre crimes usually got PCP involvement. Some woman in Southeast last year, she stabbed herself in the eyes. Her mind was gone, that's what they say. Even one time using PCP, they say it can cause "pinpoint lesions" on the brain. A bunch of times, your brain turns into mush, I guess; you don't know what the hell you're doing. Another woman a few months ago decapitated her baby and then she dismembered it. There was a history of instability there, but still, she was heavy into PCP.

On the street they call PCP boat. Loveboat. We learned all about it in training. Originally, it was used as a hog tranquilizer. Now cocaine is one thing—human beings been using coca leaf for thousands of years—but you should know you're asking for trouble if you go fooling around with swine tranquilizers. The human brain is different from the pig brain, of course. The pig brain is not evolved enough to suffer from hallucinations.

Eventually they go into Betty Ferguson's place with a SWAT team. Once they ascertain it's safe, Schwartz and I are allowed inside. The woman's not there; no one's there. I see an ashtray with a lot of cigarette butts, a Doritos bag crumpled up, beer cans around. Otherwise, the place is immaculate. Could be the kids were here partying, but it feels funny somehow. And then I see that cigarette burn in the carpet. I show it to Schwartz. I put my foot next to it. Look at this. Schwartzie, he shrugs, but that ground-out cigarette butt sticks with me. I get a shiver in my back, like someone walking on my grave.

We find out the woman is a paralegal, works at a law firm. From her secretary we learn she had a date last night. This guy is sleeping in, we wake him up. Does he ever not want to have this discussion. It was their first date. They went to an Orioles game. She'd left her car parked in the office lot and he'd driven her back to it. Last he saw her, she was driving off. He assumed she was going home.

I get back to headquarters, about eight-fifteen, and go in to see McVay. He nods his chin sit down. "So."

"I think the woman's a hostage."

He's shocked. He sits back, considers. "You think the kids...?"

"I don't think it's the kids. Here's the thing. There was a cigarette ground out into her wall-to-wall carpet, and that started me thinking. The cigarette burns on the victims, you know, plus a big ashtray full of cigarette butts at the woman's house and also, if I remember right, at the Ebinger house."

"I'm not with you."

"Did anyone think to ask? About these kids, I mean."

"You lost me, Jack."

"Here's the thing. Do they *smoke*?"

"Do they smoke." He's nodding his head. "I see what you mean. Because if they *don't*..." He nods his head some more and then he starts making calls, giving orders. Question the friends, check the girl's purse for tobacco in the bottom, matches, anything like that. Their rooms too, check the rooms.

"The thing is," McVay says, "if it isn't the kids, who the hell...?" He starts shaking his head like the numbers are never going to add up right.

Chapter Twenty-Nine

MARIAH
Engulfed

I REACH OVER TO turn off the alarm clock, but when my hand fumbles for it, I don't even find the bedside table. I keep on groping and my fingers brush up against what feels like wet grass, a sensation so unexpected that my eyes pop open. It's not what I expect: my table and lamp, the curtained window of my room. I'm looking at grass, moss, underbrush. It takes me a minute and then I remember.

Oh.

I wouldn't say my heart shrinks, but any enthusiasm for the dawning day instantly withers inside me. A weird feeling, as if I'm sinking inside my own skin. I can feel myself going down.

The beeping continues. I wish it would stop, I wish I could stay asleep, I wish I could wake up and everything would be different.

A daddy longlegs ambles into view not six inches from my face, and the sight of him so close makes me flinch. I sit up. Next to me Ryan moans and turns over. The light is green and misty; birds twitter and call overhead. Tiny droplets of dew are beaded up on everything: the grass, the moss, the red cloth of the sleeping bag. Ryan groans again and shifts up, onto his elbow. Finally the beeping noise stops. "Oh God. That's right. Got to call my mother."

We fold up our stuff, hide it, start walking toward the telephone at the marina. I feel unbelievably grubby. I wish I had my toothbrush.

We don't talk much. Ryan has a grim look and he walks purposefully. I'm in flip-flops and my toe hurts. I have to hurry to keep up. When we get to the dam, we both stop. In the mist the lake is flat and still, and there's a perfect reflection in it of the trees and the sky. It's so perfect that for a second I feel suspended between two realities. Except for the contact of my feet with the ground, I wouldn't be able to tell which are the real trees and sky and which is the mirror image. A bird rises up from the top of a tree. In the reflection it dives down, as if it's jumping off the earth. Ryan squeezes my hand; we start off again.

This time she's home, Ryan's mother, at last. She's coming. I listen to Ryan giving her directions. He doesn't tell her much over the phone, says he'll explain it all when she gets here.

All we have to do now is wait. Ryan figures maybe an hour. The johns are locked. We go down to the lake and splash water on our faces. It smells funky, and afterward I feel even grubbier than before. There's nothing to dry off with except the inside of my shirt. Ryan dunks his whole head under the water and then shakes it like a dog. While we're down there, a bunch of ducks come rushing toward us, quacking like crazy. When they see we don't have food, they settle back to just floating, waiting.

We end up in the parking lot by the main entrance, where we're meeting Ryan's mother. The lot is rimmed by those telephone-pole-type logs laid on their sides. We sit on one of them, scuffing our feet in the gravel.

Now that I feel like it's going to be over, I can't wait for Mrs. Ferguson to get here. We got to the phone before six-thirty. It's almost seven-thirty now. That's an hour already. We thought she might be here by now, but I guess you couldn't expect her to just hop into the car the second the phone rang. I'm sure she was sound asleep when Ryan called. I guess you couldn't expect her to fly out the door. You have to give even a mother time to brush her teeth.

I try not to think about my own mother, her voice on the phone, the way it got away from her: "I'm afraid you have the wrong number." I try not to think about my mother at all, or my father or any of that. If I do, little panicky breaths start up and there's a sickening, dizzy, stupid feeling in my mind. I try not to think at all. I try to just wait.

I'm hungry. I'm stiff all over from sleeping on the ground. My throat is sore. I feel so grubby I can't even stand it. Ryan too. His face is covered with stubble. His eyes are bloodshot. We're a mess.

"I love you, Ryan," I blurt out, but my voice sounds so desperate and out of control, I'm embarrassed.

"Mariah," he says slowly, and puts his arm around me and pulls my head toward his. "Oh, Mariah," he says. His body gives a couple of big shakes next to mine. I'm afraid he's crying. I kiss his cheek. I squeeze his hand. I can't think of anything to say.

We just sit there staring at the road, waiting for his mother to drive up. The entrance booth—where you pay to get in—is closed now, of course. The metal arm is down to keep out cars. The booth sits at the crest of a small hill. Suddenly, down at the bottom of the hill, a red car comes swerving slowly into view.

Ryan jumps up. "That's her, that's the car!" The red color of her car is so bright, it almost seems like a hallucination in the misty green light. We walk toward the toll gate. The car lurches to a swerving stop. "God," Ryan says, "is she drunk? Man." We're holding hands; Ryan gives mine a squeeze.

Now that we're closer, we see that there's someone else in the car.

"Who's that? Her boyfriend?"

"I guess."

His mother just sits there. It strikes me as funny. I expect her to come out and hug him, I guess, but maybe she's pissed off. Maybe she's pissed off about getting woken up or about Ryan missing his exams. Maybe we're just generally on her list.

We're at the edge of the parking lot. Ryan is acting goofy and melodramatic now, bowing to her, flinging kisses to her with both hands. He always acts a little weird and boyish around his mother. "Thank you, Mom!" he yells. "Thank you! Thank you!" Still she doesn't move, she doesn't even roll down her window. Ryan tosses me a look, a little tick of worry in his eyebrows.

We're close to the car now, maybe ten yards from it. Ryan and I both get the picture at the exact same moment because he stops walking at the identical instant I feel the breath going out of me. Through the windshield his mom's face is going through some strange contortions. Next to her is not her boyfriend, but the man who came to the door of my house, the man who said: "Mah-rye-ah."

"Oh shit," Ryan says.

The man lifts up a gun and holds the barrel against Ryan's mom's temple. We all stay where we are for a second, staring at each other. In the backseat the other man's head appears as he sits up. I'm not surprised to see him. He gets out and walks toward us.

My surprise at the men being here only lasts an instant, and then I'm saturated with fear and resignation. I feel myself giving in, all the way down to my bones. Why did I ever think we'd be able to get away?

The older man grips my upper arm tightly in his hand. It seems to me my flesh is moving under his grip, going soft, dissolving. It feels as if my bones are melting, the strength is going out of me fast. I barely have the energy to keep standing up. A little crying moan from my mouth: "Ohhhhhh."

Ryan says: "What the fuck? *Mommmmm?* What the *fuck*?"

Ryan's mom is getting out of the car, prodded by the first man. Now we can see that her hands are tied behind her with duct tape. That's why the car was swerving. The man was actually driving, not her. "Oh honey," Ryan's mother says in a voice full of regret and pain.

"On the ground," the man says. "Facedown."

"But—" Mrs. Ferguson starts, and then he gives her a shove. With her hands tied together she can't break her fall. She goes down hard.

"Hey," Ryan says, stepping toward his mother. The man lunges forward and smacks Ryan hard across the face with the back of his hand. Ryan is unprepared for the blow, and he too sprawls onto the ground.

Ryan's mother begins sobbing hysterically. She's lying on her side, her face on the gravel. In between shallow breaths she's saying, "You *said*, you said, you said, you said, you said."

The other man hasn't moved. He and I are just standing there, with him gripping my arm.

Ryan gets to his hands and knees, but then the dark-haired man puts his foot squarely in the middle of Ryan's back and pushes him hard down to the ground again. Ryan's head bounces against the ground. I lunge toward him, but the man who's holding me tightens his grip on my arm. He nudges the barrel of his gun against my ribs, a reminder.

"Hugo," says the man holding me. "Let's tie the boy up and leave them here in the car. Let's get out of here."

A low moan comes from Ryan's mother.

"Get the tape," Hugo says. "And shut that bitch up. Come on, turn over," he says to Ryan. He rolls Ryan over with his foot and then puts his foot up against Ryan's neck. Ryan keeps his eyes closed, squeezed shut. His face is bleeding, his cheek, his eyebrow, his lip. Little bits of gravel are stuck in the oozy cut above his eye. He has dirt in his mouth. The man holding me stuffs the gun into his pocket and yanks me toward the car with him. Without letting go of my arm, he reaches into the backseat and pulls out a duffel bag. He tosses it to the other man.

"Get up!" the man orders Ryan, who does as he is told. Very quickly his arms are taped together behind his back with duct tape; a roll of gauze is shoved between his teeth, two pieces of tape are slapped across his mouth. Tape is looped around each of his ankles, leaving a few inches of tape between his legs. It all happens so fast, it's like watching a cowboy at a rodeo, roping a calf. The man rips open a package, then pushes another roll of gauze into Mrs. Ferguson's screaming mouth, slaps a piece of tape across it. Her legs are bound as well, in the same manner as Ryan's. The man tells them both to lie facedown on the ground. It's hard to do that when you're bound hand and foot. Mrs. Ferguson is too slow about it and the man gives her a shove. When they're both down, he places his foot in the center of Ryan's back.

I watch everything as if I'm a spectator, as if I'm not even part of it. When it's my turn to be tied up, I don't even resist. Where did I learn to give in like this? It feels like I'm practicing to be dead.

The man who was holding my wrist does the job on me. His motions are jerky and hurried. He breathes in short, rushed breaths, almost as if he's the one who's frightened. He ties my hands in front of me instead of behind.

There's a plastic taste in my mouth from the duct tape. He grabs my arm again and I stiffen, expecting to be shoved to the ground, but he just holds my arm in his hand.

The man named Hugo says: "Well, should we do it here, *Capitán*? Or somewhere else? What do you think?"

"What? Do what?"

"You know—" He nods his chin meaningfully. "— the boy and his mother." Ryan squirms under his foot, rolling his shoulders to try to get up. Hugo raises his foot and chops his heel into Ryan's back; Ryan's body contracts sharply.

"We're going to let them go," the man who's holding me says in a clear, surprised voice.

Hugo laughs at this, an ugly sniggering sound that expands into a cackle. When he starts talking again, it's as if the other man hasn't said a word about letting anyone go. "Possibly not here, although…" He looks around with an assessing look, as if trying to decide whether this is a good picnic spot or not. "…there's nothing really wrong with right here. Maybe we'll get them in the car. Tidier that way. It's tough to cram a dead body in a car, believe me, you can't imagine how tough until you try it." He looks at his watch. "It's another hour until the place officially opens, according to the sign, but I'll bet some personnel will show up within the next half hour. We better get a move on."

He pulls out his gun and looks at it. "No real reason to put them in the car, I guess. We'll be well out of here by the time they're found. You want me to turn them over, *Capitán*? You want to see their faces?"

Without knowing I'm going to do it, suddenly I find myself hurtling through the air toward him. It doesn't accomplish anything. I just land hard on the ground, not even close to him.

"Fuck, Rolando," Hugo says. "Keep hold of her."

"Let them go," Rolando says. "Just as we said. Put them in the car; tie them together, back to back, leave them here."

"Alive?" He sniggers again. "Sure. Why not call them a cab. Or maybe—let's buy them a ticket to Disney World."

"I want to let them go."

"You are crazy, *Capitán*. There's no way. We are not going to let them go."

"We'll leave them tied up in the car. They don't know us, they don't know where we're going. In fact, I'll get them in the car, tie them together. You go and get the other car. By the time they're discovered and released—"

"You think they don't alert airports anymore? You think your face won't be on an Identi-Kit drawing inside two hours? Besides, even if we get clean away, you think this will never come back on you? It's gone too far now, *Capitán*, we have to make a clean sweep, we are not in a position to... Let me put it this way: You think they're never going to put two and two together back in B.A.? Grow up, *Capitán*. We are not going to leave behind a couple of witnesses."

Ryan thrashes hard under Hugo's foot. Hugo shakes his head disparagingly and there's a little patronizing smile on his face as he draws his gun from his waistband. In my head I start going: oh God oh God oh God oh God. My eyes slam shut and squeeze tight. There's a shot and a scream explodes in the air and I don't even know if it's me that screamed or not. Inside my head the sound of the shot seems to produce a blinding light, and for a second I wonder if it's me that's been shot.

But when I open my eyes, I see that it's not me, it's not Ryan, it's not Ryan's mother. Rolando is looking at the gun in his hand with a startled expression. And the man, Hugo, is toppling to the ground as if his bones are collapsing, as if he's dissolving from the feet up. His gun goes clattering down on the gravel and skids away from him. He tries to rise up on his hands and knees, and I see that the wound is in his chest. There's a big, shiny stain on his white shirt, spreading. His face looks gray, as if already he's lost so much blood that there isn't enough left. He manages to get up on his hands and knees only for a moment. Then he collapses again and his head sinks down to the ground, his cheek against the gravel. When he opens his mouth to speak, a pink froth comes out, no sound.

Ryan has somehow managed to get to his feet; he comes teetering toward me. The gun barrel presses into my temple and Rolando says, in a decisive voice, "Don't. Don't do it. I'll kill her, I'll fucking kill her, stay where you are." Ryan stops. We all stand there and look down at Hugo. His eyes are staring and fixed. There's a pool of blood under him. Rolando picks up Hugo's gun and sticks it in the waistband of his pants. He waves his own gun vaguely toward Ryan. "Take your mother and get the hell out of here." But Ryan doesn't move or turn away. He just looks at me, and then he actually takes a couple of steps toward us. I don't want him to. The man will kill him too. I look away. I look down at my feet.

There's a pattern in the gravel that looks like the shape of Africa. I see the cut on my toe, the dirty dried blood. I can't seem to feel my toes anymore; they're too far away. I'm very cold.

Rolando heaves a sigh and shakes his head. He walks over to Mrs. Ferguson and helps her up. He half drags her over to the car and pulls open the back door. It's awkward, but finally he swings her feet inside. Ryan goes in the other door, but at first he won't fit. Rolando has to get in the front seat and move it forward to make room for Ryan's feet. I just stand there. When both Ryan and his mother are inside the car, Rolando rolls down the windows a few inches and then from the front seat he leans over and tapes their bound hands together. They wind up slumped on the seat back to back, looking out opposite windows.

Rolando turns his attention to me. What I think is that we're going to go down the road toward the "other car" he mentioned before, but instead he takes my arm and we head toward the water. It's slow; I can only walk in tiny mincing steps, like a woman who's had her feet bound.

The rowboats are in a line, turned upside down on the sand. Rolando sticks the second gun in his belt, rolls one of the boats over until it's righted, then shoves it down toward the water. It's not easy. He has to stretch his arms out and push hard; the boat makes a grinding sound as it goes over the gravelly sand. It leaves a smooth path behind it, grooved in the center. When he's got it down halfway into the water, he heads for the rental shed. It's padlocked shut. He shakes the door, then tries to break the lock with the butt of his gun, banging at it furiously. Finally he steps back, takes aim, shoots. Once, twice, three times. The noise is incredible. It seems to drive the last shred of hope out of me.

When I open my eyes, he's coming toward me with a pair of oars. He stops a few feet from me, pulls one of the guns out of his waistband, then flings it out into the water. We both watch it go under.

He approaches the boat. The oarlocks dangle by galvanized chains. He lifts them, slides them into their sockets, fits the oars into them. Then he picks me up and sets me on the seat in the stern, pushes until the bottom stops scraping and the boat floats free. He steps right into the knee-high water in his new-looking shiny black loafers. Then he swings himself into the boat and sits on the center thwart, bracing his dripping feet. He begins to row, with firm, smooth strokes. His mouth is set hard; he doesn't look at me.

I watch the blades cut into the water, dip in and out. I watch the ripples on the water spreading out from the oars. I keep expecting that we'll glide to a stop, that this man Rolando will pull out his gun and shoot me, but instead he keeps on rowing. Every breath I take seems to push my heart a little deeper into my chest. My mind is fading too, already losing clarity. It's almost as if I'm dead already.

Chapter Thirty

MARIAH
Counterclockwise

WE ROW FOR a long time in the milky light, around and around and around the lake in a counterclockwise direction. At first I think about what I can do, how I can get away. If I throw myself at him, could I knock him down, might he hit his head? When I experiment with tiny movements, it's clear that I couldn't even get enough forward momentum to get close to him. All I'd be able to do would be to dump myself on the floor of the boat.

He rows and rows. Half-moons of sweat appear under his arms, then the sweat spreads, a darkness around his waistband. Eventually his whole shirt is wet, his face is slick, drops of sweat roll off his eyebrows and make dark splotches on his light-gray pants.

After a while my heartbeat seems to become synchronized to the stroke of the oars. We have to stop eventually, I know that; he can't row forever. I try not to think about it. I'm afraid that when we do stop, it will be time for me to die.

The glary ball of sun rises higher; we row on and on in the white morning. Birds call in the woods and sometimes the geese begin honking or the flocks of ducks rise up from the water in a ruffle of quacking. It seems as if we've been out here for a long time, at least an hour, maybe more. I realize my sense of time is unreliable, but still, other people should be here by now, I think—joggers, or people fishing, park workers—but I don't see anyone, anyone at all. Eventually someone will come and find the body in the parking lot. Eventually someone will find Ryan and his mother in their car. Eventually, someone will call for help.

I'm not sure anyone can help me.

I shut my eyes and listen to the sound the rowing makes. I concentrate on the sensation of the boat cutting through the water. Then suddenly the rowing stops. The boat glides.

My heart skips a beat, then it thuds in my ears and a thick plume of fear rises from my stomach. It floods into my throat, spreads along my arms and legs; my fingertips prickle.

When I open my eyes, I see that we're about in the middle of the lake. Rolando tilts the oars so the handles drop into the boat; the blades angle up toward the sky, dripping water.

"Do you know me?" he asks. He speaks in English. A clipped British accent.

I shake my head. No. My lips move and flatten inside the tape. My mouth tastes of adhesive.

A sigh. "I am Rolando Carrera, your uncle, from Argentina." He speaks in a polite, explanatory voice, as if we're long lost relatives meeting for the first time in the living room of some mutual acquaintance. "And you— you are María Teresa Aguilar. My sister, Gabriela, was your mother. She was a very great friend of my wife. My wife—" Suddenly he stops talking and looks away. I see his chest heave; tears glitter in the rims of his eyelids. "A very great friend of my wife, Liliana." He draws a shaky breath and throws his head back. A spray of sweat flies off his hair. He continues looking up at the sky as he speaks. "When you were four years old, your best friend in the world was my daughter...my daughter..." He squeezes the name out: "Elena. My daughter Elena." His voice breaks and he stops talking.

I close my eyes. *Argentina. Mother. Gabriela. María. Elena.* The way he pronounced the name María resonates through my memory.

I open my eyes. He's holding his face in his hands. He's strong, well-built. His skin is tan, black hairs curl up from his muscular arms. A gold watch glints on his wrist.

My uncle.

Rolando.

His hands come away from his face and he reaches toward his waistband. The breath goes out of me, but it's purely a reflex of my body; the truth is that I feel unafraid and strangely passive. I'm bound and gagged; there's no way any cagey move or brave act on my part is going to change anything.

But he isn't reaching for the gun; he puts his hand in his pocket instead and pulls out a wallet, which he flips open with a twist of his wrist. Then he shakes his head. A sad, bitter laugh comes out of him. "I forgot," he says. "I forgot."

He fishes out a photograph, a smiling little boy with buzz-cut brown hair. He looks at it, shakes his head, laughs some more and then flicks it into the water. It floats there, with its slightly curled edges. I keep my eye on it as it drifts away, as if it's important not to lose visual contact with the little boy, as if he can somehow help me.

He says: "I can't even show you."

I look at my knees.

He speaks in a flat, commanding tone: "Look at me, María. *Look at me.*"

My neck stays bent; I can't make my head move. I look at the flakes of dirt shifting with the film of water on the bottom of the boat.

Then my head snaps up, yanked by the hair. His breath is on me, warm and moist. His face is only a few inches from mine. Tears surge into my eyes and I open them. He holds the barrel of the gun against my cheek for a moment, then takes it away.

He lets go of my hair, leans back away from me, sits down. "You don't even remember, do you? I came all this way to kill you for something you don't even remember." His shoulders sag and his head wags sadly on his neck. He begins to shake with barely audible laughter.

When his bitter, dispirited laughter fades, his shoulders give another heave and he sighs, then levels a gaze at me and says: "You're going to know. I want you to know what you did." He takes a huge breath. "Don't interrupt." That starts him laughing again. "I guess you *can't*," he manages between bouts of laughter. This time there's a giddy, juvenile edge to his hilarity. It takes him a couple of minutes to get himself under control.

When he looks up at me this time, there's a distant, slightly bored expression on his face. He talks in a bland unemotional voice, as if he's delivering a lecture.

"Let's start at the beginning, María, shall we?" He presses his hands together. "At the beginning—imagine a room in a hospital in Buenos Aires. It's a private room in the best hospital in the city, and it's already crammed with bouquets of flowers, although the reason for them is only a few hours old." He points a finger at me. "You, María: it's the day you were born. Oh, all of us in that room are so happy. Your mother and father, of course. I'm glad too, naturally, but my wife Liliana is just beaming, bursting with happiness. Her best friend has survived the ordeal, the baby is perfect, and the baby is even a girl, like her own beautiful Elena, born three weeks before."

I'm thinking he's a head case, he's got me mixed up with someone else.

"My wife, Liliana, and my sister, Gabriela, were friends from childhood, you see, *best* friends, in the way that only girls seem to be best friends. They lived in the same neighborhood, they went to the same school, they were confirmed together, they did everything together. In fact, it was my sister Gabriela who introduced me to her friend. Gabi was so delighted when we got married; it was almost as if Liliana was becoming her sister."

A plane goes by overhead, but I can't see it through the clouds. The man shifts his weight and the oars creak in the oarlocks as the boat rocks. "The two women, María— they were so pleased to be pregnant at the same time. They compared bellies; they decorated nurseries together; they traded maternity clothes. Now they would have babies to stroll with, diapers to change together, stories to trade. There would be nothing to interrupt the progress of their friendship. My mother—" He looks at me. "Your *grand-mother*—was there in the hospital room too, beaming with joy to have a second grandchild within the space of a month, another baby to kiss and hold and love. We popped a bottle of champagne and toasted you, although the new mothers worried about introducing alcohol into their breast milk, so they only had a sip, for luck." He snorts derisively. "Luck," he repeats.

"The country was in a bad state at the time," he starts again, "a very bad state..." Sweat is on his upper lip. Gnats flick through the air. He brushes the insects away from his face and takes a deep breath and looks away for a moment.

There's a siren in the distance, and again the faint rumble of an airplane. I hear a funny sound, almost like static, from the shore, but he doesn't seem to notice it.

He shakes his head. "Terrible things were happening."

Suddenly I'm drowning in an unstoppable flood of memories. Tears are spilling, pouring out of my eyes. This man. His voice. His body between me and my friend. Elena. *Elena.* Her little face, her twinkling eyes, a pink comb in her hair. He's reading to us. Every once in a while he stops reading a sentence and lets one of us finish it for him. We know the book by heart: *Cinderella.* The word comes to me in Spanish: *Cenicienta.* The book is the version featuring the characters from the Disney movie. The cartoonish images float before me: Cinderella in her torn and shabby dress, the stepsisters' hair of sausage curls, their mean, frowning eyes and large, silly noses.

Now my friend Elena leans forward, past the barricade of her father's body, and bestows on me an anticipatory smile. We're getting to the best part. Her dimples. Her dark eyes shining. Uncle Rolando. He reads with animation about how Cinderella has stayed too late dancing. We know what she'll find when she rushes out. No golden coach, no footmen. The pumpkin, the mice. Uncle Rolando turns to us, first to Elena and then to me. "The prince could find no trace of her, *except,* on the stair..."

He pauses and we scream it, in unison: *"El zapatito de cristal."*

I can picture the page exactly, that little glass slipper gleaming, the prince going down on one knee to pick it up, his mystified gaze as he stares off in the direction where Cinderella fled.

I want to tell him I *remember! I remember!* but he isn't paying attention to me now, he's talking to himself. Tears keep drooling out of my eyes and I'm breathing spastically through my nose. My body keeps giving these little shaky jerks.

"Forces were set loose," Uncle Rolando says. "I know that now. When forces are set loose you can't necessarily control them." He stops, wipes his forehead.

"You were four years old, almost five, when it happened. It was some time—years—before I was able to reconstruct these events. You will have the benefit of knowing the whole story at once.

"It was 1977," he says in his strong, precise voice. "December twelfth, to be exact. A squad came to your house on Calle Valentin and took the three of you in: your mother, your father, you. The neighbors told us about it: the helicopter overhead, the cars pulling up, the half dozen men jumping out. The cars were unmarked; the men were not in uniform. They seldom were; that way, the abductions could still be blamed on terrorists. They swarmed into your house, they looted the place of course. The neighbors could do nothing. They called the police, but your house had been declared a free zone, the police had been warned ahead of time not to interfere. The three of you were stuffed into one of the cars. The cars drove away. It was all over in ten minutes.

"You were taken to a detention center. In the next few hours, your mother and father were tortured. An electric cattle prod was applied to the usual areas: gums, anuses, nipples, genitals, armpits. Your mother was raped in front of yourself and your father. They never touched you, though, that's one thing. You yourself were spared."

If my hands were free, I would put them over my ears and push until couldn't hear him anymore.

"Eventually your parents confessed to everything, to whatever their interrogators wanted: being Montoñeros, recruiting students at the university, stockpiling weapons, conspiring to overthrow the government. They signed every prepared paper they were asked to sign."

He stops. Far away I can hear the ruckus of some ducks quacking. They stop as suddenly as they started.

"Many prisoners can...bear their own pain but not the pain and debasement of their loved ones."

I'm so cold. I'm freezing to death. I don't believe what he's saying. He's whacked out. He must have this wrong; he must have the wrong person. This didn't happen to me, this never happened to me. I'd remember, I would certainly remember. I'm still shaking when I breathe; every breath makes my whole body shake and twitch.

His voice is low now, and quiet. "I know all this because years later I hired Hugo Moro to identify the responsible men and then track them down. Moro was an expert at interrogation. I don't believe anything was withheld."

Some corner of my mind has been keeping track of the photograph of the little boy as it's floated away. It's so far now, I can hardly see it anymore.

"Once your parents capitulated to the demands of their interrogators, you, María, were taken back to your house. You sat outside on the Calle Valentin in the car with two of these men and you 'recognized' people who came to visit. Your house was under surveillance, you see, a trap.

"The people who came to call at your house. You sat in the car and it was your job to say if you knew them well or not. If you knew them, they would be taken in for questioning. It was something that was done routinely, to watch a house where people had just been abducted and pick up concerned callers. The wary stayed away, of course, but most people…most people didn't know, they didn't believe it, they would stumble into these roundups…

"Liliana and Elena were expressly *forbidden* to see you and your mother, they were *forbidden*…" He starts rowing the boat again, but he's too uncoordinated, the oars keep slipping out of the oarlocks. Eventually he stops and doubles up, his head in his hands.

I'm still snuffling, making a dim, moaning sound, breathing in the jerky, rhythmic way of an inconsolable child. He hardly seems aware of me anymore, and when he resumes talking, his voice is again flat and composed.

"Imagine if you will, María…a man…whose wife and daughter are tortured and murdered. He never believed his sister, that such things were occurring. His expertise was in naval operations, he had nothing to do with internal

Argentine affairs. His sister accused him of willful ignorance..." He shakes his head. "He was perfectly sure that the persons being questioned were left-wing guerrillas, and if they disappeared—good riddance.

"He was away on maneuvers in the South Atlantic when his family disappeared, but even if he'd been there—he asks himself this to this day—could he really have done anything? Probably not. Word reached him on board ship, and he came back to join his frantic, exhausted mother in trying to find out how it could be that three adults and two young children could simply vanish off the face of the earth. It was then that he found out from the neighbors that his wife and child often visited Gabriela. His wife had defied him all along, you see; she had never abandoned her friend because of the wishes of her husband.

"On the night in question, the neighbors had seen Elena and Liliana taken away in an unmarked car, just as they had earlier witnessed the abduction of Victor and Gabriela and you. But that was it. There was no more information, there were no leads, it was as if those cars had driven off the end of the earth."

There's that funny sound again, like a rasp of static from the shore. He hears it this time, stops talking, pushes his hair back from his forehead, stares at the shore, but then he just starts talking again.

"He and his mother hired detectives, they hounded the powerful people they knew, but they might just as well have done nothing. In fact, doing nothing might have been better. Often, as he eventually learned, the missing with powerful friends were disposed of, to destroy the evidence. His efforts simply made no difference as far as his daughter was concerned; she lasted only a few hours after her abduction. By the time word got to his ship that she was missing, she was already dead. His wife lived nine days longer.

"Imagine how a man feels when he finds out that his wife was raped by five men even before she was interrogated. When she wouldn't open her legs for the first one, their daughter was picked up and swung by the legs so her head smashed into the wall. It killed her instantly. His wife was then tortured and questioned for several more days. They thought she was obstinate and courageous, but the truth was simpler: she knew nothing of interest to the men, nothing at all. Then, possibly because of his own insistent inquiries about her, she was killed.

"Picture a man, if you will, María, who learns all this slowly and gradually. The facts accumulate slowly; they accrete in poisonous layers on his mind. Each new revelation seems more grotesque. When he learns of his wife's rape and his daughter's death from a woman who briefly shared a cell with his wife, he nearly comes unhinged. Along with the rest of the country, he learns the extent of the institutionalized torture. He learns too late and the hard way that the abducted and 'disappeared' were hardly political detainees, that they were anybody—a pretty girl some cruising army officer wanted to rape, an innocent person with a name mentioned in torture, a passerby, anyone at all."

A crow squawks. I look for the picture of the little boy, but this time I can't see it at all.

"In 1984, the bones of his wife and daughter were exhumed from a mass grave in Buenos Aires. The exhumation process proved tedious. It was some months before the twenty-four sets of bones buried together were sorted out. Finally, the bones were identified. This heap of bones is Liliana. This is Elena. It was odd, some thought, the comfort he took in touching the bones. The tiny bones of his daughter he found particularly consoling. He had an urge to keep one of his daughter's bones—a knuckle, a bone from her wrist—but he resisted. He felt superstitious; he felt that the sanctity of her skeleton should not be disturbed. He fingered the shattered skull. The bones of his wife and child were not white, as he had always pictured bones, but brown.

"The truth is, by the time he held these bones in his hands, he had exited his proper mind. He seemed to be all right, given the blows he had suffered, but the truth is he was quite insane. The interrogation sessions Hugo Moro conducted all ended the same way, in the deaths of the men. The murderers of his sister and her husband were…exterminated as well. But none of this vengeance eased his mind.

"He kept thinking of his little niece, you see. Her bones were not recovered when those of his sister and her husband were found—another sad affirmation of identity, another sad ceremony to attend with his mother. He just couldn't get that niece out of his mind. The truth is that once he found out it was she who identified his wife and child to their abductors, once he found out that it was sweet little María who pointed them out to their killers, he became obsessed. He assigned the blame to her. She was the pivotal factor: without her, he would still have his wife and his daughter.

"Oh, he reasoned with himself, he told himself it was not María's fault—she was a *child*, she could not be held responsible, she was a victim herself. But he could not dislodge from his mind the image of his daughter, picked up by the legs, her skull shattering against the wall. But when he heard the men recounting the incident…of María identifying his wife and daughter, when he heard this with his own ears, he…

"And María—she was not touched, she was not harmed. He couldn't stop thinking about it. He thought of his daughter's small brown skull, and the notion of his niece María continuing to giggle, to have flesh, to walk, to have eyes—it was more than he could bear.

"Continually, he pictured his daughter's head smacking into the wall. He remembered running his fingers over the caved-in part of that little skull. He imagined the shriek of his wife, how she numbly endured the rapes that followed.

"Every year on her birthday, he thought of Elena, of course. Eventually, once she was exhumed and reinterred, he visited her grave on that date. He knelt, he touched the ground, he brought flowers, he even prayed. Her birthday always brought images of Elena freshly to his mind. He remembered her last birthday party; her little cheeks puffed out as she blew on the candles. He never imagined any more candles on the cake. Elena never changed in his mind; she remained, always, five years old. Her life stopped; he'd held the evidence in his own hands, that small, brown, cracked skull.

"Every year on *her* birthday, he thought of María. This was different. He imagined her growing, getting older. She was seven, then ten; she was eleven, she was twelve, thirteen.

"And all along, his mother was searching for this niece; he was never allowed for a moment to forget that if the little girl who sent his own Elena to her death was found, she would be kissed, she would be loved, she would be cherished."

A crow squawks again from the shore. A great sigh comes over Uncle Rolando, a huge, exhausted exhalation. When he resumes talking, his voice is very low.

"The idea of revenge entered him and it could not be resisted." He sighs again. "It's not easy, María, to explain what it is to be insane, what happens when a mind comes loose from its normal attachments. At first, it was just a fantasy. It comforted him to think of killing you, even though he knew...he knew it was wrong. But he couldn't get rid of the crazy notion that everything was out of balance because you were alive. He had the irresistible feeling that if you were dead, he could begin, he could..." His voice trails away for a moment, and when he speaks again, it is with tremendous urgency.

"Are you sorry, María? *Are you sorry?*"

It happens so fast, I don't even brace for it. The next thing I know, my face is being pushed down into the water. No matter how hard I try to struggle, try to lift my head up, it's no good. The pressure eases and my head comes up out of the water just long enough for half a breath through my nose, and again the strong hands force me under and I come up again and get half a breath and then again he forces me under and a lightness, I feel a lightness in my brain, and then suddenly I'm sitting up again, clutched against him, snorting in huge rattling drafts of air through my nose. He lets go of me and slams his hand down repeatedly against the rowing seat. Our boat rocks; little waves splash up against the side.

Suddenly, a helicopter overhead. An amplified voice jumps at us from the sky. *"Please listen and no one will get hurt."*

I feel crushed by it, as if the voice is pressing down on me, the voice of God.

Rolando lurches toward me; he holds the gun to my head. His voice is high, out of control. He speaks through his tears: *"Are you sorry?"* He rips the tape away from my mouth and almost pulls me to my feet in the process. It hurts; the lower half of my face stings like fire. I taste blood.

"Say it!"

I squeeze it out: "I'm sorry."

He begins to regain composure. He strokes his hair back from his forehead with his free hand.

I look at the light glinting off the edges of the ripples. I hear the whoop of sirens. I see a boat being pushed into the water at the marina.

"Surrender your weapon, just drop it, just toss it into the water, and I promise no harm will come to you. We'll help you."

Rolando sits on the floor of the boat and pulls me into his lap. He puts his arms around my body. From a distance we might look like lovers, me leaning into his arms.

"I remember," I tell him, but he can't understand my voice, which is distorted by my sobbing.

"What?"

A huge sob convulses me. "I remember, I remember. *Cenicienta*," I say. "*El zapatito cristal.*"

The boat shifts and rocks in the water. My body is stiff and tense against him. One of his hands still holds the barrel of the gun under my jawbone, near my left ear. The metal presses into the soft flesh there. With his other hand he strokes my hair. He runs his fingers over my face. He wipes my eyes gently with his fingers. He traces my eyebrow with his fingertip. "Tell my mother—"

"*We have marksmen surrounding the entire lake. If you injure the girl, there is absolutely no chance that you will escape.*"

"Don't worry," he whispers in my ear. "Don't worry, María, don't worry."

"*We are prepared to wait. We can send a boat with food, water...*"

"*No!*" Rolando yells. He hasn't moved his head, it's still next to mine, so his voice sounds very loud, almost as if it's inside my mind.

"Ana," he says to me. "Your grandmother's name is Ana." He helps me up, so that we're almost sitting now instead of lying down. He angles his head around slightly so that he can look at me. "The Ebingers...Moro..." Tears come into his eyes, they spill over, they run down his face. His body shakes with sobs. A thin strand of mucus stretches from his nose to his upper lip. He runs his finger over my bloody lip. He shakes his head.

Blue police lights, lots of them, whirling through the trees from the shore.

"Don't forgive me," he whispers.

"What?"

"Don't forgive me," he says in an insistent, annoyed voice. "Don't ever forgive me."

The gun barrel is still pressed into my neck. "Stand up."

"No!" I'm crying again, I can't stop crying.

"Here we go, one, two, three." I make my body limp, but he pulls me up with his strong arm around my waist. "Close your eyes, María, close your eyes."

He speaks so firmly, so directly, that I do it, I close my eyes. But then I feel the barrel of the gun go away from my neck and suddenly I know what he's going to do and I open my mouth to scream, but before I can do it there's the explosion, and when I open my eyes, water is splashing up on me, and I see him entering the water, his body crashing, flopping into the water on his back. His body bends in the middle, his head and his feet go in last. I watch his face go under and then his feet going in, his shiny black loafers going into the water, and then his body begins slowly to roll over onto its stomach. There's a little frill of blood in the water, and I feel so dizzy, I don't even realize that what's happening is the boat is rocking wildly and I'm losing my balance and the next thing I know, I'm so surprised, I'm falling into the water myself.

Chapter Thirty-One

JACK HULTIN
Securing the Perimeter

TURNS OUT I was right all along about Mariah Ebinger a.k.a. María Carrera. She wasn't a real runaway, she *did* come back home just like the good girl I'd pegged her for, she just happened to come home to a fucking nightmare. I was right about Betty Ferguson being a hostage too. That cigarette burn in the carpet, the kids not being smokers, I was right about all that shit. It's months ago now all that went down, and McVay's still calling me "Hunch" Hultin.

Of course, that day at Burke Lake, the girl, she's going under for about the fifteenth time by the time they get to her. The reason being it's a wilderness park, see. No motorized craft. Except for this puny five-horsepower runabout the rangers use for collecting litter.

It wasn't that nobody thought of the boat angle. D.C. Park Service sent a boat down all right, but when the girl goes into the water, they're still trying to launch the damn thing. What a circus that was, some asshole about drowned. Turns out the runabout's so slow anyway, two officers in a rowboat actually get to the girl first.

So they drag her out and try to revive her in the rowboat but it's just too damn cramped to administer CPR in a twelve-foot boat. They got no choice but to haul ass for shore.

When they stretch her out on the sand there, I'm telling you, she looks...*dead*. Everybody's looking around with a kind of dazed letdown look, as if to say, you mean after all that, she's going to die anyway?

I mean, there must of been forty, fifty cops at the location by that time. You had the helicopter unit, the SWAT team, hostage negotiating team, fire and rescue guys, you name it. Hell, there must of been twenty officers just out there in the woods, securing the perimeter. There's a lot of ways in and out of that park, including who knows how many paths from those big new houses backing up to the parkland, that development, what's it called—South Run. The woods were crawling with guys dispatched to intercept the kids, the joggers, the folks out walking Fido.

I was at my desk less than an hour when the call came in. I remember I just finished typing up a follow-up report for McVay about a stabbing at one of the rec centers.

So anyway, the original call is just Fairfax wanting help, you know, they had that whole lake perimeter to secure, they needed manpower. But then the report gets into the central computer, and that's when McVay gets notified this thing might be connected to the Ebinger/Ferguson case. You got to hand it to these computers, linking the Burke Lake incident up with our case so fast and channeling the information to McVay.

So McVay says you and Schwartz get your asses down there. Be a presence, that's what he says. Let them know we got prior interest. We let Fairfax get clear jurisdictional priority, we might never close the books on our cases.

This sure was a hell of a case, start to finish. The park employee who was the first one to arrive that morning at Burke Lake actually *ran over* the corpse on the entrance road, if you can believe it. Poor sonofabitch had a late night, he's hung over, thumb up his ass—you know how it is. Park access road comes up a hill. Just at the end, he's going up that hill, sees this body in the middle of the road. What happens, he panics, hits the accelerator instead of the brake, nails the victim again. Un-fucking-believable.

Victim. This was some victim. This Moro guy turned out to be quite a piece of work. When Arthur Ebinger finally recovered his faculties enough so we could take a statement off him, he identified Moro as the one who tortured him and killed Ferguson.

Back to that park service guy—this wasn't his day at all. At first he thinks he's killed this Moro guy, that Moro was just passed out or something. He doesn't see the bullet wound, doesn't have the stomach to take a close look—can't say I blame him. He gets himself together and goes and calls it in and he's there waiting for the ambulance, worrying would anyone show up at the park before the authorities get there, should he try CPR, should he cover the body, what the hell should he do?

Finally he goes over to check out the car in the parking lot, just for no reason, just to do something. He had it figured as the *victim's* car, see. And that's when he finds the kid, Ryan Ferguson, and his mother, trussed up like two turkeys in there. By that time the two of them are about dead themselves out of pure frustration. They been literally knocking their heads against the windows trying to get this guy's attention, but he was so freaked out, he just didn't notice. So he cuts the kid and his mother loose and gets the gags off them. The kid can't shut up—Mariah this, Mariah that, and he's taking off down to the lake where God knows what would have happened. Except, picture this: the mother actually tackles the kid and gets her arms wrapped around one of his legs, and while she's impeding him, that's when the rescue unit finally arrives.

The park service guy finally gets the picture, that what he ran over was a corpse, which is a load off him, I guarantee you. The kid and his mother, they're babbling, trying to say everything at once, but eventually they calm down and the situation gets sketched out: girl being held hostage, man with a gun, probably down on the lake. Soon there's a squad car there talking to the kid and his mother, and then the word goes out and the crisis management team comes into play.

So me and Schwartz, we're about the last guys to get there. It's some weird scene, I'll tell you. The place is swarming with squad cars, rescue vehicles, an unbelievable amount of communications equipment and weaponry. But down by the lakefront, I'll tell you, you wouldn't know it. Everybody keeps their cool. "A well-orchestrated effort," McVay says later; he's impressed.

See, they don't want to provoke the guy in the boat until every piece is in place, and they manage to keep all those personnel pretty quiet. Everything is finally in place except the goddamn boat, which apparently the SWAT team don't get the word about or at least the correct word, because when the order goes out to make contact with the guy—using the helicopter—our boat is still in the launch area. Element of surprise, I guess that was the thinking about using the helicopter. Plus, let him know he's covered all around, even from the goddamned sky.

It went down fast from there on in, I'll tell you. I mean it wasn't but a minute or so after the helicopter made that first announcement that the guy drilled himself.

My own feeling is that he did not intend to harm the girl at that point. He sure as shit could have shot her if he wanted to. He just didn't figure it, that when he shot himself, she'd get tossed into the lake like that.

So anyway, they drag her out on the shore and the paramedics go to work on her. I wouldn't have given you a nickel for her chances, I'll tell you that. But sure enough, about two, three minutes of working on her and she pukes up a bunch of water and starts coughing. It's a fucking miracle as far as I'm concerned. I mean they train us in CPR, but I never seen a resuscitation before. A cheer goes up like you wouldn't believe, guys punching the air. Then they hustle her off in an ambulance. By this time the big boat is finally in the water; it heads out to recover the body of the man.

It was a long time before we knew what it was all about. The girl is no help; she don't say boo for six weeks. At first they're worried they didn't pull her out in time, there was oxygen deprivation, you know, brain damage. But it turns out no, tests show normal brain activity. The way it's explained to me, she's just too freaked out to talk. Severe trauma. She ends up in the same hospital with her father—Ebinger, I mean—who turns out not to be her real father but her adopted father, which she didn't know, this being the reason she ran away that night. Ebinger sits with her hours a day, ditto the boyfriend, but nothing happens, she just stares into space.

In the meantime we try to identify these two dead men. From their clothes and all, and their effects, we know the men were foreign nationals, but that's about all. Between this kid Ryan, and Ebinger—once he's available for questioning—and the kid's mother, all they know is first names. The man in the boat was Rolando; the one on the road was Hugo.

Their papers got their names different: Arturo Rafael Escobar and Miguel Antonio Jimenez. Their passports put them as Chilean nationals. We get in touch with the Chilean authorities on the basis of that and they get to work on it. But Ebinger now, he believes the men to be Argentines.

He explains how Mariah was adopted, he explains about her possibly being a "disappeared" person. But he has no idea about the agenda of the men, no idea what their business was with his daughter. So we get in touch with the Argentine authorities too. But what do we have for them? The names Rolando and Hugo. Not a hell of a lot to go on. They're running the fingerprints.

Because the men are foreign nationals, we're not expecting anything from FBI, really. But we get lucky. National Crime Center Database out of El Paso gets back to us right away, and bingo, we got them, their prints are in the system.

It isn't these guys ever committed a crime in the United States. The El Paso database contains about every print ever taken for any reason. These two, their prints are in the system because both of them attended training sessions under the auspices of the U.S. military. The way it was explained to me, all such personnel are routinely fingerprinted, both for routine identification purposes and in case they're, you know, injured or killed during training exercises or whatever.

The Argentine consulate in Baltimore sends a guy over, Claudio Travino, he helps us contact next of kin and so on. This gets into some tricky areas here. There are budgetary concerns, for one thing. If the body is to be repatriated, see, someone is going to have to pay for it. Otherwise, we'll dispose of the remains. When we do that, the body usually goes to medical science. You want to be careful, though, you don't want to release it if there's any chance you're going to get grieving, pissed-off relatives all over you. Sometimes you got religious considerations too, you got to respect that. Sometimes the country itself will pay to repatriate the corpse. It's tricky with this Hugo Moro. Technically, he's a victim of Rolando Carrera. Technically, Hugo Moro is not guilty of any crime. A moot point, as it turns out. Moro's next of kin, some cousin or whatever, don't want him.

But we learn from Claudio Travino that Carrera's mother is coming up to take the body home. And that she wishes to "consult with the United States authorities." That boils down to this guy Ted Zinovic from Fairfax County and me.

So it's three weeks to the day after all that goes down at Burke Lake that she walks into the station, this sixtyish lady, beautiful clothes, speaks perfect English. This is Ana Carrera. Turns out Zinovic is on vacation, Bethany Beach. I'm appointed to deal with her, solo.

I never met anybody like this lady before. She's got something about her right away makes me want to help her. I actually stand up when she approaches the desk and the sergeant introduces her.

"Oh please sit down, Mr. Hultin," she says in her fancy voice. "I have a great deal to tell you."

"To tell me?"

She gives me a sad smile. "She's my granddaughter," she starts. "Mariah Ebinger I mean. How is she? Can I see her?"

"Your granddaughter? She's your *granddaughter*."

"Perhaps I'd better explain."

We're there for a couple of hours, maybe. I just keep shaking my head—it's some story.

I take Ana Carrera to the hospital. I tell her if none of the others are there, we can go in and see the girl. I know it's bending regulations, but there's no way this lady is making it up. She showed me the documents and all. We sit in the room. She croons to the girl in Spanish. Mariah, she just sits there, staring at nothing. Mrs. Carrera begins to cry.

I don't want to do it—take Mrs. Carrera to the morgue—I honestly don't, but I figure it has to be done, let's get it over with. She stiffens as I lift the sheet and a little cry escapes her. She nods once, and looks away. I put my arm around her and get her out of there.

We go back to the station, which is what she wants. I get her some tea.

I have to make it formal. "That was him? Your son?"

"That was my son, Rolando Carrera." She tells me supposedly he was on a trekking expedition in Patagonia. He had been considered missing for two weeks. Search parties were still looking for him when Claudio Travino's telephone call arrived. There had been storms in the area where her son was hiking and she had been prepared for the worst, but until Mr. Travino called, she had not given up hope. She's holding my hand as she tells me this, squeezing very hard.

It's about six weeks after that when everything gets straightened out, when the girl finally comes out of her coma or whatever it is. In the meantime, blood has been drawn, DNA typing has been done, Mrs. Carrera and Mr. Ebinger have become acquainted, the boyfriend and his mother, one of Mariah's girlfriends, they've all become quite close, along with the doctors and the nurses and the therapists and so on. They go there in shifts, talk to her, play music, rent movies, all that kind of thing. Stimulation. Even I go there sometimes with Mrs. Carrera. All along, the girl is just blank; she's there, but she's not there, I mean you look right at her and you can see no one's home.

The boyfriend is the one who's in there when she comes out of it. Apparently she looks around, like *where am I?* And then she just says, "Oh Ryan," and then she bursts into tears.

Well, she's got a lot to cry about. I mean, the poor kid, can you imagine?

Chapter Thirty-Two

MARIAH
One Real Life

I'M DOWN HERE now, in B.A. People call the city by its initials, like L.A., except it's not pronounced the way you'd think. You say the alphabet a whole different way in Spanish. So it's not "Bee Ay." It's "Bay-Ah." Spanish is coming back to me, but of course I have the vocabulary of a five-year-old.

Spanish isn't the only thing. A lot of other things are coming back to me too. Argentines are big on psychotherapy, and it's a good thing because I'm going to need a lot of help. They say this country has the second most therapists per capita in the world. The first is Brazil.

South America. I never even thought about South America and now here I am. I'm staying for the summer with my grandmother—except it's winter here. I might even become a citizen of Argentina someday. Or I might stay a U.S. citizen. I don't have to decide yet.

One of the things I'm having a lot of trouble with is the timing. I never could stand those stories where some person changes their plane reservation at the last second and they end up on a plane that crashes. There was that crash in Washington a long time ago that Darlene told me about: Air Florida, I think it was. It made a huge impression on her.

I remember her saying it wasn't even the deaths of the people on the plane that bothered her, what she couldn't get over were the people who got hit when they were driving across the bridge. If a light had been red instead of green, or if they'd had trouble with their keys, or if the elevator at their office had stopped on one more floor, or if they'd decided to get an ice cream cone, then they wouldn't have been in that exact spot at that exact time and the plane wouldn't have hit them.

It drives me crazy to think about it like that. I mean, if we'd had one less snow day and I'd overheard Elisa and Yolanda talking in Spanish one day earlier, or even one day later, or if I hadn't walked the same way that morning, or if my father had got stuck at the red light on Cameron Mills Road because then Elisa and Yolanda would have already been inside the gym—I mean, that's the kind of thing that I can't get out of my mind.

Because if my memory had come back any other day, even just one day later, then I would have been home when my uncle came for me. And then maybe my mother would still be alive. For sure Mr. Ferguson wouldn't have been there, so he'd still be alive. And nothing would have happened to my father, my father Arthur Ebinger. At least he didn't die, but terrible things happened to him. He's not the same. He'll never be the same.

I just keep thinking it's another thing that's my fault. If only I'd been there, or if only they'd come the night before. My uncle—he only wanted me, he didn't want to hurt anyone else. And when it came down to it, I don't think he would have hurt me. It makes me crazy to think about it, how it could have all come out different, how none of it had to happen.

Nana says that there's an element of the absurd in all tragedy, that grotesque timing is a part of even the simplest accident. What is an accident, she says, but the unlucky evidence of chance at work in the universe? The wrong person in the wrong place at the wrong time.

But really, I can't kid myself that what bothers me most is bad timing. For instance, Aunt Liliana and Elena going to visit my mother and me that night at our house in San Ysidro. If that had been just pure bad timing, just pure accident, if they had just come by and been abducted, that would have been one thing. But that isn't the whole story, is it? There was the secret ingredient: me.

I call myself María Carrera now, I did take the name. It still sounds funny to me and I know it'll be hard for everyone else to get used to when I go back, but it was something I had to do for my grandmother. The day she was leaving with my uncle Rolando's coffin to come back here to Argentina, and I was staying behind with my father, that's when I told her I'd decided to change my name. There she was going back with her only son, dead. I had to do something for her, and it was the only thing I could think of. I had to stay with my father, I didn't want to leave the U.S. until he was fully recovered, at least physically. Even now I hate leaving him alone. Nana invited him down but he said no; he thanked her, but he thought it would be better if I went by myself. He doesn't sound so great when I talk to him on the phone. He's still kind of stunned even though it happened almost a year ago now. It's going to take a lot longer than that for him to get used to life without my mother. I still miss her so much, too. I miss just about everything about the way it used to be.

Sometimes, I think about what it would be like if I never found out. I imagine this parallel life where I'm still Mariah Ebinger, and the past never came to claim me. What would I be doing right now? Maybe I'd have a summer job at the yogurt place with Darlene. I'd be taking an SAT prep course to get my math scores up. I'd be visiting colleges. Those would be the big things on my mind. It's so easy to think about that, how if this didn't happen, if that didn't happen, my life could have gone a whole different way.

But that's stupid, I know. You can drive yourself crazy thinking like that. There is only one real way, only one real life.

During waking hours, I can believe the excuses everybody makes for me. ("She was only a child anyway, practically a baby. She's a victim as much as anyone." "You can't hold a child responsible for something like that.") The shrinks, Nana, my father, Ryan—everyone drums it in, it wasn't my fault.

But at night, when I've kissed Nana good night, when I'm in the room that I call mine, but doesn't yet feel like mine, at night the trick is harder, the memories come back so real it's like everything is happening all over again.

I remember a lot now.

My father's body contorting as the electricity relentlessly connects, his refusal to tell them anything beyond his

name: *"Me llamo Victor Aguilar, no hay más que decir.
Me llamo Victor Aguilar. Victor Aguilar! Victor Aguilar!
Victor Aguilar!"* His defiance only lasts until they start in
on my mother, and then I remember my mother...

Then I remember sitting in that car with the men,
outside my house on the Calle Valentin. I remember the
way the men smelled, their exact body odor, the smell of the
cigarette smoke. I remember the tiny soccer ball dangling
from the rearview mirror. I remember Aunt Liliana at our
front door, bending to speak to Elena, then reaching up to
press the bell. The man is asking me: "How about it? Do
you know them?" I can still hear his voice, the exact way
he said it: *"Las conoces?"*

Why didn't I say no? How would the men have known?
But I didn't say no.

I "recognized" my aunt and my cousin. Fingered them
is more like it. Here's the worst thing. I can't get away from
it, I remember it clearly, that fat, squirmy thought: *it will
happen to them too, it won't just happen to me and my
mom and dad.*

Why would I want it to happen to them too? We talk
about that all the time—me and my therapist—because I
can't get over this. She tells me it was a normal reaction. She
points out that there's a cliché for it in English: misery loves
company. She says I have to get over this guilt, I have to
forgive myself. She shows me many examples from her collection of case histories, people who have done the same thing,
dragged other people into their own torment. She points
out to me that most of the case histories involve adults, not
children. She reminds me it's possible that I thought it was
a test, that the men knew all along who Liliana and Elena
were, that they were testing me. She says it's even possible I
thought the men could read my mind. "This is the way children think, María," she says. "They do not think logically."

We go over it and over it, how all victims, anyway,
tend to feel responsible. People who have survived concen-

tration camps, even people who survive plane crashes—it's common for them to feel guilty. They feel guilty just for surviving. They wonder what I wonder: Why was I saved? They think what I think: I don't deserve it. They think: Why am I spared? I am not worthy.

The point is that I knew terrible things would happen to Elena and Aunt Liliana and I still did it.

The man asked me: *"Las conoces?"*

I sat in the car and nodded. I said it: *"Sí."*

Then Aunt Liliana was screaming "No!" Her strong body was being dragged toward the other car, the Falcon. She struggled, she thrashed, her shoe came off, it lay there in the road, like Cinderella's lost slipper. And then Elena. I remember Elena's bewildered look as a man picked her up and hustled her roughly into the car.

I started to cry then. The man sitting next to me in the car shushed me. He was nice to me. He held me on his lap. He gave me a piece of candy.

I never saw Liliana and Elena again. I never saw my mother or father again either. The men covered my eyes and drove me to a place I don't remember well. The only thing I remember is wetting my pants because no one would pay enough attention to tell me where there was a bathroom.

My therapist expects this will all come back to me someday. I can't wait.

When I'm done with the memory of that horrible night, when it leaves me for a moment, there's always more, the recent events that never stay out of my mind for long. My mother's voice: *"I'm afraid you have the wrong number."*

And Uncle Rolando: *"Close your eyes, María. Close your eyes."* The gun going off. His loafers going under the water. The plume of blood.

Maybe I was thinking if I helped the men, or if they had someone else to do things to, they'd leave my mother and father alone. Maybe I was thinking they'd let us go. Maybe I was thinking Aunt Liliana could help us somehow. These excuses are offered to me on a daily basis, and who knows, maybe they're even true.

My father, Arthur Ebinger, says that I didn't speak for almost a year when my mother and he first got me, and that sometimes I lapsed into catatonic states the same way I did in the hospital after they pulled me out of Burke Lake, although never for that long. Now I know why.

The men in the car asking me: "Do you know them?" I remember it exactly, me saying it.

Yes.

Even then, even at that very moment, I remember feeling the excruciating discomfort of doing something I knew was wrong. Even then, I experienced the shrinking feeling that follows an act of betrayal.

No one can escape the past, I know that. Someday who knows, I may even forgive myself.

In the meantime, although I have embraced my new identity, although I am eager to find out about this country, although I love Nana, although I am not totally without happiness or hope, at night, in my sleep, here is what I dream of: I dream of being Mariah.

I dream of answering to the name Mariah Ebinger. I dream of the tidy suburban houses I lived in, I dream of my Barbie dolls, my stuffed animals, my canopy bed, my shelf of trophies, the smooth rocks I collected at the beach, I dream of my mother chopping onions, I dream of her piano students plunking away at "Twinkle Twinkle Little Star" while I color my coloring books, I dream of my soccer teams, I dream of Ryan the way he used to be.

Ryan writes to me every day and sometimes I feel like that's the only thing that's keeping me on the earth. It's amazing that our relationship has survived everything, including his mother's efforts to break us up. But the bond between Ryan and me is different now, it isn't normal. We cling together as if we're hanging on for dear life.

It's really only in my dreams that I'm happy now. Mariah never had to wade through this fog of grief and shame. Mariah never knew a world where things like this could happen. Mariah never remembered her father, his face contorted, his eyes streaming tears, screaming his name.

Victor Aguilar! Victor Aguilar! Victor Aguilar!

Mariah never saw her mother's nipple, touched with a cattle prod, and the frenzied arcing spasm of her mother's body. Mariah never saw her mother underneath a man, his pants pulled open, her mother screaming and screaming and screaming. And then the screaming stopped and the whimpering began.

Mariah never had to struggle just to get out of bed in the morning, or coax herself to lift her toothbrush. Mariah never looked in the mirror, never felt the toothbrush slip from her fingers and clatter to the floor, never thought, "Why bother? Let them rot."

This is why I spend so much time sleeping now. This is why I like to stay in bed. The therapist says I'm escaping but why not? I'm learning to live the life of María Carrera now; at least in my dreams, I still get to be Mariah.

AUTHOR'S NOTE

My idea was to write a book about "real" and received memory, about our inability to escape the past, about deception and discovery. I started out writing about a girl with memories that did not fit, a girl who possessed aberrant recollections. I'm not sure how or when the tragic events that occurred in Argentina during the Repression became enmeshed in the plot. At first I resisted—both wary of trespassing on territory that seemed more properly to belong to Argentine writers, and worried that I would find it impossible to write about the brutality of the events without feeling I was exploiting their victims. In the end I put aside my doubts, captured by the power of the story and even persuaded of its relevance. U.S. citizens, horrified by the abduction and abuse of a handful of individuals in the Middle East, can scarcely imagine the experience of a country that had more than twelve thousand of its citizens abducted, tortured, and murdered by its own government.

Unfortunately, Argentina's experience with its "disappeared" is far from unique. As I explored the matter, I learned that I could have set the "backstory" in any of dozens of countries around the globe whose governments abduct, torture, and kill with impunity. Of the examples in our hemisphere, the United States can hardly feign surprise. In 1963, U.S. Secretary of Defense Robert McNamara told Congress: "Our primary objective in Latin America is to aid, whenever necessary, the continual growth of military and paramilitary forces." This policy remains essentially in force. The U.S. government has supported and continues to back some of the most repressive regimes on earth, and that includes the juntas that ruled Argentina from 1976 to 1982.

Two books were absolutely essential to my research. The first is *Nunca Más* (New York: Farrar, Straus, Giroux, 1986), the report of the Argentine National Commission on the Disappeared. This commission was created by the Alfonsin government (which took power following the junta's demise), and headed by writer Ernesto Sabato. Its report, *Nunca Más*, is simply a litany of horror, a bald-faced accounting by victims and witnesses, describing in the least dramatic language the systematic terror that occurred in Argentina during the "dirty war." It is impossible to read this inventory of methodical torture without fear and a deep revulsion at the brutality of our fellow human beings. The second book is *The Disappeared and the Mothers of the Plaza*, written by two BBC reporters, John Simpson and Jana Bennett (New York: St. Martin's Press, 1985). It provides a survey of Argentine history and describes in detail the years of the dirty war. It focuses on the heroic efforts of a group of mothers and grandmothers of disappeared persons who, despite fear, harassment, and the loss through kidnap and murder of some of their number, insistently marched in the Plaza de Mayo, the square in front of the presidential palace, in Buenos Aires. Without resources beyond their own outrage and courage, these women, some of the least empowered of Argentine citizenry, managed to focus world attention on the horrific practices that had become commonplace in Argentina by 1979. Once that attention was focused, although the junta remained in power for years longer, the worst of the abuses ceased.

I visited Argentina in 1989. Walking through the Plaza de Mayo, it was impossible not to notice, painted in white on the bricks beneath one's feet, the occasional outline of a body, or a painted white kerchief tied around an invisible face. The first are the symbols of the disappeared; the second are the symbols of the mothers and grandmothers of the Plaza de Mayo who still gathered in that square on Thursday afternoons, and along with other concerned citizens of the world, marched in slow, dolorous circles. Some of the women wore kerchiefs stitched with the dates their loved ones disappeared; some of them had photographs pinned to their clothing.

At the time of my visit, Argentina was beset with crippling economic problems. A military that still seemed to consider itself the proper rulers of the country contributed to the feeling of political instability. Many of the symbols painted on the bricks of the Plaza de Mayo were faint and fading. The graffiti on the walls no longer concerned human rights abuses but economic matters. There seemed to be a desire in the country to "put all this behind us."

There have been four military rebellions since the resumption of civilian rule in Argentina. Because of various amnesties granted to the military by nervous civilian governments, very few of the men implicated in the atrocities committed during the dirty war ever spent time in prison. (Following the first military rebellion, in 1987, a law was pushed through the Argentine Congress absolving most officers below the rank of general of human rights violations and charges.)

A story by Eugene Robinson in the January 2, 1991, *Washington Post*, reported that even General Jorge Rafael Videla, a man who has been termed the "architect" of the dirty war, was pardoned by Argentine President Carlos Menem at year's end, 1990. Menem defended his pardon as "a way of closing a black chapter in the nation's history."

When released, Videla, far from being repentant about the brutalities that occurred during the junta's reign of terror, claimed that his time in prison ought to be considered an "act of service," and that his only crime was "to defend the nation against subversive aggression."

Nor did Menem's pardon really mollify Videla's sense of injustice at having been imprisoned in the first place. He went on to request, in his open letter to the chief of staff of the Argentine army, that the pardon was not enough vindication for him, that he still required "the reparation of military honor."

September 11, 1991
Washington, D.C.